THE TIMES
DO NOT PERMIT

THE TIMES DO NOT PERMIT

The Musical Life of Michael Mosoeu Moerane

CHRISTINE LUCIA

WITS UNIVERSITY PRESS

Published in South Africa by:
Wits University Press
1 Jan Smuts Avenue
Johannesburg 2001

www.witspress.co.za

Copyright © Christine Lucia 2024
Published edition © Wits University Press 2024
Images and figures © Copyright holders

First published 2024

http://dx.doi.org.10.18772/12024119193

978-1-77614-919-3 (Paperback)
978-1-77614-920-9 (Hardback)
978-1-77614-921-6 (Web PDF)
978-1-77614-922-3 (EPUB)

All rights reserved. No part of this publication may be reproduced, stored in a retrieval system, or transmitted in any form or by any means, electronic, mechanical, photocopying, recording or otherwise, without the written permission of the publisher, except in accordance with the provisions of the Copyright Act, Act 98 of 1978.

All images remain the property of the copyright holders. The publishers gratefully acknowledge the publishers, institutions and individuals referenced in captions for the use of images. Every effort has been made to locate the original copyright holders of the images reproduced here; please contact Wits University Press in case of any omissions or errors.

This publication is peer reviewed following international best practice standards for academic and scholarly books.

The publication of this volume was made possible by funding from the Africa Open Institute, Stellenbosch University.

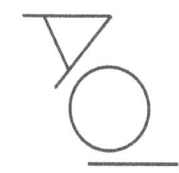

AFRICA OPEN INSTITUTE

Project manager: Inga Norenius
Copyeditor: Helen Moffett
Proofreader: Alison Paulin
Indexer: Rita Sephton
Cover design: Hybrid Creative
Cover image © Sophia Metsekae Moerane and Marumo Moerane
Typeset in 11.5 point Crimson

For John Lucia

Contents

List of Illustrations	ix
Musical Examples	xi
Acknowledgements	xiii
Map of Southern Africa showing Key Places in Moerane's Life	xvii
Timeline of Political Events: 1880–1991	xix
Preface	xxv
Introduction: Moerane in Life and Literature	1
1 The House of Moerane	17
2 Moerane the Student	37
3 Moerane the Teacher and Composer	59
4 Moerane in Correspondence	83
5 The Symphonic Poem *Fatše La Heso* (*My Country*)	95
6 Moerane and the Choral Movement in Southern Africa	113
7 Moerane's Spiritual Songs	135
8 Songs about Family, Community and Tradition	151

9	Songs of Love and Loss	169
10	Conclusion	199
	Appendix: Catalogue of Works by Michael Mosoeu Moerane	207
	Glossary of Musical Terms	211
	Notes	219
	Bibliography	253
	Index	267

List of Illustrations

Fig. 0.1	Moerane as a young man (courtesy Tsepo Moerane)	3
Fig. 0.2	The African Springtime Orchestra in Queenstown c. 1952 (courtesy Sophia Metsekae Moerane, Marumo Moerane and Jonathan Ball Publishers)	4
Fig. 0.3	Moerane teaching his son Thabo the piano c. 1964 (courtesy Sophia Metsekae Moerane, Marumo Moerane and Jonathan Ball Publishers)	7
Fig. 1.1	The Moerane family at Mangoloaneng c. 1920 (courtesy Tsepo Moerane and Jonathan Ball Publishers)	25
Fig. 1.2	The Moerane home at 10 Scanlen Street c. 1960 (courtesy Tsepo Moerane)	28
Fig. 1.3	The empty lot in 2014 (author's photograph)	29
Fig. 1.4	The house in Peka village 2014, (author's photograph)	34
Fig. 1.5	The house in Tsifalimali, 2014 (author's photograph)	35
Fig. 2.1	Lovedale students c. 1924 (courtesy Tsepo Moerane)	41
Fig. 2.2	Rhodes University Main Building 1946 (courtesy Cory Library)	54
Fig. 3.1	Choir competition adjudication comments written by Moerane (courtesy Neo Mahase Moerane)	64
Fig. 3.2	Peka High School Orchestra c. 1965 (courtesy Sophia Metsekae Moerane and Marumo Moerane)	75
Fig. 6.1	Extract from Moerane's 'A General Note on Modern Music' (courtesy Neo Mahase Moerane)	120

Fig. 8.1	*Nonyana Tse Ntle* typescript (courtesy Neo Mahase Moerane)	159
Fig. 9.1	*Ntsoaki* manuscript bars 1–8 (courtesy of the Moerane family)	182
Fig. 9.2	Thabo Moerane, Sylvia Zongola and Michael Mosoeu Moerane (courtesy Nthabiseng)	198

Musical Examples

Ex. 5.1	*Fatše La Heso* Theme I as played in bars 1–16	106
Ex. 5.2	*Fatše La Heso* Theme II as played in bars 43–48	106
Ex. 5.3	*Fatše La Heso* Theme III as played in bars 56–59	106
Ex. 5.4	*Fatše La Heso* Theme IV as implied in bars 46–55	108
Ex. 5.5	*Fatše La Heso* bars 179–193	110
Ex. 7.1	*Jehova Oa Busa* bars 1–20 melody	137
Ex. 7.2	*Vumani KuYehova* bars 17–24	138
Ex. 7.3	*Ngokuba Sizalelwe Umtwana* bars 1–14	139
Ex. 7.4	*Ruri!* bars 91–122	141
Ex. 7.5	*Nobody Knows The Trouble I've Seen* bars 1–16	144
Ex. 7.6	*By An' By* bars 17–32	145
Ex. 7.7	*Go Tell It On The Mountains* bars 17–25	146
Ex. 7.8	*Shenandoah* bars 1–20	148
Ex. 8.1	*Ma-Homemakers* bars 1–23	153
Ex. 8.2	*Pelo Le Moea* bars 1–32	154
Ex. 8.3	*Alina* bars 9–23	155
Ex. 8.4	*Seotsanyana* bars 41–66	157
Ex. 8.5	*'Mankholikholi* bars 1–25	158
Ex. 8.6	*Liphala* bars 1–18	162
Ex. 8.7	*Morena Tlake* bars 1–18	167
Ex. 8.8	*Morena Tlake* bars 52–55	168
Ex. 9.1	*Khati* bars 34–53	173
Ex. 9.2	*Monyaka Oa Pelo* bars 31–54	175
Ex. 9.3	*Paka-Mahlomola* bars 45–70	178
Ex. 9.4	*Mahakoe* bars 11–20	184
Ex. 9.5	*Mahakoe* bars 21–48	185

Ex. 9.6	*Della* bars 60–76	190
Ex. 9.7	*Sylvia* bars 17–29	192
Ex. 9.8	*Sylvia* bars 36–57	196

Acknowledgements

This book could not have been completed without financial assistance from the Andrew W. Mellon Foundation between 2016 and 2019, and a generous research grant from the Vice-Chancellor of Stellenbosch University, Professor Wim de Villiers, who is sincerely thanked. These funds were channelled through the Africa Open Institute for Music, Research and Innovation at Stellenbosch University, to whose Director, Professor Stephanus Muller, I am profoundly grateful. I also acknowledge the collegiality and support of my other colleagues at the Africa Open Institute. Stephen Gill, Tii Pitso and Mpho Ndebele provided initial help in contacting interviewees and other people made important material or contact information available, among whom I must single out Dr Fezeka Mabona, without whose persistent help I would never have had the great privilege of interviewing Moerane's last surviving sibling, Epainette Mbeki, shortly before her death in 2014. Moerane's first-born son, the late Mofelehetsi Moerane, was a rich source of information about his father's personality and his life. Moerane's daughter, Sophia Metsekae, kindly gave me material about her father's membership of the Cape African Teachers Association (CATA) and his musical production at Mfundisweni College of Education, and permissions, for which I am profoundly grateful. The late Thuso Moerane not only preserved his father's manuscripts, lists of works and two important family documents, he also gave me useful insights into his father's life and work, and put me in touch with Nthabiseng Itholeng. To Marumo Moerane I am indebted for connecting me with Moerane's first grandchild, Mosa Ndludla, for his generosity in allowing me to visit Moerane's home in Tsifalimali, Lesotho, one last time, and for his wise advice and the granting of a number of permissions.

Mpho Ndebele has been a staunch companion in the Moerane journey of many years, an invaluable linguist as well as cultural resource for all things Sotho, and I can never thank her enough. She led me to Thuso and other family members as well as four of Moerane's former students at Peka High School, to whom I am in turn profoundly grateful: Shadrack Mapetla, Victor Lechesa, Matsobane Putsoa and Zakes Mda. Stephen Gill and Tii Pitso connected me with one of Moerane's former students at Basutoland High School, Gilbert Ramatlapeng, and with two of his former colleagues at Peka High, Tseliso Makhakhe and TTE Pitso. David Ambrose and Mamhlongo Maphisa gave invaluable background and archival information. Moriee Khaebana took me to Moerane's house in Lesotho the first time and he and Lebohang Mofelehetsi provided information about Moerane's ancestry and his life in Tsifalimali. I would also like to thank Mr Ramaema, caretaker of the house in Tsifalimali, Mafothe Malaoli from Peka High School, Makonye Tiiti, caretaker of Moerane's former house in Peka village and Eric Lekhanya of Lesotho Teachers' Training College. Moerane's grandson, Tsepo Moerane, and his granddaughter, Neo Moerane, have been enormously kind and helpful throughout the process of completing the Moerane Edition and writing this book, and have provided a wealth of information in interviews, made photographs available, and given moral support and permissions. I also thank Moerane's grandson Neo Mahase Moerane for help with interviewing his father Mofelehetsi, and for images and permissions. Mark Gevisser most generously made some of his private research material available over and above the extensive Gevisser papers in the South African History Archives, for which I am deeply grateful; and Jonathan Ball Publishers kindly made available images previously used by Gevisser. Finally, without my husband, Michael Blake, I doubt I would have had the stamina to begin this book, never mind finish it. Among many other ways in which he helped, he visited Moerane's daughter, Sophia Metsekae in 2018, and shared with me what she told him. I am enormously grateful to her, and to all other members of the Moerane family and esepcially Tsepo Moerane, for their kind permission to reproduce extracts from Moerane's musical works. Finally, the Wits University Press team deserve my heartfelt appreciation for the way in which they embraced this book and its musical idiosyncrasies with such enthusiasm. Throughout

ACKNOWLEDGEMENTS

the long process of publication, I always felt supported and encouraged. It was a pleasure to work with you all. Thank you!

I sincerely thank the artists and organisations that enabled me to use live recordings from two concerts for some of the musical examples given in this book. First, Asma Diakité, Francois Venter and Bongani Njalo from the Goethe-Institut, Johannesburg, hosted a Moerane choral concert on 17 October 2023. At this event, The Chanticleer Singers conducted by Richard Cock and Quava Vocal Group conducted by Sabelo Mthembu sang 11 Moerane songs, which were recorded by Frequency Manipulation. Second, the Kyiv Symphony Orchestra, under the management of Alexandra Zaitseva and the baton of Arjan Tien, gave a wonderful rendition of Moerane's symphonic poem *Fatše La Heso* on 8 December 2023 at the Internationales Chor- und Orchestermusikfestival in Kassel, Germany, organised by the Director of the Festival, Musa Nkuna.

Among the many other individuals who also gave intellectual or practical assistance during my years of research for the Moerane Scholarly Edition and this biography, I would particularly like to express my deepest gratitude to Zayne Upton, the webmaster of www.african-composers-edition.co.za and to the following people: Susan Brown, Anriette Chorn, William Fourie, Ron and Priscilla Hall, Pamela Hicks, Mokale Koapeng, Barry Liknaitzky, Ignatia Madalane, Percy and Flesba Mangoaela, Paul Maylam, Nandipha Mnyani, Angus Moir, Kgaugelo Mpyane, Grant Olwage, Leigh Phipson, Nosipho Rapiya, Hilde Roos, André Le Roux, Cara Stacey, Thembela Vokwana and Liz Welsh.

The following institutions are also acknowledged:

Cory Library for Historical Research, Rhodes University, Grahamstown
Documentation Centre for Music, Stellenbosch University, Stellenbosch
International Library of African Music, Rhodes University, Grahamstown
Lukhanji Museum, Komani (formerly Queenstown and Frontier Museum)
Morija Museum and Archives, Morija, Lesotho
National Library of South Africa, Pretoria

National Sesotho–Afrikaans Literary Museum, Bloemfontein
South African Broadcasting Corporation Radio Sound Archives, Johannesburg
South African History Archive, Johannesburg
South African Society for Research in Music
Southern African Music Rights Organisation, Johannesburg
University of Cape Town Manuscripts and Archives, Cape Town
William Cullen Library, Wits University, Johannesburg

This book is dedicated to my brother, John Lucia, who has always been there for me, and whose generous and critical nature shows me who I am.

Map of Southern Africa showing Key Places in Moerane's Life

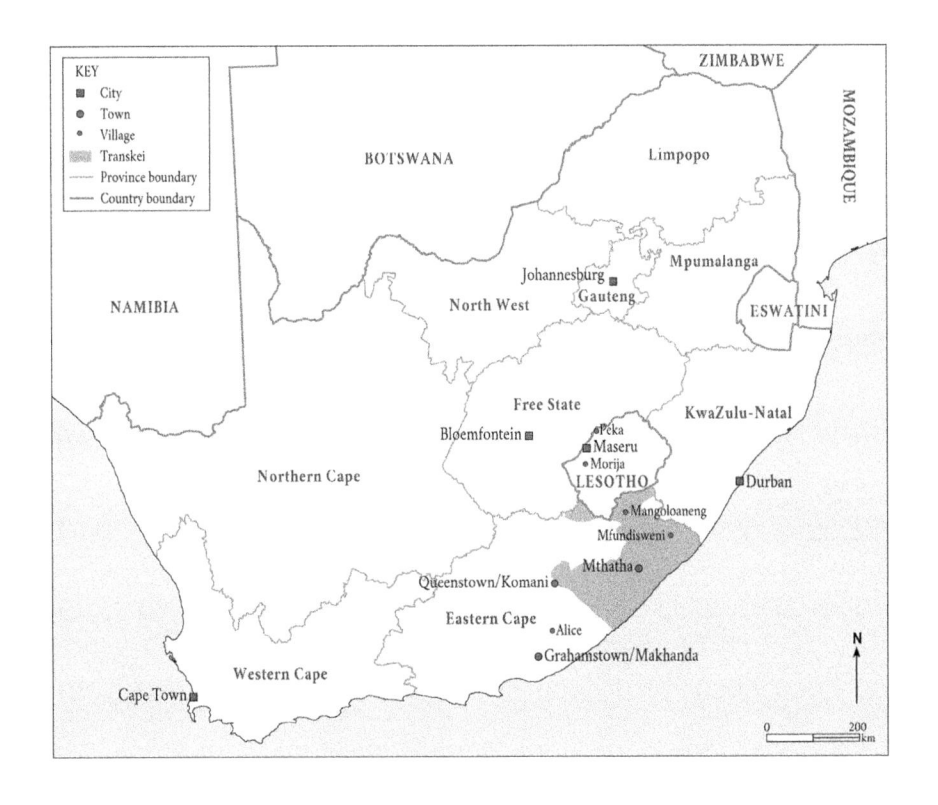

Timeline of Political Events 1880–1991

1880–81: First South African (Anglo-Boer) War
1884: Annexation of Thaba 'Nchu by the Boer Republic of the Orange Free State
1887: King William's Town Conference of Vigilance Associations (Jabavu)[1]
1891: Death of Letsie I, son of Moshoeshoe I, and ascendancy of Lerotholi
1899–1902: Second South African (Anglo-Boer) War
Early 1900s: Transvaal Congress, Orange River Colony Native Congress, Bapedi Union, Basuto Association, Cape Native Convention (Jabavu)
1904: *Naleli ea Lesotho* (*Star of Basutoland*) newspaper launched[2]
1904: Moerane born on 20 September in Mangoloaneng, Cape Colony
1905: Death of Lerotholi and ascendancy of Letsie II
1907: The Progressive Association of Lesotho;[3] Cape elections
1909: South African National Convention, Bloemfontein (Rabusana)
1910: The Union of South Africa, into which Basutoland, Bechuanaland and Swaziland resisted incorporation
1912: South African Native National Congress (SANCC, later African National Congress, ANC)
1913: Death of Letsie II and rise of Nathaniel Griffith Lerotholi; Native Land Act[4]
1914: National Party established in South Africa (Hertzog)
1914–18: World War I
1915: Socialist League of South Africa
1917–23: Russian Revolution
1918: Union of South Africa; Broederbond established

1919: Lekhotla la Bafo (The Commoners' League, Lesotho); Communist International (Comintern)[5]

1920: Native Affairs Act

1920–21: Moerane studies in Morija

1921: Communist Party of South Africa (called South African Communist Party after 1953)

1922: Moerane teaches at St John's College, Umtata

1923: Native Urban Areas Act

1923: Moerane enrols at Lovedale High School

1925: Lekhotla la Bafo associates with ANC

1927: Native Administration Act

1929: Lekhotla la Bafo affiliates with international League against Imperialism[6]

1929–33: The Great Depression

1929: National Party wins election (Hertzog); United Party established

1930: Lekhotla la Bafo establishes connections with the Comintern[7]

1930: Moerane begins a BMus degree part-time

1931: Moerane marries, first child is born

1933: Adolf Hitler Chancellor of Germany[8]

1935–36: All-Africa Convention in Bloemfontein[9]

1936: Native Trust and Land Act[10]

1936–37: Basotho miners' riots on the Reef

1937: International Committee on African Affairs (later Council on African Affairs), USA[11]

1938: Native Administration Proclamation and Native Courts Proclamation, Lesotho

1939: United Party wins South African election (Smuts)

1939–45: World War II

1939–40: Moerane teaches at Basutoland High School in Maseru

1940: Alfred Xuma ANC president[12]

1941: Moerane returns to the Cape, completes BMus degree

1942: Moerane begins teaching at the African (later 'Bantu') Secondary School, Queenstown

1943: Non-European Unity Movement (NEUM)[13]

1944: ANC Youth League (ANCYL)[14]

1945: University of Lesotho established at Roma, Maseru

TIMELINE OF POLITICAL EVENTS 1880-1991

1946: Albert Luthuli ANC president
1947: Ashby Mda ANCYL leader[15]
1948: National Party wins South African election (Malan)
1949: ANC Conference, peaceful programme of action planned
1950: ANCYL Africanist movement (Mda, Robert Sobukwe)
1950–52: Defiance Campaign
1952: Basutoland African Congress (later called Basutoland Congress Party, BCP)[16]
1953: Criminal Law Amendment Act and Public Safety Act
1954: Basutoland's first political newspaper, *Mohlabani*; Africanist Movement led by Sobukwe and Potlako Leballo
1955: Freedom Charter adopted at Congress of the People, Kliptown[17]
1955ff: Split between Africanists and Charterists; Sobukwe Editor of *The Africanist*
1956–61: Treason Trial[18]
1957: Ghana gains independence under Nkrumah[19]
1957: Moerane expelled from Queenstown's Bantu Secondary School
1958: All Africa People's Conference in Ghana;[20] BCP Conference in Maseru, attended by Sobukwe, Leballo and Madzunya; Basutoland National Party (BNP); new Basutoland Constitution
1958–59: Moerane teaches at Mfundisweni College of Education, Mpondoland
1959: Pan-Africanist Congress (PAC) (Sobukwe);[21] Constantinus Bereng installed as Moshoeshoe II
1960: 2nd PAC Conference in Maseru votes for armed insurrection in SA; Sobukwe jailed for three years; Sharpeville massacre, State of Emergency; ANC and PAC banned; pass laws suspended; PAC armed wing (Poqo) uprising in Transkei;[22] BCP majority in Basutoland District Elections
1961: South Africa leaves Commonwealth and becomes Republic; Marematlou Freedom Party, Basutoland (Khaketla), Basutoland Congress of Trade Unions; the Lesotho Communist Party; ANC armed wing (Umkhonto we Sizwe); Ciskei self-governing 'homeland'
1961: Moerane joins staff of Peka High School, Lesotho
1962: Defiance Campaign; Leballo PAC leader; PAC violence in Cape
1963: Police Mobile Unit in Lesotho;[23] British police raid PAC HQ in Maseru;[24] Transkei self-governing 'homeland'
1963–64: Rivonia Trial[25]

xxi

1964: Basotho Constitutional Conference; Zambia independence

1965: Basutoland General Election won by BNP (Chief Leabua Jonathan)[26]

1966: Verwoerd assassinated, John Vorster Prime Minister; Lesotho Independence 4 October;[27] Malawi independence

1966: Thuso Moerane served with a five-year banning order; March 1966: Moerane writes to Percival Kirby 'The times do not permit'

1967: Terrorism Act, Luthuli killed, Tambo ANC leader

1968: PAC reorients towards synthesis of Africanism and Maoism; Swaziland independence

1969: African Student Movement (later the South African Students Movement)

1970: Leabua Jonathan seizes power in Lesotho, suspends Constitution, declares State of Emergency[28]

1970s: Rise of the Black Consciousness Movement (Steve Biko)

1972: Black People's Convention (BPC);[29] South African Students Movement (SASM) organises against Bantu Education

1973: Steve Biko banned;[30] Afrikaner Weerstandsbeweging (Afrikaner Resistance Movement, Terre'Blanche)

1974: Failed coup in Lesotho; Angola independence

1975: Inkatha National Liberation Movement (later Inkatha Freedom Party);[31] Mozambique independence

1976: Soweto uprising against compulsory Afrikaans in African schools

1977: National Party 'total onslaught' strategy; Progressive Federal Party; Steve Biko dies in detention[32]

1977: Moerane's grandson Lenare shot dead by police in Queenstown

1978: PW Botha Prime Minister; Leballo chair of PAC[33]

1979: Guerrilla war in Lesotho; Bophuthatswana self-governing 'homeland'

1980: Zimbabwe independence

1980: *Moerane dies on 27 January in Bloemfontein*

1983: United Democratic Front;[34] Tricameral Parliament SA

1984–1990: Armed struggle

1985: State of Emergency

1986: Lesotho military coup (Jonathan deposed by Lekhanya)

1987: Mineworkers strike; Immorality Act repealed

1988: Explosions and killings in South Africa all year

1989: FW de Klerk replaces PW Botha as South Africa's president; fall of Berlin Wall
1990: Nelson Mandela released from prison; ANC, PAC, South African Communist Party unbanned; Namibia independence; Moshoeshoe II exiled in UK
1991: USSR dissolves; Lesotho military coup (Lekhanya deposed by Ramaema).

Preface

Books about composers are generally located in subject areas such as orchestral or piano music, opera or chamber music, jazz, electro-acoustic music, popular music, folk or traditional music. The focus of this 'musical life', Michael Mosoeu Moerane (1904–1980), wrote one short orchestral work but more than 80 short *a cappella* choral works for amateur choir, of which only about 10 were known during his lifetime. Composers in the past about whom biographies are written tended to have worked mainly in Europe, North, Central or South America, the Russian Federation and Australasia. Moerane, on the other hand, spent his whole life in rural southern Africa: first the British Cape Colony, then the British Protectorate of Basutoland, then apartheid South Africa and post-independence Lesotho, the latter, one of the smallest and poorest countries in the world.

In addition to subject area and geographical area, there is another unconventional factor in this case. This is not a detailed chronological biography, but an overview of Moerane and his music from different perspectives. A birth to death narrative, even if this were desirable, is impossible because insufficient personal and professional documentation survives to support such an account. If there were personal diaries, certificates, memoirs, notes, memos, LPs and books, they have disappeared – only a few photographs and professional letters are to be found. If much more had existed, however, would it have brought us any closer to 'the truth' about Moerane? Biography, to Freud, was an exercise in idealisation, which is why he went to some lengths to destroy his professional papers.

Peter Gay makes this claim in the Preface to his biography of Freud, where he also quotes Freud's warning: 'Whoever turns biographer, commits himself to lies, to concealment, to hypocrisy, to embellishments, and even to dissembling his own lack of understanding, for biological truth is not to be had, and, even if one had it, one could not use it.'[1] There are a couple of truths about Moerane in this book that might make some members of the family uncomfortable, but they are very far from amounting to 'biographical truth' writ large. As for dissembling my lack of understanding, some readers will no doubt find plenty of this here. (That 'no doubt' is already an example of dissembling.) There are embellishments, too, but – and this is the crux of the matter – they are not significant; there is occasional speculation, but no attempt to fabricate missing detail. Rather, there are copious explanations of the background and the circumstances from which Moerane emerged as a composer, of the times in which he lived – with the purpose of showing how important these were in shaping his life and his musical legacy as it has come down to us today. The obscurity of this black African choral composer in southern Africa in the first eight decades of the twentieth century, and the lack of documentary evidence, has shifted the focus of this book very firmly onto history, culture and place. It shows ways in which Moerane's musical life was lived in history – notably political history – in southern Africa. It explores the *preconditions* that existed for him to have had such a life as he had; and it was in many ways a successful life as a composer and teacher. It shows what he could and did do; but it also reveals what he could not do. However, the life not lived hinted at in this narrative is not presented as a tragedy of missed opportunities, but as a reminder of what happens when political systems and social circumstances fail individuals in their struggle to be creative, and prevent them from becoming widely known for their work, nationally and internationally. Moerane so deserved this kind of recognition during his lifetime. I hope this book begins the process of exploring his life and evaluating his contribution to the musical world.

Thanks to the Southern African Music Rights Organisation (SAMRO) and Moerane's sons Thabo and Thuso, much of the music written by Moerane *has* survived, including works previously unknown. This body of work was published in 2020 by African Composers Edition (ACE) and makes an overview of his music possible for the first time.[2] Moerane's personal voice remains lacking in this book, which is the poorer for it, but I hope that the voices of people who knew him, spoken through interviews and the professional letters reproduced here, partly compensate for this.

The emphasis on history, the absence of Moerane's personal voice and the desire to make his music known have shaped this book's structure. The Introduction and first three chapters concern his life and times, or rather, times and life. Chapter 4 presents professional letters to, from, or about Moerane to give his voice some small presence; the remainder of the book, including a chapter on choral music that explains the significance of this genre in African society, is given over to Moerane's music.

Note to the reader: I use the words 'African' and 'black' almost interchangeably in this book, although the former tends to mean 'born or made in Africa' and the latter refers to colour. This is not a book that uses 'black' as 'non-white' in the sense sometimes used in South Africa. It is a book about blackness in classical music in southern Africa historically – and how this kind of musical identity struggles to define itself.

The titles of Moerane's extant works published in 2020 by African Composers Edition are given in italics; only where titles refer to manuscript sources do they appear in single quotes

This book draws on many sources, in some of which spellings, diacritical marks or accents differ from those used by Moerane. This causes apparent typographical inconsistencies in the text. These are retained here rather than corrected, so as to stay as close as possible to the historical materials we had to work with.

If URL links from musical examples fail, contact info@african-composers-edition.co.za.

Introduction: Moerane in Life and Literature

Michael Mosoeu Moerane is one of South Africa's foremost mid-twentieth century composers, and was the first black South African to get a BMus degree. His extraordinary legacy has been overlooked because so little of it is known; and because the times in which he lived did not allow a black composer to gain any prominence.

In this work, which represents over a decade of detective work, trawling through archives and tracking down family members and former students, I attempt to recreate, from oral sources and fragments of archival material, a fitting portrait of one of our most compelling cultural figures. In narrating Moerane's musical life, we cover the political and social history of southern Africa during some of its most turbulent decades, presided over by the ideologies of imperialism and grand apartheid. In so doing, new light is shed on Moerane's contribution to this region's music history, and on our understanding of that history within a global context.

This introduction begins with a brief overview of Moerane's life in order to establish a few facts, with pointers to later chapters where fuller explanations are given. A survey of previous writing on Moerane follows – a 'literature review' – that reveals ways in which his life in twentieth-century colonial and apartheid South Africa and colonial and postcolonial Lesotho has been represented. In today's climate of redress for previously neglected composers, one does not always learn how marginalisation or erasure of a composer's life and music happens or how 'race' impinges on this.

Moerane's early life

Michael Mosoeu Moerane was born on 20 September 1904, the second son of Eleazar Jakane Moerane and his wife, Sofia Majara.[1] His birthplace was Mangoloaneng, a village in the Mount Fletcher district of the Eastern Cape located in the larger region of what was then the British Cape Colony, a region known as East Griqualand or Transkei (see the map at the beginning of this book).

Mangoloaneng was established as a 'French mission outstation',[2] where Moerane's father, Eleazar, who was descended from a long line of Basotho chiefs, acted both as an emissary for the Basotho royal family and an evangelist for the Paris Evangelical Missionary Society. Eleazar Jakane and his family established a homestead that grew into one of great self-sufficiency.[3]

Moerane attended his father's junior primary school in Mangoloaneng, and the Mariazell Catholic mission school a few kilometres to the north for higher primary classes.[4] Later, Moerane would travel across the border into what was then the British Protectorate of Basutoland to complete middle schooling at Morija Training Institution in 1921,[5] where he obtained a primary school teaching certificate. It was the norm in southern Africa in those days for teenagers who had not yet completed higher schooling to qualify as teachers of young children, and there was also nothing unusual about crossing the Basutoland border to do so; Morija Training Institution was the nearest middle school, besides being the most famous African mission in the region. Moerane went on to teach for a year at St John's College, Mthatha,[6] and in 1923 he enrolled at Lovedale High School in Alice, completing the level then called Standard 8, in 1924.[7] The photograph shown in Figure 0.1, which is in almost every Moerane home today, may have been taken when he entered Lovedale, and gives a glimpse of him as a youth.

In 1926, Moerane completed Standards 9 and 10, as the final two years of secondary school were then called and obtained a matriculation certificate at the South African Native College (later called Fort Hare University College, now Fort Hare University).[8] He taught at Lovedale High School while completing a high school teaching diploma at Lovedale Training School. By 1929, he was on the staff of the Lovedale Practising Schools as well, and in 1931, at the age of 27, Moerane had obtained a permanent post at Lovedale High School, which he held for the next eight years. In the same year, 1931, he married Beatrice Betty Msweli, who had

Figure 0.1: Moerane as a young man (courtesy Tsepo Moerane)

been a fellow student at Lovedale.⁹ Their first child, Mofelehetsi (Count), was born in Alice at the end of 1931, followed by a daughter, Mathabo (Lineo). A third child and second son, Thuso (Majalla), was born in 1935 in Kroonstad, where Moerane's wife was teaching at the time.

Meanwhile, in 1930, Moerane had registered for a Bachelor of Music degree part-time, through the University of South Africa (Unisa),¹⁰ which was at that time the only southern African university offering examinations to external, non-resident (black) students.¹¹ Unisa was not yet a teaching institution, and Fort Hare did not offer a BMus degree. Moerane thus took the music courses offered through Rhodes University College in Grahamstown (present-day Makhanda), studying by himself in Alice, where he was teaching, and taking the exams through Unisa.

In 1939, Moerane and his family moved to Basutoland, where he took up a post at the newly opened Basutoland High School in Maseru (now called Lesotho High School), teaching Sesotho and Commercial Arithmetic, among other things.[12] Throughout Moerane's career as an African teacher, music education and performance remained extramural activities. The couple had two more girls, Halieo (Lucinda), and Sophia (Metsekae) (born 1940), and moved back to Alice in the eastern Cape Colony in 1940.

Moerane completed his final fourth-year BMus (Honours) courses in 1941, studying with Friedrich Hartmann (who was appointed lecturer in music at Rhodes in 1939), and writing the orchestral work, *Fatše La Heso*, which was to become his most famous composition, which I discuss in Chapter 5.[13] In 1942, Moerane obtained a position at the African Secondary School in Queenstown. Here the family first lived in Victoria Road, and then moved to Number 10 Scanlen Street.[14] His last-born son, Thabo (Kabeli), was born in Queenstown in 1947.

Around 1950, Moerane received a small donation of orchestral instruments. With these, he 'organised the African Springtime Orchestra,

Figure 0.2: The African Springtime Orchestra in Queenstown c. 1952. Moerane is standing at the back, his wife Betty is seated in the middle, his son Thuso is seated on the left holding a violin (courtesy Sophia Metsekae Moerane, Marumo Moerane and Jonathan Ball Publishers)

which met after school hours, taught students to play (orchestral) instruments.'[15] Most of his children played in this orchestra, shown in Figure 0.2, which comprised stringed instruments, flutes, clarinets, trumpet and trombone. For a while, one of the other family members was his sister Epainette's son. This was the young Thabo Mbeki, a future president of South Africa, who lived with his uncle and aunt in Queenstown in 1952.[16]

Moerane's later life
Moerane lived in Queenstown until 1958, supporting the Non-European Unity Movement (NEUM) and joining the Cape African Teachers Association (CATA), which organised protests against the introduction of the South African Government's apartheid policy of Bantu Education. As a result of his political activities, he went into 'enforced retirement' in 1957, and was banned from teaching in Queenstown. He then went to Mpondoland in 1958 to teach at Mfundisweni Teacher Training Institute, but may have fallen out with the authorities there, too, and returned to Queenstown for a while. In 1961, he took up a position at Peka High School in northern Basutoland, where he formed a new configuration of instrumental players called the Peka High School Orchestra.[17] As a Basutoland Congress Party (BCP) member he opposed the conservative Basutoland National Party (BNP), led by Chief Leabua Jonathan (1914–1987). Jonathan became the first Prime Minister of Lesotho in 1966, but lost the 1970 election to the BCP. He nevertheless seized power in a coup that year, and presided over a brutal regime in Lesotho during which hundreds of people were tortured or killed,[18] before he himself was finally removed in a coup in 1986, six years after Moerane's death.

Moerane's wife Betty, fondly remembered by family members as 'Auntie Betty' was clearly a great homemaker. This was about far more than raising children and doing domestic chores. She was part of the 'Zenzele' movement in southern Africa, which was a powerful voice in gender politics, its influence spreading across large areas of Africa.[19] Moerane's mother, Sofia, as Mark Gevisser points out, had been a stalwart of this 'self improvement organisation', whose members worked 'with less-educated women to teach them how to farm, how to cook, and how to generate additional income from cottage industry.'[20] Moerane even wrote a song in praise of 'Ma-Homemakers', set to words by his wife.

In the late 1960s, the couple drifted apart and Betty Moerane went to live with their son Thuso's family in Queenstown until her death.[21] Thuso was himself a political activist who shouldered the forced removal of his family from their home in Queenstown in the 1960s, and was served with a banning order on 15 February 1966.[22] The Moerane home at 10 Scanlen Street was bulldozed under the Group Areas Act, and Thuso and his family were eventually resettled in 'Mlungisi location in Queenstown. Remarkably, Number 8 Scanlen St, where composer Todd Matshikiza lived, and Number 6, where singer Lex Mona lived, were not destroyed. It is fascinating to think of two such important musicians as Moerane and Matshikiza, the composer of the musical *King Kong*, as neighbours. They did not get along, apparently, but Moerane nevertheless tutored several of Queenstown's jazz musicians.[23] He disapproved of the 'immorality' and liquor often associated with jazz performance, and tried to stop his children from being unduly influenced by their neighbours.[24]

Moerane taught at Peka High School until his retirement, and in the 1970s he helped to establish the music department at the new National Teachers Training College in Maseru (NTTC), now called the Lesotho Teachers Training College.[25] He retired to his home in the village of Tsifalimali, in the Leribe District of Lesotho. Here he cultivated a large vegetable garden and had a small shop attached to serve the local people. His son, Thabo, who was by then working in Geneva, visited his father there and eventually retired to Tsifalimali himself after his father's death. Father and son were by all accounts very close, with Thabo inheriting his father's enormous musical talent. The photo in Figure 0.3, taken c. 1964, shows Moerane teaching Thabo at their home, then on the grounds of Peka High School.

Moerane became ill in late 1979 or early 1980, and went into Queen Elizabeth Hospital in Maseru, from which he was transferred to Pelonomi Hospital in Bloemfontein, where he died on 27 January 1980.[26] Michael Mosoeu Moerane is buried in the graveyard in Tsifalimali. Thabo, who died of cancer in 2006, is buried next to his father. The family raised Michael Mosoeu's tombstone in 1988,[27] on which occasion Manasseh Tebatso Moerane (also known as 'MT'), the distinguished educationist, journalist and cultural activist, gave an address honouring his late brother. The following extracts show the family's deep pride in the composer.[28]

INTRODUCTION

Figure 0.3: Moerane teaching his son Thabo the piano c. 1964 (courtesy Sophia Metsekae Moerane, Marumo Moerane and Jonathan Ball Publishers)

Chiefs, Honoured Guests, Ladies and Gentlemen and you the family of Pelesana.[29]

[…] The hero we are commemorating here was a real pioneer. […] Michael composed beautiful songs such as *Liphala* and some which have been prescribed for competition at different Eistedffeau, such as *Morena Tlake, Ruri, Sylvia* and his last and best *Matlala*. […] Michael Moerane was a deep non-racialist. He proscribed that his songs should not be used on Radio Bantu if they were not used on the 'white' channels of S.A.B.C. [South African Broadcasting Corporation] […] He was so active in fighting for the rights of the African child and the African teacher that he was a thorn in the flesh of the Education Department. [...] He made a worthy contribution to the struggle of our people for freedom in the Teachers' Association. Indeed, he made a contribution to the education of the Black Man in Southern Africa over a long time and a wide area, but his greatest contribution was to the cultural heritage of society. He trained thousands of music teachers-to-be and above all through his own composition[s]. We raise our hats to Michael today and say Bravo! Yet even as we do so we realise that though much has been done, much remains to be accomplished; so while we thank God for giving us Michael, we pray that he raise more Michaels to follow in his trail, so that all Southern Africa may resound with music from the united free and happy hearts.

Moerane's musical output

Moerane's musical output is discussed in detail in Chapters 5 to 9. He wrote more than eighty works, most of them for unaccompanied choir. As Chapter 6 shows, some have been lost and only a few are dated.[30] In 1936, he wrote a set of solo piano pieces called *Album for the Young* – with the same title as Schumann's set of 43 short pieces written in 1848 – and it won the May Esther Bedford Prize for Musical Composition at Fort Hare.[31] Two of his choral works, *Liphala* (*Whistles*) and an arrangement of the American spiritual *Nobody Knows The Trouble I've Seen* were published by Lovedale Press in tonic solfa notation in 1938; other than these, he saw none of his music published during his lifetime. The Southern African Music Rights Organisation (SAMRO) published *Barali Ba Jerusalema* in dual solfa-staff notation in 1998, and *Della* in 2008.[32] Only about ten of his choral works were known before 2000, as prescribed music for competitions, for which purposes they were published informally by the competition organisers. *Fatše La Heso* received several international live performances and at least one national radio broadcast during Moerane's lifetime, and has had an interesting reception history since then. A *Catalogue of Works by Michael Mosoeu Moerane* is given in the Appendix, which shows scoring, duration and key, while sources for his scores and an overview of choral works are given in Chapter 6.[33]

MT Moerane's address above expresses a pride in MM Moerane and his achievements shared by many people in South Africa and Lesotho, particularly in the African choral sector. A trophy in the house in Tsifalimali bears testimony to this. The Eastern Cape Department of Sport, Recreation, Arts and Culture (DSRAC) awarded it posthumously on 14 December 2004 for his 'contribution to Xhosa choral music', as the inscription reads. Dr Mavis Noluthando Mpola, then Deputy Director of DSRAC, was keen to counter the tendency among choirs to see choral music as belonging in the 'public domain' by making a point of honouring individual African composers; she most likely instigated the award.[34] The wording on the trophy reflects the reality that for many choralists in South Africa, *Sylvia* and *Della* – both of which have isiXhosa lyrics – represent Moerane, although it does brush over the fact that almost all his other songs are in Sesotho. Moerane may have been born in the Eastern Cape, but he thought of himself as Mosotho – a person of Lesotho – because of his family background, his mother-tongue and his culture.

Two separate communities knew Moerane's music during his lifetime, and to a large extent this is still the case. He was, and remains, well known in African communities for *a cappella* choral music written in tonic solfa notation, but there was almost no knowledge in these circles of his orchestral work, *Fatše La Heso*. This bifurcated view resulted from the entrenchment of South Africa's racially divided 'parallel streams' of music production and reception.[35] The fact that two communities knew Moerane differently is entirely due to decades of racially unequal educational and performing arts policies in South Africa.

What is less clear is how the tangled web of discourse surrounding Moerane until the present day came about, since the 'two communities' are theoretically less separated than they were before 1990. An example of a change in discourse can be seen in the way Moerane's reputation as a choral composer gained momentum in white South African musical circles during the rapidly changing political climate of 1990–1994, as South Africa moved towards a new democratic government. Historian Kenneth Grundy gives a first-hand account of the politics of this violent transition period, in which national cultural policy was thrown into complete disarray;[36] and Louise Meintjes has eloquently described what it was like to do fieldwork in Johannesburg's recording studios during these times.[37] It was an interregnum, to paraphrase Gramsci's famous remark from his *Prison Notebooks*, in which 'the old [order] is dying and the new cannot be born' and in which 'a great variety of morbid symptoms appear'.[38] Some of these symptoms are manifest in the sudden resurgence of interest in Moerane's music during this time. As explained in Chapter 6, his *Barali Ba Jerusalema* was championed by SAMRO to such an extent that they commissioned Eben van der Merwe to paint an imagined portrait of Moerane sitting at his piano holding the manuscript of *Barali Ba Jerusalema*, which is rather like the 1748 Haussmann portrait of Bach.[39] Moerane's face is based on the photograph shown in Figure 0.1.

Moerane in the literature

Moerane's name is most frequently found in the literature on African choral music in southern Africa. This has emerged sporadically since 1968, when Deirdre Hansen wrote a short monograph on Benjamin Tyamzashe, and 1969, when Yvonne Huskisson published the first survey of 'Bantu' composers, later revised in 1992.[40] Some of this literature refers to Moerane obliquely: essays by Khabi Mngoma and Bongani Mthethwa in the 1980s identify syncretic elements in choral music generally, including his.[41] In the 1990s, Veit Erlmann writes about Moerane's contemporary, Reuben Caluza, locating him within a broad sociopolitical history of popular and choral music.[42] Sibongile Khumalo and PJ Nhlapo give an overview of the choral genre,[43] and Christopher Ballantine describes the compositional process of Ladysmith Black Mambazo's leader, Joseph Shabalala.[44] In the 2000s to 2020s, Markus Detterbeck uses action research methodology as part of his study of the Pietermaritzburg Choral Society, and Grant Olwage explores choralism and (post)colonialism in the Eastern Cape.[45] George Mugovhani and I write about choral music and identity;[46] and Vivien Pieters gives an account of Moerane at Lovedale.[47] The first extended pieces on Moerane and his music are my own 'General Introduction' to the *Michael Mosoeu Moerane Scholarly Edition* and 'Catalogue of Works', as well as historical introductions to 52 of the works in that 2020 edition.[48]

Moerane's name also appears in some of the general literature on South African music. In 2007, Mark Gevisser devotes a chapter in his biography of Thabo Mbeki to Moerane's family: 'The Moeranes: Chekhov in the Transkei'.[49] Gevisser's book is not about music, and it naturally reinforces the single most quoted fact about Moerane – that he was Mbeki's uncle – but it is a significant source not least because Gevisser interviewed many family members, and also left a large archive of research documents.[50] In the general South African music literature, Moerane is mentioned in dictionary entries, reviews and surveys, correspondence in the Kirby Papers in the University of Cape Town (UCT) Archives, Rhodes University's Cory Library for Historical Research and the Yvonne Huskisson collection in the Archive of the Southern African Music Rights Organisation, as well as in unpublished essays, eisteddfod programmes and memoirs.[51] These are, nevertheless, mostly brief outlines or mere mentions, and aside from short articles on Africlassical.com and Wikipedia, it is immensely frustrating to have so little accurate information on such an important figure. Even within the minor reportage on Moerane, the bulk of it reiterates the same information, some of it incorrect.[52]

The two family documents quoted here by Moerane's brother MT and Moerane's son Thuso are an exception. These are reliable posthumous sources. I have, however, found very few family photographs showing Moerane; and there are apparently no surviving notebooks, diaries, journals or teaching materials that would testify to his thoughts and actions or confirm a host of factual details. One secondary source, journalist Carmel Rickard's interview with Thabo Moerane for the *Weekly Mail* in 1988, does quote comments on Moerane's music by Thabo, showing his sense of responsibility for preserving his father's musical legacy.[53] Thuso took on this responsibility after his brother Thabo's death in 2006; and Thuso's son, Tsepo, has done so since Thuso's death in 2020. Thanks to this caretaking, many of Moerane's musical manuscripts and typescripts have survived. His former home in Tsifalimali has nothing personal to Moerane, aside from his metronome,[54] but Tsepo Moerane has Moerane's Fort Hare blazer and his Unisa/Rhodes BMus academic gown and hood in Komani. (They show that Moerane was not very tall.) The instruments of the African Springtime Orchestra have evidently vanished. But Moerane's piano has not, because his eldest son, Mofelehetsi, took it back to his house in Atteridgeville after his father's death.[55]

The earliest dictionary entry on Moerane gives his date of birth correctly as 20 September 1904,[56] a date reiterated by writers in the 1980s;[57] but in the 1990s it became 12 September 1902 or 21 September 1904, and eventually, through publications emanating from SAMRO, 20 September 1909.[58] (The Old Mutual National Choir Festival celebrated his birth centenary in 2009.[59]) The date of Moerane's death also varies in the literature. It is correct in a notice in the *Rand Daily Mail*,[60] but other sources say February 1980 or February 1981.[61] In a recent PhD thesis, Moerane's dates are still given as 1909–1981.[62] Africlassical.com, the most comprehensive website for African and African-American classical composers, used to have an entry on Moerane that gave SAMRO's information verbatim, crediting the latter's 'Brief Biographical Notes' and an online Dictionary of African Composers at the University of Pretoria, which also had incorrect information.[63]

Moerane's religion, the places of his birth and death and his ethnicity are also reported in variable and inconsistent ways. Pallo Jordan described the family as 'practising Catholics' in an obituary of Moerane's sister Epainette Mbeki in 2014, but they were in fact members of the Protestant Evangelical Lutheran Church (from 1933 called the Lutheran Evangelical Church[64]), and in Queenstown, Moerane attended the Presbyterian Church. It does not seem a grave mistake on the face of things, but in Lesotho during the 1960s and 1970s, the two main political parties were split along religious lines: 'Protestant–BCP, Catholic–BNP'.[65] Furthermore, the Catholic Order of the Oblates of Mary Immaculate 'considerably strengthened the authoritarian influence within the [Lesotho] chieftaincy', says Bernard Leeman, 'to the detriment of the democratic tradition'.[66] So it is important to establish that Moerane was a baptised Protestant, a BCP member, and above all, a man of 'deep democratic values'.[67]

SAMRO gives Moerane's place of birth as Lesotho but it was in fact South Africa (the Eastern Cape);[68] he was said to have 'taught President Mbeki to play the violin' but it was the flute.[69] More insulting, but unsurprising in a country that racialised ethnicities for so long, people connected to the SABC designated him at different times as 'S.[South] Sotho', 'Xhosa' and 'Zoeloe'.[70] (South Sotho is not even an ethnicity, but a language within the Sotho–Tswana group of languages.) Parastatals such as the SABC, where Huskisson worked as Organiser for Radio Bantu, used these terms to broadcast separate channels to different African language groups in the country, in order to maintain and promote their separate identities and thereby uphold a cornerstone of apartheid. The SABC orchestra played *Fatše La Heso* in 1973, with this performance broadcast on the English Service on 8 August at 10 pm.[71] It was also, however, played on one of the

'Bantu' stations, with the Head of Music at the SABC writing to Huskisson, 'Perhaps you would like to announce this to your Xhosa listeners and also drop the composer a line.'[72] *Fatše la Heso* would have made more sense to Sotho listeners, given that its title refers to Lesotho, not South Africa; furthermore, Basotho are more likely to have recognised the Sotho folk themes on which it is based. But the independent sovereign state of Lesotho was a thorn in the flesh of apartheid South Africa, and playing the work on Radio Sotho would be an acknowledgement that many Basotho lived in South Africa; this would make a mockery of the SABC's (and the government's) rigid categorisation of people into separate ethnicities and places. It is unlikely that Moerane saw this internal memo, but Huskisson did tell him about the English Service broadcast, with which he was in fact utterly delighted. His letter to Huskisson on this point is given in full in Chapter 4. In general, however, Moerane 'did not want to have his music played on the SABC'.[73]

Other sources in the literature confuse places where Moerane taught and when: an early Afrikaans source says he taught at 'Maseru-Hoërskool [High School] (1938–63) [...] en sedert 1964 by Peka Hoërskool [and since 1964 at Peka High School], Gumtree, Lesotho';[74] but Moerane left *Basutoland High School* – which was called Lesotho, not Maseru High School three decades later – at the end of 1940, and joined Peka High School in 1961, not 1964. The same source gives Moerane's middle initial as 'H'. Huskisson repeats some of this: 'Since 1964, Moerane has been teaching at Peka High School, Gumtree.'[75] The notice of Moerane's death in the *Rand Daily Mail Extra* states, oddly, that he was 'survived by his wife, Mrs Mamofelehetsi Moerane, and a son, Mr Count Mofelehetsi Moerane', but Moerane and his wife Beatrice Betty had six children.[76] This Mofelehetsi Moerane, of Atteridgeville in South Africa, has been confused with a cousin, Mofelehetsi Moerane of Maseru, who was a BCP activist in Lesotho during the 1970s and risked his life in a coup attempt in 1974.[77] It is easy to confuse Sotho names, however, because in Basotho lineages people often bear the same names; and surnames may become first names and vice versa. Huskisson claims in 1969 that Moerane 'was married and had five children' (it was six) and that in his song, *Sylvia*, 'he bids his sister, to whom he was inordinately attached, farewell as she leaves home'. Moerane did indeed write *Sylvia* for someone 'to whom he was inordinately attached', but she was not his sister.

Moerane operated in several spheres simultaneously: family, school, church, black choral competitions, white orchestral culture, radio; he moved between the Eastern Cape and Lesotho, and was separated from his wife in later life; and he was by all accounts a very private man. Compounding this, he is likely to have had a strong sense of his 'double-consciousness' as a black composer living in a world of 'men who are black and whitened',[78] a consciousness that made him even less inclined to reveal or confirm personal details to establishment figures who would have no sense of his true identity. Whatever the reason, many spurious facts about Moerane have been perpetuated. Although I don't claim to have 'all the facts' correct, I have tried, in this book, to give evidence for them wherever possible. I end this chapter with one particularly confusing example of this, relating to a place called Gumtree.

This name crops up regularly in the literature as a place in Lesotho where Moerane was born, lived, taught and died. In fact, it is a tiny village in Free State Province, South Africa, a short distance across the Lesotho border from Peka High School. It comprises a former railway station and former mill, some farm buildings and a few houses. According to photographer Tessa Joughlin, Gumtree was 'a hive of activity' in the earlier twentieth century 'with a Station, a Shop, a Post Office (with its own telephone exchange), a school and right in the centre, the hub of the village, was the tallest sandstone building in South Africa, the Gumtree Mill'; but her photographs poignantly reveal Gumtree's descent into something 'forlorn and almost empty' today.[79]

Peka High School, not in Gumtree and not even in South Africa, was opened in 1961 in what was still officially called Basutoland, but was already generally known as Lesotho. The school rapidly earned a good reputation in the 1960s and 1970s, attracting African students from several countries in the region. It had prestigious results, 'with a one hundred per cent pass rate in the Cambridge Overseas School Certificate every year' although it 'looks quite dilapidated now, with broken windows and grounds that are overgrown with grass and weeds [...] It was not like this when I was a student here from 1965 to 1969,' says author Zakes Mda.[80]

The village of Peka lies several kilometres south of the school, and both are about fifteen kilometres from Gumtree. Gumtree in South Africa and Peka in Lesotho are equally poor districts of rural Africa, but worlds apart politically and culturally, separated by the Mohokare (Caledon River) and decades of history. It is difficult to imagine how they could ever have been confused, as they are, for example, on the South African History Online website: 'Michael Mosoue [sic] Moerane, pianist, choirmaster and composer, is born in Gumtree, Basutoland (now Lesotho). He died in Gumtree.'[81] According to Percival Kirby, Moerane 'became a teacher at a High School in Gumtree, Transkei'; and in the correspondence between Huskisson and the Regional Manager for the SABC in Grahamstown, Mr de Jager, Huskisson was told that Moerane's postal address was 'Peka High School, OFS'.[82] De Jager had in turn been given this information by the Principal of Lovedale, Robert Henry Wishart Shepherd – it was important, given that the SABC needed to know where to send Moerane's royalty cheques.

In Gumtree's heyday, it was a centre of communication because of its rail links and post office, and until 1963 an easy border crossing. Then in April 1963, the South African government set up 36 new passport control posts 'for the control of movement of persons between the Republic and High Commission Territories', with 12 of them on the borders of Basutoland, including Ficksburg Bridge and Peka Bridge.[83] The first principal of Peka High School, Tseliso Makhakhe, remembers that 'you did show your passport at the border post – it was next to Peka High School there, Peka Bridge – but from Ficksburg there's another bridge, which we used very freely.'[84] Perhaps because the South African-Basutoland border was relatively porous in the early 1960s, there was regular traffic between the school and the much larger range of shops across the border in South Africa. One of Moerane's students recalls that 'teachers used to go and do shopping in Ficksburg, probably 45 minutes' drive'.[85] A *Rand Daily Mail* advertisement for the post of Deputy-Headmaster at Peka on 30 June 1962 gives the school's address as 'Peka High School, Private Bag Gumtree, O.F.S.',[86] but elsewhere the newspaper refers to it as 'Peka High School (Basutoland)'.[87]

The village of Gumtree in the literature on Moerane, then, is confused with Gumtree as a postal address. Moerane and the school used this address rather than the one for Peka village in Leribe District, Lesotho 340, because Peka village is some kilometres away from Peka High School.[88] Still, Mrs RW Levine of The Institute for the Study of Man in Africa wrote to Percival Kirby that 'Mr Michael Moerane's address is as follows: Peka High School, P.O. Gumtree, O.F.S.',[89] but when Kirby wrote to Moerane a year later, it was to 'Peka High School, P.O. Peka, *Lesotho*'.[90]

In light of all this, what a wonderful irony that the composer's brother Manasseh Moerane wrote in his autobiography: 'A big tall gumtree marks out my homestead [Mangoloaneng]. You can see it for miles and miles around. On one side it bears a tear testifying that at some occasion the tree must have been struck by lightning.'[91]

1 | The House of Moerane

The placing

The house of Moerane belongs to an ancient and complex history of African chiefdoms and clans in and around the area of southern Africa known by the mid-nineteenth century as Basutoland.[1] Moerane was born in the former British Cape Colony, which adjoined Basutoland, but as historians of this region have shown, borders were far from fixed in 1904. Conflict existed between African peoples and the British colonial systems which administered both Basutoland and the Cape, as did conflict with Dutch-Afrikaner settlers trekking northwards, as well as conflict between African peoples themselves.[2] Moerane was born long before Lesotho became a sovereign state, but shortly before South Africa became a Union (1910), in a region that had experienced, and went on to experience throughout his lifetime, waves of migration and resistance to one form of oppression after another.

Moerane's family lineage is indirectly linked with that of the founding father of the Basotho nation, Moshoeshoe I (c. 1786–1870) through Moshoeshoe's son, Lebenya. Lebenya was a major chief in the Mount Fletcher district, a 'frontier zone', as Martin Legassick has termed this kind of border area between countries that did not yet have fixed and immutable boundaries,[3] and where Basotho lived side by side with other peoples, including 'their sister tribe the Batlokwa and the Hlubis with the Xhosas scattered in their midst'.[4] Lebenya's son, Thakaso, met Daniel, Eleazar and Joshua, three baptised sons of Chief Ramokopu (christened Lenare) while they were studying together at Morija Training Institution (in Basutoland). Thakaso persuaded his father to invite Lenare and his family to live in Mount Fletcher (in the Cape) in the 1880s, on what Manasseh T Moerane later described as 'an educational mission'.[5] The other attraction of the region, for Lenare, may have been the abundant land for farming. After Lenare and his wife Arianyane settled there, their son, Eleazar Jakane, 'crossed the mountains in 1899 to join his parents' once he had finished his education at Morija.[6] Jakane moved to Mangoloaneng within a few years to establish his own farm and homestead, remaining 'a lifetime pillar and counsellor' to Chief Lebenya.[7] It was therefore through Moshoeshoe I's son that Moerane came to be born in the north-eastern Cape, into a family of recently converted Christians trained as teachers and skilled as farmers. It was a form of 'placing' the Moeranes' presence in Mangoloaneng, through which they were expected 'to take charge of a section of' Moshoeshoe's following on 'the periphery of his domain, to experience responsibility, learn to adjudicate, and govern it.'[8]

The lineage

The Moeranes are descended from a distinguished family of African chiefs whose lineage goes back several centuries, during most of which time no part of southern Africa would have been thought of as 'frontier' country in the colonial sense, or Moerane's people as 'Basotho'. I trace this lineage with the help of documentation collected by Mark Gevisser and information from Moerane family members in Lesotho and South Africa.[9] These sources show that Michael Mosoeu Moerane is descended from the royal house of Bafokeng, today considered to be a nation of people in South Africa's North West Province comprising 'approximately 300,000 people'.[10] Bafokeng themselves are descended from the royal house of Bakoena, which can trace its line back to 'a Sotho leader named Koena (Kwena)' who was 'senior in rank to all the other major "tribes"',[11] and who lived eleven generations before 1800.[12] Thus the house of Moerane is linked to genealogies stretching across the whole of southern Africa and back many centuries. Indeed, according to Bernard Leeman, 'Sotho' is a 'linguistic name given to the 8 million members of a Bantu-speaking people who inhabit a crescent-shaped territory commencing in south-western Zambia and sweeping down through Botswana (encompassing small, adjacent areas of the Caprivi Strip and Zimbabwe) through Azania (South Africa) and Lesotho, to areas of the Transkei.'[13]

Basotho were one of several groups in southern Africa, including Batlokoa, Bapedi, Batswana, Lobedu, Phalaborwa and Birwa, who themselves were not fixed, stable clans, but continually evolving. Dependence on expansion into new grazing lands was vital for them all, and so it was inevitable not only that they would be in competition with each other, but that all their livelihoods would be profoundly disrupted by the disastrous sequence of events in early nineteenth-century southern Africa known as 'Lifaqane' in Sesotho ('Mfecane' in Zulu). 'Lifaqane' (pronounced 'Difaqane' and meaning 'crushing' or 'scattering') was a period of widespread political turbulence in south-eastern Africa from the late-eighteenth to the mid-nineteenth centuries, in which tens of thousands of people died or were displaced. Historians have contested the reason for this phenomenon, but mostly agree that there were several contributing factors, including Nguni expansion under the Zulu king Shaka, British colonialism, and the African ivory trade with the Portuguese. Exacerbating this 'already difficult situation', writes historian Stephen Gill, 'a severe and long-lasting drought created adverse environmental conditions in the years around 1803', there was 'unprecedented competition between th[e] emerging "kingdoms" for control over prime pasture land and other resources', and a cattle disease in 1817 that 'killed large numbers of cattle.'[14] Further periods of intense drought followed, huge numbers of Sotho refugees were created by the displacements, and as they came into contact with English and Afrikaans settlers, many of them 'became herders, general farm labourers or tenant farmers'.[15]

Moshoeshoe I was a minor chief descended from the Bakoena chiefdom via the Mokoteli clan, who owed allegiance to Chief Mohlomi of BaMonaheng, a 'wanderer, practising his skills as a healer, visionary and sage [who] possessed the power to travel mysteriously and to make rain', and who lived among various people, including Batswana (from present-day Botswana) and BaMahlabeng (from present-day Venda).[16] By the time he died, Mohlomi had 'visited and married in every part of Africa from the Zambezi southwards, and his influence was acknowledged throughout that area. His headquarters were at Mekoatleng (modern Mopeli's Spruit)'.[17] Moshoeshoe sought out Mohlomi, and among other things he learnt from him was that his power had come through the respect he had earned as a healer, visionary and sage, and through polygamy; to which skills, says Leeman, Moshoeshoe 'added his own considerable skill as a cattle raider'.[18] Thus Moshoeshoe's house should not be thought of, Leeman argues, as emanating from a minor chieftainship in the Butha-Buthe region of Lesotho (which it was literally), but as conceptually descended from 'the Mekoatleng kingdom of Mohlomi'.[19]

Moshoeshoe's hopes of expanding his Butha-Buthe chieftainship into an empire were truncated by the devastation of Lifaqane, which forced him in 1824 to accept an offer from a relative in the Ntsane clan to bring the remnants of his people to the shelter of the mountain stronghold called Thaba Bosiu in western present-day Lesotho. Moshoeshoe then incorporated the Ntsane and another small group of Phuthi warriors under Moorosi. Over the next few years, his newly formed group of Basotho, who were descended from various clans, fended off the Kora, the Ngwane, Tlokwa, Ndebele and Zulu – and, for a while, the Dutch-descended settlers (Boers). Moshoeshoe was about forty-seven years old when the first Protestant missionaries arrived from France in June 1833, and had established a 'prosperous, well-armed and expansionary' Basotho state.[20] English and Dutch settlers systematically eroded this until Moshoeshoe was forced to sign the Treaties of Thaba Bosiu (1865) and Aliwal North (1869), in terms of which most of the arable land of his new Basotho kingdom west of the Mohokare (Caledon River) was lost to the new Boer colony of the Free State.[21]

Culturally, Moshoeshoe relied heavily on Bafokeng chiefs from the Mahooana clan, 'traditionally the doctors who officiated at the *lebollo* circumcision rituals', one of the 'most renowned' being a traditional doctor named Moerane.[22] Strategically, Moshoeshoe relied heavily on the missionaries, one of whose 'earliest and most celebrated converts' was Mokhanoi, baptised Zachea.[23] Moerane was Michael Mosoeu's paternal great-grandfather, who took his Sesotho name as his new Christian surname after he was baptised; Mokhanoi/Zachea was Moerane's maternal great-grandfather.

The House of Moerane

The family tree in the Mark Gevisser research archive shows the complex line of descent from 'Tata Bafokeng', the founder of the royal house generations earlier. The tree has several levels and many annotations. On the first level, it shows, among other things, the descent from Chief Mapape, through his son Ratlali and grandson Khati to his great-grandson Mangole. On the second level, it shows Mangole's son Mahoana, and the line of descent through his son Selikane, then Tsatsi and Khabele (Mahase) to Lingate, who had two sons, (another) Khabele and Montšo. On the third level, it shows Montšo's son, Moriee, and his two grandsons, Taeli and Pelesana, and their two branches of the family. A much simpler family diagram in the possession of Lebohang Mofelehetsi of Maseru, which he kindly showed me in 2014, confirms what is shown on the fourth level of the family tree: how the lineage continues from Pelesana and his second wife, Mamofelehetsi, to their sons Mofelehetsi, Keotje, Matšasa, Moerane, Molutsoane, Kekeleng and Moesa. This Moerane (d. 1899), who seems to have been the fourteenth generation of Bafokeng chiefs, was the paternal great-grandfather of the composer. He fathered Ramokopu, who converted and was christened Lenare, and then served Lebenya by moving to Mount Fletcher; and it was Lenare who fathered Jakane Ramphoma.

One way of expressing this complex lineage very simply, through the male line, ignoring all side-shoots, is as follows:

Tata Bafokeng→Mapape→Ratlali→Khati→ Mangole→Mahooana→ Selikane→ Tsatsi→Khabele→Lingate→Montšo→Moriee→Pelesana→ Moerane→Roboame Moerane (Lenare)→Jakane Moerane→Michael Mosoeu Moerane

When Lenare took the Christian forename Roboame and his father's name Moerane as a Christian surname, he and his wife Arianyane effectively established the Christian house of Moerane. When he baptised his third son Jakane (sometimes spelled Jacane), which is the Sotho word for a Christian, he demonstrated to what extent he had embraced what Gevisser has called 'the literate, "progressive" Western world that developed around the *fora* mission stations.'[24]

Lenare Moerane (d. 1913) and Arianyane (d. 1931) had six children: Daniel (later a school principal at Qoboseoneng), Mishael (a blacksmith), Jakane (the composer's father), Joshua (a teacher), Anna and Nkau (whose son Mamala lived in Kroonstad). MT Moerane's autobiography opens with an idyllic description of Lenare's homestead in Basutoland, noting that he was wounded during the 'Gun war' (1880–1881) and that he refused to surrender his gun or 'his spear and battle-axe' to the British.[25]

Daniel, Eleazar and Joshua 'were to proceed to Morija Training Institution for a three-year Teacher Training course'.[26] Eleazar Ramaphome Jakane Moerane (1873–1938) then married Sofia Majara (1899–1938), and they had seven children, listed by Thuso Moerane in 1988 as follows, with some additional dates supplied in square brackets where known:

1. Daniel Mokhakala – a member of the Transkei Bunga. [1902–1967]
2. Michael Mosoeu – B.Mus. [1904–1980]
3. Antoinette 'Mazael Mphoma – married and died in Lesotho – a primary school teacher.
4. Fraser Masole – B.Sc. – taught and died in Bloemfontein.
5. Manasseh Tebatso – B.A. – President of Natal Teachers Union – Editor of *Drum Magazine* – joined Moral Rearmament. Son Marumo State Advocate. [1913–1989]
6. Epainette 'MaMotseki – teacher in Natal schools – wife to Govan Mbeki, B.A., B.Econ., father to president Thabo Mbeki. [1916–2014]
7. Renee Sake – lady teacher – Married to Mr Khomo – land surveyor – both employed and died in Dar-es-salam, Tanzania.[27]

The house of Moerane continued through the six children of Michael Mosoeu – known in the family as 'Mike' – and his wife Beatrice Betty (née Msweli). They were Mofelehetsi Count (1930–2018), Mathabo Lineo (known in the family as Thabs), Thuso Majalla (1935–2020), Halieo Lucinda, Sophia Metsekae (b. 1940, known in the family as Sophie) and Thabo Kabeli (1947–2006). Just as Moerane became a surname, so did Mofelehetsi. Other ancestral names were passed on as middle or 'Sotho' names, including Mosoeu. I still do not fully understand how all the Lesotho Moeranes are related to each other or to the South African ones, but is not my place to untangle what is essentially a family matter.

What I can more easily explain is the etymology of the word 'Moerane'. The standard Sesotho–English dictionary explains that '*mamōera*' is a noun meaning 'someone who goes out at night' while '*mōèranē*' means 'mantis, caddis-worm'.[28] A later edition of this dictionary has '*mo·êrane* [...] the insect Criocharacta amphiactis in the larval state, bag-worm';[29] this being an insect larva whose threads have 'powerful medicinal and spiritual value',[30] and which would have been used by Moerane the traditional doctor. The later dictionary entry also makes clear the separation of the prefix 'mo' and the stress on the first 'e'. During an interview in 2014 with TTE Pitso, a former colleague of Moerane's at Peka High School, I had a sobering lesson on the pronunciation of 'Moerane':

TTEP If you want to get some of these syllabic vowels, you isolate them: 'Mo-erane'. Just like when you talk of a nurse, you talk of a nurse as being 'Mo-uti'. You can exaggerate that and you won't go wrong. So, Mo-erane. Mo-erane. It's like there's a pause. You say, 'Mo-erane'.
CL It's almost like 'Mo-(w)e-rane'.
TTEP Yes. But once you slur it: that's where many mistakes are made in our language. Syllabic vowels. They stand by themselves. You can easily say, 'Mo-e-ra-ne', but then when you say it quickly you still have to bring out[,] separate [them.] It's especially in music that you hear those syllabic vowels.
CL At Peka you taught at the High School? Did you know Mr Mo-e[,] Mr Moerane there?
TTEP Mr Moerane. Yes! you are almost getting it now! Mo-e-rane![31]

I learnt about the possible origin of 'Mangoloaneng' during an interview with Lesotho archivist David Ambrose in 2014. For one thing, said Ambrose, 'there's a Mangolong, too, which is nearby, and Mangoloaneng is the diminutive of this.' He explained that 'ngola' is the Sesotho word for drawing, from which comes 'mangolo', the plural, and 'mangolong', the locative. 'So Mangolong in its original meaning meant, I would say, "art gallery" or place where people painted. And indeed it is that. Sehonghong, the most famous of all [rock painting] sites in Lesotho was originally called Mangolong. I'm pretty sure the one in East Griqualand is similar, and Mangoloaneng would mean either the place with less rock paintings, or a smaller place with rock paintings.' When the word is interpreted in Lesotho, said Ambrose, it means a place of letters.[32]

Which parts of Lesotho did the Moeranes of recent generations come from? According to Tseliso Makhakhe, it was from Lumokema, also called Mokema:

That village is very famous in the history of Lesotho, I don't know why. Every time the British high commissioner came to Lesotho, he would pause at Aliwal North, then from there move to Morija, and then move to Mokema, that village. On one occasion the king held a meeting, a pitso of the people. Why they choose Mokema, I really don't know. That was the Moeranes' home.[33] There are other Moeranes further south, which is not very far from my own home at a place called Likena. I don't know whether they had moved from Mokema or those at Mokema had moved from Kena.[34]

Moerane's childhood home

The home into which the composer was born was Christian and middle-class, both English and Sesotho-speaking. Mark Gevisser begins his biography of Thabo Mbeki with a description of the large framed photograph of Jakane, his wife Sofia Majara, who was the daughter of a tenant farmer from the Orange Free State, and their children that he calls a 'portrait of a country gentleman, his wife, and seven children' and which hangs in several Moerane family homes.[35] In Figure 1.1, Moerane is in the front row, second from the left.

'Not many a black South African of Jacane Moerane's generation', Gevisser points out, 'was able to send all seven of his children for tertiary education' and 'could boast four university graduates among the[m].' Gevisser lists the achievements of the next generation: business people, teachers, nurses, an engineer, an advocate, 'a senior United Nations official in Geneva' (MM Moerane's youngest son, Thabo), and 'a President in Pretoria' (Dr Thabo Mbeki), all of this notwithstanding 'the limits that apartheid placed upon black aspirations.'[36] Lesotho's political history created limitations of its own, too, notably during the State of Emergency imposed by Prime Minister Leabua Jonathan from 1970 to 1986. These terrible times, and the composer's story framed by them, are dealt with below.[37]

Aside from the intellectual and cultural life at Mangoloaneng, there were extensive lands to cultivate. An integral part of Moerane's early education was his responsibility for looking after crops and animals at Mangoloaneng, a normal part of life for children in rural

Figure 1.1: The Moerane family at Mangoloaneng c. 1920 (courtesy Tsepo Moerane and Jonathan Ball Publishers)

Africa. The extent of the estate can be gathered from Epainette Mbeki's memory of it when she visited the homestead with Mark Gevisser in 1999:

> I stood with Epainette Mbeki on the threshold of the home in which she had been born, and followed her outstretched arm across the grasslands. *'There* were the sorghum fields, and *there,* beyond, the apple orchard. Behind there was the dairy. The maize fields and the wheat fields were a good distance further. Down there was the sheep kraal; that's where we kept the cattle when they were not being grazed up at the mountains. And behind here – oh the trees have been chopped down now – here was our own orchard.' From the 130 head of cattle, there are six. Not a sheep, not a horse. Not a single growing thing – not a stalk of corn, not a tomato plant.[38]

The deterioration Gevisser describes occurred over a long period of time, the first obvious cause being The Land Act of 1913, although Gevisser attributes most of the decline to apartheid's homeland policies of the 1950s, which created the self-governing 'Xhosa bantustan' of Transkei in 1963, with its 'Xhosa mandarins' who introduced measures such as the enforced culling of cattle.

Moerane's life within a political timeline

The Land Act and the creation of the Transkei 'homeland' were just two of the major political events that impacted upon Moerane's life. The 'Timeline of Political Events: 1880–1991' in this book anchors those events, although it only hints at the hopes, failures, betrayals, cultural erosions, displacements, political and social oppressions – and resistance to all of this – that characterised southern Africa's history from well before Moerane was born until well after he died. The primary source for the timeline is Bernard Leeman's *Lesotho and the Struggle for Azania*, which shows, as no other regional history does, the connections between politics in South Africa and Lesotho, which provided the backdrop to Moerane's musical life as he moved back and forth between the two countries.[39] The timeline highlights Pan-Africanist events and leadership because this was Moerane's political orientation; it gives the names of some political leaders in brackets. It shows how intricately linked the political histories of Lesotho and South Africa were, and how African resistance to the systematic erosion of their educational opportunities, economic advancement and civil rights took the more Africanist turn with which Moerane sympathised. The timeline also shows that this period was as turbulent in Lesotho as in South Africa, and that going back and forth as Moerane did meant repeatedly leaping out of the frying pan into the fire. It is hard to know specifically how Moerane was personally affected by these events without supporting documentation, but he certainly expressed his political views through teaching: as he placed his 'colonial education in the service of an African nationalist identity' – and, as Chapters 5 and 8 show, through some of his compositions.[40] Many members of the house of Moerane were political activists; some were banned, exiled or killed during the long struggle for emancipation.

Politics in the House of Moerane

Moerane's elder brother Daniel was a member of the Transkeian Territories General Council, which became 'the largest African reserve in the country, and the pace-setter in the Bantustan scheme of HF Verwoerd.'[41] Originally, it was a great honour to be a member of the 'Bhunga',[42] but opposition to the councils gradually became fiercer, especially in East Griqualand where Daniel lived.[43] Moerane's younger brother Manasseh Tebatso was president of the National African Teachers Association of South Africa, 'a founder of the ANC Youth League [and] editor of South Africa's largest Black newspaper'.[44] Moerane's sister Epainette was one of the first women to join the Communist Party of South Africa in 1938; she 'worked as an agent for the party's newspaper *Inkululeko* and also ran the Communist Party of South Africa's (CPSA) famous night school.'[45] Her husband Govan Mbeki held leadership roles in both the CPSA and, after it was banned, the ANC. Imprisoned for 24 years on Robben Island after the Rivonia Trial, he was released in 1987 and became Deputy President of the Senate after 1994. Moerane's nephew Thabo Mbeki joined the ANC Youth league in 1956, left South Africa in 1962, became a member of the ANC National Executive Committee in 1975, underwent military training in the Soviet Union, and continued living in exile (in Zambia) until 1990. He returned to South Africa to become deputy president from 1994–1999 and president 1999–2008. His brother, Jama Mbeki, his son Kwanda Mbeki and his cousin Phindile Mfeti all 'disappeared without trace' during apartheid; the family was never able to find out the truth about their deaths.[46] Mbeki's younger brother, the distinguished journalist Moeletsi Mbeki, has remained as critical of the ANC since the end of apartheid as he was of the previous regime.

On 15 February 1966, Moerane's son, 'Thuso Majalla Moerane, of Scanlan [sic] Street, Queenstown', was 'prohibited under the Suppression of Communism Act from attending gatherings for five years.'[47] 'He was supposed to go to Robben Island', says his daughter Neo, 'but I was very young, as was my brother [Lenare], and my mother was a nurse in Port Elizabeth, so they kept him a prisoner in his own house; it was called "house arrest".'[48] He was barred from studying medicine because of the banning order, and was then 'forced to move out of [10] Scanlen Street' and his family 'forced to stay in one room; from a ten-room house.' In 1969, the Queenstown municipality gave Thuso Number T96 Soga St, situated in a part of 'Mlungisi township ironically named 'White City'. 'Empty space remains' where Number 10 stood, said Thuso in 2014.[49] Figure 1.2 shows the red-roofed Moerane family home as it was in c. 1960, set back from the road. Figure 1.3 shows the empty space in 2014.

Composer Todd Matshikiza and his family lived in Number 8, while performer Lex Mona and his family lived in Number 6, which was later bought by Mrs Margaret Naidu while the Matshikizas were still living next door.[50] Thuso's daughter Neo went to stay with her grandparents in Peka as a small child, returning to Queenstown in the early 1970s. Her mother had trained as a midwife and was looking for a nursing position there, but because of her husband's banning order, the family remained under constant surveillance. 'The police used to park outside the house, from 1970 until my brother was killed in 1977,' said Neo. Her brother Lenare was returning from Steve Biko's funeral on 25 September 1977 when he was shot by police. But 'they were after him for half a year until they killed him':

> Remember how he [Biko] used to inspire a lot of black students, even the way they were dressing, you know, he was their inspiration.

Figure 1.2: The Moerane home at 10 Scanlen Street c. 1960 (courtesy Tsepo Moerane)

Figure 1.3: The empty lot in 2014 (author's photograph)

> But the *way* they were killed ... there was no need to do that. Even his funeral was disrupted by police. We couldn't hear a damn thing because of the helicopters. Ja, they harassed us, there was no need. They had killed him. My grandfather [Moerane] was still alive but he couldn't come to the funeral; he was not allowed to come back [from Lesotho]. Remember, he was exiled? Most people could not make it to the funeral.[51]

Moerane's youngest son Thabo Kabeli was heavily involved in political activities, especially in KwaZulu-Natal. His cousin, Marumo (son of MT) joined the PAC. His father was 'an African nationalist [...] So when there was a question of making a choice between what I viewed as Marxist-Leninist ideology and Pan-Africanist ideology, I opted for the Pan-Africanist ideology.'[52]

In Lesotho, Moerane's nephew Mofelehetsi Moerane was prominent in the BCP Youth League, in 1974 leading one of the most dangerous attempted coups during Leabua Jonathan's illegal regime. The case of the 'State vs. Mofelehetsi Moerane & 31 others, 1975' tells how the 32 accused attacked police stations, captured arms and ammunition, and attacked the Maseru headquarters of the Police Mobile Unit.[53] Chief Justice JT Mapetla found Mofelehetsi guilty, but noted in mitigation of the death penalty how Crown witnesses had testified to the 'unprovoked severe and sometimes even brutal and humiliating assaults' on BCP supporters, 'and the burning and destruction of their property by members of the "Lebotho la Khotso" ["Peace Corps" *aka* Police Mobile Unit] whose activities were apparently connived at and even encouraged by the police who also themselves indulged fully in this kind of behaviour with impunity,' not stopping 'even at cold-blooded murder'. Mofelehetsi Moerane was sentenced to nine years' imprisonment, of which two were suspended.[54]

Social anthropologist David Coplan recorded a song about the Police Mobile Unit that expresses the impossible choice Basotho often felt during the 1970s and 1980s between two equally oppressive countries: *'Ke sotleba, Lesotho mona; Ke hampe, Lesotho mona [...] Ke stabile'muso oa mathata; Ke stabile Lebotho la Khotso Heela, uena ngoan'a moshanyana! Heela, uena ngoan'a moshanyana! lefatseng la makhooeng-bo!* (It's oppressing me, Lesotho here; It's awful, Lesotho here; I've fled from a government of miseries; I've fled from the 'Peace Corps'. Heeyyy, you man-child! It's better I die in the whitemen's land-bo!).[55] Moerane must have known political songs such as these; and been all too familiar with the arrests, bannings, exiles and murders of members of his family in both countries. He would also have been aware of the strong link between the PAC and the BCP, and between Pan-Africanist Congresses nationally and internationally.

Moerane and Pan-Africanism

The genre of African choralism in which Moerane was heavily involved as a composer, teacher, conductor and adjudicator often produced music that was politically oriented. His orientation leaned strongly towards the values of Pan-Africanism, and therefore he supported the BCP, which in 1965 was gearing up towards elections. Peka district in Lesotho, where he was working by then, was a known BCP stronghold, and Peka High was 'suspected to be harbouring insurgents. All that was absolute nonsense. We didn't teach our students any politics,' said Moerane's former principal, Tseliso Makhakhe. 'We allowed them to attend meetings so that they could hear what politicians were saying, but at Peka School there was nothing like that.'[56] However, Makhakhe himself became deputy leader of the BCP and was forced to flee to Botswana along with other BCP leaders in January 1974.[57]

'Quiet as he was,' former Peka student Victor Lechesa recalls of Moerane, 'he was a member of the Basutoland Congress Party. It became easy, so long as you are not outspoken, right? Keeping a low profile kept many people out of trouble.'[58] 'Through our contacts outside the school,' said another student, Matsobane Putsoa, 'we got to know that we had "a strong teacher there" [but] he would not talk about it.'[59] Putsoa went into exile in April 1970 and returned in July 1973, but 'unfortunately in January 1974 there was an uprising [...] then I spent 11 months and 11 days in detention without trial. Those were terrible times.' His friend Lechesa 'was eventually charged and found guilty of high treason. He was sentenced to six years. He came out on parole before the six years, so I left him, in Central Maximum Security Prison. Things continued bad up to the early eighties.'[60] 'We knew that [Moerane] was a BCP supporter, but I cannot vouch whether he was a member or not, I never saw his card,' says another former student, Zakes Mda. 'Moerane was less of an activist, he was not like Makhakhe, but when we talked politics he talked BCP politics. All of his relatives in Lesotho were BCP people.'[61] Moerane's loyalty to political organisations such as CATA, NEUM, the BCP, and more broadly the PAC alliance, reflects his Pan-Africanist and nationalist views, as opposed to the Marxist-Leninist approach of the ANC or Communist Party of South Africa. As suggested in the next chapter, he may have been influenced here by the politics of Fort Hare, but he clung to his views against other strongly held views in his immediate family.

Moerane might not have insisted that his wife and children subscribe to Pan-Africanism, but he imposed other views on them, including a prohibition on associating with jazz musicians. More significantly, he insisted that only Sesotho be spoken at home. 'Xhosa was not allowed. He didn't want us to forget Sesotho, and we only got it from him'; even his Xhosa wife had to speak Sesotho at home 'in his presence'.[62]

Moerane loved Lesotho: 'the other siblings were not so keen on the country, but he was proud of Lesotho,' said his Lesotho nephew, Lebohang

Mofelehetsi. There must have been a connection for Moerane between his Sotho roots and his rejection of both British colonialism and African intellectualism. The use of African languages vis-à-vis English, was another 'black-and-white' issue for Moerane. When he moved to Queenstown, Mofelehetsi recalls, 'he found out which school did not have an English influence' and got a post at Queenstown African Secondary School because 'the principal there was Xhosa and all that'. Mofelehetsi recalls that his father saw English as the 'oppressor's' language, and although Mofelehetsi 'grew up speaking English' and 'played with English-speaking children', his father 'stuck to the Sotho language'.[63]

Not only language use, but other kinds of discipline were strictly enforced in the Moerane family, especially musical discipline. 'A typical day on Scanlen Street' in 1952, Sophia Metsekae related to Mark Gevisser, 'went like this':

> We would come home from school, and then everyone had to have his or her half-hour at the piano; you would scramble to get a slot when my father *wasn't* at home. Piano practice would end at six o'clock sharp, and then there would be evening prayers, followed by dinner at seven o'clock sharp. Eight o'clock was recital time: perhaps I would be on piano and Thabo would accompany me on flute, or perhaps my father would play the piano for an hour. The entire family was required, even the tiny ones, to sit quietly and listen. Then at nine o'clock sharp, everyone goes to bed. That's it. The end. Lights out.[64]

At the same time, Moerane loved English literature and indeed taught it; two of his children, Mofelehetsi and Thabo, majored in English at university. Thabo did a Bachelor of Arts in English at the University of Lesotho; a photograph taken at his graduation is shown in Figure 9.2.

The issue of language enforcement cannot have made things easy at home. There might also have been an issue with the politics of the orthography of the language. Moerane, and indeed most composers who used Sesotho lyrics in those days, had to choose at a certain point between the old Lesotho orthography encoded by French missionaries in the mid-nineteenth century and the new South African orthography introduced in 1959. The latter was not accepted in Lesotho: 'When South Africa suggested strongly that we adopt a revised orthography, there was resistance in this country. It was during the apartheid years.'[65] Moerane's Sesotho lyrics all use the old orthography.

Moerane at home

Perhaps because of the language issue, the pressure of formal teaching and extramural music teaching, and the social unrest that increased with every year the Moeranes spent in their Queenstown home, the Moerane's marriage does not seem to have been an easy one. The couple lived apart several times – in Maseru, in Mpondoland and in Kroonstad 'where our mother taught until our father completed' his BMus in Grahamstown.[66] And in Peka, 'somehow they were not on good terms' by the end, said Thuso: 'old man not interested in her any more, and she decided to come my way. We kept her nicely here until she died. She died after the old man died. We buried her here, in Queenstown, and the old man in Lesotho. Hayi!'[67] Was their marriage in 1930 also a testimony to Moerane's Pan-Africanism? It was an 'inter-racial' one, unusual in African society at that time: a marriage across ethnicities and across not only languages, but language groups.[68] Speaking about his (Sotho) zoology teacher at Healdtown School in 1937, for example, Nelson Mandela recalls that what most amazed him 'was his marriage to a Xhosa girl from Umtata':

> Marriages between tribes were then extremely unusual. Until then, I had never known of anyone who marrie[d] outside his tribe. We had been taught that such unions were taboo. But seeing Frank and his wife began to undermine my parochialism and loosen the hold of the tribalism that still imprisoned me. I began to sense my identity as an African, not just a Thembu or even a Xhosa.[69]

Of Michael and Betty's wedding, Epainette Mbeki said, 'I was not at the wedding. There was something tricky about the wedding. People were still racialistic; she was Xhosa and he was Sotho. Ordinary people were not against it, but in the family, they were against it.'[70] Gilbert Ramatlapeng, a former student of Moerane's at Basutoland High School, felt that along with jealousy of Moerane's superior teaching skills, another reason for him leaving Maseru after only two years was that he was married to a Xhosa. 'People here in Lesotho were not familiar with [Sotho] people who married Xhosa women. They didn't like it.'[71]

In 1958, Moerane left Queenstown for Mfundisweni College in Mpondoland, leaving his wife and family in Queenstown. It was here that a student, Sylvia Ntombentsha Zongola, became very important in his life. After he moved to Peka High School in 1961 he continued a relationship with her, which is possibly what caused Mrs Moerane to return to Queenstown.[72] As a teacher, he had a house on the Peka High School premises, where he lived with his wife (at first), his son Thabo and granddaughter Mosa. He built a little red brick house in Peka village for Sylvia.[73] This extramarital 'house of Moerane' is not mentioned in the family, but in 2014 the secretary at Peka High, Mrs Mafothe Malaoli, took me to it and introduced me to the caretaker, Mrs Makonye Tiiti – who remembered Moerane. The house and the fields adjoining it are shown as they were in 2014 in Figure 1.4.

Figure 1.4: The house in Peka village 2014, (author's photograph)

Figure 1.5: The house in Tsifalimali, 2014 (author's photograph)

Moerane's own house in Tsifalimali was enlarged by Thabo after his father's death, and Figure 1.5 shows it as it was in 2014. It is looked after by a caretaker, Mr Ramaema.

After Moerane's death in January 1980, the political situation in Lesotho and South Africa gradually began to improve, leading to the ousting of Leabua Jonathan in a military coup in Lesotho in 1986, and a new multiracial democratic government in South Africa in 1994. Moerane did not live to see these changes, but neither did he live to see the decline of Pan-Africanism, which had so informed his beliefs and his work as a teacher and composer. The next chapter gives some idea as to how those beliefs may have been nurtured during the long years of his education, musical and otherwise.

2 | Moerane the Student

Mangoloaneng, Mariazell and Morija

Michael Mosoeu's first teacher was his father, at Jakane Moerane's Junior Primary School of Mangoloaneng. This went up to what was then called Standard 4, equivalent to the current Grade 6 in South Africa, in which the average age is eleven to twelve.[1] Rural children like Moerane helped with farming chores before and after school: 'the care for the calves, horses and sometimes even sheep, was our full responsibility and woe betide us if anything went amiss in these fields.'[2] Like his siblings, Moerane continued higher primary education (Standards 5–7) at the Roman Catholic Mission School at Mariazell, five miles north of Mangoloaneng.[3] Mariazell 'trained us to be hardy', remembers Manasseh: 'we woke up even in the Drakensberg winters in time for mass at 5 a.m. and we did manual work after classes and our food was simple but good.'[4]

Moerane's musical education began, as it does for most children, informally, in the family home and the community. Moerane played the harmonium in the house, an instrument that, as his sister Epainette pointed out, 'would be unusual now, but it was not unusual then'. She remembered how one's feet had to pump the pedals while 'you played on top, on the keyboard', and that 'whenever there was singing, he [Moerane] preferred classical music'. Her recollection was that among all the siblings, 'Mike' was 'the only musical one, the only one interested in music'. When I asked her where she thought this talent came from, she replied 'Goodness knows!' Moerane learnt to read tonic solfa notation at primary school; 'very elementary music', as Epainette saw it, adding that she personally 'was *so* uninteresting! ... tonic solfa ... very boring!'.[5]

The mission press at Morija published school textbooks and songbooks in tonic solfa, some of which Jakane would have bought for his school. Mariazell made use of tonic solfa songbooks published by the Catholic Mazenod Institute in Maseru. Singing and tonic solfa theory provided the staple musical education for African children in mission schools across southern Africa in the early twentieth century – and did so in state schools until comparatively recently.

Like the solfège system in Europe, the British tonic solfa system developed sight-singing and music literacy, and inculcated an understanding of scales and keys. Its introduction to southern African missions in the nineteenth century drew on a music education system that already existed in Victorian Britain, and which was exported as part of Britain's 'civilizing mission'.[6] The French-Swiss missionaries themselves grew up knowing solfège, which is used in Europe but not in Britain; but their wives were often British, and it was they who mostly taught music in Basutoland's mission stations.

There is a significant difference: in solfa, the keynote is moveable, so 'doh' can be any note in the twelve-note chromatic scale; in solfège, 'doh' is always 'C', 're' is always 'D' and so on: pitch is fixed. If students such as Moerane had learnt solfège instead of solfa, they would have been able to transfer to staff notation more easily, and they would have learnt solmization, in which a fixed pitch is associated with a particular solfège word. They would also have immediately learnt sharps and flats derived from the scale doh, re, mi, fa, sol, la, ti doh. This would arguably have developed a different understanding of functional harmony, one less dependent on the major scale and the position of 'doh'; and along with this, a more fluid sense of tonality that accommodates dissonance, minor keys and key changes more easily than the tonic solfa system allows. This 'what if' scenario is further complicated by the fact that what students learnt in mission schools was mainly how to *write* in solfa, not to sight-sing with it: they learnt it as a writing system finite in itself rather than as an aural system of solmization leading to knowledge of staff notation. The fact that solfège is such a successful system is borne out by the fact that it is still very much in use in music education in European countries.

Many homes in those days would have possessed a hymnal with tonic solfa tunes, along with a community songbook, a few Victorian parlour songs, and easy piano pieces in staff notation. As Epainette's remark about the harmonium above shows, it would not have been unusual in the 1910s for African middle-class families to have sheet music in their homes, although it would be almost unheard of a hundred years later. Given the interaction of mission teachers and families across the Cape Colony, it is also likely that a music teacher in the region taught Moerane keyboard and staff notation or gave him some sheet music. The few scores left in Moerane's son's house in Atteridgeville (listed later in this chapter), were probably gathered after Moerane went to school or began the BMus degree in 1930, but one or two may have dated from his childhood.

The harmonium was part of the desolate scene painted by Mark Gevisser when he visited the Mangoloaneng house in 1999 with Epainette, where he noted an instrument 'with rotting and broken keys, lying beneath the junk [...] carrying the memories of the after-dinner recitals of Epainette Mbeki's youth.'[7] Gevisser reminds us how normal it was for Christian African families in this era to sing in the evenings; indeed, musical evenings around a harmonium or piano were normal occurrences in many homes worldwide at this time. Historian Josias Makabinyane Mohapeloa, for example, brother of the composer Joshua Pulumo Mohapeloa, who was brought up in rural Lesotho at the same time as Moerane, recalls evening family prayers 'followed by learning how to sing hymns, especially the unfamiliar ones.'[8] The Moeranes belonged to the Lesotho Evangelical Church (LEC) and the hymns they would have sung would have been from the Paris Evangelical Missionary Society (PEMS) hymnal, *Lifela tsa Sione* (*Songs of Zion*).[9]

Traditional music also had a place in Moerane's childhood, as several witnesses have been able to corroborate. Moerane's son Thabo points out that his father was 'strongly influenced by the threshing, hunting and other songs he had heard and learned as a small boy.'[10] Friedrich Hartmann tried (in vain) 'to persuade Dr. Kerr to appoint Moerane in some form at Fort Hare in order to enable him to collect the songs of his people, a matter in which Moerane was very interested.'[11] Neo remembers that when she visited Moerane in Peka as a little girl, her grandfather 'was very strict and very concerned of the values, the beliefs that you'd pick up' from traditional ceremonies, not because of the music or words but because 'in the

Sotho tradition, if you are a girl, you wear tetani, one of these traditional regalias. He said, "No, no, don't go and wear those." Because we were not allowed to wear underwear [with tetani], and he says, "And then what?! Don't! Don't!"'[12] Moerane's protection of Neo notwithstanding, Moerane was intimate with traditional Sotho culture, music, dance, poetry and ways of life, as revealed by the songs he composed, which are discussed in Chapter 8.

After Mariazell, Moerane obtained a primary school teaching certificate at the PEMS Morija Training Institution ('Middle School') in 1920/21. At 'Thabeng', as the institution was called, 'music education was very important. A young man who completed his studies there was expected to be able to teach music in such a way that the children would know the notes.'[13] He would not only sing and learn more advanced tonic solfa theory, he would also occasionally have had lessons on the piano and instruction in staff notation, as did Mohapeloa in Morija a few years later.[14] Like Mohapeloa, Moerane came under the influence of Mr Ernest Frank Pester, the music master at Morija. Pester taught the general body of students how to conduct 'showing time and how to direct the singers with your hands' and how to sing 'with soft voices'. He chose the most talented for a quartet where 'they were trained with care and patience, such that when they sang, it was mysteriously beautiful.'[15] Miss Florence Mabille volunteered 'for many years [...] to teach those who wanted to learn how to play and read piano music' in staff notation and taught Moerane, 'one of those who chose to continue with this [until] they became composers'.[16]

After Morija, Moerane taught for a year at St John's College, Mthatha, an African high school founded in 1879. Many years later, his nephew Thabo Mbeki would attend this prestigious former mission school in the eastern Cape Colony; other future political leaders were also educated there.[17]

Lovedale Missionary Institution

Moerane enrolled at Lovedale High School in 1923 in order to obtain a Junior Certificate.[18] This indicated that the holder had completed a level of schooling roughly three years lower than university entrance level. It was the end point for most African students, some of whom went on to do vocational training. Moerane was among the few who got the Junior Certificate, and continued on at school to university entrance level.

Lovedale High School was part of the extensive Lovedale Missionary Institution in Alice. Moerane was 18 when he entered Form B (Grade 9), one of the youngest of 43 men and 12 women in his class. In 1924 he enrolled in Form C (Grade 10), becoming 'Dux' (the one with the highest marks) of his class, winning the 'Messrs. Dreyfus' Gold Medal' and passing his Junior Certificate from the Cape Education Department with a 'First Grade' at the end of 1924. He was also a 'temporary language teacher' in the high school in 1924.[19] Figure 2.1 shows a group photograph taken at Lovedale c. 1924, in which Moerane is probably the young man in the centre of the third row with the black suit, his arms folded.

The impact of fellow students on Moerane's time at Lovedale is incalculable, but among the few women in his class, one became particularly important: Beatrice Betty Msweli. Registered since 1921 at the high school as a student from Klerksdorp, in 1924 her home background is given as Qanda (a rural locality in the eastern Cape).[20] By the time they were married and had children, their son Thuso remembers only that in the family she was known to have 'come from Lovedale'.[21] Moerane and Betty were both on student bursaries: he 'was one of the first country lads to write and pass the

Figure 2.1: Lovedale students c. 1924 (courtesy Tsepo Moerane)

Andrew Smith Bursary', while Betty held a Govan Bursary.[22] One of the few other bursary students that year was Frieda Bokwe, daughter of John Knox Bokwe and the future wife of Zachariah Keodirelang Matthews. Getting a bursary was important, as the fees were steep.[23] Beatrice obtained a second-grade pass in the Junior Certificate the same year Moerane gained his, and won 'Mrs. Stewart's prize for helpfulness, interest, and good example'.[24]

Lovedale College and close-by Fort Hare were attenuated cultural spaces, bizarre to us today in their separation of African students from white students, as they were the only places where 'Natives' could obtain a higher education, and because they attracted African students from all over southern Africa. Both Lovedale and Fort Hare were multiracial in a way no other higher institutions in South Africa were at that time. At Lovedale, students and staff were nevertheless saturated in the Presbyterian ideology of their mission foundations: these were 'total institutions', as Graham Duncan puts it, with every aspect of students' lives controlled, which tended to produce a sense of 'conformity in some learners' and an equally strong 'resistance to mission education' in others.[25] The principals of Lovedale and Fort Hare played a major role in maintaining control, as they represented the authority, often authoritarianism, of both church and state. The strict regimes of William Govan (1841–1869), James Stewart (1870–1905) and James Henderson (1906–1930) at Lovedale became ossified into 'a diplomatic form of "coercive agency" under Arthur Wilkie (1932–1942) and a brutalised form under Robert Henry Wishart Shepherd (1942–1955) until mission schools were taken under the wing of the *Bantu Education Act* (1953).'[26]

Moerane entered Lovedale under Henderson's regime, but the latter died in July 1930. Wilkie faced issues that his predecessor had not: 'governmental antagonism, white public opinion, financial troubles' over farming and industrial departments and 'a more secular and heterogenous staff'.[27] One of Wilkie's achievements, however, was the promotion of the Lovedale Press, which had been established under Henderson in 1928. It became very active during the 1930s, publishing literary work and scores in tonic solfa notation by black composers such as Reuben Caluza, EAJ Monaisa, AM Jonas, Enoch Sontonga, Benjamin Tyamzashe, Daniel Marivate and even RHW Shepherd.[28] It published two works by Moerane in 1938, giving him the opportunity to learn about the practical process of publication, and to become a reviewer for scores by other composers.

Robert Shepherd was acting principal in 1931 while Moerane was teaching at Lovedale High School, but once he became principal, he was unable to control events following the reconstruction of mission schools in the 1930s after the International Missionary Conference held at Le Zoute, Belgium, in September 1926. Here the ground was laid for a vision of Christian National Education like that of the Netherlands. According to this, pupils would be prepared for life experience and the upliftment of the rural community,[29] with this 'vocational model' replacing a 'book-learning' model. It did not mean that literary teaching and activity ceased: the 'Literary Committee' under Shepherd included illustrious figures such as John Dube from Ohlange and Davidson Don Tengo Jabavu from Fort Hare.[30] However, the de-emphasis on 'book learning' had far-reaching consequences, with a profound impact on the educational climate in which black composers were trained.

On the other hand, the medium of instruction at Lovedale was English; indeed, 'only English could be spoken within the Institution grounds from Mondays to Fridays.' This gave Africans the verbal and written agility to enter into the realms of international politics and literature 'and so helped to form the burgeoning "new class" of African'.[31] That, and a variety of other factors – including the expectation of greater freedom among Africans returning from service in the armed forces during World War II – brought the climate of resistance to a head in the Lovedale riot of 7 August 1946. Although this event happened long after Moerane left Lovedale, signs of unrest had been present for many years, not limited to Lovedale and often fuelled by similar grievances: high fees, poor food, declining standards of teaching, and authoritarian governance, all of which contributed towards 'depriving the students of freedom'.[32] In 1946, nearly two hundred male students went on the rampage, smashing windows and trying to start fires. After a protest march by almost five hundred students in support of those arrested, there was a boycott of classes, and Lovedale was summarily closed. During the Commission of Enquiry into the riot, Xhosa educationist and politician Davidson Jabavu said, 'The real cause is that all present-day students grow up in homes, rural and urban, where the principal staple of conversation is the colour bar, unjust wages, lack of faith in the White man generally, and the whole gamut of anti-Native legislation and ill-treatment by public officers.'[33]

Music at Lovedale

It was not all student politics and repression at Lovedale, but most of the subjects taught were not exactly conducive to the development of a composer. Alongside carpentry, gardening, manual work, wagon-making, shoe-making, printing, bookbinding (for men), scripture and English, music theory and staff notation were taught, with piano offered to the lucky few. There were several other ways in which Moerane could have participated in music-making as well. Lovedale had choirs, and the *Lovedale Annual Report for 1924* devotes a page to 'The Brass Band' directed by Mr SW Hill, although Moerane's name is not among the 18 members listed.[34] Pieters rightly notes that such bands 'were part of the tradition of Presbyterian churches and missions [...] initiated [already] while Bokwe was at Lovedale',[35] although the music principally played would have been hymns, which – as the music by the composers listed above also demonstrates – were a strong and damaging 'colonizing force' on the musical language of composers all over Africa.[36] There was a hindrance to the progress of the brass band noted in the *Lovedale Annual Report for 1926*, which was that 'none of those joining have any knowledge of the staff notation, although they are quite familiar with tonic sol-fa.'[37] It would be interesting to know if Moerane's introduction to any of the instruments he later taught students to play in the African Springtime Orchestra was at Lovedale, and if he was asked, as a very talented musician, to help the Lovedale brass players to learn staff notation.

Moerane's name is listed among those taking up one of the collections at Presbyterian church services on Sunday afternoons offered in 'Sesuto and Sechuana' (Setswana). This may have given him an opportunity to broaden his knowledge of church music, although it is probably more likely that he used his own musical talents to enrich the services musically in some way. He participated in extramural activities such as the (choral) Musical Association, whose vice-conductor and secretary in 1930 was Bennie Mashologu, a neighbour of Mohapeloa's from Morija, and Moerane's classmate throughout their Lovedale and Fort Hare years. He attended meetings of the Literary Society, which held gramophone concerts and 'pleasant musical evenings', and debated topics such as 'What constitutes a lady or gentleman?', 'Is it profitable for those who have to learn English to spend much time in learning classical languages?' and 'Should music occupy more time than history in the school curriculum?'[38] Moerane seems to have been active in the Literary Society long after he had stopped being a student, giving a lecture on 2 May 1930 before one of their debates.[39]

By 1934, the Musical Association had merged with the Drama Society to become the 'Musical and Dramatic Association', with Moerane a committee member, although we do not know if he acted in plays.[40] Mandela remembers acting 'in a play about Abraham Lincoln', and both Mandela and MT Moerane recall the Students Christian Association, 'which taught Bible classes on Sundays in neighbouring villages'.[41] MT also remembers singing in a vocal quartet and participating in tennis, athletics and rugby.[42] I somehow doubt that Michael was the sporting type, and there were other activities he may or may not have participated in, such as ballroom dancing. 'To a crackly old phonograph in the dining hall,' recalls Mandela, 'we spent hours practising fox-trots and waltzes, each of us taking turns leading and following. Our idol was Victor Sylvester […] In a neighbouring village there was an African dance-hall known as Ntsekamanzi, which catered to the cream of local black society.' Such sophistication made Fort Hare unique, says Mandela, a 'revelation to a country boy like myself', with its toilet soap and toothpaste, 'water-flush toilets and hot-water showers'.[43]

Moerane evidently put his knowledge of carpentry and gardening to good use later on, for Epainette Mbeki recalls that 'he was a very good carpenter. He made the table and chairs at his home. It was a beautiful table.'[44] Moerane's agricultural skills were always put to use, as several people remember. There 'was a big garden' next to Moerane's house on Peka High School grounds in the 1960s where he was 'planting things and growing things'; 'he planted vegetables there at Peka High School, cabbage, tomatoes, green beans, squash, pumpkin. We didn't have to buy those things, we just used to pick them from the garden.' Next to his house in Peka village, he 'was allocated a huge field. It was like a farm. You know, in the past, you just went to the chief and he said, "Where do you want land? How much?", so he just ran from here, there, there, there.' On this farm, Moerane had 'potatoes, flowers, a whole lot of things'; 'he had fields where he planted mealies, beans, wheat. There was a gentleman – he used to own a tractor, my grandfather – and he used to go there, this man was working for him, helping him with the farming.'[45]

One thing that Lovedale did not provide Moerane with was a piano, and so he bought one in 1928 while he was living in Alice, from the firm Darters in Cape Town. It was a solid overstrung upright German piano made in Berlin by Adolf Ernst Voigt, 'Koenigl. Span. Hofleiferant' (by Royal Warrant of Appointment to the King of Spain) and probably brand-new. Moerane took it with him wherever he lived, and his son Mofelehetsi, who fetched it from his father's home in Lesotho after he died, testified to its importance in Moerane's life.

> When I was born it was there, at Alice. I've always known it. [...] I remember my time was at three o'clock. Without *fail* I should be on that piano, daily except for Saturday and Sunday. Out of habit, even on Saturday, if one did not have anything to do, one would just sit down and start practicing. Only if he was not playing himself, because he was at it daily, and he tested his compositions on the piano. He tested on the piano most of the time in the evenings, but weekends when we felt free, we would sit down. I remember we heard one night, [something] being repeated – these composers, they repeat a phrase twenty times if [...] it's not correct according to them.[46]

The few scores left in the piano stool in Mofelehetsi's house in Atteridgeville may be only the remnants of a larger score library, but they are revealing nonetheless. The solo piano music includes Schumann's *Album For the Young, Novelletten* and *Phantasiestücke*, Handel's *Harmonious Blacksmith, Das neue Klavierbuch* vol. 1, *The Leschetizky Method*; 'Souvenir' by G Karhanoff (page 176 of what was probably a large book of piano music by various composers); the *Home Series of the Great Masters* No. 8 (Liszt), and one of Liszt's *Liebesträume*. Vocal scores include Schumann's *Frauenliebe und -leben*, the Novello vocal score of the oratorio *The Holy City* by AR Gaul, and five solo songs with piano accompaniment: *Sincerity* by Emilie Clarke, *On Wings of Song* by Mendelssohn (with tonic solfa letters written by Moerane above the melody), *Passing By* by Edward Purcell, *Garden of Happiness* by Edward Lockton, and the English folksong

O No, John! arranged by Edith Braun. The latter, a yellowed and much sellotaped-together score, has as its second page a section from the slow movement of Beethoven's *Piano Sonata* No. 4 Op. 7 ('Largo, con gran espressione') despite the fact that 'O No, John!' is written at the top.[47] The chorus, 'Rejoice, O Daughter of Zion' in the piano stool is nothing to do with the Soprano aria from Handel's *Messiah* but a chorus (No. 3) from John Witty's sacred cantata written c. 1950. This cantata, *From Manger to Cross* (c. 1950), is transcribed into tonic solfa by James Broadbent & Son,[48] and was prescribed for the church choirs competition that most likely took place in Maseru, according to an adjudication form headed 'African Catholic Church'. There is also a tonic solfa score of 'Sweet and Low' by Barnby, and other pages or fragments of manuscript in Moerane's hand or in typescript. The most interesting item in the eponymous piano stool is 'A General Note on Modern Music', written by Moerane and discussed in Chapter 6. Finally, the stool contained Dvořák's *Humoresque*, which was to become an important piece in Moerane's later life: he arranged it for school orchestra, for violin and piano, and as a duo for flute and piano, which he played with Zakes Mda.

Prizes for 'Bantu Literature, Art and Music' at Lovedale were announced in 1935 'for a period of three years in the first instance', having been made available by 'Dr. and Mrs. Mumford, formerly of Tanganyika Territory and now of London University'. In January 1937, the May Esther Bedford music prize-winner was announced, and although Moerane was already teaching at Lovedale by this time, it testifies to what he had learnt and how this was acknowledged, albeit grudgingly:

> Twelve competitors entered for the May Esther Bedford Prize for Musical Composition. Mr S.J. Newns, B.A., the [Cape] Departmental Inspector of Music, who kindly adjudicated, has awarded the Prize of £20 to Michael M. Moerane of Lovedale for an Album for the Young, comprising ten pieces for the piano-forte. Below is an extract from his report. We would especially call the attention of Bantu musicians to his recommendation that they learn to read and to use the Staff Notation and to his advice to attempt simple themes and harmonies before anything more elaborate.

[Extract:] It must be insisted upon in future that the music be written in Staff Notation [...] There is no picture of the piece in sol-fa, and each note has to be read separately in laborious fashion. Many of the entrants hoped to be awarded the prize on the bulk of the work submitted rather than on the quality of it! There is a great deal of loose and unsuitable part-writing, and much of the harmony could never be accurately sung, even apart from harmonic errors. In view of [this] criticism, I have awarded the prize to the compositor [sic] who has written out, plainly and fairly accurately, what he has in mind, with some idea as to form and musical expression. From a musical point of view, the compositions leave a good deal to be desired. As a general suggestion, the Native people should aim at simplicity of writing, rather than try to tackle composition too elaborate for their technical abilities.[49]

The facilitator of the prize and author of the above (anonymous) article must have been Basutoland Director of Education, Mr Oswin Boys Bull, who not long after this invited Moerane to teach at the new Basutoland High School.

South African Native College, Fort Hare
Moerane enrolled at the South African Native College, Fort Hare, in January 1925. This was the only college in South Africa where Africans could complete the last two years of high school (Standards 9 and 10), and obtain a Senior Certificate or a university matriculation certificate (matric). Moerane obtained a university matric pass, Class II, in December 1926.[50] Alongside this, he taught part-time at Lovedale High School in 1925, was an assistant at Lovedale Training School, and in 1926 completed a high school teaching diploma at Lovedale Training School.[51] By 1929 he was on the staff of the Lovedale Practising Schools, and by 1931 he obtained a permanent post at Lovedale High School, where he taught for the next eight years.[52]

Fort Hare and Lovedale in combination made 'a great impact on the wider Southern and East African renaissance'; moreover, Fort Hare 'was a cradle of Pan-Africanism' and of struggle politics generally, attracting, many years later, the archives of the ANC, the PAC, Azapo, the Unity Movement and the Black Consciousness Movement.[53] Fort Hare offered university degrees and diplomas as well as matric, a combination which benefited the matriculants – although Manasseh Moerane felt that 'the standards of Fort Hare as a *University* were compromised by this set up.'[54]

Like Lovedale, Fort Hare registered black matric students from all over southern Africa.[55] 'It was completely non-racial,' said Marumo Moerane when he arrived in 1959, 'except they didn't accept white students'.

> There were Africans, Indians and coloureds amongst the students and faculty. Students were drawn from the whole of Southern and Central Africa. We had a lot of students from what later became Zimbabwe and what later became Malawi and what later became Zambia. Many students from Swaziland and Botswana and Lesotho. And the student body was completely integrated as far as Africans and Indians and coloureds were concerned [while] there was no obvious apartheid within the staff.[56]

At one level, it must have been something like a 'Sixth Form College', an academic space between secondary and tertiary education, and there was a uniform or at least a blazer. Tsepo Moerane has kept his grandfather's blazer from Fort Hare, which despite its age, is still in beautiful condition: thick material, dark brown with gold stripes. 'For young black South Africans like myself,' said Nelson Mandela, Fort Hare 'was Oxford and Cambridge, Harvard and Yale, all rolled into one.'[57] It was also a hotbed of political activity. Professor ZK Matthews, Fort Hare's first graduate, taught social anthropology and African law 'and spoke out bluntly against the government's social policies', while Professor Jabavu taught Xhosa, Latin, history and anthropology, later becoming 'the founding president of the All-African Convention in 1936, which opposed legislation in Parliament designed to end the common voters' roll in the Cape.'[58]

Michael's brothers Fraser and Manasseh and his sister Renée did post-matric degrees and diplomas at Fort Hare after matriculating.[59] (Renée was in the same class as Mandela.) Manasseh and Fraser graduated on the same day, along with Archibald Campbell Jordan. Moerane's parents, Eleazar and Sofi, attended the graduation and were invited to lunch afterwards with Alexander Kerr, the first principal of Fort Hare, who during his long tenure (1916–1948) was noted for the rigidity of his dealings with politicised students.[60] He told the Moerane boys: 'You fellows think that with your degrees and education you are wonderful and knowledgeable but I can tell you that your father is better than all of you put together.'[61] Moerane did not stay on at Fort Hare to do a degree after he matriculated in 1926, presumably because the degree he wanted to do was in music – the BMus – which was not offered there.

The University of South Africa and Rhodes University College

Moerane could not register for music at a white university music department full-time because of his race, but he could register part-time at Unisa, and may have done so through one of its satellite campuses, Rhodes University College in Grahamstown, which was not that far from Alice where he taught. Moerane completed the degree between 1930 and 1941,[62] his successful progress noted in *The South African Native College Calendars*.[63] Moerane studied all the first-, second- and third-year subjects by himself, at home, without tuition but with textbooks. As a black student, he graduated at a ceremony on the Fort Hare campus, not at Rhodes,[64] apparently visiting Grahamstown for private tutorials with Hartmann in his fourth (final) year.[65] He must also have written his exams at Fort Hare, but there were practical exams as well, demonstrations of musicianship common to BMus degrees in Europe and the colonies before World War II, which would have included score-reading on the piano and aural tests. Where did he do those? Did Rhodes staff travel to Fort Hare to examine one black student? This seems unlikely. 'He did his music theory under U.N.I.S.A. [and] for the practical part he was allowed into Rhodes University', is how Thuso Moerane puts it, although he may have been referring to his father's fourth-year studies with Hartmann, described below.[66]

Moerane completed the degree after spending two years teaching in Maseru (1939–1940), where he went with his wife and children, and 'from there went to Kroonstad where our mother taught until our father completed [his] degree at Rhodes.'[67] Moerane seems to have spent all or a great deal of his final year, 1941, in Grahamstown.[68] Writing to Percival Kirby in

1968 about depositing the score of *Fatše La Heso* at Rhodes, Moerane says that he had 'most pleasant memories of the place'.[69]

He took five years (1930–1934) to complete the first three years of the degree, following the 'Courses prescribed by the University of South Africa'.[70] In 1930, the only full-time music lecturer at Rhodes listed in the *Calendar* was Miss KM Paterson, and there were very few music students. The first-year BMus courses listed for 1930, which were presumably Unisa's requirements, are '(1) Practical Aural-training, including Musical Dictation, (2) History of Music (1700 up to date)', for which the prescribed book was *Style in Musical Art* by Charles Hubert Hastings Parry, '(3) Studies in Phrasing and Form, particularly Beethoven Sonatas', for which the prescribed book was *Form* by Stewart Macpherson, '(4) Harmonisation of Melodies and Figured Bass up to 4 Parts, Instrumental and vocal (for pianoforte, string quartet, or voices, in short score), Dominant and Chromatic 7th and Augmented 6th [chords and] Simple Sequences in Figured Bass', with Macpherson's *Harmony* as the textbook.[71] Moerane's student record, obtained by Kirby in 1962 from Unisa, gives the names of courses actually passed. Aside from English I, the first-year subjects listed there are 'History of Music, Harmony & Counterpoint and Elements of Sound'.[72]

The second-year Rhodes BMus syllabus in 1931 had two components: '(1) Studies in the History and growth of (a) Symphony or (b) Opera. Students will be required to study the works and characteristics of the principal composers of these works', and '(2) Advanced Harmony, using Open Score, for String Quartet or Voices, and with contrapuntal treatment of the harmonisation of Melodies', using Macpherson's *Harmony* and Percy Buck's *Unfigured Harmony* as textbooks.[73] The courses Moerane passed through Unisa that year were 'Counter Point, Score Reading, Advanced Harmony using Open Score for String Quartet or Voices and with contrapuntal treatment of the harmonisation of Melodies, Composition'.[74]

Third- and fourth-year BMus

The third-year syllabus in 1933 was 'Study of selected classical works from score. Advanced Harmony, *C.H. Kitson*. Elements of Acoustics. Form and Analysis. Sight playing from four-part score'.[75] Moerane passed exams in 'Orchestration and Instrumentation, Double Counterpoint and Fugue'.[76] The difference between the course and the exams is greater here than in the first two years, and the wording of the course itself raises a question: was there a 'sight playing' exam and if so, where did Moerane do it? Also known as score-reading, playing a previously unseen score at sight on the piano requires considerable skill: mentally arranging what you see on the page, music written in several staves on a score, for two hands on the piano. It might be a four-part vocal score, but could also be a four-part brass, wind or string score. It would involve transposition, and at the very least, a high degree of keyboard facility, along with excellent music reading and aural skills.

Score-reading was a normal part of a music degree in those days, linked to advanced harmony, counterpoint and orchestration, and harking back to a centuries-old European tradition of learning musicianship through the keyboard and church music scores. This tradition ossified in nineteenth-century Europe through newly introduced BMus courses in Paris, Leipzig and Oxford. 'Harmony and Counterpoint, Fugue, Canon, Formal Analysis, and Musical History, in addition to the submission of written composition of prescribed nature' became a 'pattern generally adopted' by other universities.[77] Perhaps because Rhodes University College had modelled itself on Oxford since its inception,[78] such courses naturally found their way into curriculum. There were clearly insufficient staff to teach all aspects of a complex degree at a high level, and probably insufficient library holdings as well, and so the standard British music textbooks of the day (Parry, MacPherson, Buck and Kitson) filled the gaps. This was to Moerane's advantage in some ways: as long as he had the prescribed textbooks, some scores, a piano (and almost certainly a gramophone and a few of his own records), he could study at home relatively easily.

No fourth-year music syllabus appears in any Rhodes *Calendar* before Hartmann's arrival at the college in February 1939, and so it is difficult to guess the contents of the course 'Advanced Composition, 4th year', which Moerane passed in 1934.[79] However, an examination paper has survived, in the famous piano stool in Mofelehetsi's house in Atteridgeville, which is headed 'University of South Africa, B.Mus. Examinations, 1935. Third Year. Paper 3, Composition'. (Perhaps '4th year' on a Unisa Student Record produced long after the fact might be a misprint.) The three-hour paper contains only one question: 'Set to music, as a song for voice and piano, either of the following poems', with a 'Note' to say that 'The Candidate must have the use of a Piano in this Examination'. The examiners were Percival Kirby and Douglas Mossop. The first poem is 'Gibberish' by Mary E Coleridge, and the second a heavily bowdlerised version of 'A Dream of Death' by WB Yeats. Both poems have two stanzas.

Two short lines written on the exam paper marking the second stanza of the Yeats may indicate that this was Moerane's choice for setting. The music that was expected of students was presumably expected to match the focus on poetry of the British Isles. Certainly the examiners, Kirby and Mossop, were knowledgeable about British music in the early twentieth century: a concert organised by the Contemporary Music Society in Johannesburg in which Mossop played music by Arnold Bax, Frederick Delius and John Ireland was reported in August 1936; and Kirby was mentored by Parry, who wrote music in an early twentieth-century English style, and whose *Style in Musical Art* was a prescribed textbook at Rhodes.[80]

In a letter to Kirby long afterwards, in 1958, Hartmann said that Moerane 'completed also the fourth year subjects […] except the subject composition' and that through the intervention of Fort Hare principal, Alexander Kerr, 'Moerane had asked various university music departments in the country to help him' with composition – but that 'such assistance was not given to him'. Dr Kerr asked Hartmann to help, and on Kerr's recommendation he 'undertook to do so. Moerane came to Grahamstown where I gave him tuition for a full year' – presumably 1941.[81] This was informal private tuition, outside of Hartmann's regular teaching at Rhodes, and it was the only tuition Moerane received for his degree.

The student record gives only two courses passed in 1941: 'Composition III' and 'Exercise', with *Fatše La Heso* submitted as the 'Exercise'.[82] Moerane clearly made strides in composition through courses such as these – after all, he won a prize for *Album for the Young* in 1937 – but it is puzzling that the student record lists a third-year course in 1941, a fourth-year course in 1934, and nothing for 1935 even though the exam paper kept in the stool is dated 1935.

Rhodes in the 1930s and 1940s

It was amazing that Hartmann agreed to allow Moerane to study with him at all, even as a part-time non-resident (Unisa) student, given the 'strict racial segregation enforced at Rhodes', an image of which in 1946 is shown in Figure 2.2, 'until the late 1940s.'[83] Even admitting part-time white students was unusual: when part-time students at Port Elizabeth Technical Institute asked 'to become affiliated students of Rhodes [and] so enabled to take the examinations conducted by Unisa', concern was expressed at Rhodes about the tail wagging the dog, and 'the request was referred to a Committee, a procedure which ensured that for some time at any rate nothing more was heard of it.'[84] Perhaps 'the recession of the late 1920s' that caused South African university students in 1930, male and female, to 'easily qualify for admission to a university, by examination, at 16' helped to create the climate in which it was possible for Hartmann to invite Moerane to study with him.[85]

In 1937, before Moerane had met Hartmann and completed his degree, a new Master (or Vice-Chancellor as we would say nowadays) was appointed – John Smeath Thomas from the University of Cape Town who was to be responsible for the biggest and most expensive scandal Rhodes had seen thus far. Paul Maylam devotes 20 pages of his *Intellectual, Political and Cultural History* of Rhodes University to an account of the 'The Field Case' in the Music Department, which flowed directly from Rhodes

Figure 2.2: Rhodes University Main Building 1946 (courtesy Cory Library)

Council's summary appointment of Smeath Thomas (without advertisement or interview), and the latter's appointment of Hartmann in the same way in 1939.[86] In 1941, Hartmann in turn summarily appointed a piano teacher, Leslie Field, but by the end of that year, he was accusing Field of poor teaching. Field in turn filed complaints against Hartmann's teaching in 1942. This set in motion 'a damaging chain of events that would last another five years', almost bankrupting the university.[87]

It is extremely unlikely that Moerane was not privy to the start of this debacle, although he may not have experienced, during his sessions with Hartmann, any of the allegations made by students: that he 'liked to lecture on the sex lives of European artists' and frightened students with 'his talk about hypnotism, telepathy and ghosts'.[88] Described in the *Rhodes Calendar* as 'F.H. Hartmann, M.Mus., L.L.D. (Vienna), late Professor of the Theory of Music and Director of the Great String Orchestra, State Academy for Music and Dramatic Art, Vienna',[89] Hartmann was far more musically qualified than any previous lecturer at Rhodes; without his influence, Moerane would almost certainly not have written a symphonic poem infused with the language of early twentieth-century European music, a language that no amount of Parry, Macpherson, Buck and Kitson could have developed.

Moerane graduated with a Unisa – or, one might say, a Rhodes University College of Unisa – BMus degree in 1942 in a class of two. His graduation gown and BMus hood have survived,[90] and Figure 9.2 shows Moerane wearing these at his son Thabo's graduation, 26 years later.

Fatše La Heso, the subject of Chapter 5 and the crowning glory of Moerane's BMus degree, was seen immediately as an extraordinary work; Professor Jabavu of Fort Hare claimed that 'the University was hard put to find in South Africa, persons with enough advanced knowledge to examine Michael Moerane.'[91] Hartmann turned to the most illustrious composer and composition teacher in South Africa at that time, William Henry Bell, as external examiner. Bell (1873–1946) had emigrated to South Africa from England in 1912 to take up the position of Principal of the South African College of Music in Cape Town,[92] becoming the first Dean of the College in 1923. Bell reported to Hartmann that 'he never had expected such a work to be written in South Africa, and less so by a Native.'[93]

While studying for the BMus degree, Moerane continued to compose: two works for unaccompanied choir by Moerane were published in tonic solfa notation by Lovedale Press: *Liphala* (*Whistles*) and an arrangement of the spiritual *Nobody Knows The Trouble I've Seen*. They are listed in Lovedale's 'New Books Published at the Cost of the Lovedale Press 1927–1937', but were actually published in 1938.[94] Moerane also completed his first version of *Della* in 1938.

Friedrich Hartmann and Michael Moerane

Friedrich Hartmann (1900–1973) studied in Vienna and published books on 'music theory, harmony, and theory pedagogy in Vienna in the late 1930s.'[95] He fled Austria after 1938 because he was 'an outspoken opponent of Nazism with a part–Jewish wife', says Maylam, but his story 'was not as straightforward as it might appear'; he seems to have been 'an Austro-fascist, a supporter of the regime of Engelbert Dollfus and Kurt Schuschnigg'.[96] Nazism was not only viewed from very different perspectives within Austria in the 1930s; it was also viewed very tolerantly in South Africa by those who opposed Jan Smuts's pro-British government. Young Afrikaner intellectuals such as Hendrik Verwoerd and WWM Eiselen were sent 'to study Nazi ideology and organizational tactics' and upon their return 'developed structures that paralleled the Nazi SS and Brown Shirts in the form of the Osse-waar-brandtwag and the Gray Shirts.'[97] Indeed, the same year Hartmann escaped from Nazism for one reason, South Africa's Defence Minister, Oswald Pirow visited Hitler for another: to affirm ties with South Africa's right-wing National Party, which would come to power in 1948.[98] Hartmann's flight was of a very different order, then, from the flight of other musical refugees, including Hans Adler, Hans Kramer and Joseph Trauneck, from Nazi Germany to South Africa at around the same time.[99]

Hartmann had not been in Grahamstown for long when Moerane came to study with him; he had barely rewritten the BMus syllabus with additional composition in fourth year when he had what was probably his first experience of a composer of colour. How did they work together? Perhaps they studied scores by late nineteenth-century Austro-German romantics such as Liszt, Brahms, Wagner, Bruckner, Mahler, Richard Strauss and Zemlinsky – not only for their orchestration, but for their musical language. 'The influence of Hartmann on Moerane's musical language is most obvious in his use of chromaticism and fugato writing', as Jeffrey Brukman says, reminding us that Hartmann codified a system 'for the analysis of music in the style of late-romantic composers, such as Wagner and Richard Strauss, whose use of chromaticism and shifting tonalities are apparent in the harmonic vernacular of Moerane.'[100] Moerane's musical education peaked at Rhodes during what must have been the most intense period of musical study in his life. There is no doubt that Hartmann came at the right time for Rhodes, elevating the BMus to a professional level. He went on to become Head of Music at Wits, exerting a strong influence on the Unisa syllabus as well, before returning to Europe after World War II.[101] His political stance did not prevent him from being a good teacher, but it prevented him from tolerating Moerane's political views; years later he describes meeting Moerane and finding him an 'embittered' man with 'communistic' tendencies (see Chapter 4). Even sadder than this view is the reality that Moerane was unable to put most of the advanced knowledge he had gleaned from his music degree either into high school teaching – because of the restricted or non-existent music syllabus in black schools – or into choral composition, because of the restricted music education of conductors and choristers. He never obtained a post as a university lecturer. Music remained extramural for Moerane: throughout his life, it was an addition to his teaching load. Perhaps it gave him more satisfaction than he found in other aspects of high school life, especially after 'The Eiselen Commission on Native Education' (the same Eiselen sent to study Nazism in Germany) was set up under Malan's Nationalist Party government in 1948.

One of the strongest statements made in the Eiselen Report was that the function of education was to 'transmit the culture of a society from its more mature to its immature members and in so doing develop their powers' while at the same time 'protecting' the community and the culture of a people. By this time, Moerane was firmly enmeshed in the state school system for Africans; he would have felt the effects of a tightening noose whereby the 'increased emphasis [...] placed on the "mass of the Bantu" would "enable them to co-operate in the evolution of new social patterns and institutions".' The term 'Bantu Education' was coined and considered vital by the Eiselen Report, 'because after school the African child returned to his own community and when he reached maturity his concern would be for the development of his own people. So the aim of all African [Bantu] Education should be for the type of individual that would function most efficiently in African society.' This theory was based on 'theories of differentiation' put forward by Charles Templeman Loram, Lovedale Councillor and first President of the South African Institute of Race Relations: 'Loram's views were to be political dynamite in the hands of the new Nationalist Government [and] particularly important because they emanated from an educationalist who was generally sympathetic to the missionary cause.'[102] Moerane's experience of mission education, then, was to haunt him in a ghastly new form as he launched his career as teacher.

3 | Moerane the Teacher and Composer

Moerane was born into a family of teachers who 'irradiated' education throughout southern Africa 'and beyond':

> In South Africa the most outstanding schools are Lovedale, Healdtown, St Matthews, St Peters-Rosenttenville, St Johns [Umtata], Kroonstad High, Tiisetang [Bethlehem], Adams College, Ohlange Institute, Inanda Seminary, Tseki High, Bonamelo College of Education, Phiritona, Lora, Peka High, Basutoland High, and at all these at some point a Moerane has taught.[1]

The enormous pride expressed here is fully justified. Yet teachers at these few elite schools for African scholars worked against all odds. Moerane spent most of his teaching life in the Cape Colony working in the environment of mission education during the poverty-gripped colonial late-1920s and throughout the 1930s; then in a climate of increasing state repression in black schools during the 1940s and 1950s, as apartheid took control of every aspect of life. Even in his final years in Lesotho, he operated in a country rife with political interference and economic impoverishment. Not only that, but by the time he was fully educated and musically trained, and had produced an orchestral work that belongs firmly within the orchestral culture of the Western metropolis, Moerane was obliged to teach only in rural schools, which were largely without resources, and without a formal music curriculum. This while negotiating a national educational ideology that separated schooling from urban life and dictated that students aspire to be little more than agricultural or industrial labourers. That he not only survived these odds, but did such a huge amount of good as a teacher is clear from the evidence presented in this book. But first we must ask: how did the odds become so stacked against such an achievement?

In the landmark 1984 publication, *Apartheid and Education: The Education of Black South Africans*, one author after another documents policies that had remained unchanged for a hundred years prior to that, and were, in the 1980s, still excluding the black majority from any aspirations.[2] In 1903, the year before Moerane was born, they were expressed thus: 'Habits of obedience and cleanliness and order are what [the native] most wants, and these must be the foundation not only of the usefulness of his school life, but of the life for which the school is but a training'; in 1936, while he was in the midst of a BMus degree: 'we must give the Native an education which will keep him in his place'; in 1946, as he launched his career in Queenstown: no African 'should be given education based on the assumption that one day he shall cease to be an employee of the whiteman' [sic].[3] In 1954, when Moerane was active in the Cape African Teachers Association (CATA), the Bantu Education Act decreed that 'there is no place for [the Bantu] in the European community above the level of certain forms of labour [...] for that reason it is of no avail for him to receive a training which has as its aims absorption in the European community, where he cannot be absorbed', aims that 'drew him away from his own community and misled him by showing him the green pastures of European society in which he was not allowed to graze.'[4]

As Moerane entered the teaching profession, intellectual restrictions in black education were becoming more severe. This was the result of escalating class populations, a 'vast imbalance in the number of primary and secondary schools', closure of nursery schools, insistence on both English and Afrikaans in primary school from the 1950s onwards, and a system that was altogether 'seriously underfinanced'. African teachers' salaries were much lower than those of white teachers, and although black communities tried to make up the shortfall by 'raising money for extra teachers' salaries, classroom buildings and equipment', to be an African teacher in Moerane's day was more than a vocation: it was a daily sacrifice.[5] Throughout Moerane's working life, not surprisingly, schools were sites of protest against both the institutions and regional and national government.

The tonic solfa books that constituted music education in black schools took students only so far, causing a permanent 'state of arrested development' that lasted for decades, and which has left a detrimental legacy.[6] As Khabi Mngoma put it in 1985, five years after Moerane's death, citing Todd Matshikiza: 'In my segment – back of the moon – the position of music education is gloomy indeed.' School authorities ignored the wealth of traditional music in the community, not even exploiting it in the interests of 'keeping Africans in their place', just as they ignored popular music and jazz, never mind the solfa repertoires of African choral composers since John Knox Bokwe (1855–1922) that would have been useful as educational material. Choral competitions kept music alive, but also confirmed the notion that the voice was the only 'instrument' an African student should have – which, of course, cost nothing. Ironically, this has come back to haunt South Africa as one glorious vocalist after another has become famous on the world stage – Pumeza Matshikiza, Pretty Yende, Simon Shibambu, Masabane Cecilia Rangwanasha – all having started life against odds not unlike the ones just described. The extramural 'choral contests' were the only thing that 'helped to keep music literacy alive in schools'.[7]

No wonder African teachers and composers were, like Moerane, often one and the same person. No wonder instrumental composition never became a normal part of a black composer's output, and that choral music proliferated instead, developing relatively little during the twentieth century compared to the enormous development of popular music and jazz, and of classical music in white society. No wonder it was difficult for Moerane's isolated symphonic poem to counter the narrative that prevailed during his life and for years afterwards – that Black composers did not possess musical knowledge – a narrative that prevailed for decades as a reason for keeping African composers out of the greener pastures in which they were 'not allowed to graze'.

The teacher-composer at Lovedale High School
Moerane taught at Lovedale High School for ten years, from July 1929 to December 1938, resigning only 'on [his] appointment to the new High School at Maseru'.[8] Exactly what Moerane taught at Lovedale is not known, but he composed alongside teaching; and the fact that the Lovedale Press

published music was surely an incentive to do so. *Liphala* and *Nobody Knows The Trouble I've Seen* (1938) are confident in their melodic, rhythmic and expressive detail, and interesting for the way in which they seem to have been written as teaching pieces – in this bar you learn triplets, in this bar mezzo-forte, here crescendo, there how to write a cadence, and so on. What else he may have composed with Lovedale students in mind is anyone's guess.

Years after Moerane left Lovedale, when the SABC regional manager in Grahamstown, Mr de Jager, was trying to track him down, the former principal, RHW Shepherd, came up with this surprising piece of information: 'Dr Shepherd remembers him as being a teacher on his staff and for an oratorio which Moerane wrote.'[9] 'Oratorio' may be an exaggeration, given the lack of an orchestra or even instrumental ensembles at Lovedale (other than the brass band), but a cantata-like series of unaccompanied works for choir, perhaps with some solo passages, is not an inconceivable work for Moerane to have written. Whatever his 'oratorio' was, it is now lost. Bokwe himself had written a collection of choral songs, *Amaculo ase Lovedale*, and Bokwe must still have been used as a model at Lovedale in the 1920s. Even though his hymn-tune 'Lovedale' or *Msindisi Wa Boni* (*Saviour of Sinners*) was written half a century earlier in June 1875, it was 'the first known notated composition by a black South Africa' and the first music that Lovedale published;[10] it would thus have been the pioneering work in the route that Moerane followed.

The *Lovedale Reports* tell us that in 1924, while Moerane was in Form C (Standard 8/Grade 10) he served as a 'temporary language teacher' in the high school, although this does not indicate whether he taught English, Latin or an African language.[11] He must have studied Latin at Lovedale, as he taught it at Peka and perhaps also at Lovedale. In 1925, Moerane taught part-time at Lovedale High School and was an 'Assistant' at Lovedale Training School.[12] There was a total enrolment of 138 students that year, across all three years, and four full-time and two part-time teachers, as well as another two teachers who each worked a half-year.[13] In 1926, the year he passed matric at Fort Hare, Moerane taught at the training school.[14] The training was for lower and higher primary-school teaching, across four years of study. The staff comprised a headmaster and 14 'Assistants', and there were 215 students.[15] By 1929, Moerane was on the staff of the

Lovedale Practising Schools, which means that he must have been teaching educational methods as well as curriculum content, and possibly supervising those students doing teaching practice.[16]

By 1931, he had obtained a permanent post at Lovedale High School. When he resigned at the end of 1938, together with 'Miss C Nikani, B.A.', who left 'for new work in Moroko High School, Thaba 'Nchu', it was recorded that she and Moerane had both 'given notable service, an appreciation of which is given by the Head of the School in his report.'[17] In the *Lovedale Report* for the previous year (1937), we read that he and two other teachers, Mrs Geddes and the same Miss Nikani, had jointly produced a school operetta, *Prince Ferdinand*, a work that had been published by Novello in London in 1896, with music by Richard D Metcalfe and words by HJ Ashcroft.[18] Twenty years later, at Mfundisweni College, Moerane produced another operetta in the same vein, as discussed later. Many students must have proceeded to Fort Hare with Moerane's help, as Lovedale and its neighbouring Methodist mission school, Healdtown, produced half of 'the African students passing Cape Senior Certificate', while 'a majority of students at Fort Hare were by the early 1950s from these two institutions.'[19]

Part of Moerane's work at Lovedale must have involved choirs: rehearsing and conducting them, teaching conducting and rehearsing, and adjudicating competitions. There is not yet any national historical archive of choral scores or books of prescribed competition songs, but once it exists, Moerane's name will often appear there. We know that several of his works were expressly written for competitions, and once works were in the competition circuit, they tended to appear over and over again in successive years, and in different parts of southern Africa. We also know that he adjudicated competitions – an instance in Lesotho is mentioned below – and in Mofelehetsi's piano stool is a copy of the chorus 'Rejoice, O Daughter of Zion' that was prescribed for the Church Choirs Competition, according to the adjudication form that has survived with it. This must have been a rough copy, and it is indeed incomplete, but the extract in Figure 3.1 gives an idea of what adjudicators were looking for. Other pages show the marks Moerane roughly allocated to the 12 competing choirs, and his comments on the 'African Catholic Church' choir's performance of 'Rejoice, O Daughter of Zion'.

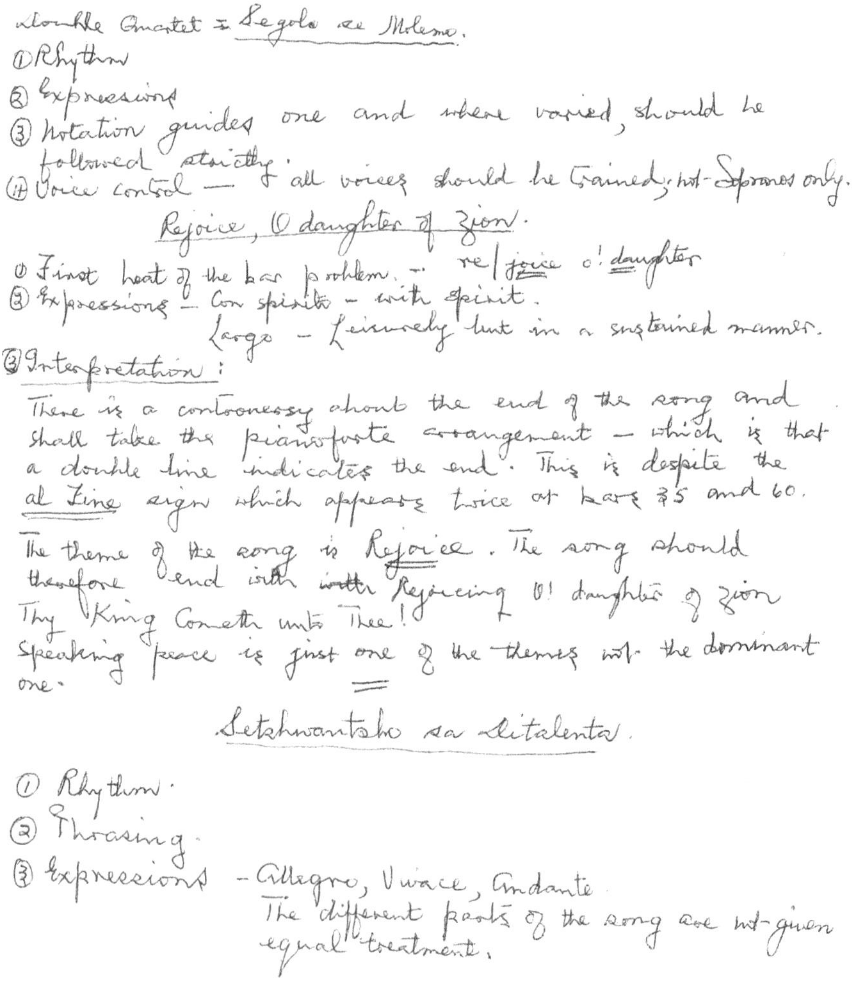
double Quartet = Segolo se Molemo.
① Rhythm
② Expressions
③ Notation guides one and where varied, should be followed strictly.
④ Voice control — all voices should be trained, not Sopranos only.

Rejoice, O daughter of Zion.

① First beat of the bar problem. – re/joice o! daughter
② Expressions — Con spirito – with spirit.
Largo – Leisurely but in a sustained manner.
③ Interpretation:
There is a controversy about the end of the song and shall take the pianoforte arrangement – which is that a double line indicates the end. This is despite the al Fine sign which appears twice at bars 35 and 60.

The theme of the song is Rejoice. The song should therefore end with Rejoicing O! daughter of Zion Thy King Cometh unto Thee!
Speaking peace is just one of the themes not the dominant one.

Setshwantsho sa litalenta.

① Rhythm.
② Phrasing.
③ Expressions – Allegro, Vivace, Andante
The different parts of the song are not given equal treatment.

Figure 3.1: Choir competition adjudication comments written by Moerane (courtesy Neo Mahase Moerane)

Basutoland High School

The move to Lesotho at the beginning of 1939 to take up a post at the newly opened Basutoland High School (now Lesotho High School) must have been a huge upheaval for the Moeranes, with young children, new teaching commitments, and Moerane's BMus degree still incomplete. Perhaps the attraction was life outside South Africa, given how racial tensions had increased during the 1920s and 1930s. According to one of

Moerane's former students at the school, Gilbert Ramatlapeng, Moerane 'was specially recruited from Lovedale [...] hired from the Cape by the [Basutoland] Director of Education. Specially invited by that man.'[20] 'That man' was the Director of Education, Mr OB Bull, who had administered the May Esther Bedford award which Moerane had won while he was at Fort Hare. This was a period of educational renewal in Basutoland, as Bull points out in the first issue of his *Basutoland Teachers' Magazine* launched at the end of 1937: 'A new era is beginning in Basutoland' with 'new enterprises [seen] in almost every department of the Territory's life'; hence the need for improving 'the standards and suitability' of education.[21] This was not South Africa, and such improvement included book-learning. During his two years at the school (1939–1940), Moerane taught Sesotho and Commercial Arithmetic among other things, and formed an extramural choir and a vocal sextet, which 'sang all sorts of songs, all types'. Ramatlapeng remembers how popular Moerane was, despite the fact that he was 'very strict': 'in the whole school, he was the best teacher, of *all* of them'. He also remembers Moerane as 'very handsome, with a very nice voice. Not high, but well-modulated. Very nice tone. He was a wonderfully gifted man, well versed in music. He was very, very intelligent. We liked him so much. And most of the time we were there at his house, singing.'[22]

Moerane and Betty's daughter, Sophia, was born in Maseru in 1940, and the family left at the end of that year. It may have been because of his 'being from the Cape', at a time when Basutoland was 'at this stage of new beginnings'. 'Black people were beginning to find themselves', as Ramatlapeng puts it, 'and that was a problem':

> So they kicked him out. And we were so sorry. He called us to the hall and explained that 'Boys and girls, I am going.' 'Going where?' 'No, going back home. People don't need me.' 'What d'you mean, they don't need you?' We were shocked. Such a tiny school. Because, you know, in 1940 we were just over 40. The whole school was just over 40. They just left. He was a threat. So they wanted to get rid of him. The other teachers were jealous of him. We were so sad that he had to leave so early, when the school was still in its infancy. It was a terrible thing.[23]

Queenstown African Secondary School

Moerane must also have applied for a position in Queenstown during or after the year he completed his BMus in Grahamstown (1941). Once again it was not a music teaching post, but he made music a strong extramural feature at the school. Moerane could easily have started a music department at Fort Hare at this stage in his life, or at least have taught part-time there and developed the beginnings of such a department – just as Reuben Caluza later did in the Education Department of the University of Zululand in 1962, which developed under Khabi Mngoma into the Music Department during the 1970s. The differences between Caluza's and Moerane's life trajectories are marked in other ways as well. Caluza's most enduring works, such as *Si lu Sapo* or *iLand Act*, were published by Lovedale in the same few years as Moerane's two pieces. However, Caluza had compositions recorded by HMV in London in 1930, and had studied at Hampton Institute, Virginia, and Columbia University, New York, between 1930 and 1935. In 1936 he had 'assume[d] the leadership of the newly formed School of Music at Adams College in Amanzimtoti, near Durban' – a real music teaching post, with funding from 'members of the American Congregationalists'.[24] No such opportunities were given to Moerane. Was it because the Transkei was less conducive to such things than Natal? Did Kerr, the principal of Fort Hare, block his appointment or involvement? Was it because of Moerane's politics, or because, unlike Caluza, he was not at all interested in jazz and popular performance?

Queenstown was known in those days as 'That Great Little Jazz Town'. 'Can I ever forget', wrote Todd Matshikiza, 'the Darktown Darkies, the Versatile Six, the Harmony Kings and above all the Darktown Strutters in blazing red blazers and melton Oxford bags?'[25] It was also as 'renowned for its choral and classical music scene': 'every night there was a choral event of some kind or another, and Michael Moerane was at its very centre'.[26] Moerane must have begun teaching at Queenstown (African) Secondary School in Victoria Road (later called Queenstown Bantu Secondary School and now called Luvuyo Lerumo Senior Secondary School) in about 1942.

According to Mofelehetsi Moerane, 'I suppose he found out which school did not have an English influence' and chose Queenstown because 'the principal there was Xhosa and all that. So he got a post there and we left Kroonstad for Queenstown.'[27] Thuso Moerane, younger at the time, remembered that the 'Principal was Chisholm [and] by the time I got there, it was Mr Noah, a black man this time, after Chisholm.'[28] At first, the family lived in Victoria Road, but then Moerane bought the house at Number 10 Scanlen Street. The children attended the Moravian mission school. It must have been exciting for them, says Gevisser, to live in this bustling town with a 'frontier feel to it'.[29] It must have been more stimulating for Moerane, too, although the choirs in the region were isiXhosa-speaking. Plus it cannot have been easy to have Todd Matshikiza at Number 8 and Lex Mona at Number 6 Scanlen Street: 'Moerane, upright and classical, thought the jazzy Matshikizas were dissipated ne'er-do-wells' and they 'no doubt [viewed] the Moeranes as teetotalling prigs.'[30] Mofelehetsi used to sneak out and play jazz 'in the house the other side of Matshikiza's, second house from us, in the evenings.' His brother describes how one day, 'he [Mofelehetsi] was singing with one group there at the location, at the old hall':

> Old man got wind that he was there and went and fetched him in the course of the performance. At the door, the doorkeeper didn't want to admit him. The old man pushed him aside, I'm told – I wasn't there – and went straight to the stage. So the chap couldn't help running away, my eldest brother [...] Rushing like that, straight to the stage! So he had just run away. I don't know who told the old man that he was at the location.[31]

As Mofelehetsi put it:

> I had been recruited and fell victim to a jazz group [which led to him being] sent to Durban, to Ohlange, to get me away from mischief. [So] at age thirteen, I was sent from Queenstown to Durban, via East London, in the *Athlone Castle* [ship]. I struggled my way to Ohlange Institute, which institute my uncle later joined: MT. So most of the time I was away from home. It was because of that behaviour. He didn't care for jazz. I suppose he wanted to keep me for classical music.[32]

It is odd, somehow, that even though Thabo was by far the most musically talented of Moerane's children, his father should have forbidden him to study music at university. 'I could not understand it, why the old man did not allow Thabo to train as a musician, go to university or wherever and train and get certificated. He didn't allow that.'[33] Moerane must have been somewhat galled when Thabo later became such a good jazz pianist.

Another reason for Mofelehetsi's banishment was probably the affair he had with one of the Mona girls, who subsequently gave birth to Mofelehetsi's daughter and Moerane's first grandchild, Mosa, in 1952:

> What happened is that I was an illegitimate child. I was born there in Queenstown, from there my mother was Mona, the surname. They lived not far from us. We were neighbours. When I was born, because my mother was from a well-to-do family, for her to fall pregnant, it was such a disgrace, it was a shame, so they took me to live in the rural areas. Then, when my grandfather, Mr Mona, came to visit me, he didn't like the conditions I lived under, he spoke to my [other] grandfather [Moerane], to say they must please take me. Then I came to the Moeranes, they fetched me from that family there in the rural areas, I don't even know what that area is called, in the Eastern Cape. So then I lived with the Moeranes – my grandfather, grandmother, and Uncle Thabo – in Queenstown, and I attended the Roman Catholic School in Scanlen Street. When M.M. relocated to Lesotho, I was about nine years old; he took me there.[34]

The African Springtime Orchestra

Moerane was in Queenstown when his *Fatše La Heso* was broadcast by the British Broadcasting Corporation (BBC) Symphony Orchestra in 1944. Whether it was because of this, or through the church, through the contact he made with the Council on African Affairs (which led to the 1950 American performance of *Fatše* in New York, described in more detail in Chapter 5), or through his brother MT's connection to the Moral Rearmament movement in the United States,[35] Moerane received a small donation of orchestral instruments and used them to start the African Springtime Orchestra in Queenstown. 'Well, it was a family thing, that orchestra,' said Thuso. 'I was playing the violin.'[36] (Figure 0.2 in the Introduction shows Thuso sitting on the left.) 'He taught all of us. All of it. All instruments. And he was mainly on the piano. He played the piano and we followed on.'[37] Moerane included students outside the family, too, and 'the orchestra performed at the location hall and town hall.'[38] In addition, 'his school choir performed in various places in and out of town.'[39] Students from the high school 'would come for rehearsals. He used to produce these cantatas. Many students used to come [home] and practice. He played accompaniment, he gave them accompaniment and all that.'[40]

Mofelehetsi had left home by the time the African Springtime Orchestra was underway and didn't play in it, but 'took up clarinet playing' in the holidays. 'In fact it was the old man himself who taught me, so that I should learn how to play the thing quickly. He taught all the instruments. Oh yes, he was a wonderful musician, and he played the flute.' On one occasion:

> We were from Lesotho, him and I, on the train. He liked public transport. And why? He would be able to play that instrument of his among his people, get criticism if there was any, and pleasure where necessary. So he played that thing one evening in the train and an old lady who was there, she had tears, she cried. [The] 'old man' [was] very strict when it came to us and the piano […] when it came to us and learning, he was very strict […] Only the super-intelligent among the family became great friends of his. The last-born [Thabo] and the sister that comes after me [Mathabo] [were] his favourite[s].[41]

'Super-intelligent' meant the most musical ones, and even as an old man, Mofelehetsi was still highly conscious of the fact that his father had not considered him as such. At the very beginning of our first interview in 2014, he said:

> There is something that worries me when it gets to music. There was a training school at Everton. I composed two songs, sent them to the old man […] His letter after I sent him my two compositions was a surprise to me; for him to write a letter to me like that. To me, and actually send me a few [books] on music, and recommend certain others on harmony and counterpoint and all those things […] He said I should keep on. Because the harmony I used was not this common

thing that we hear from the radios. I don't think it was very far from his; I don't think so. That's why I feel very bitter.'[42]

Mofelehetsi's bitterness stemmed from the fact that he gave the two songs to a white choir conductor and never saw them again, a loss made all the more painful because such praise from his father was extremely rare. All told, I got the impression that Mofelehetsi's relationship with his father was fraught. Mathabo, his musical sister, played the piano almost until she died: 'He was on his way to Lovedale from Queenstown, when she went off her senses in the train. Well, they managed to get her home [...] But piano: any time. She's *very* good, *very* good [...] Yes, she's in a home in Queenstown, and in December – Christmas – Thuso brings her home and we discovered she has not forgotten *any*thing about piano playing, many years after she had fallen ill.'[43]

Teaching and politics

MT's address in 1988, at the unveiling of Moerane's gravestone, stressed the threefold importance of Moerane's activities and contribution: teaching, composing and politics. 'He made a worthy contribution to the struggle of our people for freedom in the Teachers Association. Indeed, he made a contribution to the education of the Black Man in Southern Africa over a long time and a wide area but his greatest contribution was to the cultural heritage of society. He trained thousands of music teachers-to-be and above all through his own Composition.'[44] 'Like many black schoolmasters from the Cape, Michael Moerane belonged not to the ANC but to the rival Non-European Unity Movement (NEUM)', which 'developed, through the 1940s and 1950s, an uncompromising anti-collaborationist stance', calling for boycotts not only of the schools, but also of the Native Representative Council and the Transkei Bhunga, on which his brother Daniel and brother-in-law Govan Mbeki served.[45] 'Uncle Govan would come to Queenstown to see the Reverend Gawe [the ANC leader in the town], who lived on the same street as us, but would not even come to visit us, because we were not ANC.'[46]

Moerane joined the Queenstown branch of CATA, which was affiliated to the All-Africa Convention and NEUM. CATA, together with The Natal African Teachers' Union, The Orange Free State African Teachers' Association, The Transvaal African Teachers' Association and The Transvaal African Teachers' Union, which collectively constituted the

Federal Council of African Teachers' Associations, submitted a memorandum to the South African government on Bantu Education in 1955.[47] CATA's Executive Committee issued a statement around this time, 'The choice before the Cape African Teachers', in which they rejected the notion of education for servitude.[48] Sophia remembers that writer AC Jordan and his wife Phyllis Ntantala visited the Moerane home in Queenstown during these years, and in 2015, Sophia gave me the relevant pages in her autobiography, *A Life's Mosaic*, with a note saying that they would 'give one an idea as to how my father came to be involved with CATA.' She also remembers the seminal 1948 CATA conference in Queenstown, at which CATA vowed, Ntantala recalls, 'that our struggle [as educated middle-class African teachers] is inextricably bound up with the struggle of the African labourer' and indeed 'the general political struggle for the emancipation of the African.'[49] CATA thus fiercely resisted Bantu Education when it was introduced after 1954,[50] their resistance taking various forms, including the boycott of classes.

Tensions in education in the 1950s were part of a broader sociopolitical onslaught against inter-racial mingling. The creation of a centralised Department of Bantu Education and Development set the scene for confrontation, manifested as a widespread schools boycott, an action seen as one of the only protests left open to African people. This created major rifts in the anti-apartheid movement: 'The schools' boycott itself caused divisions as to the merits of the strategy. A.B. Xuma, a former President-General of the A.N.C., considered the boycott to be a negative plan', and even the African press came out against it.[51] When Moerane's 'relations became shaky with the Education Department' in 1958, 'he left Queenstown and taught at Emfundisweni Institution in Pondoland in 1959.'[52] 'Shaky' was one of Thuso Moerane's typical understatements: the Education Department 'decided to force him to retire prematurely' along with several of his colleagues,[53] and he may even have been in physical danger: 'He belonged to the teacher's association. That is what got him to Lesotho. They chased him away. They were happy to [do so].'[54] According to Moerane's granddaughter, Neo, there was a raid at 10 Scanlen Street, after which her grandfather left for Lesotho. 'He was exiled,' she said.[55] But before he went to Lesotho, he moved to Mpondoland in 1958 to teach at Mfundisweni Teacher Training Institute for at least a year.

Mfundisweni College of Education

The spirit of resistance was just as strong in Mpondoland. Publications such as *The Torch* and *The Student* had been distributed in Faku Training Institution and Mfundisweni College of Education hostels in 1953, and complaints by women students at Shawbury and Mfundisweni in 1957 about their hostel conditions had led to the expulsion of the entire student body; moreover, 'African teachers who had intervened to try and resolve the 1957 dispute [at Mfundisweni] were reported to the authorities for inciting the students.' Even though the issues mainly concerned food and discipline, the Bantu Education Department increasingly 'sharpened' them 'by their confrontationist stance'.[56] It is no surprise, then, that Moerane was forced to leave Mpondoland, and he must have returned to Queenstown in late 1959 or early 1960.[57]

Moerane's daughter Sophia, known in the family as Sophie, was a student at Mfundisweni while he taught there. So was a young woman called Sylvia Ntombentsha Zongola. Sylvia was born in Matatiele in the Eastern Cape, and attended school there before going to the training college.[58] She later worked as a teacher in Ficksburg, Orange Free State, just across the South African border from where Moerane taught at Peka High School in Lesotho.[59] Again, I do not know what subjects Moerane taught, but at some point, Sophia recalled, he conducted a performance of the operetta, *Princess Ju-Ju or The Golden Amulet (O Mamori)*: 'A Japanese Operetta in 3 Acts; Book, Music and Lyrics by Clementine Ward.'[60] Sophia's friend, Nonceba Lubanga, sang the part of the Princess. Moerane's score of this work, which he must have owned, has not survived, but there is a page in tonic solfa headed 'Hail to the Land' (in the piano stool), which is the chorus 'Hail to the land of the rising sun' from Act I. Moerane must have ordered this and other such works during his life as a teacher from overseas, no doubt through a music shop such as Darters in Cape Town (where he bought his piano), and then transcribed the whole operetta into solfa – unless a solfa score was available in those days. Moerane staged several other concerts at Mfundisweni College, and, according to Thuso, 'bought the [college] a piano', but 'at the end of the year he was served with early retirement papers', a euphemism for getting the sack.[61]

Why were works such as these performed in South African schools and colleges? Clementine Ward was an American composer who responded to the 'emerging market for children's operas' in the second half of the nineteenth century. These were written by composers such as Marian Arkwright, Lucia Contini Anselmi, Jessie Love Gaynor, Louise Le Beau, Florence Marshall, Hendrika van Tussenbroek, Ward herself and Marie Wurm.[62] When Robin Malan was doing research in the early 1960s into drama in southwestern Cape high schools for a BEd thesis, he discovered that 'there was an extraordinarily large number of schools producing operettas' (and not only African schools). Malan was 'nonplussed' by their scripts: 'I really did not know [what] the point and purpose and value of our doing them were. I am thinking of things like Clementine Ward's *Zureka, the Gypsy Maid, Pearl, The Fishermaiden, Princess Juju*, and, in Afrikaans, *Sneeuwitjie, Prinses Rosalyn, Repelsteeltjie, Kom Dans Klaradyn*.' Why not do 'the Mozarts, the Holsts, the Benjamin Brittens and the Humperdincks of the world', he asks, and create 'the kind of experience [...] which so excites or disturbs or fills one with joy that one leaves the theatre a different person from the one who came into it.'[63] Perhaps Moerane would rather have done *Bastien und Bastienne* or *The Little Sweep* but could not, due to, among other things, a lack of instruments to accompany them. And at the very least, such musicals as he did produce gave students a genuine musical experience, and one that children of other races were getting. This must have been rare in apartheid South Africa.

Peka High School, Lesotho

Moerane got to teach at Peka High School in Lesotho through Thuso. 'Thuso had applied, got a post at Peka. They'd accepted him by letter, which he gave to our father, and our father had no job, so Thuso decided, "You go". Ja. Thuso remained in Queenstown; the old man went to Peka.'[64] 'My grandfather had a car', Mosa Ndludla remembers. 'My grandfather, my grandmother and Uncle Thabo also went [to Peka]. We were four in the car.'[65] 'He arrived in 1961,' recalls headmaster Tseliso Makhakhe, 'sometime after I arrived. I began to reorganise the staff and sort of employed my own men, most of whom came from South Africa. I don't know where Mr Moerane came from; he just emerged when he was most wanted [...] I had heard about him for a long time. I'd heard his song *Liphala*':

> I got him to teach English language and literature at the School Certificate level and History, and a little bit of Latin in the junior

school. I think he enjoyed teaching English literature, and certainly History. And he did very well. I knew he was a musician, but I don't know how he managed to get so involved, so interested in English and History, and Latin for that matter […] The medium of instruction was English; even in Sesotho [lessons], that was the amazing thing.'[66]

By the time Victor Lechesa was Moerane's student later on in the 1960s, 'he was teaching Maths and Latin and later English'.[67] His wife was there with Moerane at first, Thabo attended the high school, and Mosa the local Senior Primary School: 'Pretty girl. She caused quite a storm among the boys!'[68] Moerane took his orchestral instruments to Peka and started a group called the 'Peka High School Orchestra' as shown in Figure 3.2. 'He owned a small orchestra, personal instruments, you know. They played that at his house, some of the staff joined him, and he was training students there. They enjoyed that. It was after hours.'[69]

Moerane is seated in the middle, playing the violin, with his son Thabo standing just behind his right shoulder, playing the clarinet. Other players are (back row L-R:) Mpho Phakisi; Hodges Maqina; Thabo Moerane; Tseliso Tsenoli; Dugmore Hlalele; ? (front row L-R:) Takatso Shake; Morabane Makatse; Moorosi Ralitapole; ?; Joshua Nkuebe (with gratitude to Mpho Ndebele and Zakes Mda for identifying most of the players).

Moerane's affiliation to the Basutoland Congress Party (BCP) was something he downplayed in the classroom, probably out of concern for the safety of his students. 'I never heard him talk politics in class. I heard him talk about politics a lot when I was with him at his place, or when he was with other people', says former student, Zakes Mda.[70] Yet another former student, Matsobane Putsoa, remembers how he put current politics into a broader cultural and historical perspective in class, relating it to what they were studying. One day, says Putsoa, 'a local politician came and addressed us at school':

Mr Moerane was listening, and afterwards, he raised his hand, and said, 'This is for my history students. These are the facts.' And he told

Figure 3.2: Peka High School Orchestra c. 1965 (courtesy Sophia Metsekae Moerane and Marumo Moerane)

them. 'What we've been told here, the things we've been told, are not true. These are the true facts.' It was just before the 1965 elections, so politicians were coming to the school to address us. The staff would be listening and gave comments, but these were his only comments, that 'this was not historical fact, these are the facts.' Just said like that, and then kept quiet. This was an unpopular politician, because even the students fired him with questions. When he left he was not happy at all. I remember he thought we were influenced by Dr Moerane, but it was not true.[71]

Putsoa recalls what he learnt in English lessons, which gave the students 'a different perspective' compared to anything they had encountered before. 'I was thinking of the things he taught us for matric. That book by Thomas Hardy, Everdene [*Far from the Madding Crowd*].[72] Those farm hands, calling "neighbour, neighbour, neighbour". That's the first time we heard the word "Valentine". And that book by Charles Dickens, Forefathers [*A Tale of Two Cities*].[73] And plays: *Julius Caesar*, *Macbeth*. He taught us English literature, not language. The school had a library, and there were prescribed textbooks [which] we owned.'[74]

Neo Moerane, Thuso's daughter, recalls going to visit her grandfather in Lesotho when she was a little girl:

> We used to go to Tsifalimali on weekends. That was before I went to school. We used to stay near the police station [in Peka]. Our hope was to go and see all those who were arrested, talk to them, take food, wherever, feed them. Because they were not so strict as they are today. You could talk to prisoners. And they would ask us to do a lot of things and we would do that for them. It was a small community. The village [Peka] was a bit far from where we were [Peka High].[75]

Moerane also employed as many people as he could at his house on Peka High School grounds, said Neo, 'out of sympathy, because there's high unemployment in Lesotho':

> We had a lot of people working in the garden. He liked flowers, so the garden was well kept. He had people working in the house, so there was a lot of movement of people, in and out. He was a people's person, in his own way, so there was a lot of high traffic to the house, even in the evenings. Then Saturday we'd go to the farm [Tsifalimali], Sunday we'd go to church. He used to be a choirmaster in church. Yes. In Peka. LEC Church. We were expected to be there every Sunday. I remember we used to run around trying to dodge him and not go to church, but we would get a hiding. So his activities really were school-oriented, music church, family, and also business.[76]

Another granddaughter, Mosa, remembers that Moerane 'liked exercise, early in the morning. Because he liked classical music, before he would go to shower you'd hear him with his music, very soft. Listening to records. He would listen to the music, then do exercises, also to the music. Every morning! Then he would go and have his shower, and then eat porridge, then go to school'.[77]

Impressions of Moerane by students and colleagues

Moerane made a profound impression on his students and colleagues at Peka High School. I was fortunate to be able to interview some of them, and from each of these interviews, a brief story is related here that tells us more about Moerane the man and the musician.

Thabo Pitso (colleague)

He was very humble, very devoted to his work. He also organised music classes and there were choral groups organised on a voluntary basis. He had a piano, but for the choral group they used other instruments.[78]

Tseliso Makhakhe (Principal)

He was the oldest member of the staff except for one Englishman, Mr Burton. Highly respected, highly regarded, excellent teacher, very able, very good disciplinarian. He was very reserved and he never went out of his way to speak about what he was doing. He really kept to himself. He was sort of detached. There was never an occasion when we sat down and enjoyed an ordinary friendly talk [...] He was not loud, he was not turbulent in any way and he was very stable; somehow short-tempered [...] Anything trivial, anything stupid, he would blare out, as he did to me one day, 'if I can just tell you the story!' It was a rare event. Mrs Moerane kept some pigs on the premises, because a lot of extra food, you know, from the kitchen had to be thrown away: he thought he could exploit that. That was good. And then I realised that there was an awful smell coming from where the pigs were. The wind would waft that towards the kitchen, towards the dining hall. One Saturday I wrote Mr Moerane a short letter saying, 'Mr Moerane, I wonder if you could tell Mrs Moerane to do something about the pigs,' and I used an unfortunate word, 'They are *polluting* the atmosphere.' Moerane was working in his garden, and he walked to my house, he knocked on the door and when I appeared he said: 'You, you, look at you, boy! I can trample on you. You're not going to write that stuff to me!' He was very serious. He was so much older than me. I was his senior as headmaster, but outside school he was really my father. So I didn't reply, I didn't do anything at all. I just looked at him and then when he had blown himself out, he walked back to his house. Then we went on again as usual, as if nothing happened. There were no repercussions at all. He loved me, he loved my family, my wife was a friend of Mrs Moerane, and so on. He was one of the teachers who bought the first car. It was a tiny, tiny little car! I don't know what it was. It was so small. I had never seen a car that small. The school had a kombi, and then Mr Moerane bought this toy that was travelling around the country! And then all of us followed, bought cars. He set an example.[79]

Victor Lechesa (student)

He was a soft-spoken man but a very good teacher. Strict. You would never see him smiling. He was always impeccably dressed. I enjoyed his lessons in Latin and English, and of course practicing the hymns so that when we got to church we would be able to sing nicely. There was a nickname, 'Mafifing', because of his very dark complexion. 'Mififi' in Lesotho means darkness.[80]

Mantoa Putsoa (student)

We staged something, some acting with music. That evening, we sang the new release, 'Teele'. Yes! 'Khati'! That's it, that's the song. Mrs Matebisi, Mr Tsie Pekeche, Mr Teboho Mofubela, myself. A very nice song. It was 1964, '65. He was quite an interesting old man. We called him 'After Lights' because he was very dark in complexion. He looked younger than his years. He was not hated like some staff members. When he was on duty, he would come into the square in the morning to look and see that we were up. A boy would go up to him, tease him, then he'd chase him with a stick and the rest of us would run out of the square. The one being chased would outrun him and we'd all run away. He just laughed it off.[81]

Shadrack Mapetla (student)
During the week most of the students would do manual work, but those who played in the orchestra did not have to. He always said, 'If you had spare time, even if it's half an hour, just come in [to his house] and play.' We played classical music. Once, I think it must have been Saturday morning, I don't quite remember, he drove off and we thought, 'He's gone to Ficksburg.' When we saw him go, we called the other guys and we started blowing the stuff that boys like, jazz and so on. Some time later the car appeared again. Ooh, I tell you! 'What rubbish are you playing? What is this!' We were terrified! He hated it! He hated that with passion! He said, 'Not my instruments! Not playing this music. That's not music!'[82]

In rehearsal, Mr Moerane would suddenly stop us and then he would go straight to the guy in the corner and he would say, 'You there, go two bars back and play that again.' And the guy would play and he says, 'That's not the way it should be; that's a sharp. That should not be "fa", that should be "bé" [sings].' I always wondered how he did that! But he was a hopeless singer. When he sang in rehearsals we wanted to laugh because really, music was in the head, the voice, no. It was a very light voice.[83]

Zakes Mda (student)
Even though I didn't meet him until I got to Peka High School, I knew him, particularly the music but also the BCP connections. He taught me Latin and then I played the flute in the orchestra, because it just happened to be the instrument that everybody else did not want to play. I had been playing the penny whistle when I was growing up in Johannesburg as a street tsotsi, and so Moerane said, 'Okay, you, penny-whistle guy, you'll be more comfortable there.' I remember Boccherini, I remember Dvořák's *Humoresque* and that's where I would shine because there's a lot of flute there. I became so good, it was in that *Humoresque* that he noticed me, and then I played works with him on the piano. I went to his house and we would rehearse there, just playing for fun and at some of the school occasions. He was a very nice old man. Maybe because we were establishing a relationship that was more than just teacher-student, he was more like some nice old man, who was soft-spoken, who would not be riled up easily. I don't remember listening to music in his house. I remember there would be the radio playing. During the news he would say, 'Okay let's listen to the news', especially

when there was some political event happening in Lesotho, because he was highly invested in the politics of Lesotho.

He just had the sound in his head, he would write it down. He'd say, 'Oh now, when we get to this part, just try it this way.' He would write those notes and I would play them and then, 'Ah, that's wonderful! Actually, this is a better way of playing it so that it combines well with his piano.' He had to rearrange [music] so that we are able to work together as a duet. I would even have solos there. So it was a whole rearrangement and it was written in staff notation, of course. He composed by ear. He just wrote it, he didn't try the notes on the piano to hear first if they work or not. We were quite familiar with his choral music and knew when he had a new song, for instance, *Tsatsi la Pallo*: 'Tlong Rothothang' [sings], it sounds like raindrops, 'Rethethang, rothothang'. When that song was new, you would hear a lot of it from the choirs.

On those Sundays when the orchestra was playing in church we had to go to the LEC church. I myself was a Catholic, which means that if the orchestra was not playing at the Protestant church, I had to walk many miles to my church, a Catholic church. Because of the politics of Lesotho at that time, the LEC was generally known to be supportive of the BCP. The Roman Catholic church was supportive of the BNP because they believed that the BCP was communist. The BCP was supported by the People's Republic of China, Mao Zedung, you see. I remember Mao Zedung once bought us about 14 Land Rovers, to go out to campaign. Yes! So anyway, it happened that when this contestation was at its peak, I innocently went to [the Catholic] church. The priest, Father Hamel, saw me sitting there as he as conducted the mass and he kept on looking at me. Immediately after he was done, he rushed out and when I walked out, he stopped me and said: 'You, communist! I don't ever want to see you in this church again. You are terrorists, there at that communist high school of yours.' I laughed in his face and said, 'Well, you can stay with your church. Who cares?' – as I was walking away. I was happy, actually, because now I would have no reason to go to church! But Makhakhe sent me back there on Monday with Mr Moerane, to find out exactly why was I expelled. The priest saw us from some distance and rushed to his office, sat there, closed the door. Then we knocked. The priest opened, but there was this meshed wire door. We spoke from outside. The priest didn't want to talk with us because we were communists. I was angry, especially when this priest was talking like that to Mr Moerane, but Moerane, he just stayed cool and tried to negotiate, in a much more civilised manner than I myself would. Well, to cut a long story short, I had to go to church still, the Anglican church on Peka High School campus. It was a chapel.

Moerane was still teaching there in 1969 when I left. By 1970 I was in Mafiteng and I taught at 'Mabathoana High School, walking distance from the NTTC. Moerane would come and visit me, because we'd established a friendship which continued.[84]

It's these sorts of memories that help to give us a much richer sense of Moerane's personality and how this functioned in the pedagogical sphere. However fleetingly they are mentioned, the details of compositions being performed, the response to them, and the way students rehearsed and performed, offer invaluable glimpses into Moerane's life as a composer and teacher. Although the voices here are closer to us in time, one cannot help feeling that Moerane's impact would have been felt equally strongly and remembered with equal affection by students from all his earlier teaching positions.

National Teachers Training College, Maseru

Lesotho's National Teachers Training College was founded in 1975. Moerane helped establish the Music Department there, and according to Eric Lekhanya, who later ran the Department, he also 'set up a small instrumental band'.[85] Perhaps he had retired from Peka – in 1975 he would have been 71 – and brought his orchestral instruments down to the college. Moerane may have helped until Mohapeloa took over;[86] perhaps they even worked at the college simultaneously.[87] After Moerane died in 1980 and Mohapeloa in 1982, someone from Ghana took over until Eric Lekhanya was appointed in 1986.

Moerane's death

His long and productive teaching career notwithstanding, Moerane's passing was in some ways symbolic of his life of erasure and near-invisibility in terms of his work as a composer. In the last few weeks or months of his life, he developed a condition that was serious enough to take him to Pelonomi Hospital in Bloemfontein, where he died.[88] There is a lack of clarity surrounding his final illness and death, mainly because Thabo was in Geneva, and other people in the family were not close by, or did not realise that his condition was serious – perhaps because he himself played it down. Thabo told Nthabiseng, after his father's death, that 'even when he got to the hospital, he didn't give them the correct information':[89]

> That's how they battled to trace him. He almost got a pauper's funeral. I think at that time he was alone. And with Thabo being overseas, no-one knew where he was. Thabo was adamant he drove himself there, he got admitted, with the hope that once he'd signed in, he would just let them [treat him] and go home. So when he got there, he didn't give them too much information. He probably thought he would come back home.[90]

A mighty tree had fallen, but with no one to bear witness. Details of Moerane's death had to be painstakingly uncovered (and may indeed not be correct), just as much of his body of work risked being lost, and has had to be carefully recuperated. In this case, posterity has been fortunate in that Moerane's family have been punctilious in preserving his work as a composer.

The piecemeal and sometimes fractured nature of the materials pertaining to Moerane's life and career that remain mean that we risk seeing him and his work at too many removes. This is why it is the few pieces of correspondence by, to and about him are vital in restoring his voice and a sense of the man as known by his contemporaries. In the next chapter, I present these materials as a form of foregrounding his voice and presence.

4 | Moerane in Correspondence

Letters can tell us a great deal about a person both between and in the lines, and it would have been invaluable to be able to quote from Moerane's own personal correspondence throughout this book. One must be grateful, however, that in the archives of the few figures to whom he wrote, or who wrote about him, there remain a handful of professional letters. These are reproduced here so that Moerane's 'voice' has a presence in this book. Aside from the letters by Huskisson, Hartmann and Kirby to, from or about Moerane, there are three letters in the WEB Du Bois Papers about Moerane, which are quoted from in Chapter 5 but are not included here because none of them is from or to Moerane himself. The letters presented here involve only eight people aside from Moerane: Dean Dixon, Anton Hartman, Friedrich Hartmann, Yvonne Huskisson, Percival Kirby, Mrs RW Levine and Marie Slocombe. They cover only the years 1958 to 1973. There are replies without the letters they reply to, long periods between letters, and one or two very brief exchanges. They are presented here in chronological order with explanatory footnotes, and exactly as found in the archives.[1]

Letter 1: Friedrich Hartmann (University of the Witwatersrand, Johannesburg) to Percival Kirby (4, Constitution Street, West Hill, Grahamstown), 11 March 1958[2]

CONFIDENTIAL
Dear Percival,
Thank you very much for your letter of the 4th March. Regarding *Moerane*, I can give you the following information: He has taken the first three years of the B.Mus. course at the University of South Africa, studying by himself

without tuition. He completed also the fourth year subjects, again studying by himself, except the subject composition. This latter he could not manage without guidance because, among others, also a full orchestral score had to be submitted by him according to the regulations. Dr. Kerr informed me at that time that Moerane had asked various university music departments in the country to help him in this respect but, again according to Dr. Kerr, such assistance was not given to him. Dr. Kerr asked me whether I would be prepared to help Moerane. On the strength of Dr. Kerr's report and recommendation I undertook to do so. Moerane came to Grahamstown where I gave him tuition for a full year, pro deo of course. During this time he wrote also his symphonic poem "My Country", which is based on tunes of his people. In due course he received his B.Mus. degree, and I was at his graduation at Fort Hare. I then wrote to Dr. Gordon who at that time was in charge of the Overseas B.B.C. broadcasts. I sent him the score which created rather a sensation in London among the B.B.C. experts and conductors, and was duly performed there.

Moerane never was a student of Bell, but Bell was the external examiner in his final examination in composition. When Bell had seen the score, he wrote to me that he never had expected such a work to be written in South Africa, and less so by a Native. I gave this letter to Dr. Kerr, who read various passages from it at the graduation ceremony. Where the full score is now, I do not know. I understand that Moerane is now a teacher of mathematics, I believe in one of the Queenstown locations. I have tried to persuade Dr. Kerr to appoint Moerane in some form at Fort Hare in order to enable him to collect the songs of his people, a matter in which Moerane was very interested. Unfortunately Dr. Kerr did not see his way clear to do so. This is in brief what I know about Moerane and his symphonic poem 'Fatse la Heso'. Many years ago I have seen Moerane once more and also received a letter from him. He was then a very embittered man with clear communistic tendencies. I therefore did not wish to keep further contact with him.

Letter 2: Michael Moerane (P.O. Box 20, Mfundisweni, Pondoland) to Percival Kirby (Rhodes University, Grahamstown), 21 April 1958[3]

Dear Prof. Kirby,
The piece you are asking about – 'Fatše la Heso', as we call it, is quite a short one, taking just about ten minutes to perform. It is scored for Strings,

Woodwind (2 fl. 1 picc. 2 ob. 2 clar. 2 fag.), Brass (4 horns, 3 trumpets, 3 trombones, 1 tuba), Bass Drum, 2 Kettle drums, Cymbals, Triangle, Pianoforte and Harp. The score is at my house in Queenstown, as also orchestral parts which were copied out in New York when the Negro conductor, Dean Dixon, had the work performed there in a concert of Negro orchestral music. That was some years ago. The same man also rendered the work in Paris on one of his usual rounds. No doubt the BBC made a copy of their own. They also recorded the piece (for what they call their transcription service) and sent records to ten British colonies. The work is built mainly around three traditional African themes – a war song, a work song and a lullaby. A more or less adequate analysis accompanies the score. I see that you neither grow old nor lose interest in these matters.

    Best wishes
    Yours sincerely,
    M.M. Moerane

Letter 3: Unisa Registrar (University of South Africa, 263 Skinner Street, Pretoria) to Percival Kirby, 24 October 1962[4]

Dear Prof. Kirby,
I acknowledge receipt of your letter of 16th October and regret to inform you that the University does not have a copy of the relevant composition in the library. Unfortunately I cannot provide you with Mr Moerane's address and refer you to the enclosed statement of courses passed by him at this University.

    Yours faithfully,
    REGISTRAR.

Letter 4: Percival Kirby to Dean Dixon (Musical Director, Symphony Orchestra, Sydney, Australia), 9 January 1964[5]

Dear Mr Dixon
I am taking the liberty of writing to you, and of seeking your help to solve a small musicological problem in which I believe you played a part. About 1944 (I think it was) one of our African musicians, a man named Michael M. Moerane, wrote an orchestral work entitled 'My Country', which was based on melodies sung by the Basotho people, of whom he was a member.

The score of this work was sent to the BBC in London, and a set of orchestral parts were made from it (these are still in their Library, where I have seen them), and a performance was broadcast by its Symphony Orchestra. This performance was recorded, and eleven processed disks of it were made and distributed throughout the Commonwealth of those days. One was sent to South Africa, and broadcast there. Unfortunately I was not in the country at that time and so did not hear it. And, since under the copyright laws such records have to be destroyed after, I believe, three years, I am still unable to hear the work. But I have recently ascertained that you conducted a performance of 'My Country' in America, and it has occurred to me that you may possibly have had the score and parts copied (and may still know where they are), and may even have had the performance tape-recorded.

I should be most grateful if you could give me any information you may have regarding this matter, which I referred to, though briefly, in the article on 'South Africa, Music in', which I contributed to the latest edition of *Grove's Dictionary* at the request of my friend, the late Eric Blom. Incidentally, I may say that you can find a good deal about me in my biographical entry in the fourth Volume of that work.

With kind regards, I am,
Yours sincerely,
Percival R. Kirby (KIRBY)
Professor Emeritus, University of the Witwatersrand.

Letter 5: Dean Dixon (Hessischer Rundfunk Anstalt des Offentlichen Rechts, Frankfurt/Main 1) to Percival Kirby, 25 March 1964[6]

Dear Professor Kirby,
Thank you for yours of the 1st of January 1964. Concerning your request I am very sorry to have to report to you that I have no memory of how the score and parts to the Michael M. Moerane 'My Country' arrived to my hands. And too, there was no tape made of the performance of it. If it is of any interest to you I would say that I found the work finally very weak. The 'folk material' was genuine, as far as I could ascertain at the time, but the so called 'symphonic treatment' of it was far below normal modern standards. It represented quite mediocre mid-nineteenth

century level. Sorry that I can be of no greater help to you than as contained above.

With kind regards, I beg to remain,
Sincerely yours,
DEAN DIXON

Letter 6: Marie Slocombe (The British Broadcasting Corporation, Broadcasting House, London, W.I) to Percival Kirby, 22 May 1964[7]

Dear Professor Kirby
Thank you for your letter of 23rd April. I am glad the recordings reached you safely in the end, but sorry indeed for all the trouble and expense you have had in getting the packets through the Customs. We sent them off with the usual paperwork, which we hoped would facilitate clearance. It would, I see now, have been much better to have sent them by surface mail (and cheaper for us as well as you) but I was worried you had been kept waiting so long already. About Moerane's Tone Poem, 'My Country', I have managed to trace the London broadcast: there were two studio performances by the BBC Symphony Orchestra conducted by Clarence Raybould, both the same evening, 17th November, 1944. The first was broadcast in the BBC's African Service, the second in the BBC Home Service. I have not been able to find out much about what was said of the work at the time, but the following extract from 'The Listener' of 30th November, 1944, may interest you (it is from the weekly article by the Music Critic, at that time W. McNaught):

> Since both Fela Sowande from West Africa and Michael Moerane from Basutoland are trained and professional musicians in our Cecilian line there is no call for indulgence towards their compositions. Their most obvious shortcoming was lack of connection and direction. Mr Sowande, too, needs to acquire a finer judgment in sifting his own ideas from those he has assimilated. Yet I found both works enjoyable throughout. Mr Sowande's West African Negro Mood-Picture had an indefinable quality of appeal that arose from temperament, contour and colour of thought, fresh and clear sound, and a succession of little adventures in composition that went to no goal but were pleasant in themselves; and a certain

tone of voice that crept in now and then was none the less welcome for dropping hints of Dvořák. A similar type of appeal ran through Mr. Moerane's 'My Country', although the composer's more stylised language implied more stringent organisation than he was able to maintain. His best bits seem to come by accident, which is after all not such a bad way.

The recording made from the above transmission was for the London Transcription Service and it was part of the copyright and contractual arrangements that the recordings must be destroyed after use, so I'm afraid they really have gone. We still have the parts in the BBC Music Library, but the full MS score was returned to Mr. Moerane in November 1948. I hope this is of some help.
Yours sincerely,
Marie Slocombe
BBC Sound Archives

Letter 7: Percival Kirby to Marie Slocombe, 7 June 1964[8]

Dear Ms Slocombe,
Thank you very much for your air letter card of 22 May, 1964, which I received a few days ago. The information that you have found me about Moerane's tone poem 'My Country' is very valuable to me. The review from 'The Listener' confirms my opinion of the work from the look that I had at the orchestral parts in London, and the opinion of it sent to me by Dean Dixon, the Negro conductor now in Germany who directed a performance of it in New York. I managed to trace Mr. Dixon, at work – asking for his personal opinion of 'My Country', and he sent it to me quite frankly. I had hoped that perhaps a tape-recording of it might have survived in America, but Dixon certainly did not know of one. The only thing I can now do is to try to trace the composer, and to persuade him to let me peruse the orchestral score, but this isn't easy. With many thanks once again, and kind regards, I remain
Yours sincerely,
Percival R. Kirby

Letter 8: Mrs RW Levine (The Institute for the Study of Man in Africa, Hospital Street, Johannesburg) to Percival Kirby, 29 June 1965[9]

Dear Professor Kirby.
Thank you for your letter of the 17th June, 1965. Mr Michael Moerane's address is as follows: Peka High School, P.O. Gumtree, O.F.S. I am sure he will be pleased to hear from you. Mr M.T. Moerane [younger brother] delivered a most interesting lecture last evening and although it was absolutely freezing he had quite a good audience. We are most interested to learn that your book on 'The Musical Instruments of the Native Races of South Africa' is again available, and, too, that your 'Biography of Sir Andrew Smith' is in the press. These are two works that would be most valuable additions to the ISMA library – do you think it is at all possible that you could spare a copy of each of these for us? (my father always used to say: 'It is rude to ask – and those that do not ask do not want!') I do hope you and Mrs Kirby are in better health and that you are not finding the winter too trying. Please give her my kindest regards.
With every good wish,
Yours sincerely,
(Mrs) R.W. Levine

Letter 9: Percival Kirby to Michael Moerane, 21 January 1966[10]

Dear Mr Moerane,
I am going to ask a great favour of you, and I do hope that you will be willing to grant it. As you will remember, away back in 1958 I wrote to you, asking for information about your 'Fatse la Heso', and you very kindly sent them to me. Since then I have worried the Broadcasting authorities both here and in London about the transcription records that were made of your work in 1944. I was, however, assured that the eleven copies were all destroyed after a year or two in accordance with copyright arrangements. I even contacted Dean Dixon to see if a tape recording might have been made when he did the work, but without success. However, I did contrive to examine the set of orchestral parts that were made for the B.B.C. which they have wisely preserved in their library. From these I suppose that a score could be made, but that would take time, and for me it would have been a long job, especially as I was then engaged on a

number of musicological topics. Now, I have just completed a concise survey of the music of the African peoples of our country for the now official Music Encyclopedia that is being prepared, and I have naturally included a paragraph about you, as I did in the article on 'South Africa, Music in' which I was commissioned to write for the latest edition of 'Grove's Dictionary of Music and Musicians'. But what I am now afraid of is that your autography score may be lost or mislaid, or at any rate lost sight of. This has happened to far too many documents which are of importance to our country's history. To prevent this from happening in your case, I should very much like to have your manuscript photostatted, so that a facsimile, at any rate, will be preserved.

Would you, then, be willing to entrust your score to me for this purpose? If you would, and could have it transmitted to me here in Grahamstown, I should arrange for a photographic facsimile to be made, which I would see deposited in the great Africana collection in the Johannesburg Public Library, where I myself have deposited my personal collection of African and other musical instruments. I have in the past seen to it that as many as possible original scores and similar documents are placed there, one of the latest being the autograph of the 'patrol-march' called 'Piekniekliedjies' by the late Leslie Heward, which I found knocking about Cape Town. In this instance we were allowed to preserve the original, but replaced it by a facsimile. If you will agree to this suggestion of mine, I shall be most grateful; and I will see to it that every care is taken of your score until it is returned to you. As you said in your letter to me (1958), which I still have, I neither grow old (except physically) and still retain my interest in these matters.

Meanwhile with best wishes and kindest regards, I remain,
Yours sincerely,
Percival R. Kirby.

P.S. I have typed this instead of writing it by hand because I am not sure of your correct address, and am therefore sending copies to the two that have been given to me.

Letter 10: Michael Moerane (Peka High School, P.O. Peka, Lesotho) to Percival Kirby, 16 February 1966[11]

Dear Prof. Kirby,
It is a most pleasant surprise to hear from you again after such a great lapse of years. I left Pondoland some six year ago but cannot forget the restful

greenness of it which persists practically throughout the year. I have the greatest pleasure in sending you under separate cover the score of Fatše la Heso. My own efforts to get the piece published ended in complete failure, with the publishers always regretting the smallness of the market for such things. Your idea of making a photostatic copy for the archives certainly lifts a great burden of anxiety from my shoulders; the thought of losing, one way or another, the score of this particular piece has haunted me for a long time. I wish you, therefore, every good success in this project as well as in all other good works of which you never seem to tire.
    Thank you again,
    Yours sincerely
    M.M. Moerane

Letter 11: Percival Kirby to Michael Moerane, 22 February 1966[12]

Dear Mr. Moerane,
Thank you very much for your letter of 16 February, and for your kindness in entrusting your score to me. It has arrived here safely, and I was very much impressed by it. Since your music script is so [word illegible] it may not be easy to secure a good photographic reproduction of the work, but I shall do my best for it. I have, however, one more request to make of you. Would you be agreeable to let me have an account of your personal [illegible] – your family origins, your [illegible] – and so on.* I have, of course, your University records, but it is good to have a concise and accurate biography of you, such as one has for John Knox Bokwe and others. I am not surprised that you still yearn for the greenness of Pondoland, which I know well through my work on the [illegible], but I think the climate there is too humid for my old bones! You tell me that you had no success with publishers with your tone poem. I know that this is a common complaint, from which I too have suffered. But photostatic copies are now increasingly common, and are as useful as print. Once again, then, many thanks for your kindness. I shall report to you what has been done about your score as soon as I have got going with it.
    Yours sincerely
    Percival R. Kirby.
    * including date & place of birth

Letter 12: Michael Moerane to Percival Kirby, 9 March 1966[13]

Dear Prof. Kirby
I regret I cannot oblige with the particulars for which you have asked. I cannot even explain the reason why. Please be satisfied with the bare statement that the times do not permit. (Rather cryptic, I know, but all that is possible for me at the moment.)
   Best wishes
   Yours sincerely
   M.M. Moerane.

Letter 13: Michael Moerane to Percival Kirby, 27 June 1968[14]

Dear Prof. Kirby,
Last night I dreamt such a terrible dream about you that I was shocked into remembering that I owe you a reply to a letter of long ago in which you were asking if I could not give over my score of 'Fatše la Heso' to the Rhodes University Library. Well, there's nothing I can deny you, and Rhodes is as good a place for keeping such documents as any other, apart from the fact that I have most pleasant memories of the place. Fortunately I did make a copy of the work and also have playing parts which they made when they performed the work in New York. Some time ago I learnt that you had published your autobiography. I have not laid my hand on the book, but it is bound to be very interesting.
   Best wishes
   Yours sincerely
   M.M. Moerane

Letter 14: Percival Kirby to Michael Moerane, 3 July 1968[15]

Dear Mr Moerane,
Thank you very much for your kind letter of 27 June, 1968, to which I should have replied sooner but for the fact that the extremely cold weather has obliged me to keep indoors as much as possible, since at 81 I dare not risk getting a chill. How strange that you should have been reminded of me in a dream! However, the result has been particularly gratifying to me, and I am very happy to think that the original full score of your symphonic poem will be preserved

in Rhodes University Library. I am also glad to know that you yourself have a copy of it and of the orchestral parts. I have informed the Rhodes Librarian of your generous gift, and doubtless he will acknowledge it later on, but at present he is on holiday. I may say that several years ago I handed over my collection of orchestral scores (published), numbering over 500, to Rhodes, for the use of students, as well as my quite large collection of musical rarities, now being catalogued. And my own manuscripts (now being photostatted) will go to Johannesburg Public Library, though copies will remain at Rhodes eventually. You alluded to my autobiography, which I called 'Wits End', and express your interest in it. I must try to arrange for a copy to come your way, for I am sure that you will be amused to read of my early struggles, and the curious circumstances which led me to become a musician and a South African.

With kindest regards and best wishes, I remain,
Yours sincerely,
Percival R. Kirby.

Letter 15: Michael Moerane (PO Box 77, Leribe, Lesotho) to Yvonne Huskisson (Radio Bantu, PO Box 4559, Johannesburg), 20 May 1973[16]

Dear Dr Huskisson,
I believe you must be at the bottom of the intrigue which has caused Mr Edgar Cree and his excellent band of artists to undertake the fine transcription of my patriotic song 'FATŠE LA HESO' which I have received. I must say that I am really thrilled by the whole exciting performance put up by these people who somehow seem to know just what I was driving at. Referring to this piece, a Zulu friend of mine once addressed me as 'a poet of our sorrows'; another, writing about the last few bars called them a 'blazing defiance' of etc. etc. Well, Edgar Cree and his wonderful people are a rare lot to be able so fully to sympathize with the 'sorrows' and 'defiances' (if such they be) of strange folks such as your humble servant. Please tell them I love (or like) every one of them (however incapable of such a wild sentiment your correspondent may have appeared to be up to the present moment), and I truly wish them all success in their high calling. As for you, you must surely deserve whatever you can get by way of honour and esteem from

Your faithful, obedient and sincere acquaintance,
M.M. Moerane

P.S. Delay in replying due to my absence from this place when the parcel came. Thanks.

Letter 16: Anton Hartman (SABC, Internal Correspondence, Subject: Bantu Music) to Yvonne Huskisson, 17 July 1973[17]

This is to inform you that the National Symphony Orchestra conducted by Edgar Cree recorded Michael Moerane's tone poem 'Fatse la heso' some months ago. The first broadcast will take place on the English Service on 8 August at 10 p.m. Perhaps you would like to announce this to your Xhosa listeners and also drop the composer a line. A copy of the tape can also be made for use on Radio Bantu.
Anton Hartman
HEAD: MUSIC

Letter 17: Yvonne Huskisson to Michael Moerane, 19 July 1973[18]

Dear Mr. Moerane,
This is to let you know that your tone poem, FATSE LA HESO will be broadcast on the English Service of the SABC on the 8th August at 10 pm. We trust you will enjoy listening to it.
With best wishes.
Yours faithfully,
DR. Y. HUSKISSON, SUPERINTENDENT, BANTU MUSIC.

This sparse handful of letters tantalises as they amplify voices otherwise only available to us second-hand – and also point to the spaces left between them. This is the biographer's dilemma, where so much is unsaid, or rather, possibly written or recorded, but lost to posterity.

What we do have is much of Moerane's musical work, and most of that in complete form. I now turn to a detailed scrutiny of his work *Fatše La Heso*, his symphonic poem – possibly his most significant composition, and certainly a rare creation in a context that barely allowed for the existence of such works by an African composer.

5 | The Symphonic Poem *Fatše La Heso* (*My Country*)

The symphonic poem *Fatše La Heso* (*My Country*) is Moerane's only extant orchestral work.[1] As an orchestral composition by a black South African that makes extensive use of traditional music, it remains unique. The preconditions for the work to exist are unusual and it stands in quite sharp contrast to the orchestral work produced, for example, by African Americans William Grant Still, William Levi Dawson and Florence Price. The 1930s and 1940s in the United States were 'a time of rebirth in the Black literary arts known as "The Harlem Renaissance"', when 'Black artists of all mediums – writers, poets, painters, and musicians – were encouraged by black leaders to draw upon their own African cultural heritage and events of recent black history […] for inspiration in their own respective artistic media.'[2] Many black South African writers and artists were inspired by the Harlem Renaissance to reconcile modernity with the preservation of black cultural traditions,[3] and it is highly likely that Moerane was too, when he set about reconciling orchestral writing with traditional music from Lesotho.

The inspiration behind his symphonic poem was not only the Harlem Renaissance; there were many factors at play in the genesis of the work, including musical influences. A number of African-American and African composers admired Dvořák (1841–1904): not only had he helped to shape the genre of the symphonic poem as an expression of nineteenth-century nationalism, but through his promotion of 'the wealth of American material found in the melodies and harmonies' of spirituals, he had inspired Grant Still, Price, Levi Dawson and others to incorporate styles such as the spiritual into their classical compositions.[4] Dvořák had lived for a while in the United States and worked closely with the famous black collector of folk songs and spirituals, Harry T Burleigh (Henry Thacker Burleigh), some of whose arrangements Moerane knew (see Chapter 7). Notwithstanding the racialised world in which African-American composers in the 1930s and 1940s operated, it was still possible for them to study at university and to contemplate symphonic writing. For Moerane, it was almost unthinkable, given the 'parallel streams' of music production and reception in South Africa described in earlier chapters.

Black South African artists, writers and musicians at this time nevertheless did have opportunities to become familiar with classical orchestral music through radio and LP recordings, often listening to the latter in appreciation societies. As journalist Walter Nhlapo noted in 1947, 'Natives have formed associations to introduce the classics to their fellows and recitals and symphonic concerts have been well patronised.' His comments pointedly rejected the idea, which he attributes to Hugh Tracey, that Africans should be excluded from such cultural experiences.[5] For Africans influenced by the ideas coming out of North America in these decades, there was no contradiction between love of classical music and championship of traditional music. This only began to happen after the Nationalist Party came to power in 1948, and the divide was deepened by the power exercised by the SABC,[6] the four provincial Performing Arts Councils, the white colonial public and private school system, the Grade Examination system,[7] and university music curricula and appointments. All venues and facilities such as halls, theatres, schools, churches – anywhere in which people might gather to listen to music – were strictly racially segregated. Most buildings where music might be learnt, heard or played were for 'whites only'. All these agents and elements helped to exclude black people from the classical music industry in various ways, and to establish orchestral culture as an overwhelmingly white phenomenon. White composers mostly did well within these parastatal organisations, as Peter Klatzow has shown.[8] Black composers were prevented from similar achievements by Acts of Parliament that reduced their musical development to the minimum and excluded them from attending racially segregated concerts, although they were not prevented from buying recordings.

THE SYMPHONIC POEM *FATŠE LA HESO (MY COUNTRY)*

The music of *Fatše La Heso* has been performed and recorded several times, and the work has been mentioned in the scholarly literature.[9] Moerane wrote no other full orchestral scores and, as Veronica Franke notes, although 'the post-apartheid era has, in fact, produced a number of classically trained black composers' they have 'compos[ed] few works for full orchestra.'[10] *Fatše La Heso* has been subject to little scrutiny until now, which is why it warrants an entire chapter here.[11] I first briefly consider the work's production and reception, and then examine its musical structure.

The genesis of *Fatše La Heso*

Moerane was unable to teach music in a white school, move in white composers' circles, or obtain a position in a university music department – not even at Fort Hare, despite his supervisor's recommendation to the principal at the time, Alexander Kerr. The white BMus student who graduated at the same time as Moerane, Betty Moyra Sullivan, on the other hand, was appointed to the Rhodes University College music staff as a 'Demonstrator' even before she had completed her degree.[12] It seems extraordinarily courageous for Moerane not only to have completed a degree in music, but to have written an orchestral work that was performed internationally.

Rhodes provided the opportunity for *Fatše La Heso*'s anomalous appearance in 1941 as part of the requirements for a new fourth-year BMus course, as described in Chapter 2. There had been provision for fourth-year 'honours' courses in Rhodes degrees since 1918,[13] but none had been created in music until Friedrich Hartmann arrived. If Moerane had not returned from Maseru to the Eastern Cape, and been able to complete the degree under these new requirements and Hartmann's tutelage, he might never have composed *Fatše La Heso*.

Hartmann was proud enough of the work to want to promote it, but could not do so nationally: the work had emerged into an environment in which no other black South African orchestral music existed, because of the restrictions on 'opportunities in education and work' for Africans.[14] As Mzilikazi Khumalo puts it, in writing about the fact that he was unable to arrange Princess Magogo's Zulu *ugubhu* bow songs himself 'into a narrative song cycle for alto and piano': 'for a black composer of my generation in South Africa, it was impossible for me to make the complete arrangement myself, owing to the fact that the appropriate musical training was unfortunately not available to me in my formative years.' He goes on to mention that until the early 2000s, 'the only major figure trained at tertiary level in the full tradition of world music and its literature, together with the complete range of its accepted compositional techniques and conventions, was the Sotho composer Michael Mosoeu Moerane.'[15] Moerane could write *Fatše La Heso*, in other words; but he could not establish any kind of South African black orchestral tradition in which to embed it. There was no-one to pass the baton onto. Nor did any professional context of compositional collegiality – such as the one that existed in the United States for Price, Levi Dawson and Grant Still – exist for Moerane. As a result, *Fatše La Heso* has had a strange reception history.

A reception history of *Fatše La Heso*, part 1

A performance of the work was not required for degree purposes, and so orchestral parts were not made in 1941. Three years had to pass before its first live performance by the BBC in its wartime venue north of London, with parts made by the BBC.[16] This came about through Hartmann, who sent the score to Dr Gordon, at that time 'in charge of the Overseas BBC broadcasts' and the work was 'duly performed' by the BBC.[17] Marie Slocombe, the music librarian at the BBC during the 1960s, found recordings of 'two [live] studio performances by the BBC Symphony Orchestra conducted by Clarence Raybould, both the same evening, 17th November, 1944. The first was broadcast in the BBC's African Service, the second in the BBC Home Service.'[18]

The Home Service broadcast is confirmed in Alistair Mitchell and Alan Poulton's *A Chronicle of First Broadcast Performances of Musical Works in the United Kingdom, 1923–1996*,[19] which shows the celebrated company in which Moerane's work was heard by listeners – Saint-Saëns, Prokofiev, Britten, Shostakovich, Bartók, Bliss, Rawsthorne, Busch, Hindemith, Berkeley, Coates, Bax, Martinu – in the weeks before or after Moerane's piece, which was already regarded as unique by the BBC. Mitchell and Poulton highlight it in their Preface as a particularly memorable premiere of a work from overseas:

> History was made at Bedford on 17 November 1944 when the first ever European performance was given of a work by a Basutoland-born

composer, Michael Mosoen [sic] Moerane.[20] The work was his symphonic poem *My Country*, and the performance was given by the BBC Symphony Orchestra conducted by Clarence Raybould. Moerane's work was brought to the attention of Dr Hartman [sic], head of Rhodes University College, Grahamstown in 1944 who was quoted by a *London Evening Standard* Reporter, on 15 November, that the work was that of '… a self-taught native. It is phenomenal.'[21]

The other work on the programme that evening was 'Accricania', No. 1 from *West African Negro Mood-Pictures* by Fela Sowande. This is what the BBC called the work in 1944, although there is no longer a work by that name in Sowande's catalogue.[22] It may have been a movement from (or reworked into) what later became known as the *African Suite* for string orchestra and harp, which has remained a popular work by Sowande.[23]

Music critic William McNaught reviewed the Home Service broadcast in the BBC magazine *The Listener*, a review quoted by Marie Slocombe in her letter to musicologist and retired Wits professor, Percival Kirby (quoted in full in Chapter 4).[24] He treats Moerane and Sowande as 'trained and professional musicians in our Cecilian line [with] no call for indulgence towards' them, and although he finds 'a lack of connection and direction' in their works, they were nevertheless 'enjoyable throughout': 'a certain tone of voice that crept in now and then was none the less welcome for dropping hints of Dvořák. [In] Mr. Moerane's "My Country" [the] composer's more stylised language implied a more stringent organisation than he was able to maintain. His best bits seem to come by accident, which is after all not such a bad way.'[25] There is something very British here in the way the work is damned with faint praise, although hearing Moerane's language as 'more stylised' than Sowande's is an interesting response. Maybe it is because each composer made use of 'African elements' differently; perhaps these sounded more embedded, in Moerane's case, in Western orchestral texture and chromaticism.

Back in South Africa, the 'BBC's African Service' broadcast was anonymously reviewed under the heading 'BBC Broadcasts Work by Bantu Composer.' Notwithstanding the epithet 'Bantu' and the fact that the work is called *Fatse La Hezu*, the review is positive: 'It proved to be a work of warm vitality, strong in its rhythm and markedly African in its inspiration. It was not merely imitative of European music, and its melodic line seemed to derive directly from Bantu folk music, though refined by Western forms. The orchestration made particularly good use of the wind instruments.'[26]

Fatše was performed live the following year, October 1945, in Manchester at, remarkably, the opening of the Fifth International Pan-African Conference.[27] This 'major event in the twentieth century',[28] has also 'been described as the zenith of the Pan-African movement and perhaps the most important of all the Pan-African meetings held outside the African continent.'[29] According to Moerane's nephew, Izak Khomo, the performance of *Fatše* was at the request of the conference organiser, 'the Great Pan Africanist leader W.E.B. Du Bois', who was one of the major speakers at the conference alongside Kwame Nkrumah, Jomo Kenyatta and George Padmore.[30] Of the six sessions, one was on 'Oppression in South Africa', and two resolutions from the conference overwhelmingly condemned imperialism and urged 'educated colonials' to join in every mass action in support of 'complete social, economic and political emancipation'.[31] This was global Pan-Africanism after half a century (the first international Pan-African Congress was in 1900), although the Pan Africanist Congress of Azania (PAC) was founded only in April 1959 by Robert Sobukwe and Potlako Leballo, after they broke away from the ANC.[32]

Moerane must have been aware of international Pan-Africanism and of the 1945 performance in Manchester, and through the 1945 conference he would have known of the activities of the Council on African Affairs, founded in New York by Paul Robeson and WEB Du Bois in 1937, and until 1941 called the International Committee on African Affairs.[33] Clearly, Moerane was an outstanding example of a Pan-African composer: an educated black colonial subject who had composed an orchestral work, which had never been done before in southern Africa. Almost certainly because of the 1945 performance, another performance of *Fatše La Heso* was organised in New York in 1950 by the Council on African Affairs.[34] *The Carolina Times* reported it as a significant cultural and political event:

> In the first concert of its kind ever presented in New York City, symphonic works of African, Cuban, and South and North American Negro composers were heard in an extraordinary program at Town

Hall, May 21, sponsored by the African Aid Committee [and] directed by the noted Negro conductor, Dean Dixon. The concert featured the American premiere of 'Fatse la Heso' (My Country) by Michael M. Moerane of South Africa [and works by Amadeo Roldán, Samuel Coleridge Taylor, Ulysses Kay, Ingram Fox, and William Grant Still]. It was announced by the chairman of the [African Aid] Committee, Dr. W.E. Du Bois, that proceeds of the concert would be used primarily to support a health clinic directed by an African physician in the poverty-ridden Ciskei Province in South Africa [the region in which Queenstown is situated] and to aid in promoting the work among African youth being carried on by Mr. Moerane, in the same country, who sent the score of his tone poem to the Committee specifically for this concert. A letter from Mr. Moerane, received just a day before the concert, was read to the audience during the intermission period by Dr. Du Bois. Moerane wrote: 'Please tell the Americans we believe in them, in their humanity, in their great-heartedness. Africa needs to be saved – salvaged in all ways – physically, spiritually, economically. It is a big task, requiring large resources, but we do not despair.' The audience gave the conductor, Dean Dixon, a loud ovation, expressing appreciation of the high quality and cultural significance of the program and the splendid manner in which he directed the 54-piece orchestra. The concert was hailed by reviewers as 'a memorable and historic affair'; 'a cultural event of major significance'.[35]

Moerane was not at the concert; indeed, he never left southern Africa,[36] although he very likely saw this review. The Secretary of the Council on African Affairs, Alpheus Hunton, wrote to Moerane soon afterwards enclosing 'a copy of the program and a collection of reviews and press items', and although this letter is lost, Hunton mentions it in a memo to Du Bois.[37] Hunton tells Du Bois in the same memo that there were no 'proceeds of the concert' because expenditure had exceeded income. He also mentions Dr RT Bokwe from Middledrift, Cape Province, who seems to have been involved in the fundraising effort in some way, and is very likely the 'African physician' mentioned in the above review. In another letter, dated 30 November 1951, Du Bois explains to Moerane that the 'pieces of music' that Moerane had sent him before the concert were handed over to

Dr Hunton, who 'is now in jail', but once he is 'back in his office next month [this] matter will be called to his attention.'[38] In a third letter, from Hunton (now back in his office) to Du Bois, it is clear that Moerane was asking for pieces that were sent before the concert to be 'turned over to Dixon so that he could select which to use', and they must have included *Fatše*; but what else might have been included is hard to imagine.[39] We do not know if he knew of Dean Dixon's less than flattering opinion of the work (quoted in full in Chapter 4), one that contrasts with Bell's, Hartmann's and the BBC's, and which did not deter Dixon from 'also render[ing] the work in Paris'.[40]

'The times do not permit'

After the BBC performances, 'the full MS score was returned to Mr. Moerane in November 1948'.[41] After the New York performance, it was also, evidently, safely returned to Moerane, who at that time (1950) was still living in Queenstown; and despite all his subsequent moves, Moerane kept the manuscript of *Fatše La Heso* safe. The correspondence in the previous chapter outlines the story of Kirby's interest in Moerane's music, and his concern 'that your autograph score may be lost or mislaid, or at any rate lost sight of', a fate that 'has happened to far too many documents which are of importance to our country's history'.[42] Kirby's gratitude in receiving the score of *Fatše* caused him to write back asking Moerane for some biographical details, for the archives perhaps, or because he was thinking of writing something about the work. But in response to this request, he received a curt brush-off: 'I regret I cannot oblige with the particulars for which you have asked', wrote Moerane, 'I cannot even explain the reason why. Please be satisfied with the bare statement that the times do not permit. (Rather cryptic, I know, but all that is possible for me at the moment.)'[43]

Moerane's very English understatement about the times speaks volumes to the political chaos in South Africa and Lesotho in 1966 (as already described). Closer to home, it was most likely to have been the banning order served on Moerane's son, Thuso, that affected his willingness to continue corresponding with a member of the white South African establishment such as Kirby. After a silence of two years, however, Moerane agreed that the Rhodes University Library 'is as good a place for keeping such documents as any other, apart from the fact that I have most pleasant memories of the place' (Grahamstown). He further said that he had made a copy of the work before he sent it to Kirby in 1966.[44] That copy has disappeared, as have the parts copied in New York that were in Moerane's possession, but thanks to Kirby, the manuscript is currently safely housed in the Rhodes University Cory Library; and the full score has now been published for the first time, by ACE, along with a new set of parts.[45]

A reception history of *Fatše La Heso*, part 2

Yvonne Huskisson told journalist Carmel Rickard in 1988 how 'the tone poem was recorded and broadcast by the SABC Orchestra under Edgar Cree "some time during the late 1960s"'.[46] I can find no evidence of this, only of a 1973 performance recorded for broadcast which Huskisson informed Moerane would be played 'on the English Service of the SABC on the 8th August at 10 pm'.[47]

The SABC knew of the work as far back as 1944, because the BBC sent transcription records to several of its colonies. Kirby 'worried the Broadcasting authorities' from 1958 to 1966 about the existence of these records, but whether or not the work was broadcast before 1973, Moerane was certainly delighted by the 1973 performance, and at receiving the transcription recording (now lost). 'I believe you must be at the bottom of the intrigue', he wrote to Huskisson, 'which has caused Mr. Edgar Cree and his excellent band of artists to undertake the fine transcription of my patriotic song "Fatše La Heso" which I have received [in the post].'[48] Moerane was 'thrilled by the whole exciting performance' by 'people who somehow seem to know just what I was driving at', referring to the way he had been described by a friend as 'a poet of our sorrows' and the description of the last few bars of the work as a 'blazing defiance'. It is an extraordinary letter, continuing: 'Please tell them I love (or like) every one of them (however incapable of such a wild sentiment your correspondent may have appeared to be up to the present moment).' Perhaps such a rare public success in Moerane's life made him relax his usual reserve.

According to Carmel Rickard, the SABC archives show that this recording 'was broadcast again in 1984' (after Moerane's death), although again I have not been able to confirm this.[49] In 1991, the Cree/SABC National Symphony Orchestra recording was released commercially along with five works by white composers.[50] By this time, South Africa was locked into a turbulent transition towards black majority rule, and no doubt because of impending political changes, the time was now 'right' for Moerane to cross the invisible line that separated black choralism as a compositional practice from white orchestral music. As is well known, at the beginning of 1990, anti-apartheid movements were unbanned, Mandela was released from prison, and many exiled individuals were allowed back into South Africa. Between 1990 and 1994, there was a transitional government of national unity and at the same time, a ferocious backlash against impending political changes: 'More people died in the unprecedented levels of violence during 1990–94 than during the preceding thirty years.'[51] The rapidly changing political climate created havoc in the cultural sector, as the ANC cultural desk flexed its muscles.

During this violent interregnum, Phil du Plessis's liner notes for the 1991 recording stress the 'meeting between the cultures of Africa and the colonising West'.[52] He notes (with some surprise) how Moerane 'has not been followed into the symphonic repertoire by any other black South Africans', celebrates the fact that 'Africa is now also being heard in orchestral sound' and ends by hinting at a kind of restorative justice: 'Michael Moerane would have had much joy of it'.[53] It is hard not feel cynical about such statements, however well meant. Orchestral 'Africa' – is Du Plessis referring to Moerane's work or his colour? – had been heard in South Africa as early as 1973, if not earlier; and the reason Moerane had 'not been followed into the symphonic repertoire' was because of the dire music education system in black schools. The 1991 CD recording had a sequel: *Fatše* was re-recorded in 1994 with a new performance by the National Symphony Orchestra of the SABC under a different conductor, Peter Marchbank.[54]

The country of *Fatše La Heso*

Izak Khomo claimed that 'Our Land', as he calls *Fatše* (Moerane's own translation is *My Country*) was 'the Clarion call of the Pan Africanists in South Africa' and came directly out of the experience that Moerane and his siblings had of 'witnessing the gradual destruction of their father's property and wealth [in South Africa] by settler colonial laws which saw loss of farm land, the culling of the large heads of cattle and also flock of sheep under the pretext of land conservation.'[55] This terrible destruction notwithstanding, the country of the title is not South Africa, however, but Lesotho; which, at the time Moerane wrote *Fatše La Heso*, was still the British Protectorate of Basutoland. Moerane was born in the Cape Colony, but was Sotho by descent and culture, spent half of his working life in Lesotho, owned several properties there, and is buried there. He was a man of the land, a man of the people. Basutoland was the land of Moerane's father, Eleazar Jakane Moerane, and of many of his predecessors. The area just across the border in Matatiele where Moerane was born is predominantly Sesotho-speaking, and Moerane insisted that Sesotho be spoken in his home. Only 5 of Moerane's 51 extant choral works have isiXhosa texts and 8 English; the other 37 are in Sesotho. It was with Sesotho culture and language that Moerane identified, not colonial or apartheid South Africa; the country Lesotho was and still is an integral part of Moerane's 'House' (see Chapter 1).

The work's 'defiance' and 'sorrow' are indeed reminiscent of similar expressions in Sibelius's *Finlandia*, or Smetana's *Má Vlast* (*My Homeland*), works that Moerane might have known through recordings, or studied with Hartmann. It is indeed celebratory and dignified, as Du Plessis observes. It stands in a long line of short orchestral tone poems from Franz Liszt onwards that share a voice of national longing, emanating as they do mainly from countries politically oppressed in the nineteenth and twentieth centuries. It imagines (in 1941) the emancipation of the entire continent of Africa. This is why he sent the score to Du Bois in New York, and why he was shocked and delighted in 1973 – at the height of apartheid – that the SABC orchestra managed to realise the spirit of the work so well. But to co-opt the work as 'nationalistic' for everyone in South Africa in 1991, and hitch to it a slew of works written by white composers as a way of expressing a new cross-culturalism in the 1990s ahead of the first democratic government, seems opportunistic. One has to ask, as Abiola Irele has asked of some African literatures: what 'national status is being canvassed' here? given that the English language and European literary genres were, as Irele puts it, 'neither indigenous to the societies and the cultures on which they have been imposed [nor] national in any real sense of the word.'[56]

The music of *Fatše La Heso*

Moerane positions himself as a Sotho patriot in *Fatše La Heso* by using transfigured folksong, just as the composers mentioned above did in similar works. 'The work is based on thematic material derived from genuine

African songs', Moerane says in a preface to the manuscript in which he also writes out the four 'main themes'. Theme I: 'This is a transfiguration of a warrior song of my country'; Theme II: 'In its original form (which is quite pentatonic) this is used by the reapers as they thresh the corn with their knob-kerries'; and Theme III is 'A very free transformation of a cradle-song'.[57] These three themes are given in examples 5.1, 5.2 and 5.3.

Here Moerane forges three very different types of Sotho traditional music into Western melodic frames of 16, 6 and 4 bars respectively. We do not know where, when or indeed how he heard this music in its traditional setting, whether he transcribed it directly from performances he himself witnessed, or from memory. What we do know is that after he

Ex. 5.1: *Fatše La Heso* Theme I as played in bars 1–16 (courtesy of the Moerane family). For a live recording made by the Kyiv Symphony Orchestra conducted by Arjan Tien, visit https://tinyurl.com/2hcnxprf[58]

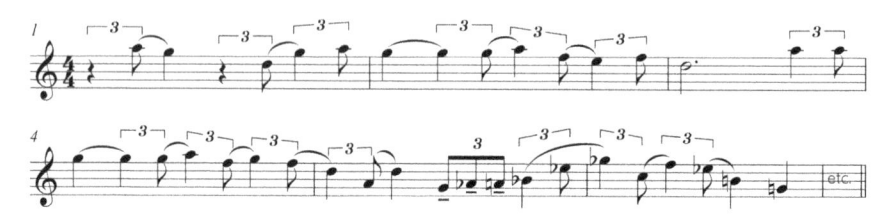

Ex. 5.2: *Fatše La Heso* Theme II as played in bars 43–48 (courtesy of the Moerane family). For a live recording made by the Kyiv Symphony Orchestra conducted by Arjan Tien, visit https://tinyurl.com/33js5kje

Ex. 5.3: *Fatše La Heso* Theme III as played in bars 56–59 with octave displacement in the first two bars (courtesy of the Moerane family). For a live recording made by the Kyiv Symphony Orchestra conducted by Arjan Tien, visit https://tinyurl.com/yryfeuxc

graduated in 1941, Friedrich Hartmann tried to persuade the Rector of Fort Hare University to 'appoint Moerane [in] order to enable him to collect the songs of his people, a matter in which Moerane was very interested.'[59] Ethnomusicologist Robin Wells spent years in Lesotho collecting and transcribing music, and it is in his comprehensive *Music of the Basotho* that possible source material for Themes I, II and III can be found.[60] Three of his transcriptions, an 'example of *mokorotlo* style', an 'example of a *pina ea polo*', and an example that 'illustrates the style of [the] lullabies, *lipina tsa kooetso*',[61] allow us to see how Moerane fashioned the pentatonic beginnings of Themes I, II and III before transforming them into symphonic themes that bear no resemblance to Sotho music.

Moerane's designation of Theme I as a 'warrior song' points to its origins in the male Basotho genre, *mokorotlo*, slow men's dance-songs sung by leader and chorus, and one of the 'reminders of the once great heroic community that the Basotho constituted'.[62] Theme I opens the symphonic poem, and is a long and mostly pentatonic melody for double basses and bassoon that recurs in different forms throughout the symphonic poem. It can be seen as lending the work, to use Wells' words, the dignity of *mokorotlo* as 'performed by a great body of men moving in one accord' with 'slow and fluid movements'.[63]

Theme II is a much lighter theme in a dance-like rhythm, initially stated by oboe with string accompaniment. It is derived from a Sotho threshing song that 'in its original form' would have been sung much lower as a work song sung when 'sorghum was thrashed by men to separate the grain from the stalks'.[64] It is slightly breathless, fragmented, as if Moerane is representing the short vocal phrases and gaps heard in beating the corn with sticks.[65] Theme III is very short and simple, and seems to accord with Wells' example of a Sotho women's *lipina tsa kooetso* (song of sleep),[66] in which a dactylic rhythm (long-short-short) prevails.[67] The basic motif has only four pitches, which in Moerane's short example rise once, then fall twice, although when the theme first appears in the orchestra, the pitch rises twice, then falls once. Its simplicity allows it to be adapted in many ways during the symphonic poem, and when it is first stated it emerges accompanied by fragments of Moerane's Theme IV: 'A hymn-tune used in this work to supply the harmonic structure'.[68]

Theme IV is not a tune so much as hymn-like material, which 'appears throughout the work and undergoes many changes', as Moerane puts it.

The form in which he writes it in the preface to the symphonic poem's manuscript is, he says, 'the simplest in which it appears'[69] (Example 5.4) but it never really appears exactly in this form, and as a harmonic progression it is far from simple: it is a 12-bar sequence of shifting chords that begins and ends in the same key (F), but the chords meander so chromatically in such a way as to make the material seem keyless. It is hymn-like rather than a recognisable hymn tune, and slides into the music in fragments: the first fragment appears, for example, between Themes II and III.

Its restless late nineteenth-century European quality sets it apart from Themes I, II and III, which so obviously come out of rural Lesotho. It is also very different from Moerane's hymn-like choral pieces discussed in Chapter 7. By calling it a 'hymn', however, Moerane reminds us that as a genre, the hymn is the most ubiquitous and hegemonic musical trope in colonial Africa. By making it so dissonant here, he almost seems to be subverting the deadening effect it had on so many composers in Africa as a 'colonising force'.

After setting out these four themes, Moerane outlines the work's structure in the manner expected of a composition student. He describes what happens in what he calls the first section (bars 1–89), the second section (bars 90–129), the third section (130–178), and the final section (179–end). In the latter, 'all four themes appear' in C major. At this point, Theme I is

Ex. 5.4: *Fatše La Heso* Theme IV as implied in bars 46–55 (courtesy of the Moerane family). For a live recording made by the Kyiv Symphony Orchestra conducted by Arjan Tien, visit https://tinyurl.com/56zr9h3p

played sonorously by bassoons, tuba and lower strings, Theme II by upper woodwinds, Theme III by trumpets, and Theme IV 'on the remaining forces', as Moerane puts it, while harp and piano play lush arpeggios. At the coda (189) the third trumpet enters for the first time, and Moerane takes the whole orchestra through a whirlwind harmonic journey that is driven by a powerfully stated, slowly descending, chromatic bass line. Then follows the 'blazing defiance' of the ending. Example 5.5 gives bars 179–193 in reduced score.

The basic structural conception of the symphonic poem, like similar works by nineteenth- and twentieth-century composers, is that of 'sonata form', in which an opening section states the main themes, a middle section develops them, and a final section restates them. In this case, the themes are set out at the beginning, and Moerane develops them in what he calls sections two and three, but at the same time there is a sense towards the end of section three that we are in a process of restatement as well. The final section (bar 179) is a masterly restatement of all four themes simultaneously, after which the music launches into a whirlwind coda. The result, to the listener, is one of passages in the middle of the work where less seems to happen, and passages in the last part of the work where everything happens at once.

The orchestral language in which Moerane locates his patriotic transformation of themes is worlds away from rural Lesotho: it comes from the European metropole, and it belongs to the world of Dvořák, Wagner or Zemlinsky. Moerane's son, Thabo, told Carmel Rickard that 'his father was influenced in form by Mozart and in the harmonies of the symphonic poem by Wagner',[70] and the 'use of chromaticism and shifting tonalities' does indeed recall Wagner; but it also speaks to a concept of expanded tonality that Moerane learnt from Hartmann. Hartmann was not only a composer steeped in late Romanticism and early Modernism, he was also a music theorist who codified an 'expanding chromatic scale' system 'for the analysis of music in the style of late-romantic composers'; thus 'the harmonic vernacular of Moerane', as Bruckman calls it, was probably indebted to Hartmann's teaching as much as it was to a study of orchestral scores or any other material that might have been available to Moerane.[71]

The strongly diatonic if transfigured 'thematic material derived from genuine African songs' is what the listener remembers, however,

Ex. 5.5: *Fatše La Heso* bars 179–193 in reduced score (courtesy of the Moerane family). For a live recording of bars 177–218 made by the Kyiv Symphony Orchestra conducted by Arjan Tien, visit https://tinyurl.com/yc3majey

and what McNaught, the *Rand Daily Mail* critic, Du Plessis, and Khomo all hear as African. This is what gives the work its dignity, and there is nothing tokenistic about its use. It is mainly the medium of the orchestra that makes it possible to say, as Huskisson said of the work, that it 'has elements of "Sotho folk music"' worked into 'an orchestral composition which is very Western'.[72] It is important to remember, however, when we listen to this work in the twenty-first century, that it was not the product of someone professionally trained in Europe or North America, familiar with Western orchestral concert culture and the world of new music, and whose first orchestral effort grew out of preceding instrumental works that had already been performed, critiqued and even perhaps published. It was the product of a largely self-taught musician in rural Africa whose chief compositional milieu was choralism, who had had little access to scores and recordings in order to learn what a symphonic poem could do, and who wrote it in order to complete an undergraduate degree.

For Hartmann, a symphonic poem of roughly ten minutes was a suitable genre through which final-year music students could prove what they had learnt in harmony, counterpoint and orchestration courses. It had long been the case in British music degree curricula that final-year exams comprised 'Harmony and Counterpoint, Fugue, Canon, Formal Analysis, and Musical History, in addition to the submission of written composition of prescribed nature',[73] a pattern first established in 1855 at Oxford that set the tone for university music curricula in many countries for the next 150 years. As apartheid ended, Larkin suggests, the symphonic poem had a new lease of life as a vehicle for 'essays' in 'cross-cultural blends'.[74] As Thomas Pooley has pointed out, however, in relation to post-1994 South African orchestral music, the model of the genre is one thing; the model of nationalism that the genre emulates – the 'nineteenth century "nationalist" movement in Europe' – quite another, and works often remain 'just that, European'.[75] *Fatše La Heso* does not. Its African material holds up against – or bursts out of – its European frame, almost deliberately subverting Western music, as Matildie Wium has suggested.[76]

How Hartmann and Moerane collaborated is an enigma, given Hartmann's political beliefs. Yet a white man with apparently right-wing political views took on a student who had already 'asked various university music departments in the country to help him [but] such assistance was not given to him'. (How poorly this reflects on those departments.) Yet Hartmann and a black South African Pan-Africanist managed to work together for a whole year, with a successful and unique outcome, of which both men were proud.

6 | Moerane and the Choral Movement in Southern Africa

The orchestral work discussed in the previous chapter is anomalous within Moerane's output and struggles, to be seen as on a par with similar works in any country's classical orchestral repertoire. Moerane's choral music, on the other hand, emerged in a very different way, along a very different trajectory – the other of the two 'parallel streams' of composition in southern Africa. Moerane composed short unaccompanied choral works throughout his life, and had a ready platform for their performance and reception: choral competitions in African communities. However, the skills Moerane learnt during his BMus studies placed him in a class of his own here too, even though he was on familiar performance terrain. The reason why many of the works that he wrote were never performed or even known until recently may have been because they were too 'difficult' in their harmonies and vocal writing.[1]

The *Catalogue of Works by Michael Mosoeu Moerane* given in the Appendix (hereafter the *Catalogue*) and on the ACE website, lists for the first time all Moerane's known works. They are presented by genre: the orchestral work, followed by original choral works for SATB (soprano, alto, tenor, bass), then SSAA, SAA, SA, and Moerane's eight arrangements of American spirituals, which are scored for various voices. This is a publisher's grouping, made for sales purposes, so it says nothing about the style of the music, the subject matter of the lyrics, or how the music was originally performed. Let me begin, then, with a sociocultural grouping based on the musical and textual expressions in the songs. For this purpose, I adapt Thembela Vokwana's categorisation of African choral music generally into three successive historical 'expressions':

- Expressions modelled on European music with texts often borrowed from the literature of the English canonic masters read in schools as well as the Bible, and identifying strongly with the work of the European mission.
- Expressions based on European models with texts of an independent and often more secular orientation, inspired by social themes in African societies and related to a burgeoning African nationalism.
- Expressions derived from European models with sections incorporating components of traditional music or based throughout on such components, and related to protest against political and social injustice.[2]

This shows the overwhelming starting point of 'European models', although it doesn't take into account jazz and popular music models from outside Europe. Nor can it be assumed that there is a common understanding of what 'European models' meant for mission-educated black musicians scattered all over southern Africa. It must be borne in mind how much the colonisation of culture, education and consciousness occurring in mission stations throughout the nineteenth and early twentieth centuries was reliant on the idiosyncratic training of individual missionaries, as Philip Burnett has shown.[3] The models that were introduced in mission stations were often those known in religious or community circles rather than in European concert halls: hymns, psalms, a few choral extracts from oratorios by Handel and Haydn or masses by Mozart, a few other extracts from light operettas such as *Prince Ferdinand* or *Princess Ju-Ju*, and Victorian or Edwardian parlour songs, rather than piano sonatas, symphonies, suites, operas, masses, motets, cantatas, or chamber music. Moreover, it was the limited form of the hymn that prevailed, not the more experimental and improvisatory forms such as da capo aria, etude or fugue. The composers introduced in mission stations were not, by and large, masters such as Josquin, Bach, Beethoven, Mozart, Chopin, Berlioz, Schumann, Brahms or Wagner; and instrumental works were rare.

In short, an extremely limited fare passed for 'European models' and even these were available only to an extremely limited number of black musicians – including Moerane – who were able to attend mission schools and colleges. This limited fare nonetheless formed the basis for subsequent choral composition throughout the southern African region. As Kofi Agawu points out, in a scathing indictment of 'tonality as a colonizing force' in Africa, the imposition of such bland, often watered-down music – hymns written in four voice parts and in four-bar phrases, and relying heavily on the doh scale and three chords, I, IV, V – upon young black composers constituted 'musical violence of a very high order'.[4]

Moerane almost certainly learnt the piano and staff notation at Morija, and so his diet would have been more challenging than the one just described. But he must have encountered the songbook in which the choral repertoire promoted was almost anything but 'major European models', and which, for all those who studied at Morija, must have perpetrated significant musical violence. I am referring to *Lipina tsa Likolo tse Phahameng (Songs for High School)*, which has no author, printed in 1907 'for Morija Sesuto [sic] Book Depot by the Religious Tract Society'.[5] This was a product of the French-Swiss missionaries, and it contains 98 pieces or extracts by a swathe of minor nineteenth-century composers from southern France, Switzerland, Austria, southern Germany and northern Italy. I list them to prove the point about 'European models': Abt, Astholtz, Baebler, Bordese, Bortniasky, Bory-Lysberg, Bost, Chwatal, De Weber, Grast, Gross, Gungl, Himmel, Huber, Immler, Klein, Kreutzer, Kucken, Laur, Lefebure-Vely, Letang, Lindpaintner, Masini, Muller, Naegeli, Paliard, Pesca, Piguet, Rau, Root, Silcher, Spaeth, Speier, Spofforth, Strunz, Tolber, Vogt, Winter, Work, Zedtler, Zwyssig, Zwissig.[6]

The missionaries pooled their knowledge in order to produce this book, based on what they in turn had been taught at school in provincial nineteenth-century Europe. Interspersed amidst the names listed above are a few items by Bellini, Haydn, Adam, Mendelssohn, Mozart, Franz, Beethoven, Flotow, Rossini, Mehul and Weber, along with a few Tyrolean folksongs. Everything is simplified and written in tonic solfa, with keys given (interestingly) by their English letter names with the solfège name in brackets – for example 'Key G (sol)' (5), rather than 'Doh=G'. This version remains in print to this day, a book whose purpose was partly music-educational; but in the broader sense, it furthered the purpose of conversion to Christianity.

Choral music written by African composers in southern Africa based on European models like this was nevertheless part of a major musical initiative on their part to achieve some kind of syncretism between the colonial and the traditional, the old and the new. European music was 'new' – previously unknown to African students, even if 'old' in Europe. Bearing this in mind, the progress made by choral composers was and remains astounding. Although I have misgivings about the way Mzilikazi Khumalo claims choral music as African 'serious' or 'classical' music, I largely agree with his comment that contributions by earlier composers were 'of inestimable value in advancing the choral genre from mere hymnody into the realm of genuine art music.'[7]

Theirs was an expression of middle-class aspiration, as Vokwana points out, but its reach did not extend beyond the church and the classroom, with the result that choral practice has been closely associated with schools, churches and community halls almost ever since. These were initially situated in the developing African townships around Johannesburg, Pretoria, Kimberly, Durban, Port Elizabeth, Bloemfontein and Maseru, as these centres expanded under the impact of industrialisation in the early twentieth century. Competitions organised by African teachers grew more substantial as time passed. Modelled on Welsh eisteddfodau, these originally included instrumental categories, but choral music came to dominate.

The choral work, as it developed in this context, was not primarily a commercial artefact, unlike genres of jazz and popular music, which developed in tandem. Rather, it was an educational one; a genre made for untrained, unamplified voices by untrained, unrecognised composers. Choral music was a sector operating almost entirely outside the recorded music industry, funded not by concerts or sales of recordings, but by corporate sponsorship of competitions. Sponsors over the decades have included the Ford Motor Company, Telkom (the South African telephone parastatal), and Old Mutual (a prominent insurance company). Composers who wrote 'vernacular' or indigenous prescribed pieces found their work in competition, internally, with 'Western' music (choruses by Haydn or Handel), and more recently with an additional category for traditional music. There was never any getting away from European models, even though the competitions were entirely African-run. They were a great incentive for composers, but must have inspired more music than was ever performed. Some of it, however, was sung outside of these competitions, most notably in schools.

From the 1960s onwards, the SABC regularly recorded choral competitions, mainly in schools in South Africa and Lesotho. The SABC Radio Sound Archives in Johannesburg (Auckland Park) has thousands of such recordings made over the decades, most of which are now digitised from original LP transcription records. A list of Moerane performances generated for my research in 2014, however, shows very few compared to the dozens, even hundreds, by other composers; perhaps because only about ten of his works were known. Almost none of the analogue recordings are dated, but among these historic school, church and adult choir recordings at the SABC – and the choirs are all listed, often the conductors too – seven are of *Sylvia*, six of *Matlala*, five of *Ruri!*, four of *Della*, two of *Morena Tlake*, two of *Lesedi La Hao*, one of *Paka-Mahlomola*, and one of *Barali Ba Jerusalema*.

Gradually, the new genre of African choir music settled into a structure that became somewhat formulaic, with all of the pieces expected to be short – a couple of minutes in the early years at first, now longer – with sections, or at least a contrasting middle section. Works were written in tonic solfa notation with a firm sonic basis in four-part European harmony, and often with final sections where the pace increased and more thrilling rhetoric was employed, which baited the audience to give a resounding ovation at the end. This was (and remains) music for vocal display, celebration, and competition in the sporting sense. Sometimes extra voices were added to compositions, as were solo passages; nowadays, piano accompaniments are sometimes used. Notes, lyrics, tempi and formal aspects of compositions were often altered to suit conductors, voices or particular situations.

African choral music as it emerged in the early twentieth century was subject to a range of musical and textual influences, in a region with several indigenous languages and many different oral traditions – not to mention the influence of recordings, radio and television, and eventually, social media. Everyone could, and can, be involved. It was, and continues to be, a democratic practice. 'Choral contests', as Khabi Mngoma put it in the mid-1980s, had 'an elaborate organizational structure [...] tiered in such a way that the whole of the Republic is divided into branches, districts, zones and regions, culminating in national finals where the provincial finalists vie with each other for national honours in the form of trophies and other prizes. All levels of the school population are catered for.' Mngoma adds a significant reminder about the educational value of competitions and the music prepared for them: 'This is more than the education departments, with all their financial resources, have been able to achieve.'[8]

African choral competitions

How did African choralism become such a knock-out, corporate-driven affair, given its modest beginnings in mission stations and with African teachers? How has it remained separate as performance practice from other kinds of South African music? One starting point has been identified as 1929, when 'Mark Radebe, an important interlocutor in twentieth-century black choralism and "one of the chief theorists of African national culture, together with the two well-known black composers, Benjamin Tyamzashe and Hamilton Masiza"', convened a meeting of interested parties in Kimberley.[9] It is clear from the meeting's statement of intent, issued by Masiza, Radebe and Tyamzashe, that their watershed 'Conference of Musicians' on 29 June 1929 was seen as part of a way to solve 'the Bantu's economic and political problems through "Art".'[10] The South African Bantu Board of Music was set up after the Kimberley Conference and undertook, among other things, to 'Research and collect Bantu Folk Music' and 'Encourage and publish Bantu Composers'.[11] The Board failed to do so effectively, however, resulting in what Mokale Koapeng sees as a missed opportunity 'for the development of a canon of modern African choral composition, one founded on a new aesthetic reality facing Africans, informed and inspired by the confluence of African and European aesthetics no doubt, but leaning towards (one would have hoped) a basis in African aesthetics and materials.'[12]

> Subsequent events of the Association, in the form of choral competitions like the ones organised by the Transvaal African Eisteddfod, provide us with further proof of the failure of the Association's avowed Africanist and Africanising programme. That choral practitioners were not self-aware of this failure is because to the mission-educated *amakholwa*:

'choral music was the supreme manifestation of improvement and progress [...and] [p]roof of how far these communities had advanced toward this goal was to be found in the precision with which early church and school choirs imitated English turn-of-the-century musical events.' In other words, the class identity of choralism prevented a progressive (and more Africanist) development of its compositional discourse.[13]

However, the Africanist discourse *was* there for some composers: the first book of songs published by Mohapeloa in Morija in 1935, for example, is heavily indebted to traditional music; and in his preface to the second edition of that book in 1953, he explicitly states that it is an archive of the traditional.[14] Perhaps, living in Basutoland, Mohapeloa did not entirely share the 'powerful interlocutor' Radebe's (South African) aspiration towards social and political advancement along Western lines. Nor was he, perhaps, as limited in his view of what African composed music should be, nor of Radebe's determination 'to exterminate the influence of "musical intoxications" like jazz, marabi and isicathamiya' on choral competitions and repertoire.[15]

Moerane may have embraced Radebe's view of such 'intoxications', but his music shows that he definitely embraced the Africanising impetus. He proceeded to shape a choral repertoire from the 1930s to 1970s that is very different from choral music in any other part of the world, and indeed from Mohapeloa's: a repertoire in which he employed Western harmonic and contrapuntal techniques to a degree that no other composer in the choral sector could have done, and to an extent beyond Radebe's wildest dreams. So much so that the majority of his works were never performed, or did not even see the light of day – and those that did are among the most challenging in the repertoire. This, I have no doubt, is because Moerane was not only drawn towards Western musical models, but because he knew far more Western models than his peers; also, because of his BMus training, he was drawn towards a certain kind of modernist European musical language. A small example of this: in the famous piano stool mentioned in Chapter 1, there is a sheet of manuscript paper headed 'A General Note on Modern Music' written in Moerane's hand. The focus is on scales such as the whole-tone scale (Debussy) and unconventional ways of building chords and unusual tonality, with the analysis applied to a piano piece by Finnish modernist Selim Palgrem, *May Night* (Figure 6.1).

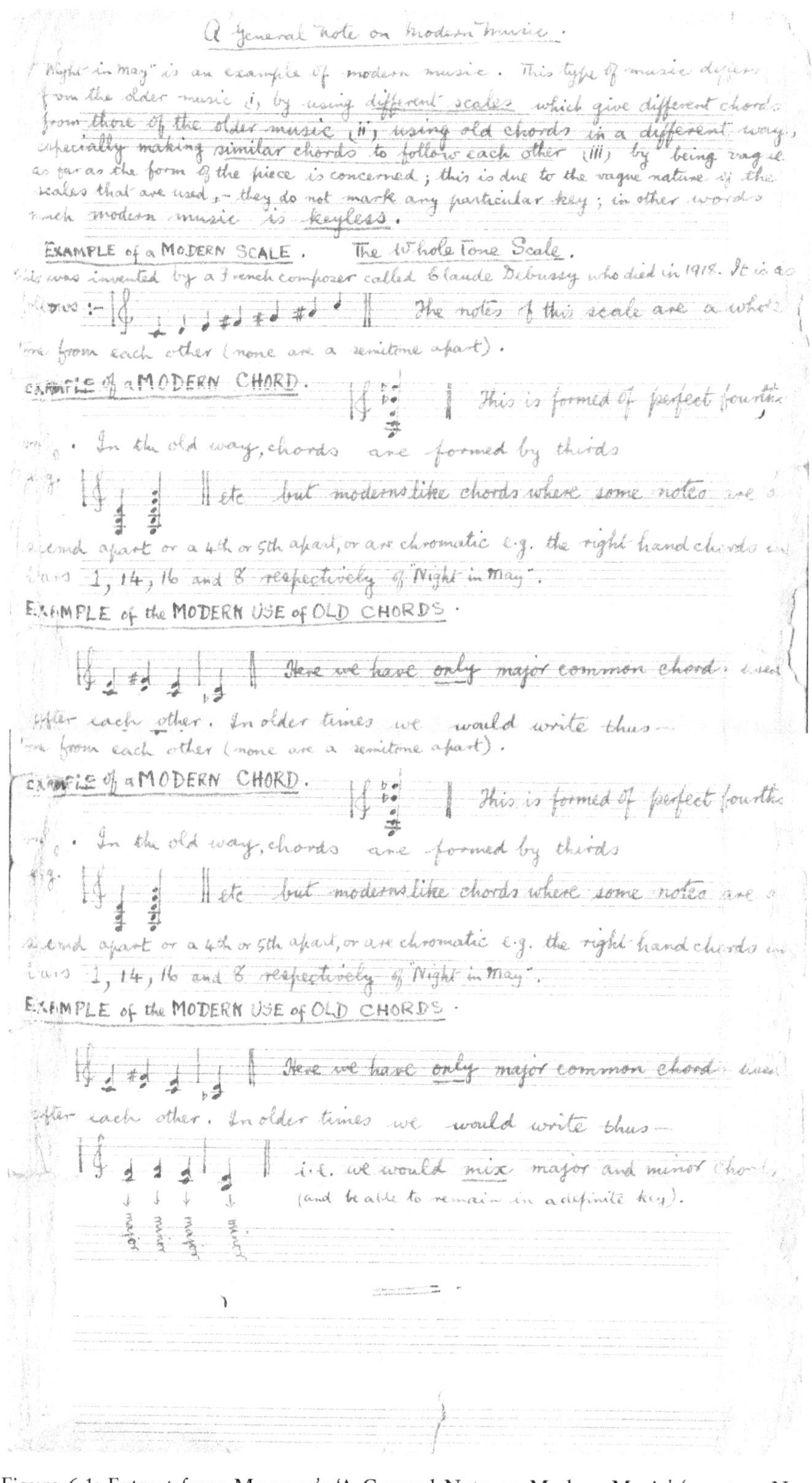

A General Note on Modern Music.

"Night in May" is an example of modern music. This type of music differs from the older music (i) by using different scales which give different chords from those of the older music (ii) using old chords in a different way, especially making similar chords to follow each other (iii) by being vague as far as the form of the piece is concerned; this is due to the vague nature of the scales that are used, – they do not mark any particular key; in other words much modern music is keyless.

EXAMPLE of a MODERN SCALE. The Whole Tone Scale.
This was invented by a French composer called Claude Debussy who died in 1918. It is as follows:– The notes of this scale are a whole tone from each other (none are a semitone apart).

EXAMPLE of a MODERN CHORD. This is formed of perfect fourths only. In the old way, chords are formed by thirds e.g. etc but moderns like chords where some notes are a second apart or a 4th or 5th apart, or are chromatic e.g. the right hand chords in bars 1, 14, 16 and 8 respectively of "Night in May".

EXAMPLE of the MODERN USE of OLD CHORDS.
Here we have only major common chords used after each other. In older times we would write thus–

tone from each other (none are a semitone apart).
EXAMPLE of a MODERN CHORD. This is formed of perfect fourths only. In the old way, chords are formed by thirds e.g. etc but moderns like chords where some notes are a second apart or a 4th or 5th apart, or are chromatic e.g. the right hand chords in bars 1, 14, 16 and 8 respectively of "Night in May".
EXAMPLE of the MODERN USE of OLD CHORDS.
Here we have only major common chords used after each other. In older times we would write thus–

i.e. we would mix major and minor chords (and be able to remain in a definite key).
major minor major minor

Figure 6.1: Extract from Moerane's 'A General Note on Modern Music' (courtesy Neo Mahase Moerane)

Surveying Moerane's choral music

In Chapters 7 to 9, I explore where and how Moerane felt able to implement his grasp of Modernism – more evident in some of his pieces than in others – but as Koapeng says, an African modernist discourse is largely absent from African choralism as a whole. It was not on the agenda of the majority of African composers because their schools or colleges could give them no access to the modernist languages of Schoenberg or Stravinsky.[16] Even more significantly, in their music education, composers seem to have had no access to Kodaly, whose music and educational methods, with their emphasis on solfège and choral music, would surely have had a profound impact on choral music in southern Africa.

Given all that has been said so far about the context for Moerane's choral and orchestral work, added to which that it has been unknown in its entirety until recently, it is daunting to attempt the first survey. How does one approach these works? A division according to when they were written does not work, because Moerane dated few pieces; nor does it work to categorise according to language, because 37 have Sesotho texts, 8 English and 5 isiXhosa. Vivien Pieters groups them according to the 'classical, religious and traditional' inspiration she attributes to them.[17] But there is little overt reference to 'traditional music' in Moerane's choral works (unlike the symphonic poem); and 'classical' is a very broad term in this context. The category 'religious' is viable, however, because of formulations in texts used and aspects of vocal writing.

Bearing all caveats in mind, I group the 51 choral works into three overarching 'themes': spiritual songs; songs about tradition, family and community life; and songs based on literary texts that deal with love and loss. Chapters 7 to 9 discuss works under each theme in turn. I continue with an explanation of how Moerane's extant choral works, at the time of writing, come to be 51 in number, and end with a consideration of their performance contexts.

In the *Catalogue* created for the ACE Moerane Edition in 2020,[18] each work is assigned a number based on the composer's initials (for example, MMM 001), a number representing its position in ACE's publisher's list for example, ACE 401), and a unique identifying International Standard Music Number (ISMN). Only the 51 extant works are listed; Moerane is not only the composer of the music, but also author or adaptor of the lyrics. There are, however, many scores of which we know that have not yet been found, according to the two main sources that were used to compile the *Catalogue*.

Source 1: The SAMRO archive

Moerane signed and returned 'Two Deeds of Assignment' of his music to the Southern African Music Rights Organisation (SAMRO) when he joined this royalty collection agency in 1973. Gideon Roos, the first head of SAMRO, also notes that Moerane returned notification forms on 29 June 1973 'with the details of 65 compositions composed and/or arranged by you.'[19] This was seven years before Moerane died, and he would have composed more works by the time of his death in 1980, and undoubtedly sent them to SAMRO. SAMRO's 'Catalogue: Works by Michael Moerane 1909–1981' (2003) lists 89 titles, but some are arrangements *of* Moerane's works by other people, or reproductions of Moerane's music made after his death. SAMRO's 'Catalogue' only lists 64 original titles, listed alphabetically:

> Alina; Atamelang; Ba Tsabang Molimo (Yizani Nive); Banoyolo (Ke Tla Bina); Barali ba Jerusalema; Bokang Jesu; Bonukunyana; Boputsoa; Chorale (Etude) for school orchestra; Della; Ea Folisang Maloetse a Hao (Mbonse Uyehova); Ea Hlolang; Fantasie from Sunny South […] for piano;[20] Fatse La Heso for orchestra; Ha Ke Bale He; Hobane Re Tsoaletsoe Ngoana (Ngokuba Sizalelwe); Hoja Ke Nonyane; In Hout Bay for piano; Jehova Oa Busa (Psalm 93); Joy-Ride from Sunny South; Ke Rata Jehova; Khati; Lebili; Leribe; Leseli Le Hao (Thumo, Ukukhanya Kwakho) (OT [Old Testament]: Psalm 93); Letsatsi; Liflaga; Likholo; Liphala; Lonesome from Sunny South for piano; Mahakoe; Mankholikholi; Mankokotsane; Matlala; Mehauhelo Ea Hao; Mitsa Mahosi; Moea, Oa Ka (Psalm 119); Mohokare; Mohokare Monyako Oa Pelo; Monyaka Oa Pelo; Moratuoa; Morena Tlake; Mosele (Musele); Naleli Ea Meso; Naleli Ka Ngoe; Ngeloi La Me; Nonyana Tse Ntle; Nyene Le Bosiu; Paka Mahlomola; Paki Ha Li Eo; Pelo Le Moea; Pina Ea Masole; Qhafutso; Rosalia [for] violin & piano; Rosalia [for choir]; Ruri; Satane A Tsema; Sunrise for flute, 2 clarinets, piano, 2 violins, viola, cello; Sylvia; Tsatsi La Palla; Utloahatsang Lifela (Ndiya Kubulela Kuyehova); Vizani Kum (Tlong Ho Na); Vumani Ku Yehova; Why Worry for flute, 2 clarinets, string quartet.

There are some misspellings here: among them, 'Hoja Ke Nonyana' 'Leseli La Hao, 'Likhohlo' and 'Tsatsi la Pallo'. Two works are listed twice: 'Mohokare' and 'Monyako Oa Pelo' are also listed as 'Mohokare Monyako Oa Pelo'. Not all the dual Sesotho–isiXhosa titles make sense as translations. Sources for the text are sometimes written as subtitles ('Psalm 93' and 'Psalm 119'), while on the scores there are no such subtitles: these words indicate the texts used. 'Psalm 93' as a subtitle for 'Jehova Oa Busa' turns up again for 'Leseli Le Hao (Thumo Ukukhanya Kwakho) (OT: Psalm 93)'; 'OT' here means 'Other Title'. But the text in fact comes from Psalm 43, not 93, written as 'XLIII' on Moerane's score. This list, with all its errors, was the official record of Moerane's music made by the national music collection agency for performing rights in South Africa and other countries. On such a list, titles denote not only 'work' but works in copyright; that is, those owned as intellectual property where royalties are due when they are performed, recorded or broadcast.[21]

Moreover, SAMRO's 'Catalogue' has only 24 titles for which 'call numbers' (accession numbers) are given, meaning that files exist at SAMRO under those numbers and contain scores; there are in fact only 22 original scores in the files on the SAMRO archive shelves, with more than one score occasionally put in one file. This suggests careless filing or even the disappearance of works from SAMRO. The originals that do exist in files are all typed or handwritten by Moerane on foolscap paper with 'MMM' or 'M.M. Moerane' in the top right corner. Most of these have '29.6.73' written in pencil at the top, the date of Gideon Roos's letter and the date SAMRO would have received them.

Source 2: The Moerane family
When I visited Moerane's son Thuso in May 2014, I found that he had some of the same manuscripts or typescripts, as well as a number of others not at SAMRO, including some not even in SAMRO's 'Catalogue'. Thuso also had four lists of his father's songs: three he had made in order to keep track of his father's music; and one made by his father. Thuso's most complete list is called 'M.M.M. Compositions and Harmonized Negro Spirituals' and covers two pages, with 68 titles on page 1 and the 23 titles for which he did not have scores listed on page 2. This list has been retyped below in three columns just as Thuso typed it, showing the songs for which Thuso did not have scores in italics.

M.M.M. COMPOSITIONS AND HARMONIZED NEGRO SPIRITUALS

Junior – SCC	Medium – SATB	Senior – SATB
1. Pelo le moea (SC)	1. 'Mankokotsane	1. Alina
2. Mohokare (SCC)	2. Hoja ke Nonyana	2. 'Mitsa-mahosi
3. Mosele	3. *Naleli ea Meso*	3. Ruri
4. Ngeloi la me	4. Letsatsi	4. Morena Tlake
5. *Boputsoa*	5. Lebili	5. *Matlala*
6. Paka-mahlomola	6. Monyaka oa Pelo	6. Barali ba Jerusalema
7. *Bonukunyana*	7. Likhohlo	7. Satane a tseha
8. Lia qhomaqhoma	8. Khati	8. Seotsanyana
9. Sekolo se koetsoe	9. Paki ha li eo	9. *Thaha e tala*
10. *Kepe sa me*	10. Ha ke balahe	10. *Qhafutso*
11. *Nonyana tse ntle*	11. *Leribe*	11. *'Mote*
12. Maholotsane	12. *Sylvia (Xhosa)*	12. *Tumeliso*
13. *Sentebale*	13. Naleli ka 'ngoe	13. *Kajeno (sacred) TTB*
14. *Ngakana-ntsonyana*	14. I got a home (Negro)	14. *Della (Xhosa) (SATB)*
15. *Botleng ba naha*	15. I stood on de Ribber "	15. Leseli la Hao (sacred)
16. Ntsoaki	16. By an' by "	16. Jehova oa busa (sacred)
17. Sa 'Mokotsane	17. Shenandoah "	17. *Merabe, rorisang (sacred)*
18. *Liflaga*	18. Its me, O Lord "	18. *Ke rata Jehova (sacred)*
19. Ma-Homemakers	19. Witness "	19. *Yizani kum (Xhosa)*
20. 'Mankholikholi	20. Go tell it on the mountains "	20. *Moea oa ka*
21. Tsatsi la pallo		21. Liphala (SATB)
		22. Ntate ea mohau (sacred)
		23. Mahakoe
		24. Letsatsi
		25. Ea hlolang (Hymn)
		26. Vumani kuYehova (anthem)
		27. Ngokuba sizalelwe umntwana (sacred anthem)

Thuso also lists *Maholosiane* and *Rorisang lebitso la Jehova* among songs he does not have – but they don't appear on the above list.

Titles on Thuso's lists that are not in the SAMRO 'Catalogue' include 'Lia qhomaqhoma', 'Sekolo se koetsoe', 'Kepe sa me', 'Maholotsane', 'Sentebale', 'Ngakana-ntsonyana', 'Botleng ba naha', 'Ntsoaki', 'Sa 'Mokotsane', 'Ma-Homemakers', and six of the 'Negro Spiritual' arrangements. However, 'Nobody Knows The Trouble I've Seen' is not listed in either Source 1 or 2 given above.

Another of Thuso Moerane's lists, headed 'Lipina',[22] looks like an earlier version of Thuso's list above; it comprises one column and was attached to a *Mail & Guardian* article published in December 1980 on the 'lost' music of Moerane.[23] 'Michael Moerane's compositions and music harmonised by him', the third of Thuso's lists,[24] is typed in blue ink and dated 20-06-2008, with the comment: 'The most popular at the moment are Sylvia and Della in R.S.A. [South Africa] In Lesotho is Matlala. Compiled by his son Thuso (Mofekeng) residing – T96 Soga Street, Mlungisi Location, Queenstown 5320. Phone (045)838 4550', followed by Thuso's signature and typed name. It lists Junior (19), Medium (34) and Senior (20) songs – 73 in all. This was two years after Thabo Moerane's death in 2006, and because Thuso gives his clan name, Mofekeng (the Moerane house is descended from the royal house of Bafokeng), it suggests that he made this list for the family's benefit.

Moerane's own list, handwritten in blue pen on a strip of lined foolscap paper, is headed, 'Price 15c plus postage', which indicates that it was made after the change of South African currency from pounds sterling to South African rands in 1961. It has 32 numbered songs and one unnumbered. Some titles have 'III' after them, meaning that they are for three female voices. I do not know what * and " before some numbers denote:

1. Boputsoa III, 2. Mohokare III, 3. Bonukunyana (Pelo le Moea) III (25c), 4. Ngeloi la me III, 5. MOSELE III, 6. Paka Mahlomola III, 7. Liflaga III, 8. Mankokotsane, 9. Hoja ke Nonyana, 10. Ha ke balehē, 11. Naleli ea Meso, 12. Satane a tšeha, 13. Letsatsi (Lebili) (25c), 14. Monyaka oa Pelo (Likhohlo) (25c), 15. Khati, 16. Sylvia, 17. Alina, 18. 'Mitsa-mahosi, 19. Paki ha li eo, 20. Morena Tlake, 21. Ruri, 22. Matlala, 23. Barali ba Jerusalema, *24. Jehova oa Busa, *25. Leseli

la hao, *26. Rorisang lebitso la Jehova, 27. I got a Home (Negro), 28. I stood on de Ribber ("), 29. By an' By ("), 30. 'Mankholikholi III, 31. Nonyana tse Ntle III (a) (with accomp) III b, 32. Tsatsi la Pallo III, X Shenandoah.

This list includes 'Matlala' and 'Barali ba Jerusalema', both written in the mid- to late-1960s, and so it must date from that period. It is much shorter than the 65 works that Moerane listed for Gideon Roos when he joined SAMRO in 1973, and appears to be something of a promotional list. Three titles combine two songs in one: Bonukunyana–Pelo le Moea, Letsatsi-Lebili, and Monyaka oa Pelo–Likhohlo. This is because on the typescript, one song ends on the same page that another begins; perhaps for this reason. they were sold together. Interestingly, 'Rorisang lebitso la Jehova' is listed by its Sesotho title only, the isiXhosa title (which is the main title at the top of his manuscript) being 'Vumani ku Jehova'.

Missing works by Moerane

Without being able to make perfect sense of the discrepancies between the above tallies, I have identified 36 works for which there are titles, but the scores are missing. Nine are instrumental or piano works that do not appear on any of Thuso's lists, but are in the SAMRO 'Catalogue':

> Rosalia for violin & piano; Chorale (Etude) for small school orchestra; Sunrise for flute, 2 clarinets, piano, 2 violins, viola, cello; Why Worry for flute, 2 clarinets, string quartet; Album for the young for solo piano; In Hout Bay for solo piano; Fantasie from Sunny South for solo piano; Joy-Ride from Sunny South for solo piano; Lonesome from Sunny South for solo piano.

Twenty-seven of them are for choir:

> 'Mote; Atamelang; Ba Tsabang Molimo (Yizani Nive); Banoyolo (Ke Tla Bina); Bokang Jesu; Boputsoa; Botleng ba naha; Ea Folisang Maloetse a Hao (Mbonse Uyehova); Kajeno; Kepe sa me; Kerata

Jehova; Leribe; Maholotsane; Mehauhelo Ea Hao; Moea Oa Ka (Psalm 119); Moratuoa; Naleli Ea Meso; Ngakama-ntsomyana; Nyene Le Bosiu; Pina Ea Masole; Qhafutso; Rosalia; Satane A Tsema; Sentebale; Thaha e tala; Tumeliso; Yizani kum.

These 36 works, together with the 51 extant works, bring the tally of known choral works composed by Moerane, to the best of my knowledge, to 87.

How Moerane composed

The scores Moerane wrote are the outcome of a process of which we know very little. 'Well, you never knew what he was doing until he could call us to come and sing,' said Thuso:

> It was a quiet shop. No disturbance until he decided, come and sing – Mofelehetsi, Mathabo, myself, Halieo, Sophie. Then you would sing and get corrected on the spot! Yes, any mistakes were corrected on the spot. But composing? I couldn't say. I didn't know really when he was composing, until he'd call you to come and sing. The songs were written by hand, and then he typed it. Nobody was helping him.[25]

Thuso reiterated this process in 2017: 'Got family around the piano when done, and said, "come and sing". He composed any time. Sons were the bass and father was the tenor.'[26] His tenor voice, the subject of mirth among students at Peka, was not only used to try out compositions. 'Thabo remembers his father', says Carmel Rickard, 'as a shy man with a fine tenor voice which he heard when the family sang hymns in the evenings.'[27] It is very likely that he modulated his voice when singing during rehearsals or trying pieces out, and it is clear that Moerane used the piano at least at the end of the process of writing music down, if not during it: 'He tested his compositions on the piano. He tested on the piano most of the time in the evenings, but weekends when we felt free we would sit down. I remember we heard one night, being repeated [...] these composers, they repeat a phrase twenty times [...] if it's not correct according to them.'[28] How he came to choose texts or what inspired his music is even less clear. One of his Peka students remembers that:

> On Saturday afternoons or Sunday afternoons you would see him walking along the river, the Caledon River, because Peka High School is on a plateau like this, overlooking the Caledon down there. He would be walking there, pacing up and down the river. At the beginning we didn't know what he was doing there, until somebody told me, 'No, what he is doing there, he is composing.'[29]

This walk could have inspired *Mohokare*. Tseliso Makhakhe remembers that *Mohokare* was indeed composed at Peka High School, 'because he was so close to the river. He could see the river anytime. He could see the river down there, and then he composed that song.'[30]

Moerane also tried out new songs at Peka:

> He formed a small choir, and they sang 'Matlala'. A typical Sesotho song. It was amazing. We were really surprised, and excited, that at the same time, our teacher has composed such a song. Later on, it became so popular. Yes, we were told that this was the first performance of this composition. I remember one of the singers there was the wife of one of our Maths teachers, Mrs Matebesi. They also came from the eastern Cape [...] That choir was teachers and some students, about six, eight.[31]

How Moerane's songs were used

Sung by six or eight family members, students, colleagues: this was how some of Moerane's songs were first heard. It raises the question of how he imagined them, as school choirs were larger than that, and competition choirs came to be standardised as having either 40 or 60 members. It is difficult to imagine the syntactical detail in many of Moerane's songs working well with such large choirs, and yet, as his brother noted in December 1988, some of his songs 'have been prescribed for competition [such] as *Morena Tlake*, *Ruri!*, *Sylvia* and his last and best *Matlala* was the competition piece a fortnight ago at the Ford music competitions at the Standard Bank arena, Johannesburg.'[32]

Tseliso Makhakhe recalled singing *Liphala* while he was 'doing teacher training in 1947' in Morija, where his music teacher was 'Mr Mashologu', the man with whom Moerane went through Lovedale and Fort Hare. He 'brought *Liphala* along and we tried our hands on it. It was such noise! It was too difficult for us.' Another thing Makhakhe noticed about Moerane's music was that there was 'not very much in the form of language, [un]like in Mohapeloa. Pulumo Mohapeloa tells a story in his music, but Moerane repeats; like in the "Hallelujah Chorus." In the "Hallelujah Chorus" as you know, there's no language. There's just one word!'[33] *Matlala* is discussed in Chapter 8 below, and perhaps the repetitions have to do with the invocation of traditional poetry and music, but the translator of the Sesotho texts for the Moerane Scholarly Edition, Mpho Ndebele, also noted how very different Moerane was from Mohapeloa, (whose texts she had previously translated for the African Composers Edition of Mohapeloa's music) in respect to their deployment of words.[34] Makhakhe goes so far as to say that 'practically all his songs are like the "Hallelujah Chorus"' and yet, as he puts it, 'you're not aware that it is just one word. The music is very, very complex. Very beautiful indeed. Ageless. So you find that in *Liphala*, you find that in *Matlala*':

> Moerane is more difficult, but once you have mastered that, then you find it's a mastery; you have achieved something. Yes, very worthwhile. They are long, but the 'Hallelujah Chorus' is long, and you're not aware. You get bewitched in listening to the music, and you're not aware that you're saying the same thing all the time [...] Well, *Ruri!* [too] is phrases, just phrases, but it's the most beautiful thing. At the competition we won here in Maseru, before exile, Mr Moerane said after our choir sang, he said "Those voices are most beautiful", because *Ruri!* is very sweet. Moerane was an adjudicator [at that competition].[35]

As I show in Chapters 7 to 9, words are for the most part subservient to the music; and it is the music, especially the melodies, that choirs and listeners remember. Moerane did not often paint a picture or convey a landscape, but he was expert at expressing emotion, and at stirring it in the listener. 'I think his songs were not so popular', said Makhakhe, 'because you've got to sing them many times before it sinks into you. You don't hear that it's beautiful music until you have really mastered it, sung it many, many times.'³⁶ *Matlala* was popular in Lesotho, perhaps because it is more immediately graspable, perhaps because the words relate to the custom of appeasing the ancestors, and undoubtedly because of the way Moerane builds excitement through multiple repetitions of the same phrase. 'He was asked by the teachers' organisation to prescribe a music piece for the competition [for] three consecutive years [1966–1968]', says Makhakhe. The first year, he set *Matlala*. 'It was amazing. Everybody wanted that song, sung many times, outside the set programme.' The second year (1967), it was *Ruri!*, which had been composed in the 1940s. It 'was well liked and was selected by the Lesotho African National Teachers Association.'³⁷ Tseliso Makhakhe recalls performing it with a new rural school in Matsieng, 'which was totally on the brink of collapse' but they 'won the competition with that piece! People in the country were surprised that a school that had no future at all, could [win] at the end of the year.' The third year (1968 or possibly 1969), it was *Barali Ba Jerusalema*:

> Mr Moerane did something that I could never understand. He set a piece, *Barali Ba Jerusalema*. It's transitions! All the way, it's transitions. You move one page, it's a transition; you move from that one, it's another transition. And then you think, 'Oh dear me. This is terrible!' Many schools could not manage, and in that one, we got first position with another school. We tied. It was awful, awful piece of music. Mr Moerane set such a piece! For a competition for schools! I could never understand. I never had time to discuss that with him.³⁸

It is hardly surprising that school choirs struggled to cope with *Barali Ba Jerusalema*: it is full of wide intervallic leaps and harmonic twists and turns, as is *Della*. When this was prescribed at the Ford Choirs Competition in 1979, journalist Harold Staefel commented that an octave upward leap towards the final phrase that had to be sung quietly 'seemed to be something of a hurdle' for some choirs, although the winning choirs managed the difficulty 'without any trouble'.³⁹ Yet the downward octave leap at the beginning of *Sylvia* didn't seem to pose problems.

Songs were sometimes performed outside of competitions. Thanks to Basil (Doc) Bikitsha's regular column in the *Rand Daily Mail Extra* (the Township Edition) we know, for example, that on Sunday 23 March 1981 at Mohlakeng Methodist Church in Randfontein, 'three works by Mohapeloa' alongside works by 'Myataza, Khunou, and Majola' were performed by the 'Mohlakeng Methodist Church Choir under Mr Nehemiah Ramasia' in the first half of the concert; and Stainer's *Crucifixion* was conducted by Michael Masote with the Soweto Symphony Orchestra in the second half.[40] This extraction of choral music from its competition environment has become increasingly common since the 1980s. The Stainer was repeated the following year, 1982, by the same forces in a five-part concert on Sunday 29 March at Ramosa Hall in Mohlakeng. *Nobody Knows* was on the programme (perhaps in Moerane's arrangement, but it doesn't say) along with 'these ditties: Sweet Day, Ave Maria, Linoto by JP Mohapeloa, and Della by MM Moerane.'[41] Mohlakeng Methodist Church Choir was one of the best church choirs in South Africa at the time, winning 'the JMB Championship, SW Tvl District Synod Championship, Ford Choirs in Contest Trophy in 1979, and Radio Sotho's Mohapeloa Songs Prize.'[42] This reminds us that church choirs were as heavily invested in competitions as school, student and adult choirs.

Moerane's *Liphala* was prescribed by the Transvaal United African Teachers' Association in 1976, according to Bikitsha, together with '"Rarely, Rarely Comest Thou" by F.A. Ogilvy, the "Pilgrim's Chorus" by Wagner, "Die Here is My herder" (Anon), "Lehesheheshe" by J.P. Mohapeloa [and] "Dashing away with the smoothin iron" by C.J. Sharp.'[43] Books of prescribed music printed over the years would show many more performances of works by Moerane. *Liphala* and *Ruri!* are noted by SAMRO in their 'Catalogue' as having been 'prescribed music for massed choir festival on 24 September 1995'.[44] Dozens more examples could be found, both in and outside of competitions.

One can only imagine how Moerane navigated choral scenes in South Africa and Lesotho in schools, churches and community halls, from local to national level. He was so well known in the community that people must have often asked him for scores, asked him to adjudicate, asked him to help them with prescribed music. But how did he deal with the criticism – or simply the reality he encountered at competitions – that his music was 'too difficult' to perform? This view of Moerane as a community-minded figure, often seen and heard in public, defending his music when he had to, or at least explaining it, is slightly at odds with the comments I heard in interviews with family members about Moerane as a person. 'He was very reserved. He would only speak when he was angry, which was seldom. He was not easily taken up to anything.' 'He was very reserved and he never went out of his way to speak about what he was doing.' 'He was not a talker. He was reserved, definitely.' 'Mr Moerane apparently was a very private person, very secretive.' 'Well, we never listened to him. He was not outspoken.' 'My first memory of Uncle Mike was when my family, that's my father, my mother, my two sisters, drove down to the eastern Cape in the early 50s [...] He was a very private person, reserved. He didn't talk much.'[45] This was interpreted as 'Moerane was a recluse' by people who did not have the family's perspective.[46] A man who participated for decades in churches, classrooms, and such public spaces as choral competitions, a man of the community who operated over a wide region of southern Africa, a man who taught rowdy teenagers Latin and English – he cannot have been too much of a private person when it came to public music performance.

The death notice of Moerane in the *Rand Daily Mail* tells us among other things that 'people will remember him as the prolific composer of songs like "Sylvia", "Della" and especially "Morena Tlake" which was sung by black South African school choirs during the early 1970s.'[47] The word 'prolific' is interesting, given how few of his songs people actually knew during his lifetime. Perhaps it was known that he had composed a great deal more, but it is more likely the case that his advanced music education set him apart, musically; he therefore only made available works that would stand a chance with choirs. At the same time, the teacher in him wanted to give them challenges that, once met, made knowledge of the music hugely rewarding.

On the other hand, because so little is known about so many other composers' entire repertoires in southern Africa, it might be that making only a few works available to choirs from many more compositions is the norm among African choral composers.

Much of what I have said here is preliminary, because the history of African choral music in southern Africa, especially during deep apartheid, remains unwritten. This is not through lack of interest in the music, which has been sung and enjoyed by millions for decades. It is because the history of music in African communities is not taught in schools, because very little choral music has been published or is easily available, because choral music has operated in a competitive field dominated by a few key figures who are not always composers themselves, because books of prescribed music are not yet collected into a comprehensive archive; and above all, because it is an enormous and diverse field. Moerane's position within this field has only been suggested in this chapter, a context for viewing his choral music merely sketched. Further interviews with those who knew him as a colleague, chorister or adjudicator would shed more light on the way he operated in the field, just as it would on the way the field itself works.

What I have been able to show here is that only a small proportion of his music was known even within this large field of cultural production – and I have tried to introduce him as a major player in the field. In the next three chapters, I provide more specific insight into individual pieces in Moerane's output, giving the first historical and analytical overview of a major choral composer's entire oeuvre, and showing ways in which he deserves to be credited with far more significance as composer – not only in this field, and not only in South Africa, but even in more global terms.

7 | Moerane's Spiritual Songs

Moerane wrote 16 works that are a direct product of his Christian upbringing and lifelong faith. Alongside his knowledge of and respect for traditional cultural values, he wholeheartedly embraced the culture and theology of the Protestant church, but because of his fairly advanced education in Western classical music, his style of writing goes far beyond the rather simple style of the hymn. His considerable polyphonic skill and a creative use of voices and harmony reveal themselves in a number of works that show his deep spirituality. Four different categories of spiritual songs are distinguished in this chapter, not in order to be prescriptive but simply by way of introduction to his music. They are distinguished not only by their texts, but also by their musical style, and are organised here into four categories: hymns, anthems, sacred songs and spirituals.

The three hymns are simple four-part harmonisations of existing or newly composed congregational melodies: *Ea Hlolang* (*The Triumphant One*), *Jehova Oa Busa* (*Jehovah Reigns*) and *Ntate Ea Mohau* (*Lord of Mercy*).[1] The three anthems are more challenging in their vocal part-writing: *Leseli La Hao* (*Your Light*), *Vumani KuYehova* (*Sing To Jehovah*) and *Ngokuba Sizalelwe Umtwana* (*For Unto Us a Child is Born*). The two sacred songs, *Ruri!* (*Truly!*) for SATB (soprano, alto, tenor, bass) and *Tsatsi La Pallo* (*Judgement Day*) for SAA can be sung in any type of venue and on any kind of occasion, including a church service. The eight spirituals are in English and are written for varied voices. One of them is an arrangement of a sea shanty, *Shenandoah*, for SSATTBB, while the rest are arrangements of African-American tunes: *By An' By* for SATB, *Go Tell It On The Mountains* (*Christmas*) for SATB soloists and SATB choir, *I Got A Home In-a Dat Rock* for SATB, *I Stood On De Ribber* for Soprano solo and SATB choir, *It's Me, O Lord* for SATB, *Nobody Knows The Trouble I've Seen* for SAA, and *Witness* for SATB.

Hymns

Brought up in the practice and faith of the Paris Evangelical Missionary Society (PEMS) church, which later became the Lesotho Evangelical Church (LEC), Moerane was extremely familiar with the PEMS hymnal *Lifela tsa Sione*. This was first published in Morija in 1844, 11 years after the French–Swiss missionaries established the Protestant mission in Basutoland,[2] and it continues in print to this day. The latest version with music (in tonic solfa) is the 53rd impression of the 24th edition, and contains 448 hymns.[3] Many of the texts written by Lesotho missionaries are still included and sung to music originally drawn from eighteenth- or nineteenth-century European composers, or music composed by the missionaries themselves. Moerane was naturally drawn to write new melodies and harmonisations for the old texts, but his music for hymns 122, *Ea Hlolang (The Triumphant One)*, and 152, *Ntate Ea Mohau (Lord of Mercy)*,[4] has not been taken up, not even in the latest edition of the hymnal. The original tune of *Ea Hlolang* was written by – or, more likely, taken from a work by – nineteenth-century Austrian composer, publisher and piano maker, Ignaz Pleyel (1757–1831). The words are by Louis Duvoisin (1835–1891), a second-generation missionary 'educated in Basel, Lausanne and the Oratoire in Geneva' who joined the PEMS in 1862.[5] *Ntate Ea Mohau*'s original music was by Samuel Wesley Martin with words by 'Moruti S. Rolland' – Rev. Samuel Rolland, a British missionary who immigrated with other British settlers to southern Africa in the early nineteenth century and joined the French Protestant Mission in Lesotho.

Moerane's *Ntate Ea Mohau* (three verses) and *Ea Hlolang* (four verses) more or less adhere to the original lyrics: he just adds diacritics (ō and š) and punctuation, separates some syllables and capitalises some letters. Both of Moerane's new hymn tunes are attractive and highly suited to congregational singing. *Ntate Ea Mohau* is a simple syllabic setting of the words with some syncopations, while *Ea Hlolang* is antiphonal, with alternating Tenor solo and choir phrases.[6] Three versions of *Ea Hlolang* have survived: the composer's handwritten manuscript, one step away from the original hymn

[Musical notation with lyrics:]

Je - ho - va o - a bu - sa o a - pe - re bo kha - ba - ne, Ma - tla ke se a - pa - ro sa Je - ho - va Le se - nye - pa sa ha - e, Le se - nye - pa sa ha - e; Ka ba ka le - o le - fa tse le ti - i - le, le ti - i - le, le - fa - tse le ti - i - le, Le ke ke la si - si - nye ha.

Ex. 7.1: *Jehova Oa Busa* bars 1–20 melody (courtesy of the Moerane family). For audio, visit https://tinyurl.com/36mybjys

and still headed 'Hymn 122', corrected to 'Ea Hlolang'; a typescript revision of that manuscript; and a four-bar fragment of the same, transcribed into staff notation in Moerane's handwriting (in blue pen). The latter looks as if it might have been the beginning of an instrumental arrangement or keyboard accompaniment. Perhaps this was one of the hymns he arranged for the Peka High School orchestra to play in church.

Moerane wrote an entirely new melody, harmony and text for *Jehova Oa Busa* (*Jehovah Reigns*). The text draws on verses 1, 4 and 5 of Psalm 93, which Moerane adapts by deleting some words, adding new ones and repeating others. The beautiful melody, with its extended fourth phrase – a typical feature of Moerane's melodic style – is eminently congregational; but the accompaniment, with short passages where the Alto or Bass divide in two to decorate the repeated harmonies, is fairly complex, indicating that perhaps he had a church choir or an accompaniment in mind. The complete 20-bar melody is given in Example 7.1.

Anthems

The difference between Moerane's hymn and anthem style becomes clear in *Leseli La Hao* (*Your Light*). Based on verses 3–5 of Psalm 43, it dwells on the idea of light guiding the soul to the holy mountain, opening with a 17-bar Soprano solo while the choir hums. They begin singing in bar 18 to the words, '*Ke finyelle altareng ea Molimo*' ('And ultimately reach the altar of God'), and with a change of key from F major to A minor.[7] With its constantly changing vocal scoring and dynamics and frequent chromatic harmonies, the music sounds almost atonal at times.

Moerane gives both *Vumani KuYehova* (*Sing To Jehovah*) and *Ngokuba Sizalelwe Umtwana* (*For Unto Us a Child is Born*) the subtitle 'anthem'.[8] They have isiXhosa rather than the more prevalent Sesotho texts, and since the second page of *Vumani*'s typescript shows part of the chorus from Mendelssohn's *I Waited for the Lord* in Moerane's handwriting, it is possible that the two works were performed on the same occasion. The typescript also has several examples of a typographical phenomenon typical of Moerane: a short handwritten straight stroke for the lower tonic solfa octave (d₁ s₁ and so on). These straight strokes above or below a tonic solfa letter to indicate an octave higher or lower had to be added after a typed song was finished in order to distinguish them from the commas (d, s,) that would indicate the duration of a note. The clarity of these handwritten strokes varies, and sometimes only the musical context can tell us when a stroke is a lower/upper octave or simply a tiny mark on the paper. If, as Thuso Moerane believed, his father's Xhosa songs 'were composed when he had retired already' and was in Lesotho, this suggests that *Vumani KuYehova* and *Ngokuba Sizalelwe Umtwana* were written in the late 1960s.[9] The music of *Vumani* is Handelian in the way it uses short, declamatory chordal phrases, sequences and fanfare-like motifs. Written in a sarabande (triple) metre, it even hints at Handel's aria 'Lascia ch'io pianga' in bars 17–24, as Example 7.2 shows.

On the top left-hand corner of the typescript of *Vumani KuYehova* one can just make out the words 'Ps. 105 vs 1–5', although Moerane's text is actually from Psalm 98; and there is an alternative Sesotho title, '*Merabe, Rorisang*' next to the isiXhosa title, although neither of these additions look as if they are in Moerane's handwriting. These and many other examples show that his use of words was quite free. His music expresses the emotional meaning implicit in the words and sometimes their literal meaning, but the words can be adapted at will; for Moerane, musical expression was paramount.

Ex. 7.2: *Vumani KuYehova* bars 17–24 (courtesy of the Moerane family). For audio, visit https://tinyurl.com/bdea6vh7

Ex. 7.3: *Ngokuba Sizalelwe Umtwana* bars 1–14 (courtesy of the Moerane family). For audio, visit https://tinyurl.com/43n3xvpu

Ngokuba Sizalelwe Umtwana (*For Unto Us a Child is Born*) uses the same text from Isaiah 9:6 that Handel uses in the chorus 'For Unto Us a Child is Born' in *Messiah*. Moerane uses JJR Jolobe's translation of this text into isiXhosa from the King James version that Handel used.[10] But Moerane's setting is very different from Handel's. His *Ngokuba* is in the style of a motet, and its many long, slow-moving notes and harmonies are even occasionally reminiscent of passsages in Bruckner's motets. The African element in the piece is therefore all the more surprising, especially as it occurs right at the beginning. The opening declamatory phrase, sung in unison, is almost a quotation of 'Ntsikana's Bell', the opening section of the great early nineteenth-century Xhosa hymn, 'Ntsikana's Great Hymn'. Moerane would probably have known this hymn from the transcription made by John Knox Bokwe and published by Lovedale.[11] Moerane even repeats the declamatory phrase, but then gradually integrates it into a progression of slowly unfolding harmonies that continues for 74 bars. Example 7.3 gives the first 14 bars of *Ngokuba Sizalelwe Umtwana*, which includes a repeat of the opening phrase as the audio fades out.

Sacred choruses
Tsatsi La Pallo is a song about the Day of Judgement, which Moerane represents through a rousing evocation of joy. The lyrics refer to beating,

shouting and dancing in twos and threes: *'Na hase lee tsatsi la nyakallo?'* ('For isn't this a day of joy?'). The dactylic rhythm – ⌣ ⌣, written as semiquaver, semiquaver rest and two semiquavers – is repeated innumerable times in this anthem; and, as with all Moerane's songs for three voices, he takes pains to handle harmony, counterpoint and phrasing ingeniously. Instead of dynamic and expression marks there are *staccatos* and *tenutos*, so that articulation becomes the main feature of the music, as indeed it does in another 'school song', *Sekolo Se Koetsoe* (*School's Out*). Moerane's student Zakes Mda recalled that *Tsatsi La Pallo* was sung at Peka High (see Chapter 3), a boys' school in those days, which means that this Soprano-Alto-Alto (SAA) song could just as easily be sung by Tenor-Bass-Bass (TBB).

Ruri! (*Truly!*), composed in the early 1940s, is probably the most loved and enduring of all Moerane's songs. His son Mofelehetsi, a teenager at the time, remembers that it was composed in Scanlen Street (Queenstown) and that his father struggled with it: 'Oh, he loved it! Some of them from him … God was making a favourite.'[12] It has a long-breathed, hymn-like melody, in the way that many themes in nineteenth-century Western classical music have, whether in piano, chamber, orchestral or vocal music. It is a deeply emotional piece about the beauty of creation. The key is G-flat major, and it mainly comprises beautiful successions of slow-moving chords, with little counterpoint or voice leading. A short middle section temporarily lightens the mood before the main theme returns, and when it does, it soars to greater heights in all four voices, the phrases extended so much that there is a feeling the song will never end. In this respect, and in the key, the lighter middle section, its late Romantic style and rather instrumental way of treating the voices, it has something in common with Moerane's *Della*; and especially with his much later *Sylvia*. Example 7.4 gives the last section, from bar 91 to the end – bar 122.

Ruri! is about the proof of God's love, his benevolence and mercy, which are visible in the stars, the dawn, reptiles and lions, even in rocks covered with snow. The crocodile is the only creature that the lyrics present as something awesome and terrifying – perhaps a reflection of its importance in Lesotho as a royal totemic animal.

Ex. 7.4: *Ruri!* bars 91–122 (courtesy of the Moerane family). For a live recording made by The Chanticleer Singers and Quava Vocal Group conducted by Richard Cock, visit https://tinyurl.com/242jac3r

African-American spirituals

Moerane was influenced, as were many other composers, especially African and African-American composers, by the huge new repertoires of African-American spirituals emerging from north America during the later nineteenth century. These originated from various sources: field hollers, plantation songs and other folk songs sung by slaves who brought them to north America (mainly) from Africa, and which were orally transmitted over several generations. The most important collector of such songs was the African-American musician Harry T Burleigh (1866–1949), who wrote down and arranged dozens of them. Burleigh admired the 'spontaneous outbursts of intense religious fervor', as he put it, which 'had their origin chiefly in camp meetings, revivals, and other religious exercises.'[13] Growing up as the descendant of slaves himself, Burleigh had learnt much of this music from his grandfather.[14] He arranged more than two hundred melodies, and through these and the published arrangements of others, 'Negro' spirituals became widely disseminated and popularised in the twentieth century. African Americans and continental Africans particularly identified with their powerful messages of freedom from oppression.

Sheet music arrangements of spirituals found their way to the British colonies, including South Africa, along with recordings, which appeared from the 1920s onwards, notably those made by the singer and political activist Paul Robeson. WEB Du Bois, with whom Moerane communicated when *Fatše La Heso* was performed (see Chapter 3), devotes Chapter 14 of his book *The Souls of Black Folk* to 'The Sorrow Songs', as he called them; and James C Scott's *Domination and the Arts of Resistance: Hidden Transcripts* shows how spirituals could become perfect examples of secret channels of communication on several levels.[15] They were an inspiration to many political movements worldwide, including Black Consciousness in southern Africa.

Moerane made one arrangement of what is strictly speaking a sailors' shanty rather than a spiritual: *Shenandoah*. The other seven 'Negro Spiritual[s] harmonised by MM Moerane', as he called them, are *By An' By*; *Go Tell It On The Mountains*; *I Got A Home In-A Dat Rock*; *I Stood On De Ribber*; *It's Me, O Lord*; *Nobody Knows The Trouble I've Seen*; and *Witness*. All have English texts. Only *Nobody Knows* was published, in tonic solfa notation, by Lovedale Press in 1938. Perhaps Moerane wrote the others, which are undated, at the same time; but they are very different from each other in their use of voices and textures, as well as different in character from other spiritual songs discussed in this chapter so far. There is no record of any performance of these arrangements during Moerane's lifetime.

We know more about the background to *Nobody Knows* because of the correspondence around its publication, and because it is one of the most famous of all spirituals. 'Who could fail to be touched by "Nobody knows the trouble I see, Lord", which is here adapted from the version used by the Fisk Jubilee Singers?' asked the anonymous reviewer of Hugh Walford Davies's *The Fellowship Song Book* in *The Musical Times* in 1916.[16] It was promoted by the Fisk Jubilee Singers in the 1870s and later by the Virginia Jubilee Singers, who, as Veit Erlmann points out, 'spent almost five years in South Africa between July 1890 and June 1898' and 'aroused interest in spirituals and Afro-American folk music'.[17] Other black South African composers were also drawn to spirituals. Soon after Reuben Caluza joined Adams College in 1936, for example, he 'requested permission from Hampton's President Arthur Howe to transcribe [Nathaniel] Dett's *Hampton Book of Spirituals* into Tonic Sol-fa.' The book never materialised, but around that time Rev. Alexander Sandilands had already started collecting material for his tonic solfa book of spirituals. He 'might have discussed his idea with Caluza at an African Authors' Conference convened by the South African Institute of Race Relations [in] 1936', suggests Erlmann, where 'issues relating to literacy, literature, and publications arising from the most recent debates in liberal circles on ethnicity and culture in South Africa' were discussed. Caluza 'trained a choir and Male Voice Quintette to perform the "sorrow songs" on a more regular basis' and promoted the relationship between them, Stephen Foster's songs and other minstrel tunes, and ragtime, which 'circulated in sheets and records in the vernacular. The Wilberforce Institute Singers [for example] recorded a Xhosa version of "Susannah" (Columbia OE 9).'[18]

It is doubtful if Sandilands' book, which only appeared in 1951, prompted any of Moerane's arrangements. Sandilands writes in the introduction that he 'began to compile this book of Spirituals about eight years ago', which means c. 1943, quite a long time after the African Authors' Conference mentioned by Erlmann. His own 'simple' and 'original' arrangements include 'It's Me, O Lord' and 'Nobody Knows',[19] but Moerane's melodies and lyrics differ substantially from his. Moerane found his sources elsewhere. His version of *Nobody Knows*, written for Soprano and two Altos, shows a detailed use of passing notes, rhythmic variation and dynamics, and is all the more haunting because of the fairly high female voice registers used.[20] Example 7.5 gives the first 16 bars.

The tune of *Nobody Knows* that Moerane uses had appeared in one of the songbooks of Burleigh's arrangements published by Ricordi, a book

Ex. 7.5: *Nobody Knows The Trouble I've Seen* bars 1–16 (courtesy of the Moerane family). For a live recording made by The Chanticleer Singers conducted by Richard Cock, visit https://tinyurl.com/phnhyu64

that Moerane himself must have owned, for he wrote to Ricordi on 25 October 1937. They replied, granting him permission to 'publish your tonic sol-fa arrangement for female voices of our publication, "NOBODY KNOWS THE TROUBLE I'VE SEEN", as per manuscript submitted for our perusal.'[21] This was written from their London office, although Ricordi's African-American songbooks were published in New York.[22]

Other correspondence in the Lovedale Press archive shows that Moerane initially tried to get *Nobody Knows* published by the Morija Sesuto Book Depot, but they turned him down: 'We are sorry to say that we do not take single songs for publication' (although in fact they occasionally did), but they also had 'on hand several song mss which have been recommended for publication by our Committee, and it would therefore be impossible to consider yours at present.' When Moerane turned to Lovedale Press, their Director of Publications, RHW Shepherd, first wrote to the Morija Sesuto Book Depot asking why they had rejected the song. He was given a different response: 'The chief reason was that Mr. Moerane asked a sum of £10 for the M.S. In view of the probable very limited sale of this song we did not consider publication on these terms a business proposition.' Moerane had just won £20 for the May Esther Bedford prize for *Album for the Young*, and so ten pounds may have seemed reasonable to him; it is the equivalent in purchasing value of about £853 today (2024). Nobody knows what Lovedale Press paid Moerane after he signed an agreement with them to accept the work in November 1937, but they did eventually publish it, in May 1938.[23]

Ex. 7.6: *By An' By*, bars 17–32 (courtesy of the Moerane family). For audio, visit https://tinyurl.com/46newej9

    Aside from *Nobody Knows*, four of the other melodies Moerane arranged are in the Ricordi songbook with almost the same spelling that Moerane used: *By An' By, Go Tell It, I Got A Home, I Stood On De Ribber Ob Jerdon*, although he changed *De Mountain* to *The Mountains* and *In A-Dat Rock* to *In-a Dat Rock*. In *By an' By*, Moerane may also have been inspired by a 1925 HMV Victor 78rpm recording for 'duet with piano' sung by Robeson with Lawrence Brown at the piano.[24] The title on the recording is 'Bye and Bye', but the words are identical to Moerane's, except for the omission of the third verse. The melody is also almost identical, barring a few tweaks of pitch and rhythm. Moerane's harmonisation is subtler; and the structure is simpler than most of his other arrangements, at 32 bars with no repeats or *Da Capos*. Nevertheless, *By An' By* is poignantly expressive, marked 'Slowly' at the beginning, and 'Very slow' and *dolce* near the end, with several different

THE TIMES DO NOT PERMIT

dynamics written in by hand and two short Alto *divisi* passages. Example 7.6 picks it up in the middle and takes it to the ending in bar 32.

Burleigh was the major source of spirituals for Dvořák,[25] who famously adapted 'Go Tell It' in the first movement of his *Cello Concerto* Op. 104. Moerane's setting of *Go Tell It On The Mountains* is only 24 bars long, but it is elaborate and joyful, moving from SATB choir to a 'Quartet' of four solo voices and then to eight parts – soloists and choir. He subtitled the piece 'Christmas', and may have envisaged it as a church anthem. Example 7.7 shows *Go Tell It On The Mountains* bars 17–25, at the moment where the soloists join the choir.

Ex. 7.7: *Go Tell It On The Mountains* bars 17–25 (courtesy of the Moerane family). For a live recording made by The Chanticleer Singers and Quava Vocal Group conducted by Richard Cock, visit https://tinyurl.com/3d39vka8

In *I Got A Home In-a Dat Rock*, the Sopranos carry the melody throughout, and the accompanying voices hum or sing the lyrics. The tempo, *Tranquillo ma allegramente* (peaceful but keep it moving) is unusual for Moerane; there are no dynamic or expression marks aside from two hand-written hairpin *crescendos* and all four of the eight-bar verses are the same. *I Stood On De Ribber* is scored for SSATB. Moerane gives the 1st Sopranos the text in the three verses, while the remaining SATB chorus hums a cascading sequence of chords, like bells ringing, creating musical contrasts between the verses and the more rousing choruses of 'O mourner don't you weep', while a briefer version of the chorus occurs at the end as a Coda. There are two versions of the typescript, the second one clarifying that both verses 1 and 2 and the chorus are sung before verse 3 and the Coda. The chorus-verse structure of *It's Me, O Lord* is simpler, with three choruses and two verses between them, and two-bar phrases constantly shared between Sopranos and SATB. The music is seamless, with increasing harmonic and contrapuntal elaborations of the theme as the piece progresses.

The typescript of *Witness* simply says 'Negro spiritual' at the top of the first page rather than 'Negro spiritual harmonised by M.M. Moerane', as his other arrangements do. The harmonies are the most diatonic of Moerane's eight spirituals, and in *Witness* they are antiphonal, as in *It's Me, O Lord*, except that the question-answer phrases are only one bar long. The Soprano leads, and the chorus hums or echoes the words 'for my Lord'. The four-verse-plus-chorus structure of the song is somewhat complicated, however, and so in the ACE publication the song is written out in full and lasts 70 bars in all.

Shenandoah is the only one of Moerane's arrangements of North American songs that is not a 'Negro spiritual' but a folksong, attributed to the white 'voyageurs' and traders who sometimes intermarried into indigenous American families. In Source 2 (see Chapter 6), the words 'Br. Sea shanty' are typed next to the work as listed there, although it is possibly not British in origin. Iraqois Chief Shenandoah was an indigenous chief from Virginia, the state whose major river is named for him. The likely source that Moerane used is a book of *Sailor Shanties* compiled by Richard Runciman Terry and published by Curwen in the 1920s or 1930s,[26] because at the top of the score, Moerane attributes the 3rd stanza to

'R.R. Terry with John Curwen and Sons' permission', although it is unclear what source he used for the other verses. Moerane's begins TTBB with the tune in 1st Bass; the second verse is for SATB with the tune in the Soprano; in the third verse, the Sopranos divide and the tune is sung by the Altos with the four other parts humming 'with half-open mouth', as Moerane notes at the foot of the score. Example 7.8 gives bars 1–20, which is most of the song, to illustrate these changing textures and the way the melody shifts between high and low voices.

Ex. 7.8: *Shenandoah* bars 1–20 (courtesy of the Moerane family). For audio, visit https://tinyurl.com/299ncmsz

Moerane's spirituals are not only quite varied, musically, they also confirm how aware he was of the links between African aspirations and African-American aspirations. They connect him with a host of other composers since Burleigh who used spirituals in South Africa, in Africa and throughout the African diaspora.

8 | Songs about Family, Community and Tradition

Moerane was a family man who spent much of his life in rural communities and was attuned to their traditions. This chapter explores 17 songs about family, community and traditional life. They have features in common with songs discussed in Chapters 7 and 9, but their lyrics and musical styles – sometimes drawing on traditional sources – set them apart. Moerane was knowledgeable about Sotho folk music, although he explicitly quotes it only in his symphonic poem *Fatše La Heso*. Because Western elements dominate his choral language, his use of traditional elements elsewhere are at risk of being overlooked. Half the songs discussed in this chapter are for female voices, with content associated with children or children's games.

Moerane uses SATB in eight songs: *'Mankokotsane (The Rain Game)*, *Alina, Ha Ke Balahē (Who Says I'm Running Away?)*, *Letsatsi (The Sun)*, *Liphala (Whistles)*, *Matlala (Matlala)*, *Morena Tlake (King Vulture)* and *Seotsanyana (Rock Kestrel)*. He uses four female voices (SSAA) in *Liflaga (Flags)*, three (SAA) in *'Mankholikholi (Yellow-billed Kite)*, *Bonukunyana (My Little Baby!)*, *Ma-Homemakers (Ingoma Ka Zenzele) (Homemakers)*, *Mosele (Mosele)*, *Sa 'Mokotsane (Wailing)* and *Sekolo Se Koetsoe (School's Out)*; and two (SA) in *Pelo Le Moea (Heart And Soul)* and *Nonyana Tse Ntle (Beautiful Birds)*. I begin with the smallest social unit in these 17 songs, that of 'family', and proceed outwards to works that speak of community, tradition and history.

Songs about family

Bonukunyana, Ma-Homemakers, Mosele, Sa 'Mokotsane, Pelo Le Moea and *Alina* all tell of family love. *Bonukunyana* survives as a fragment (the ending), but this and the title indicate a song composed to soothe a baby. (One of the folk songs Moerane quotes in *Fatše La Heso* is a lullaby.) Under 'Remarks' in *Bonukunyana*'s listing in the SAMRO 'Catalogue' are the words 'From "Setsoto" Junior Poems'.[1] Moerane attributes the lyrics of six other songs to 'Setsoto', which implies drawing on the traditional: *'Mankokotsane, Ha Ke Balahē, Mosele, Letsatsi, Pelo Le Moea* and *Ngeloi La Me*. These songs all have short texts and relate to a Sotho children's story, rhyme or game song.

'Mosele' is a generic Sesotho name for a girl child, normally the youngest in the family. In Moerane's *Mosele*, the narrator chides her for messing up her hair: *'Jo 'na! Mosele, ngoan'a ngoan'a ke Moriri oa hao, O tsabeha hakakang!* [...] *Tlisa lehare ke o kute, jo 'na! jo 'na!* (Hey, Mosele, my grandchild! Your hair is dreadful! [...] Goodness! Bring scissors and I'll cut it off!). These lines illustrate the humour of 'Setsoto' texts, their repetitions and the use of the word 'jo', a common expression of shock that punctuates the song and dramatises the scene. Moerane uses capital letters every few words, as he does in all his choral music to denote the beginning of a new line in a poem.

Moerane's wife Betty wrote the lyrics of *Ma-Homemakers*, and it is the only song by Moerane written in both their respective mother tongues: Sesotho and isiXhosa. It probably dates from the late 1940s or early 1950s when the Moeranes were living in Queenstown with six growing children, a time when Mrs Moerane's homemaking skills would have really 'shone', as the lyrics say. The song begins, *'Vukani, vukani ma-Afrika! Velani nilibone ikhwezi le-Afrika, Homemakers'* ('Arise, get up, African people! Come and see the morning star of Africa, our Homemakers'). It may pay tribute to the Zenzele movement in Lesotho, founded in the 1940s as the Basutoland Homemakers Association with Bernice Mohapeloa (a relative of the composer Mohapeloa) as its first president.[2] Basutoland Homemakers Association activities were concerned with, among other things, helping refugees to enter Lesotho from apartheid South Africa.[3] The music is for female voices and is in perpetual motion, often repeating the word 'Homemakers'. Knowing that Moerane was familiar with Wagner, one is tempted to compare the opening bars given in Example 8.1 with the women's 'spinning chorus' from Act II Scene I of *The Flying Dutchman*.

Ex. 8.1: *Ma-Homemakers* bars 1–23 (courtesy of the Moerane family). For a live recording made by the Quava Vocal Group conducted by Sabelo Mthembu, visit https://tinyurl.com/yh3njswf

Sa 'Mokotsane has a serious text even though the music is cheerful and full of syncopations. 'Sa 'Mokotsane' is a lamentation: if you '*ho lla sa 'mokotsane*', you 'cry bitterly, loudly'.[4] The lyrics outline the advice an adult gives a younger person on facing difficulties and disappointment with courage, and staying positive when friends desert you. The word 'thuso' (help) features prominently in the text. Thuso is the name of Moerane's second-born son; perhaps the song indirectly refers to the hardships Thuso faced when his family were forcibly removed from their home at 10 Scanlen Street, Queenstown, and he was given a banning order. One page of the manuscript is numbered '33', which suggests that Moerane initially wrote his scores by hand in a foolscap exercise book, a practice not uncommon among African teacher-composers of his generation.

Pelo Le Moea is a simple statement of love in two short verses. The first begins: *"Me oee! Ere ke u joetse se ratoang ke 'na: Ke uena le ntate'* ('Dearest Mum, Tell you what I really love, It's you and Dad') and the second verse ends: '*Ke tla thaba pelo le moea, 'Nete bo! pelo le moea*' ('It makes me overjoyed, In truth, heart and soul!'). It is a perfect study in two-part counterpoint, with all 32 bars given in Example 8.2.

The homely style is reminiscent of Schumann; indeed, the last few notes could almost be a quote from Schumann's gentle piano piece *Waldscenen* No. 6: 'Herberge' ('Inn'). Moerane gives the option of E-flat or F as the key, to allow for variation in children's voice ranges.

Alina is a long, dramatic narrative (57 bars), very different from the simple domestic pieces just described. The lyrics are written from the point of view of an anxious family calling their daughter (Alina) home for the evening, and their fear that she might fall prey to 'Mr Bigmouth' ('*kheleke*

Ex. 8.2: *Pelo Le Moea* bars 1–32 (courtesy of the Moerane family). For audio, visit https://tinyurl.com/3s86re9d

Ralipuo'); a cautionary tale advising young women to beware of men. The setting is rural – streams and valleys are often mentioned – and the music is restless and full of expressive harmonies, rising and falling sequences and long melodic lines. Example 8.3 gives bars 9–23.

This is yet another demonstration of how instrumental Moerane's vocal writing can be (where does one breathe?), and in addition to this, the vocal ranges are wide – the Bass part covers almost two octaves. Why Alina? According to Mpho Ndebele, who translated the lyrics, it was once a fairly common name in the townships of Johannesburg.

Although both *Ngeloi La Me* (*My Angel*) and *Ntsoaki* (a name) are about family, they use existing poems rather than lyrics adapted from 'Setsoto', and are therefore discussed in the next chapter.

Ex. 8.3: *Alina* bars 9–23 (courtesy of the Moerane family). For audio, visit https://tinyurl.com/yrv6u3zc

Songs about community

The five songs *'Mankokotsane, Ha Ke Balahē, Letsatsi, Seotsanyana, 'Mankholikholi* and *Nonyana Tse Ntle* are about games (the rain game, cat-and-mouse) or natural phenomena (the sun, the kite, the rock kestrel, beautiful birds). The lyrics of *'Mankokotsane* are adapted from 'Setsoto'. In the *Southern Sotho–English Dictionary* the word is spelt "Mankōkōsanē' – without the 't' – and means 'a game which takes place under rain'.[5] As with *'Mankholikholi*, the words of *'Mankokotsane* draw on an outdoor game that children play in Lesotho when it is raining. They say a rhyme as they hop in the rain, through which they learn that work must go on even when it rains. An important lesson, given that rain is not so plentiful in Lesotho that one can afford to interrupt work for it – especially true for farmers, who constitute most of the population. The song begins in a leisurely fashion and then speeds up, its style far from child-like. It has strong melodic lines that rise and fall as different sections of the song succeed each other, catchy syncopated rhythms and several modulations.

Ha Ke Balehē also has a 'Setsoto' text; in fact, the same tale is found in Sepedi as 'Segwaga' and 'Tselane', songs that children learn in kindergarten. It is scored for SATB, however, so perhaps Moerane had a high school choir in mind, or realised that adults would also enjoy its humour. It is a dialogue between a cat and a mouse, in which the cat tries to trick the mouse by asking why he's running away (with the intention of pouncing when the mouse stops to answer). The mouse doesn't fall for this ploy, repeating 'I'm not running away' countless times as he runs, claiming (as he reaches safety) that he's 'just energetic'.

Letsatsi's 'Setsoto' humour arises from the way the sun, as narrator, declares himself king of all good things in the world, including plants, animals, clouds, heat and cold – the king of everything, in fact. But while the sun may control people's lives, it does not control their opinions of the weather, which in this song are parodied in the form of community complaints: it is never just hot or cold, but always 'too hot' or 'too cold'; either way, people are never satisfied.

Moerane attributes the words of *Seotsanyana* to 'a Mosotho', meaning a person from Lesotho (plural Basotho). This suggests that he learnt the words and perhaps even the tune from a particular person rather than from his general knowledge of Sotho folklore. It describes a symbiotic relationship between two very common birds of prey in southern Africa: the rock kestrel and the hawk. *Phakoe* is a generic name for hawk in Lesotho, although the falcon is actually more common in southern Africa.[6] The rock kestrel is recognisable by its russet colouring and the way it 'hovers frequently, hanging motionless in wind' before diving on its prey.[7] It catches prey, in fact, as much as the hawk does. However, in this song, the kestrel shares the kill just made by the hawk, as they sit amicably side-by-side – or so goes the story, but if the moral is intended to be 'You scratch my back, I'll scratch yours', it doesn't quite work (for the hawk). It is 90 bars long and Moerane composes it as a series of contrasting sections with very little repetition of previous bars, but with two repeated sections. It thus feels like quite a long song. There are some unexpected chromatic harmonies and dissonances, and a number of stop-starts in the rhythm, including two bars rest at one point, which is where Example 8.4 begins – in the middle of the song – which also

Ex. 8.4: *Seotsanyana* bars 41–66 (courtesy of the Moerane family). For a live recording made by the Quava Vocal Group conducted by Sabelo Mthembu, visit https://tinyurl.com/25455vws

illustrates how quickly the music can change. The last four lines hint that this may be a children's game song with clapping involved.

'Mankholikholi is the Sesotho name for two other common southern African birds of prey: the yellow-billed kite and the black kite.[8] In the 1950

Ex. 8.5: 'Mankholikholi bars 1–25 (courtesy of the Moerane family). For audio, visit https://tinyurl.com/2b3ejxm4

Sesotho–English dictionary, 'mankholikholi is spelled 'mankholi-kholi, or even 'mankholi, and its meaning is given as 'black kite, Milvus Korshun' and metaphorically, 'a fabulous person supposed to be in the air'.[9] It is also the name of a mythical creature with whom children in Lesotho communicate when they lose their milk teeth, requesting that 'Mankholikholi send them strong permanent teeth. (In Sepedi culture, children are told to leave their tooth in a shoe under the bed, so that the rat will come and leave money for it.)[10] According to cultural historian Zacharias Matšela, children in Lesotho play a game involving 'Mankholikholi without reference to the tooth, and 'in that case the children merely ask 'Mankholikholi to give them unripe sorghum [talane] to plant on the hillside [to which] 'Mankholikholi responds by saying "I can't give you talane because you have no large grain basket"'.[11] This game is referred to in the song lyrics, and the music clearly reflects the fun of a game, including the call of the kite – 'heea!', and there are many repeated words in the text. If *'Mankholikholi* is not an actual folksong, then Moerane has written something very much like one, as Example 8.5, with its declamations and jaunty rhythms, shows.

Nonyana Tse Ntle is one of only two extant songs by Moerane for SA or 'SC' (Soprano, Contralto), as he writes on the score.[12] It is also one of his shortest songs, at 26 bars: the complete typescript shown in Figure 8.1 is

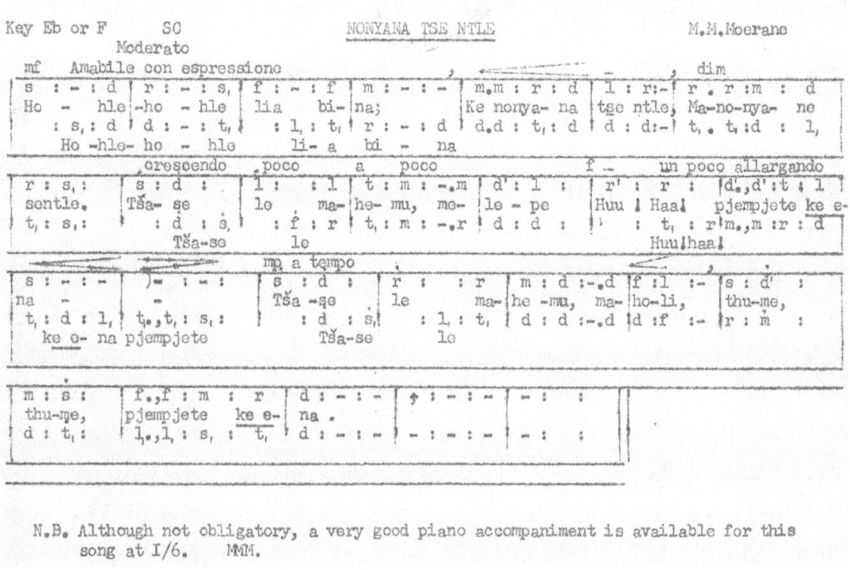

Figure 8.1: *Nonyana Tse Ntle* typescript (courtesy Neo Mahase Moerane)

only half a page long. Moerane writes such ingenious melodies and counterpoint that one wonders why he suggests (on the manuscript) adding piano accompaniment to this perfect miniature. Perhaps he was thinking of inexperienced voices struggling to keep pitch.

Despite its brevity, *Nonyana Tse Ntle* contains many different expression marks and dynamics, as well as introducing a number of common southern African birds: an ornithological as well as a musical lesson. The birds mentioned range in size from small (pipit) to medium (rock thrush, bokmakierie, starling) to large (crane). The bokmakierie, which is also sometimes called 'pjempjete', is a shrike; the crowned crane (*lehehemu*, plural *mahemu* in Sesotho) is only found in eastern South Africa.[13] Perhaps this is a hint as to when the song was written, as Moerane worked in that part of the country in 1959. Perhaps, given that the birds 'are everywhere and they are singing', as the first line says, the song was composed in spring. The price of one shilling and sixpence shows that the piece was written before 1961, anyway, which was when South Africa abandoned the British pound for the rand. (Lesotho abandoned the pound in 1966 for the loti.) That Moerane charged for his accompaniment is not surprising, given that his list of works (Source 2 in Chapter 6) shows a number of prices.

The note also suggests that it was not entirely unusual to accompany tonic solfa songs in Moerane's day, and that some African school choirs might have had access to a piano. He hints that the piano part would enhance the song, calling it 'a very good piano accompaniment', although he does add that it is 'not obligatory'. A more interesting question: did Moerane write this note only intending to produce a piano accompaniment on demand? Because one has not survived.

Liphala and *Sekolo Se Koetsoe* are songs about school. All the songs here, in a sense, could be 'school songs', as Robin Wells called them in 1994. This implies that they are for two, three or four voices with texts that appeal to children, and music that when originally 'fostered by missionaries' was 'based around the hymn style they had imported from Europe'. As the style progressed, what became obvious was that this kind of song was 'important as a medium of instruction'.[14] The composer Mohapeloa is the example Wells gives of what such songs are like, but in Moerane's case they stretch musical conventions and voices more than Mohapeloa's do, although they still seem highly suitable as (if not intended as) teaching material.

Moerane's *Liphala* is a fine example of a school song. It was one of his earliest pieces and because it was published, we know a little more than usual about its origins. As explained in Chapter 7, the first print run of *Liphala* at the Lovedale Press was 1 500 copies; and this can only have been because it was destined, as all Lovedale songs were, for the school market. The reviewer's report, anonymously written (although the author was very likely the Cape school music inspector, Mr S Newns), gives 'criticisms' as the points below are called, that nevertheless led to the conclusion that the work was satisfactory enough to 'continue' (i.e. publish):

a. More marcato than moderato. Has 7th chord transition. Rhythmic staccato. Harmony good. In secondary 4 parts chords come in regularly in after-beats in B part [2nd section].

b. Employs different chords for same note & tempo is regular. Chords are minor in B part.

c. Employs rapid triplets in his C part & ends of [sic] with a smooth cadence. Suggests finale – major and minor parts interwoven. Towards his cadence he employs augmented chords. Very good ending – suggests grand finale – Orchestral. An interchange of same notes between sopran[o] & bass. Is a perpetual movement. Music + words suited. Continue.[15]

Moerane simplified a few rhythms and harmonies in his revision, making the latter less chromatic in places, but even so, the song is not at all easy. It is cast in fast quadruple tempo with many triplets, dotted figures and repeated notes, a middle section in the relative minor that relies heavily on staccato quavers, constantly changing dynamics throughout, and passages that seem dedicated to perfecting intervals in a major scale from unison to octave. Moerane's principal at Peka High School, Tseliso Makhakhe, who was himself a choral conductor, had found it 'very complex […] beautiful but too difficult for us', when his school choir sang it.[16] The style is indebted to operetta; indeed, the year in which he wrote *Liphala* was the year Moerane helped produce *Prince Ferdinand* at Lovedale. *Liphala* is a song about singing and about school: the name can translate as 'whistle' or, in the case of a song by Mohapeloa of the same name, 'Horns'. Moerane's

Ex. 8.6: *Liphala* bars 1–18 (courtesy of the Moerane family). For audio, visit https://tinyurl.com/5abrk9hs

score demonstrates ways in which tonic solfa notation deals with some of the musical complexities he had in mind, and the song clearly shows what he wanted children to learn through singing it. The first section, given in

Example 8.6, seems to mimic a boy whistling to his friends as they join each other in walking to school – as is common for children in rural Africa, who sometimes travel miles on foot. Here is the text in English, as translated by Mpho Ndebele:

> Come, let's teach ourselves songs which are played by whistling, at our school, When we walk along the road in line: Our school, whistling, They go: 'Tha-thatha-ba', be happy, joy to all; happiness. They go: 'Tse-tse', laugh! They say, 'Let's laugh and be joyful' Come, let's learn the songs the young men of our school sing, Let's enjoy ourselves, even in Heaven they love these songs. Let's celebrate, we're so happy! Rejoice!

Sekolo Se Koetsoe (*School's Out*) is another take on school days, but does not present the unrestrainedly joyful picture painted in *Liphala*. Ostensibly, it is about school holidays, but it hints at leaving school altogether, and the anxiety attached to that. Here are the last few lines: '*Ho thoe re tla hloella lihlorong tsa thaba Re bone mosi oa kepe tsa ntoa Ha re theoha teng re tla-bi-tlabikela Na re sa tla fihla lebopong la leoatle. Tsatsi le liketse re sa le hole Hantle-ntle re ea kae? Hantle-tle re ea phomolong.*' ('Maybe we'll climb high mountains And see the smoke of battle-ships. As we walk down, scrambling clumsily, Will we ever reach the beach? The sun has set and we still have far to go. Where are we really going? After all, we are on vacation.'). The imagery progresses from the local to the global, from close to home to far away, as the poem becomes a metaphor for life's potential joys and threats. The music is in the style of a jaunty gavotte, and therefore not all that far from the sound-world of *Liphala*, but it changes towards the end, matching the more portentous words.

Songs about history and tradition

One of the three songs discussed in this final section is completely unknown: *Liflaga* (*Flags*). It is the only extant work for SSAA, although the two Soprano parts sometimes double up. The lyrics strongly suggest that it was written around the time of Lesotho's independence, 4 October 1966 – the day the Union Jack was lowered over what had once been the British Protectorate of Basutoland, and the Lesotho flag raised. This is a joyful victory: *'Hure! Helang! lona liflaga tsa moo, Rea bitsana, Rea thusana!'* ('Hooray! Hey! you flags over there! We call to each other, help each other!') *'Ba hlotsoe, rea hlakisa; Nala ke nala, nala e teng Eona e teng ke phetho.'* ('They are beaten, it's clear; It is time to reap the harvest, We've done it, it's all over!'). It is three minutes long, a difficult piece moving at a brisk tempo, full of syncopated rhythms and semiquavers. This may be the reason there is no record of its being sung by the school choirs for whom it was probably intended.

Morena Tlake and *Matlala* are in a class of their own. They are two of Moerane's most magnificent choral works, widely known and much admired ever since they were first prescribed for competitions in the late 1960s to early 1970s. *Matlala* is popular with choirs because it feels like 'a typical Sesotho song', as Victor Lechesa puts it.[17] The lyrics may well have been inspired by a traditional source, but they are written by Moerane. As with *Morena Tlake*, there are few words. Only three sentences are repeated for 92 bars: 'The ancestors long for matlala. How do they see it if they're dead? They see it through cracks in their graves.' The word 'Matlala' literally refers to choice cuts of meat from an animal slaughtered during a ritual. These cuts are often set aside for a special category of people, in this case the ancestors, who hold a special place in Africa culture. On a literal level, the song is about appeasing the dead and acknowledging the things that happened to them during their life, according to Mpho Ndebele, who translated the text. On a metaphorical level, it is about atonement – or the way deeds may come back to haunt you.

Matlala has a droll side: the dead (*'Bonkgono'* literally means 'Grannies') hanker after meat, even from the grave; the entire second section, which includes a long musical repeat, is about the dead grannies peeping out. The song's rhetorical and celebratory style is shot through with rapid call-and-response declamations, relying heavily on modal writing and diatonic harmonies. Unlike most of Moerane's songs, it is harmonically simple (one chord sequence sounds like the beginning of the 'Hallelujah Chorus'). Both music and text celebrate reconciliations between past and present, the living and the dead. According to Tseliso Makhakhe, it was an immediate hit when the Lesotho school choir competition prescribed it in 1966. As we saw in Chapter 3, a group of teachers at Peka premiered it in front of the whole school. The pupils 'were really surprised, and excited, that our teacher has composed such a song'.[18] The first performance of *Matlala* must have been sung almost one voice per part, then, because of the frequent *divisi*; the feeling of intimacy this must have generated is remarkable to think of. It makes one wonder how Moerane imagined his music, what density of sound he had in mind, what kind of acoustic. We do know that his music was composed for what we would now think of as amateur choirs, much of it for children – and that is even more remarkable to consider, given the musical challenges he poses.

Morena Tlake is one of the few Moerane songs with two Altos throughout, and Soprano and Bass sometimes divide as well. Not surprisingly, Moerane's writing for this rich contrapuntal texture is virtuoso. Indeed, it relies more than any other work of his on changing textures. Although not as chromatic as some of his other works, it is rhythmically and texturally his most 'modernist' piece. The opening motif is declaimed in unison in the key of D minor or 'lah mode', which is rarely used by Moerane – or indeed most tonic solfa composers, who often stay within the safer terrain of the 'doh mode', the major key. A relentless *ostinato* figure in the lower voices provides the energy for long-breathed phrases in the upper voices that tell the story of 'King Vulture'. Tseliso Makhakhe explains *Morena Tlake*'s text:

> Whenever there is carrion, the crows would smell that and identify it. Then they would fly in that direction and the vultures would see the crows, the white-collared crow, who would then call upon the vultures to follow, to go there and to open up the carcass. 'Phunya malana re', 'Open up' so that you can have access to the entrails. Because the crows can't do that, and because the vultures [...] will do the vivisection.[19]

The carcass is a dog: '*Hng! Ke'ng hoo? Monko o monate Ntja e shoele, lekokotoana.*' ('Hng! What's that? Nice smell! A dead dog, his skin is tough.'). The music relies throughout on declamations such as this – one group calling another to the feast of blood. It is shorter than many of Moerane's other well-known songs (55 bars), and there are no repeated sections, although choirs may be tempted to repeat them in performance. There are many repeated notes and phrases, yet not a single note feels wasted. In its minimal simplicity, the work perfectly combines Moerane's knowledge of Western classical musical momentum and phrasing with his understanding of rhetoric in traditional music. His additional Alto or Bass voices flesh out the rich harmonies from time to time into five or six parts. The first D minor section (marked *Con energia* – with energy – in Moerane's score) leads to an E minor for the middle section (bar 34), then touches briefly on D major before the work ends in G major. None of his other songs has such a remarkable tonality, and few of his works use chromatic harmony so relentlessly.

The opening phrase hints at the beginning of Wagner's 'The Ride of the Valkyries', marked *mezzo forte* at the beginning and *forte* at the end, with a pause on the penultimate note: very detailed expression marks, even for Moerane. The next few bars of declamatory chords call upon Morena Tlake 'to come and dissect the bowels'; a *ritenuto* for two bars of a descending chromatic motif ends in a dramatic pause. Then, *a tempo* and *mezzo piano*, begins the frenetic *ostinato* that dominates most of the piece: a five-note rhythmic figure to the words 'mo-re-na tla-ke', tossed between lower voices. Over this almost *sotto voce* accompaniment, as Example 8.7 shows, Moerane begins a slow, sustained chromatic melody, all the more chilling for being sung to the Sesotho word, 'Hng!': a difficult syllable for choirs to sustain on long notes, which means, 'What's that?' and refers to the 'nice smell' of the dead dog.

Unusually for Moerane, but not surprising in such a defiant song, he quotes from the end of Enoch Sontonga's African anthem *Nkosi Sikelel' iAfrika* in the final cadence of *Morena Tlake*, which gives a triumphant resolution to this highly dramatic song, as shown in Example 8.8.

Morena Tlake first gained prominence in choral competitions during the early 1960s, while Moerane was teaching at Peka High School. When it was prescribed for the 'Ford–Old Mutual Choirs National Finals' in December 1987, Trod Ledwaba wrote in the programme notes that Moerane adapted the words from 'a street song that was popular in the 1940s', which he quotes, in tonic solfa notation:

| .m : s | f . f :–m | r . r :–m |–d : | .m : s | f . f :–m | r . r :–m |–d : |
| .d : m | r . r :–d | t$_1$. t$_1$:–d |–d : | .d : m | r . r :–d | t$_1$. t$_1$:–d |–d : |

Ledwaba also claims that the work was written 'for the occasion of [Moerane's] celebration party in honour of his graduation',[20] in which

Ex. 8.7: *Morena Tlake* bars 1–18 (courtesy of the Moerane family). For audio, visit https://tinyurl.com/8atmyvfw

case it would date from 1941 rather than from the 1960s – unless he was referring to his son Thabo's graduation. The song is experimental enough, at any rate, to belong to the 1930s, the period when Moerane

Ex. 8.8: *Morena Tlake* bars 52–55 (courtesy of the Moerane family). For audio, visit https://tinyurl.com/mvsx2d86

was studying advanced harmony, counterpoint and composition at university. To me, the lyrics are a political allegory for the tearing apart of people's lives in Lesotho during the 1960s, one party set against another, with countless political killings in the run-up to elections in 1965 and independence in 1966.

9 | Songs of Love and Loss

The 18 songs in this chapter are distinguished from songs in Chapters 7 and 8 by their texts, which are in almost all cases drawn from Sotho authors, and are intensely personal. They are the most 'literary' of Moerane's songs, as it were. He was very well-read in Sesotho and English literature, as has been shown. Thirteen songs are for SATB: *'Mitsa-Mahosi (A Call To Kings), Barali Ba Jerusalema (Daughters of Jerusalem), Della, Hoja Ke Nonyana (If I Were a Bird), Khati (Skipping Game), Lebili (Wheel), Likhohlo (Gorges), Mahakoe (Jewels), Monyaka Oa Pelo (A Joyful Heart), Naleli Ka 'Ngoe (One Star at a Time), Paki Ha Li Eo (No Witnesses), Satane A Tšeha (Le Joe-leputsoa) (The Devil Laughed (Johannesburg))* and *Sylvia*. Five are for SAA: *Lia Qhomaqhoma (They Frolic), Mohokare (The Caledon River), Ngeloi La Me (My Angel), Ntsoaki* (a girl's name) and *Paka-Mahlomola (Creator of Sorrow)*.

Because they are so diverse in their musical character and textual themes, I group and discuss these works according to the authors of the poems that Moerane drew upon. Bennett Makalo Khaketla is the poet for five songs: *'Mitsa-Mahosi (A Call To Kings), Khati, Lia Qhomaqhoma, Likhohlo* and *Monyaka Oa Pelo*. The work of Khaketla's wife, 'Masechele Caroline Ntseliseng, is used in one song, *Hoja Ke Nonyana*. Five songs are based on poems by Kemuel Edward Ntsane: *Ngeloi La Me, Mohokare, Paka-Mahlomola, Paki Ha Li Eo* and *Satana A Tšeha (Le Joe-leputsoa)*. 'Mabasiea Jeannette Mahalefele is the poet whose work is used for *Ntsoaki*.[1] The words of *Barali Ba Jerusalema* are from the Old Testament's 'Song of Songs'. *Della* uses a poem by the Xhosa poet, Sampson Synor Mputa,[2] and Moerane himself wrote the lyrics for *Mahakoe* and *Sylvia*. Moerane rarely uses an original poem in its entirety, preferring to extract verses that must have inspired his musical sensibilities.

All of Moerane's songs are about love, one could say: love of parents, children, siblings, the love between lovers and friends, love of nature, country, community, home, and love of God or one's ancestors. Some of the songs in this chapter are 'love songs' in a more specific and personal sense, addressing a woman, whether she be lover, mother or child. *Della* and *Sylvia* are women's names, and the songs celebrate the person named. As already mentioned, Moerane was most remembered as the composer of these two songs, along with *Morena Tlake*.[3]

Songs set to poems by Bennett Khaketla

Bennett Makalo Khaketla (1913–2000) was 'arguably the most significant writer from Lesotho after Thomas Mofolo'.[4] He wrote scathing critiques of both British colonialism and Leabua Jonathan's post-independence coup, as well as stories, novels, plays and poems. One of his pupils was Tseliso Makhakhe, who remembers him not only as a prolific writer but also for the way he 'revolutionised the approach to the teaching of Sesotho. And today [2014] the approach used is called "Khaketla's Sesotho". He made it so interesting, and so easy to understand', says Makhakhe.[5] His name appears in the Timeline as one of the co-founders of Basutoland's first political and pro-BCP newspaper, *Mohlabani* (*Warrior*), and he was a declared Pan-Africanist who had joined the PAC in 1959,[6] an 'African nationalist' who was 'to some extent influenced by the writings of Frantz Fanon, and one concerned with the role of African intellectuals in the continent's anti-colonial and revolutionary movements.'[7] In 1961, he decided to break away from the BCP and form a new party, the Freedom Party. This merged in 1962 with the Marema–Tlou Party to form the Marematlou Freedom Party. His 1970 book, *Lesotho 1970: An African Coup Under the Microscope* is a courageous critique of Chief Leabua Jonathan's politics, written during those turbulent times. Khaketla's writing is vivid and journalistic. Here is an extract from his description of the coup:

> The declaration of the state of emergency [on 30 January 1970] was as unexpected as the explosion of the first atomic bomb on Hiroshima. No one had ever thought such a thing could happen in Lesotho.

> After our long and close association with the fountainhead of modern democracy [Britain], we all thought everybody understood the meaning of democracy [even] Chief Leabua [...] Thus when our turn to become independent came our breasts swelled with pride, for although a small nation, we had an unshakeable belief in our capacity to show the rest of the world that had become contemptuous of African independence, that democracy can and will work even in dark Africa. But at one stroke of the pen our alabaster pot of democratic ideals and concepts lay shattered at our feet. Our modern Solon [Leabua] had, overnight, become a constitution-buster. Thus was ushered in one of those awful periods which occur in the history of men. The noble Basotho nation fell from its high pedestal with a bang and a crash, and lost all trace of sense or purpose.[8]

Khaketla was not only a writer but also a choral conductor, and in 1975 his choir, the St James's Church Choir of Maseru, was prohibited from entering South Africa in order to sing in Soweto.[9]

Moerane chose poems of Khaketla's that reveal his concern with the relationship between language, culture and politics. 'Mitsa-Mahosi is a love poem, probably known to Moerane from Khaketla's collection, *Lipshamathe*.[10] Moerane's musical dramatisation in 'Mitsa-Mahosi of a young man struck down by love is expressed in a sudden change of key from F major to B-flat major, voices jumping up an octave, dynamics suddenly moving from *piano* to *forte*, and a catchy rhythmic tune that appears unexpectedly in the middle. These features exemplify Moerane's mimetic approach to word setting: his music often serves to portray or enhance the meaning of the words. In 'Mitsa-Mahosi, Moerane writes for the choir syllabically, as if they were bemoaning with one voice the dire effects of the onset of love.

Khaketla must have adapted a folk tale in the poem of his that Moerane uses in *Khati*. The song describes a skipping rope made from the Cape tulip, a ubiquitous plant of the genus *moraea* that in this song goes by the Sesotho name of *teele*. (As we saw in Chapter 1, Khati is the name of one of Moerane's early ancestors, and in Chapter 3, Matsobane Putsoa described the first performance of the song at a Peka High School.) The reed-like part of the plant is used to weave many things, in this case a skipping rope; both the rope and the game associated with it are called *'khati'*. Grass is very important in the culture and economy of Lesotho: the house-roofs, mats, buckets, brooms and beer-strainers are all made from grass;[11] cattle and sheep depend on it, and thus so do humans. *Khati* has an infectious melodic line and is full of syncopated rhythms and contrapuntal movement. One imagines it making a perfect action song for children, or a song for skipping. The section from bar 34 to the end given in Example 9.1 is effectively a 'final chorus', with some voices humming and others singing. The Altos and Basses sometimes subdivide here, although not at the same time. All of this indicates that those five teachers who originally sang the 'new release', as Putsoa called it, must have been extremely versatile musicians.

Lia Qhomaqhoma is an evocative description of young lambs frolicking in the spring, written from a child's point of view. As is customary in rural Africa, children usually look after the family's livestock, and it is men's work to manage the livestock, hence 'father's lambs'. It is common for African children to do this over weekends, during school holidays, and even before and after school, as a way of helping with the family chores. Moerane, who wrote this text, almost certainly did this himself as a boy, growing up on the family farm in Mangoloaneng. The music is full of staccatos, accents and repeated notes, as if describing the frolicking lambs. At the same time, Moerane is developing an awareness among the singers of the techniques that music uses. Like all Moerane's SAA songs, *Lia Qhomaqhoma* was almost certainly intended for primary schools or girls' schools.

Moerane adapts a poem by Khaketla in *Likhohlo* in order to emphasise the way light creeps into the deep valleys and gorges created by Lesotho's towering mountains. According to *Encyclopedia Britannica*, '"maloti" means merely "mountains" or "in the mountains" as far as people living in Lesotho are concerned. To people in the country's western lowlands, which themselves are more than 3 300 feet (1 000 metres), in elevation it signifies the mountainous eastern two-thirds of Lesotho. This contains the tallest mountain peaks in southern Africa, the highest of which, Mount Ntlenyana, is 11 424 feet (3 482 metres) above sea level.'[12] The lyrics begin 'An easterly wind is blowing, The dew has settled like diamonds, The sun is an enchanting circle Shimmering on the dew', which suggests sunrise

Ex. 9.1: *Khati* bars 34–53 (courtesy of the Moerane family). For audio, visit https://tinyurl.com/z9s8jbnb

rather than sunset, as does the line, 'The birdsong is simply breathtaking.' The poem is not just about the beauty of nature, even in such deep, cold valleys, but about the fact that 'Rivers, gorges, and valleys Are the creation of the one on high'. In line with the reverence of the last line, the music has a gentle hymnal feel from beginning to end, with regular phrasing throughout its 22 bars, simple harmonies, and homogenous writing for the four voices. There are two surviving versions of the score: the composer's original one-page foolscap lined manuscript, numbered page '6'; and a two-page copy of the typescript. The latter has the final few bars of another song to words by Khaketla, *Monyaka Oa Pelo*, at the top of the page, suggesting that Moerane may have worked on the two songs at the same time; or perhaps he finalised them at the same time, as it was his custom to write first by hand and type the final version. The manuscript, on which the Soprano part and the lyrics are written in pen and the other voices in pencil, has handwritten dynamics and expression marks that do not appear on the typescript.

Monyaka Oa Pelo is based on a beautiful love poem in rhyming verse from Khaketla's *Lipshamathe*.[13] Moerane chooses only the first two verses of a seven-verse poem, then cuts out some words and repeats others. Using only selections from Khaketla's much longer poem doesn't make for a short song, however. Moerane's *Monyaka Oa Pelo* is 75 bars long, full of syncopated rhythms, rapid contrapuntal exchanges and bright major harmonies. The music expresses the joyful innocence of young love, and completely ignores the hint in the last line of the lyrics about tears and regret. Moerane's metronome mark of crotchet=138 is very fast, verging on *Presto* rather than the *Allegro* he actually writes for the tempo at the beginning of the score. Moerane gives three options for the key at the top of the typescript: G, G-flat or F. In such cases, the ACE edition always uses the first key, G major, which is higher than the other two, on the basis that it was probably Moerane's first choice, and he might have offered the other keys for the sake of choirs who couldn't easily reach the high notes. Example 9.2 illustrates a section in the middle.

The poem by Khaketla that Moerane uses in *Naleli Ka 'Ngoe* has proved hard to trace; the original perhaps comes from one of Khaketla's Sesotho story books. Just as the manuscript of *Likhohlo* has the page number '6' at the top of the page, so *Naleli* has '7' on the first page in pencil (but nothing on the

Ex. 9.2: *Monyaka Oa Pelo* bars 31–54 (courtesy of the Moerane family). For audio, visit https://tinyurl.com/2a886atr

second). *Sa 'Mokotsane* has pages '33–34' and *Sekolo Se Koetsoe* has '35–38' in blue pen, suggesting that Moerane wrote out fair copies of songs in sequence in an exercise book he took with him as he moved around during his teaching career. The lower number for *Naleli* does not necessarily mean that it is an earlier song, however. The numbering may simply have to do with Moerane's readiness to copy and sell songs. It is scored for SATB and is one of Moerane's most harmonically unadorned songs, almost austere in character. The slow tempo (*Lento*) and stately, syllabic setting convey a mysterious mood appropriate to nightfall and speculation as to what the movement of the stars means as they become visible after dark. 'As if by negotiation', the lyrics end, 'each star seemed to move around others, to shine in its own beauty.' Hence the title 'One star at a time'. Unlike *Monyako Oa Pelo*, then, where words are secondary to music, here the metaphorical inferences in the text are allowed to resonate and to take effect gradually. This is a fairly unusual approach to text setting for Moerane; and the key, G-flat, the modulation to D-flat major in the middle, as well as the long periods when the Bass does not sing, all contribute to the ethereal effect of the piece.

Songs set to poems by Kemuel Ntsane

The best-known works by Kemuel Edward Ntsane (1920–1983) are his 53 poems in the two volumes *Mmusa-pelo I* (Heart-Restorer I, 1946) and *Mmusa-pelo II* (Heart-Restorer II, 1954).[14] He wrote a number of other books, not all of which are still in print, including *Bana ba rona* (1954), *Makumane* (1961), *Nna sajena Kokobela, C.I.D.* (1963), *Bao batho* (1968), *Maqoqo oa Abiele le Johannes* (n.d.), *Masoabi: ngoan'a Mosotho 'a kajeno* (1957), and a Sesotho translation of Shakespeare's *The Merchant of Venice* titled *Mohwebi wa venisi* (1961).[15] Ntsane's work provides evidence, says Ketlalemang Maimane, of the way 'the religious, traditional and western [blend] in modern Sesotho poems',[16] words that could easily be applied to Moerane's songs.

These poems are very different from Khaketla's, not only in this respect, but in terms of subject matter – if one judges Khaketla by the poems that Moerane set. Moerane chose poems that foreground the political history of Lesotho as seen through Ntsane's strong and sometimes stark images, especially poems that concern the country's borders with South Africa. *Ngeloi La Me*, *Mohokare*, *Paka-Mahlomola* and *Satane A Tšeha* are all tales of the mighty Mohokare (Caledon River), the boundary between Lesotho and the Free State province of South Africa. A huge area of the border on the South African side was once part of Moshoeshoe I's lands, as discussed in Chapter 1, and remains contested to this day. Ntsane's poems tell of the many sorrows that people crossing this border from Lesotho had to endure.

Ngeloi La Me is a deeply emotional song based on the poem 'Ha Eso' ('My Roots'), as Moerane writes at the top of the score. It tells of the nostalgia for rural Lesotho homesteads felt by migrant workers in South Africa, who lived in appalling conditions in hostels near the mine dumps. Even though only three female voices are used, the song is 81 bars long and full of changing moods, short phrases, expressive harmonic gestures, dissonances and contrapuntal overlaps of the voices in an effort to represent the words as they unfold. The poem is an address by a migrant worker to his beloved (*'lona baratua'*) describing *'Botle ba heaso, Botle bo hlollang, Moo ho phelang'* ('My home, my roots, my amazing background'), then *'mme mmoratua, mme moratua, mme, Ngeloi la me, le mpaballang'* ('And the place where my dear mother lives, my beloved mother, My angel, who takes care of all my needs'). The force of the emotions expressed comes partly through the repetition of the Sesotho words for 'beloved', 'heart', 'mother' and 'home'. The vivid remembrance of mountains, valleys and rivers only torments the narrator further, as he longs for home while living in foreign lands (*'lichabeng'*). Mother and land become synonymous in this outpouring of sadness. Moerane allows Ntsane's poem to speak for itself, with few changes.

Mohokare is about both the Mohokare (Caledon river), and the Maloti (Drakensberg mountains). Ntsane's poem focuses on the source of the river, a terrifying 'place of nightmares' in the peaks of the Maloti's eastern edge, which creates the border between Lesotho and the South African province of KwaZulu-Natal. The gentle undulation of the music seems to reflect the Mohokare at its western edge rather, where it forms the meandering border between Lesotho and South Africa's Free State province before flowing west towards the Atlantic Ocean and creating a large delta where it meets the sea in Namibia. Something potentially huge and ancient bred in darkness leads to something potentially enormous and destructive in the poem, capable of devouring people and cattle. One interpretation of this metaphor might be 'Don't underestimate the power of nature', but the poem could also mean 'don't underestimate the power of humans to destroy'. As shown in Chapter 6, the song might have been composed when Moerane was teaching at Peka High School and 'could see the river any time'.[17]

Paka-Mahlomola is based on the traditional oral form of praise poem called *'lithoko'*, an example of the blending of traditional and Western forms discussed in Ntsane, as mentioned above. The Mohokare in this poem is a 'creator of sorrow', as the title says, rather than a powerful force of nature. In the first place, it is the historically contested border; second, it forms the natural barrier that people from Lesotho cross, by rail, bus or on foot,

Ex. 9.3: *Paka-Mahlomola* bars 45–70 (courtesy of the Moerane family). For audio, visit https://tinyurl.com/5n7zpjn7

in order to seek work in South Africa. The poem refers to the physical and psychological damage that people suffered because of the border, the tragic damage done to family and communal life by a migrant system in which workers left behind a huge gap in the lives of their loved ones, whom they saw only once a year when returning home for Christmas. To black and white people, the river sings a very different tune, and for Ntsane, the river stands for the longing for home that 'a Mosotho' feels, as soon as they have crossed to the South African side. As with *Ngeloi La Me*, Moerane uses three female voices very effectively in this setting, often repeating words and phrases as if to emphasise the sorrow, dwelling on the words '*paka-mahlomola*' (creator of sorrow) and '*kolieamala*', which literally means 'funeral song'. The repetitions are a way in which Ntsane evokes the form of the oral praise poem, which generally relies heavily on these. Again, it's a long song, 70 bars, composed in several sections with few modulations and without a repeat of the opening section (a *Da Capo*). It is written in a major key and relies, as Moerane so often does in his songs for three female voices, on chords in their inversions rather than in root position. In this song, this use of chords gives the music a restless, provisional quality that profoundly matches the sadness of the lyrics. This is particularly so towards the end of the song, as Example 9.3 shows. Moerane uses more syllabic divisions than usual. These include 're-'ng' in bar 2, which is short for 're-eng', and 'N-ka_u' in bars 4–5, 8–9, 10–11 and 12–13. The word 'mmae' is divided into two or three syllables ('m-mae' and 'm-ma-e') in bars 35–36, and the word 'Kolieamalla' is separated into six: 'Ko-li-ea-ma-l-la'.

Moerane adapts Ntsane's words in *Paki Ha Li Eo* to suit the musical setting, as if he thought of the music first and then found the words. It is deceptively simple and syllabic at the beginning of the score, but as the song proceeds for the next 59 bars, it becomes increasingly chromatic, and persistent syncopated rhythms emphasise the second beat. The poem tells a frustrated story of love that somehow cannot be expressed: 'There are no witnesses, I don't count, I am related'; it seems that the relationship with the loved one cannot be acknowledged. 'The only witnesses are my lungs and heart, drumming in my chest, tolling bells inside of me, ringing all the time even when I'm asleep, Ding! Dong!'. The constant emphasis is on the same emotion, experienced by a person whose heart is bursting with love that cannot be acknowledged. It is quite hard to fathom what is going on, even in the last line: 'A ringing that shows someone's child is loved.' The music is written in the style of a church hymn, except that the words are secular and drive it on for far longer than a hymn would last. Much of the time the vocal registers are fairly low, as if representing suppressed emotion, until they rise up to an elevated pitch with a kind of outburst in bars 39–42. Then they break up into alternating pairs of voices, and the Alto divides at the words '*teu, teu*' (ding dong), and the hymn-like mood is restored for the final few bars.

Ntsane's poem *Satane A Tšeha (Le Joe-leputsoa)*, written during the height of apartheid in South Africa, is about the menace and danger that confront people from Lesotho when they crossed the Mohokare. The border guards are 'laughing devils' who represent white South Africa and treat

Africans heading for 'Le Joe-leputsoa' (Johannesburg) as second-class citizens. The short text is drenched in irony:

> *Ra tšela Mohokare: Satane a tšeha, A phutha mohatla, A rakalla, Li khahla Satane le mangeloi a hae. Lia rateha, lia khahleha, Li monate-nate, Ra ngoloa bukeng ea lihele, ra amoheloa. Re tšetse Mohokare, Re siile bohlale morao.*

> We crossed the Caledon: And the devil laughed, He coiled his tail, Stiffened his muscles, And said how great our language is. It impresses him and his angels. They think it's really great, Really super! Thus were we registered in the book of hell, As we crossed the Caledon River, Knowing nothing could help us now. (Translation by Mpho Ndebele.)

I take this to mean that the language – Sesotho – stigmatised those passing through border control as workers headed for the hell of 'Le Joe-leputsoa'. This word is ambiguous, too. It might derive from the adjective '-putsoa', which means 'grey, bluish', or from the noun 'leputsoa', meaning 'grey-haired, old person': might this be a reference to the white border guards?[18] Or it could simply refer to Johannesburg. Notwithstanding the ominous text, Moerane's music is cheerful. This is a song for entertainment. Despite its sombre moments, the music suggests that Moerane is playing up the irony – the comedy almost – of people's experience of border guards, rather than the underlying tragedy of migration.

Songs set to texts from other sources

Barali Ba Jerusalema is a religious work because of its text, which Moerane takes from chapters 1, 5 and 6 of the Old Testament 'Song of Solomon' and translates into Sesotho.[19] ('Song of Songs' is a more common title, drawn from a phrase in the first line of 1:1.) Mark Gevisser goes so far as to call these lines 'proto-Black Consciousness': 'Daughters of Jerusalem, I am black, but beautiful as the tents of Kedar. Do not stare at me because I am black – Because I am darkened, darkened by the sun.'[20] It is of a different order, musically and poetically, from the hymns and anthems discussed in Chapter 7, and somewhat different from the songs based on Sesotho poems discussed so far in this chapter. It is a strange piece in Moerane's output and was not understood when it was first heard in Lesotho in the 1960s, as we saw earlier ('it's all transitions, terrible, awful piece!'). Mzilikazi Khumalo, who 'discovered' it in the SAMRO archive in 1996 as a 'previously unknown' work,[21] found it 'one of the loveliest of our African "serious" music choral masterpieces, both melodically and contrapuntally; but few impartial musical experts would specifically identify it at a first hearing, and without prior knowledge, as the work of an African composer.'[22] Its early nineteenth-century qualities and word-painting do make it sound like Schubert,[23] and the very close attention to phrase-by-phrase word setting is intense even for Moerane. This detail tended to be overlooked in some beautiful arrangements made of the song for the nation-building Sowetan Caltex Massed Choir Festival in 1996, and in 1997, for Soprano or Tenor and piano, for soloist and orchestra, and for choir and orchestra.[24]

Ntsoaki is unusual because of its metre, in which there are five beats in a bar compared to the norm of 2, 3 or 4; Moerane doesn't use this metre anywhere else. The word *ntsoaki* in Sotho culture refers to a girl child who comes after the birth of several boys in a family, and comes from the verb *tsoaka*, meaning 'to mix'. In the song, this is a proper name, meaning 'one who mixes'. Moerane has taken the words from the poem 'Ntsoaki' by 'Mabasiea Jeannette Mahalefele, whose lyrics are not used by Moerane in any of his other extant songs. She is well known in Lesotho, having had her first work, a play called *Lireneketso (Transactions)* published in 1971,[25] and she continued to produce literature long after Moerane's death in 1980. Moerane set verses 1 and 4 of her poem as it appears on page 10 of *Lireneketso*. The text begins with a disclaimer, '*Ha kena khaitseli, ke ana lejoe*' ('I don't have a sister, I swear') and ends with a complete turnaround: '*Ntsoaki o tsoetsoe habo bahlankana, Le ka re bona ka ho bososelaka*' ('Baby Ntsoaki just joined the boys, And we are full of smiles'). The music's 5-beat metre gives the piece an extraordinary sense of flow; the key is E major, which Moerane rarely uses; he keeps the voices rather low in pitch as if the news about the birth is being whispered; and the two lower voices, Alto 1 and 2, often cross above or below each other. Figure 9.1 shows these features, in a rare example of a Moerane manuscript.

Moerane does not in fact designate the voices for this song, which is unusual for him. In the ACE edition, it is transcribed for SAA, because musically it seems to fit with other songs for SAA. The manuscript shows how Moerane notated the five beats in tonic solfa as three beats plus two. The diagram below gives the rhythm of the first four bars of the Soprano. In tonic solfa rhythm, the longest vertical lines are bar lines that enclose all five beats; the shorter horizontal lines separate the first three beats from the second two, the colons separate the beats, and the full stops divide certain beats into two.

(beats:) | 1   2 3 4 5 | 1 2 3 4 5 | 1   2   3   4   5 | 1   2   3   4   5 |
(tune:) | m .f : m : r | r : d | s₁ : s₁ : s₁ | s₁ : s₁ | l₁ . l₁ : l₁ : m | m : r | d . t₁ : d : r | d : t₁ |

In *Hoja Ke Nonyana*, the lyrics overflow with imagery of nature – earth, sea, sky, clouds – with an especially powerful metaphor of the setting sun as a nesting bird, which the narrator imagines finding after flying far enough to see where the sun sets. Repetitions in the text reiterate the importance of nurturing new life. Renewal of the day, renewal of the seasons, and renewal of life are thus beautifully intertwined. Moerane attributes authorship

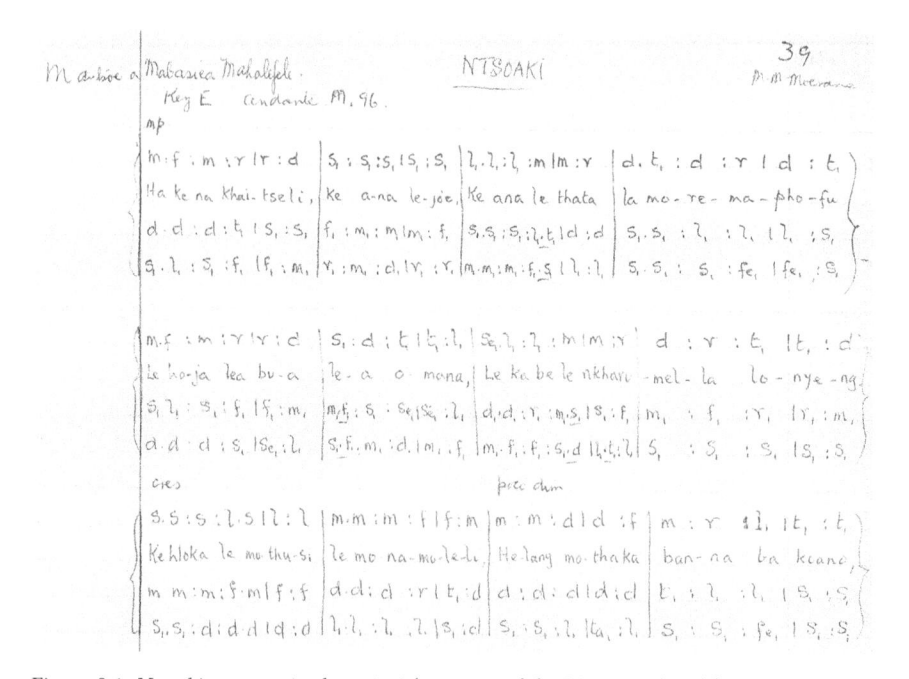

Figure 9.1: *Ntsoaki* manuscript bars 1–8 (courtesy of the Moerane family)

to Bennett Makalo Khaketla, although on both pages of the typescript, the initials before 'Khaketla' are partially erased. This suggests that the poem is likely to be by his wife, 'Masechele Caroline Ntseliseng Khaketla (NM Khaketla), who in fact wrote more poetry than her husband, as can be seen on the webpage 'Sesotho Publications'.[26]

Mahakoe

Mahakoe is an intense, impassioned work and without a doubt Moerane's most atonal or modern-sounding piece on account of its harmonic dissonances. Moerane wrote the words, which are clearly inspired by WB Yeats' poem, 'He wishes for the Cloths of Heaven' (1899), but in Moerane's case they are darker in tone. Compare Yeats and Moerane below:

He wishes for the Cloths of Heaven (Yeats)
Had I the heavens' embroidered cloths,
Enwrought with golden and silver light,
The blue and the dim and the dark cloths
Of night and light and the half light;
I would spread the cloths under your feet:
But I, being poor, have only my dreams;
I have spread my dreams under your feet;
Tread softly because you tread on my dreams.[27]

Mahakoe (Moerane)
If only I had gold And other precious metals, high quality stones! But I am destitute, I am poor, I have no possessions, I am in dire trouble, I am embarrassed, A destitute among destitutes, A poor indigent. And so I will lay at your feet all the dreams and nightmares of my soul. (Translation by Mpho Ndebele)

Original Sesotho: *Hoja ke na le gauda,*[28] *Mahakoe a benyang, mahakoe, gauda tsa bohlokoa, tse rorisehang! Empa joale ke mohloki Kea sitoa, Kea hloka, Ke tsietsoe, Ke soabile, Ke mohloki ea hlokang, Mofumanehi ea sitoang 'Me ke tla ala maotong a hao litoro le maloro a moea le pelo.*

There are two notions of poverty and riches here: in Moerane, riches are gold or diamonds (mined in South Africa) and poverty is utter destitution; in Yeats, two intangibles are contrasted – the 'cloths of heaven' and 'my dreams' – and poverty is not emphasised. In an even darker twist, Moerane offers to lay his 'dreams and nightmares' rather than his dreams (as in Yeats) at the feet of the beloved. This is Moerane's most experimental work, musically; its chromatic language borders on the Expressionist, suggesting that the work might have been written during the late 1930s to early 1940s while he was studying advanced chromatic harmony with Friedrich Hartmann during the writing of *Fatše La Heso*. Example 9.4, the opening of the work (which is repeated – Example 9.4 gives the repeat) illustrates the dissonant harmony and the instrumental, almost attenuated quality of the phrasing.

In a few places the four voices divide, and in bar 21 the 2nd Tenor part has a four-note rising chromatic motif that is a quotation from Wagner's

Ex. 9.4: *Mahakoe* bars 11–20 (courtesy of the Moerane family). For a live recording made by The Chanticleer Singers conducted by Richard Cock, visit https://tinyurl.com/yc4c2trf

Ex. 9.5: *Mahakoe* bars 21–48 (courtesy of the Moerane family). For audio, visit https://tinyurl.com/m843tw8b

opera *Tristan and Isolde*, sometimes called the 'Tristan' motif. This acts as a transition to the central section of the piece, shown in Example 9.5, which contrasts in texture, rhythm and tonality with the two outer sections. It begins with a hemiola rhythm, meaning that a persistent two-beat rhythm goes against the overarching metre of three beats in a bar, something that Moerane might have learnt from Schumann.

Tempi, dynamics, phrasing and expression marks are unusually detailed, even for Moerane, occurring every bar or two, and typed or handwritten between the lines of music. Moerane uses the word 'ten.' for the *tenuto* lines that occur towards the end of the middle section, and there is a change of key in bar 22 that lasts for some time, with brief modulations within it. There is a rare lower double-octave note (t_2) in one bar, and the last two quavers have rests in the lower voice, as if to express a kind of fading away. The vocal writing is unlike any of Moerane's other choral works; the song could easily work as a string quartet. The only other work with such an advanced harmonic and contrapuntal idiom, and material so instrumental in conception, is his symphonic poem. It is a fine example of African musical modernism.

Della

The last two songs considered in this chapter are *Della* and *Sylvia*. *Della* was much vaunted during the time of South Africa's dramatic political changes, and the dismantling of apartheid under the transitional Government of National Unity (1990–1994). It is a more diatonic work than many of Moerane's songs, quite dramatic, and also somewhat archaic in musical style. This at times feels almost Baroque, both vocally and in its use of counterpoint. One of the arrangements made as a solo vocal work for Mezzo-Soprano and orchestra, is particularly effective.[29] Although *Della* shares with *Barali* a reliance on a pre-existing text, it is a very different work, much older in origin. The history of the song goes back to 30 September 1937, when the writer Sampson Synor Mputa sent his isiXhosa poem 'Della' to Lovedale Mission Press, and requested a musical setting.[30] The ensuing correspondence between Mputa, the Lovedale Director of Publications (Rev. RHW Shepherd) and Moerane does not tell us if Mputa asked for Moerane specifically, but Moerane was assigned the task, and Mputa gave permission for 'unnecessary words [to] be altered'. He also offered to pay for the setting, and asked only that he be able to see it before it was published.

Moerane found the text 'mostly unsuitable' but 'endeavoured to extract and adapt the little that is singable', and Mputa readily agreed that 'if there are some unsuitable words for music they must be cut off without making any delay.' On 4 February 1938, Moerane sent Shepherd his completed score of *Della*, to 'words adapted from the "poem" of the same name by Mr. S.S. Mputa', as he put it. He asked Shepherd to 'kindly ask Mr. Mputa to preserve [the score] with great care' as it 'is the only complete one in Tonic Sol-fa', and to 'return it to you for publication if you accept it.'[31] Shepherd suggested charging Mputa £3 3s. in advance for the setting, with Moerane waiving all rights to royalties, but the fee was too steep for Mputa, who did not want the royalties in any case. Shepherd thus returned the score to Moerane on 30 April 1938 'for safe-keeping', without publishing it, and its whereabouts remains a mystery.

The handwritten manuscript of the work in the SAMRO Archive[32] is very unlikely to be the one dating from 1938. First, it is not typeset but handwritten, and sending a handwritten manuscript for publication would be unusual for Moerane. Second, the handwriting is not Moerane's, although it is somewhat similar. Third, on the top right-hand corner of the first page it says, 'Music by M.M. Moerane', while Moerane always signed himself simply 'M.M. Moerane' on page 1 and 'M.M.M.' on subsequent pages. However, no other manuscript or typescript has survived.

In 2008, SAMRO published a version in dual notation that differs even from this SAMRO manuscript, without noting what source was used. Remembering that Thuso Moerane said his father wrote the isiXhosa songs after he retired, this version might date from the late 1960s. Yvonne Huskisson notes that *Della* was prescribed for the national interschool choir competitions in 1969,[33] and Moerane may well have reworked *Della* for that purpose. Unusually, then, we have two surviving versions of *Della* to compare, as well as being able to compare the original poem by Mputa with Moerane's lyrics. Mputa's poem is indeed more 'poetic prose' than 'poem', as Moerane implied, written in old isiXhosa that draws upon archaic expressions and spellings no longer used today, and possibly even unusually 'poetic' in the 1930s. It is written out in short lines below, with an English translation kindly made by Thembela Vokwana.

Qudeni, Mthembu, utsho u Lunika.	Qudeni, Mthembu, so says Lunika.
Isithembise u sapule,	You have broken the promise,
Inthiziyo yam iwile.	I am crestfallen.

Kumbula mhla wa funga,	Remember when you vowed while we were
sihleli e nthlanjeni	seated by the valley
xa ilanga li bantu bahle,	just as the sun was about to set,
usith noba umthu u pase i B.A.	saying that even if someone has a B.A.
akuko'omthanda nje ngam.	there is no-one you love more than me.
Della, mhla nge mini e banda kakulu,	Della, it was a very cold day,
ilanga lobusika, nemitha yalo liyangqina,	as the winter sun and its beams attest,
inthaka zezulu ziman'u ku papazela	birds of heaven sometimes fluttering
pezu kwenthloko zethu. ziyangqina.	above our heads, also bear witness.
Ndikedamile, ndakumkanya,	Dejected, I look on,
ndixeli mfene ndala.	like an old baboon.
O. Hayi udano endi nalo.	O! What disappointment I have.
Della! Della! Ndi-ndi-mbi-ndinzakele,	Della, Della, I am-I am bad, I am hurt,
inene ndibuhlungu ngawe.	you have made me truly sad.
Makaukau u lahlekelwe mfondini	Makaukau, you have lost a man,
ulithwele ihlazo.	you must bear the disgrace.
Yenza intsholo enkulu, yithi,	Shout out loudly, say,
Della! Della!	Della! Della!
Kukupela kwako wedwana?	Are you the only one?
Yo! Yo!	Yo! Yo!
Yehake – kanene bendikuthanda,	Yea – Indeed I loved you,
ubu fana ne ndyathyambo kum.	you were like a flower to me.

Below, one can see how Moerane adapted Mputa's poem, ignoring many expressions in the original and concentrating rather on a few images (the birds, the cold) while discarding others (the disgrace, the BA degree, the baboon), and repeating the exclamation, 'Della!' more often, to bring out the emotion of the poem. The English translation is by Nosipho Rapiya.

Della! Khumbula mhla wawufunga.	Della! Remember the day you made a promise?
Della! wawuyindyatyambo kum.	Della! my flower.
Della! Khumbula! Iintaka ze zulu.	Della! Remember! Those heavenly birds.
Zaman' ukuphaphazela	How they hovered, flapping their wings

phezu kwentloko zethu iintaka zezulu.	above our heads, those heavenly birds.
Hai! ndidanile.	Oh! I am heartbroken.
Ngaloo mini, min' ibandayo	On that day, that chilly day,
Ngaloo mini, mini yobusika.	That winter's day.
Ngaloomin'ibandayo	It was a cold winter's day,
Wawufunga entlanjeni wawusithi	Down at the meadows you vowed that
noba kutheni awusakuze undilahle.	no matter what, you would never leave me.
Is' thembiso usaphule.	You broke that promise.
Della, ndidanile, ndilithwele ihlazo.[34]	Della, I am heartbroken, I am mortified.
Della, ndibuhlungu, Ngawe ndidanile,	Della, I am devastated with pain,
Ndilithwele ihlazo;	I am mortified;
O! Della, kanene bendikuthanda.	Oh Della, I really loved you.
Della! Ndidanile.	Della, my heart is broken.

Both SAMRO versions show an overall three-part ABA structure, but their published version ignores most of the manuscript's tempi: the opening *Andante sostenuto* (crotchet = 88) in the manuscript becomes *Adagio* (crotchet = 80), for example, while the tempo change to crotchet = 138 at the end of bar 19 becomes crotchet = 88. The publication also ignores many expression marks, dynamics and accents that are assumed to be Moerane's (and in this he was very particular, as we have seen), and converts the last note of several phrases in the Soprano from dotted crotchets to minims, in bars 2 and 4, for example. The publication also has different pitches or rhythms in several places and some different octave doh' placements, resulting in a note becoming an octave higher or lower; for example, in bar 8 the manuscript has an octave leap in the Soprano, but the publication does not.

As the entire song, in a version made from the SAMRO manuscript, can be heard on the African Composers Edition website,[35] the analysis here focuses on the difference between the two middle sections. The rather awkward counterpoint in the SAMRO publication casts doubt on the authenticity of this passage. Moerane was skilled at contrapuntal writing; moreover, the outer sections are also rather contrapuntal, and he generally wrote contrasting material in a middle section. The middle section of the SAMRO manuscript, on the other hand, has gently syncopated

Ex. 9.6: *Della* bars 60–76 (courtesy of the Moerane family). For a live recording made by The Chanticleer Singers conducted by Richard Cock, visit https://tinyurl.com/mwkje79x

rhythms, like the middle sections of *Sylvia* and *Ruri!*, and this does provide a contrast. Example 9.6 gives this middle section prefaced by the two-bar lead into it from the first section. The manuscript version is seven bars shorter than the SAMRO publication, and maintains the tempo of the outer sections.

Sylvia

Sylvia is Moerane's most loved and often sung work – so popular, indeed, that Moerane must have loaned it out countless times; and so the original manuscript and typescript have both vanished. It was prescribed for the South African national interschool choir competitions in 1968.[36]

Moerane presumably composed it fairly late in life because it is addressed to a young woman he knew as a student in 1959. It is possible that he had also known her previously as a schoolgirl, as they both came from Matatiele. Her name was Sylvia Ntombentsha Zongola. Sylvia was born in Matatiele, attended school there, and then studied at Mfundisweni Teacher Training Institute in Pondoland.[37] Perhaps Moerane wrote the song when Sylvia graduated from Mfundisweni College, because the lyrics talk about her 'going away'. She might have finished her teacher training in Mokhotlong or Qacha's Nek, and there is some evidence that Moerane might have paid her fees.[38] Sylvia visited the Moerane family at Peka High School, where her presence caused some consternation. 'This Sylvia,' according to Moerane's granddaughter Mosa Ndludla, who lived with her grandparents as a child, 'he introduced her to us as *"mchana"*, meaning "my niece". She used to come for the weekend and go back, just like that. Then, later on, as I was getting older and realising things, then my gran also would ask us and my uncle [Thabo Moerane], "Tell me, people, how are we related to this person?" And I would say, "Granny, you should be asking, I don't know."'[39]

After Sylvia married and moved to Ficksburg, she and Moerane saw each other regularly there, so much so that it became a source of great discomfort for Mosa, who used to accompany her grandfather on his car trips to Ficksburg.[40] Sometime afterwards, Betty returned to Queenstown to live with Thuso. This affair was without a doubt a great love, but it was clearly very hard for the family to deal with. Sylvia had two children: a daughter, Nthabiseng, and a son, Lerato. Nthabiseng remembers that when she was a girl, living in Peka village and going to the nearby Catholic mission school (St Rose), the pair had a huge argument, after which they parted ways.[41]

Sylvia is a profound love song. Musically, its late-Romantic yearning phrases, reverential style, and use of harmonic language and sequences hints at the fifth and final song in Mahler's *Rückert Lieder*, 'Liebst du um Schönheit' ('Do you love beauty?'). A performance of the Mahler by Jessye Norman on YouTube gives an idea of how Moerane's *Sylvia* should be sung: very slowly and with great restraint.[42] As Thuso Moerane pointed out, 'a common fault in *Sylvia*: they seem to cheer it, some conductors, I don't know why; make it sound "better", I mean, "sweeter", but it is actually a very sad song.'[43] The opening is a typically long-breathed Moerane melody and accompaniment, with phrase extensions that give a sense of urgency, even as the rhythms seem at the same time to hold the music back. Moerane writes much more simply and directly here than in many of his other pieces: there is little counterpoint, the textures are homogenous, the tonality mostly diatonic; it is the harmonies that dominate, rising and falling

Ex. 9.7: *Sylvia* bars 17–29 (courtesy of the Moerane family). For a live recording made by the Quava Vocal Group conducted by Sabelo Mthembu, visit https://tinyurl.com/yc8j33ck

like waves breaking in a slow rhythm, creating an atmosphere of profound devotion.

The middle section, marked '*Agitato*', begins at the words 'crashing waves'. It is lighter in mood than the outer sections and has a piano ragtime feel, rare in Moerane. Example 9.7 gives the end of the first and beginning of the second section.

Is this a reference to Pondoland, as the border area close to the sea between Xhosa and Zulu people in south-eastern South Africa, land of the 'Mpondo', was known? Was Moerane thinking of that older popular category of Zulu music called 'iRagtime', one of the African-American minstrel styles 'recognized by Zulu-speaking urban performers and audiences', found 'in the repertoire of the Ohlange Choir' and used by choral composers such as Reuben Caluza?[44] The change is subtle and short-lived, however – 8 bars in a song of 57 bars; a gentle interruption rather than a striking contrast, in which the key centre of G-flat major does not change. The return of the opening theme is a breath-taking moment. The 'real' Sylvia did not emigrate across the ocean as far as we know; she left college, set out on her career as a teacher, got married, and went to live in Ficksburg in what was then the Orange Free State,[45] close to the border at Peka Bridge. The crashing waves are metaphors for powerful emotion, obviously reciprocated.

Sylvia in the song is referred to as 'sibling' (*mtakwetu*) and 'home girl' (*ntomb'asekhaya*), but women are often referred to as 'sister' in Xhosa culture. '*Ntombi*' (girl) in the first line is elided into the next word, '*asekhaya*' (of home or from home) by shortening it to '*ntomb*'. This word refers to an adolescent girl or teenager: no longer a child, but not yet a mature woman. It is close to Sylvia's isiXhosa name, Ntombentsha, and she and Moerane indeed came from the same area of the Eastern Cape. This perhaps explains the first line: '*Sylvia mtakwetu ntomb'asekhaya*' ('Sylvia, my girl, my sister'). This is the longest continuous song lyric that Moerane wrote, set to music with hardly any word repetitions, and his most personal utterance. Here is the whole poem, extracted from his manuscript and translated from isiXhosa into English by Mantoa Motinyane and Nosipho Rapiya, with the phonemic translation given as well in order to show the literal meaning of the isiXhosa.

THE TIMES DO NOT PERMIT

Sylvia mtakwetu ntomb'asekhaya,
Sylvia my sibling girl of-home,

Sylvia, my girl, my sister,

Kazi ndothini ukuthetha nawe,
Wonder I-say to-speak to-you,

I wonder what I will say to you,

Xana kunamhlanje sosala sodwa
When today we-remain alone

After we're separated today?

Ewe ke namhlanje sizinkedama
Yes so today we-are-orphans

Yes, today we are orphans,

Kazi kunamhlanje soba yini na
Wonder today we-become what

And I wonder what will become of us.

Kambe sitsho sithi ndlela ntle.
Perhaps we-say we-say farewell.

Perhaps we simply have to bid farewell.

Sylvia mtakwetu ntomb'asekhaya,
Sylvia my-sibling girl-of-home,

Sylvia, my girl, my sister,

Uzuyubuye kwakamsinya noko,
You-should-come-back quickly,

Please go and come back soon,

Wen'ukad'usifundisa indlela
You have-been teaching way

You have shown us the way,

Indlela zobulumko nobungcwele
Ways of-wisdom and-holy

The wise and holy ways.

UThix'azabe nawe ngase lwandle
God may-be with-you over ocean.

May God be with you near the ocean

Kambe sitsho sithindlela ntle.
Perhaps we-say we-say farewell.

Perhaps we have to say goodbye.

Sithi Vuthuza wena moya waselwandle
We-say Blow you wind of ocean

We say, Blow, you ocean wind,

Vuthuza moya khawgqume ke lwandle
Blow wind go-on rumble then ocean

Go on, blow and rumble, you ocean,

gqumani ke nanima'zasolwandle,
rumble then you sea-water,

rumble, you waves,

SONGS OF LOVE AND LOSS

Bethani nasemaweni,
Beat even-on-rocks,

Beat those rocks!

Dedani elunxwemeni.
Retreat from-beach.

Then, retreat from the beach.

Make nizolel'istandwasetu.
Please you-be-calm for our love.

Be calm for our love.

Sylvia mtakwetu ntomb'asekhaya
Sylvia my-sibling girl of-home

Sylvia, my girl, my sister

Kazi ndothini ukuthetha nawe,
Wonder I-say to-speak to-you,

I wonder what I will say to you,

Xana kunamhlanje sosala sodwa
When today we-remain alone

After we're separated today?

Ewe ke namhlanje sizinkedama
Yes so today we-are-orphans

Yes, today we are orphans,

Kazi kunamhlanje soba yini na
Wonder today we-become what

And I wonder what will become of us.

Kambe sitsho sithi ndlela ntle.
Perhaps we-say we-say farewell.

Perhaps we simply have to bid farewell.

Sylvia, Kambe sitsho sithi ndlela ntle.
Sylvia, Perhaps we-say we-say farewell.

Sylvia, perhaps we have to bid farewell.

UThix'azakuphe amathamsanq'onke,
God should-you-give blessings all,

May God shower you with blessings,

Ntomb'entle thembalihle kum
Girl who-is-beautiful expect-good from-me

Beautiful girl, I will look after you,

Ntomb' e nkulu sthandwa sethu.
Girl who-is-big love of-ours.

Great girl, whom we love.

There are many extant versions of the score in circulation, copied manually or electronically over many years. An interesting example in circulation is a handwritten manuscript in the possession of Mandla Kala

Ex. 9.8: *Sylvia* bars 36–57 (courtesy of the Moerane family). For a live recording made by the Quava Vocal Group conducted by Sabelo Mthembu, visit https://tinyurl.com/ysx8w569

in Pretoria, which bears the subtitle, 'Sonata for S.A.T.B.'[46] The tempo, dynamics and expression marks on this copy, which vary on other copies, may not be Moerane's, although the initial tempo, *'Con espressione'*, is characteristic of him. Adding 'Slowly with feeling' in brackets afterwards, however, is not.

The ending is unlike Moerane's other unexpected shifts and turns. After repeating the 'first verse' (bars 1–12) with a few minor embellishments in bars 13–24 (the 'second verse'), and after the short middle section, a two-bar transition calms the music down; then he repeats the main theme almost exactly as before (the 'third verse'). He could have ended the piece at that point, in bar 47, but he draws it out for another ten bars, playing with fragments of the theme until the music reaches a final cadence, one that has already been reached three times before. And then he stops, just before the very final cadence and clings to the chord of G-flat major for four bars during a short pedal point over the tonic chord of G-flat, as shown in Example 9.8. Two or three notes are repeated by the choir as it sings, 'Young lady, I will look after you, beautiful girl whom we love.' It is as if Moerane could not bear to let go, to bring the music to a close; and the lyrics, after all the anguish about parting, end with a commitment to love.

Sylvia died of cancer in January 1980; Moerane knew of her death.[47] Moerane died a few weeks later in hospital in Bloemfontein, South Africa, and is buried in Tsifalimali, Lesotho. His wife of 50 years, Beatrice Betty, died a few weeks after he did, and was laid to rest near her grandson Lenare, in Queenstown, South Africa. The little house that Moerane built Sylvia in the village of Peka is still there and belongs to Sylvia's daughter, who did not know until she was an adult, who her real father might have been. She became friendly with Moerane's son, Thabo, her half-brother; and the only photograph of Sylvia with Moerane that her daughter has is the one shown in Figure 9.2, of Thabo Moerane, Sylvia Ntombentsha and Michael Mosoeu. It was taken at Thabo's graduation ceremony at the University of Botswana, Lesotho and Swaziland (precursor to the University of Lesotho at Roma) in Maseru, in 1968.

Figure 9.2: Thabo Moerane, Sylvia Zongola and Michael Mosoeu Moerane (courtesy Nthabiseng)

10 | Conclusion

In drawing the main themes of the book together, I argue that the phrase Moerane used in 1966 in a letter to Percival Kirby – 'the times do not permit' – describes his life and musical output all told. He had no precedents or successors as an African composer of classical music in southern Africa during his lifetime – and for years afterwards. As a result, he was often simply not known or misrepresented. Not until the 2000s did young black South African composers of classical music emerge who had actually trained *as* composers. Moerane could almost be described as a 'misfit': he was highly trained musically in an environment – southern Africa in the twentieth century under deep apartheid – where no-one else like him existed.

One result was that he produced many works that were never performed. Among these are works whose use of tonality and harmony belong to a modernist language that no-one else in the genre of African choral composition had embraced before or understood – and which he himself was only beginning to develop. Their Sotho and Xhosa musical elements and lyrics, indeed, render them unlike any choral compositions in South Africa or other parts of the world.

It is almost impossible to imagine what motivated Moerane to continue writing music year after year in the kind of compositional vacuum in which he lived and worked. His belief in himself, despite the loneliness of his position as a composer, must have been extraordinary. Moerane could not belong to any white social groupings for attending new music performance and composition, and would not have known most of the music that was being composed by white South Africans or composers overseas. I doubt whether or he had any colleagues on an equal footing with whom he could talk about his work, either complete, or in progress, and particularly his symphonic poem. He touched base only tangentially with the white musical establishment through individuals such as Yvonne Huskisson and Percival Kirby, and could reap no benefit as a teacher from his excellent music education because he could not teach music formally in school, although he did teach it informally.

A black South African in a family of political activists, and a firm believer in Pan-African values, Moerane was harassed to the point of losing his house and his job, and ultimately forced to leave South Africa. He spent his later years in the extreme poverty of rural Lesotho; and although some white South African composers of his generation also lived in rural areas – one thinks of Arnold van Wyk's years in Calvinia – there is really no comparison in terms of lifestyle, opportunities, status, and income. Moerane was lucky not to lose his life, as so many of his activist family and friends did. As a Mosotho he lived for much of his life in the Eastern Cape, where his home language, Sesotho, was not a majority home language; he even taught in isiXhosa. He was a classical music lover who lived in African communities where many people preferred lighter music – which may have partly explained his antipathy to jazz, although this was also due to his distaste for the alcohol associated with its performance. Had he spent his life in the vibrant black urban communities of Johannesburg and its surrounds, even, the trajectory of his life might have taken an altogether different turn.

Moerane never left southern Africa, and so had none of the benefits that other African composers on the continent have had, of studying and living in the United States or Europe, and making contacts there that could help to support and develop careers in their home countries. One thinks here of Fela Sowande of Nigeria, or Ephraim Amu of Ghana, for example, who were almost contemporary with Moerane, and who have had considerable international exposure.

Regarding the more positive aspects of his life: Moerane began life in an almost ideal home environment. His strong, uncompromising character was formed within a middle-class, well-educated, cultured and relatively affluent family on a well-stocked, well-run farm. He had a better education and more opportunities than most Africans of his generation, including the chance to become highly educated musically. He won a school bursary at a time when few were offered, and an award for composition while still studying – something very few Africans have achieved until the present day. He had a work for large orchestra performed, recorded and broadcast several times nationally and internationally. He developed a strong following and earned enormous respect in the very large amateur black African choral sector in southern Africa (it must embrace at least a million people in the region, and probably did so even in his day) – just for the handful of works known to his contemporaries. He probably influenced a number of composers (a topic that cries out for research), although I could find no record of him having a 'composition student' as such. He married and successfully raised a family, and his extended family and successors are aware of his importance and proud of his achievements. And I am sure that his Christian faith sustained his spirit throughout the many difficulties he faced in life.

Moerane was by all accounts a rather strict but tremendously well-liked and highly successful teacher. He was reserved, intelligent, occasionally moved to outbursts of anger, but generally cautious – and one can only guess what an influence his wise and intellectual personality alone must have had on the generations of students whom he taught, and colleagues with whom he worked. He navigated the fragile and narrow pathways between authority and opportunity under successive regimes of political repression and fear. There is something staunch, determined and immensely courageous about the way he dealt with all these challenges. This is not to idealise the man or exaggerate his importance: he was no saint; and he produced an interesting body of work among which there are a few really good pieces that are highly unusual for their time and genre. I would hesitate to call him a genius, however – a word that has lost currency through over-use in in any case; but he was a remarkable if largely 'hidden' figure in the compositional world of his time. As in the case of the American Modernist composer Charles Ives, real recognition came only many years after his death.

In 1980, SABC Bantu Music Organiser Yvonne Huskisson described Moerane as a recluse. Percival Kirby described him as modest,[1] which may be nearer the mark. What we know about Moerane from the research

I conducted, and which I discuss in the Introduction and Chapters 1 to 3, is that his family and students found him reserved and 'quiet' unless riled – which is different from being reclusive. It was not his personality so much as his political views that made him evasive in communication with parastatals such as the SABC. When Carmel Rickard quotes Huskisson as saying Moerane went off the radar after 1964, for example, and when Percival Kirby received a sudden brush-off in the middle of a fairly lively correspondence in 1966, such incidents speak to Moerane's situation rather than his personality.

Digging a little deeper into the consequences of the restrictions he faced, unable to make a connection with the world of 'new music' nationally or internationally, even at the choral level, he still has no profile outside southern Africa. Even within it, because he died in 1980 and was not a jazz or popular musician, he remains relatively unknown to the majority of South Africans. The choral sector in which Moerane worked hardly ever releases commercial recordings, there are almost no recordings of his music, and his Afro-modernist choral style is not what some people hear as or consider to be 'African'. The brief overviews given in Chapters 7, 8 and 9 can do little to mitigate that perception, although I hope that they go some way to explaining *why* his music sounds the way it does; why it *is* African; and why a conversation about what such music means in a global context is now an urgent priority.

To set such a conversation in motion has been one of the main purposes of this book, but first we must ask: what would such a context be? Hopefully not one of sheer opportunism or tokenism: it is no use occasionally dropping a piece by Moerane into a programme of choral or orchestral music without the context of a sustainable vision of cultural education to support it. Such 'one-off' moves, which would reflect on the programme organiser more than the composer, can do little to promote real understanding of where Moerane (or others like him) came from in the past; or what his music could therefore mean in the present. Even the performance of *Fatše La Heso* that took place in New York in 1950 was solely in the context of promoting 'Negro' classical music, and black conductor Dean Dixon's response, for one, was to find it too 'romantic'. What does this say?

One conclusion that follows from all of this is that Moerane's 'times' came and went, never 'permitted' him to operate as a composer as fully and professionally as he might have done – and that they never will. This gloomy thought is partly what I have tried to dispel in this book. But I have not been entirely successful, because assessing the preconditions for Moerane to compose reveals historical truths that are still difficult for some to acknowledge. There has been a great deal of emphasis on politics here, and on how much governments, leaders and policies have to answer for in the case history of Moerane – along with thousands of other potential Moeranes. Moerane was a political animal, and the political contexts described are intimately linked to every stage of his life and his beliefs as a human being. He lived his life according to his political as well as his religious beliefs, and the violence he witnessed was real. The politics of Moerane's *musical* history persisted throughout his life, and the politics of music history still prevail for his afterlife as a composer. And they continue to have an impact upon composers in southern Africa today, albeit in new forms, which include a lack of funding for new music and too few qualified music teachers.

Once Moerane's music is more fully known, more recordings of his works are made, and both scores and recordings are in greater circulation, they can become talking points at least; and this is where a shift in the way we think about Moerane can begin to occur. A historically informed re-evaluation of Moerane's music is not hard to imagine in schools, colleges, universities and the media. Even a retrospective evaluation would afford him some kind of posthumous recognition, similar to that given to South African black writers Sol Plaatje and Es'kia Mphahlele and black artists George Pemba and Gerald Sekoto, and already afforded to African continental composers such as Fela Sowande, Ephraim Amu, Akin Euba, Justinian Tamusuza, African-American composers William Grant Still and Florence Price, and British composer Samuel Coleridge-Taylor.

Is there still time to do this? In terms of a discourse of 'memory and forgetting',[2] one can argue that Moerane has had little or no influence on South African music (or even on choralism) so far, never mind further afield. This loss is incalculable, even unimaginable. One can only speculate how Moerane's creative experiments with texture and dissonance might have helped to mitigate the 'musical violence of a very high order' imposed by four-part, 16-bar, 3-chord hymns on so much African choral music.[3] However, it is now possible to study, analyse and discuss his music, not for what it does not do or does not 'sound like', but for what it *does*: and to use this as a way into a larger discussion about what is nowadays viewed as 'normal' in musical compositions of the past.

Moerane's case also offers an example of how to view a composer's life and music from the perspective of the composer and their times: to turn the spotlight back to the viewer, and ask what it is that clouds our view of the past. Money for reparations is one thing. Money to ensure that today's Michael Moeranes get a balanced music education, that more composers are trained, that composition study moves beyond its musty starting point in four-part harmony, and that schoolchildren learn about other people's musical histories, is another.

The tragedy of Moerane's lost life – the one not lived – does not end here. It is replayed, daily, for far too many other Michael Moeranes. The kind of music education he received at mission schools in 1910s and 1920s South Africa and Lesotho has almost completely disappeared. For the vast majority of children, nothing as good as (even) he had can now be found in state schools in South Africa, generally speaking. Private schools offer wonderful music tuition, and in the future, this is where composers are going to be made, unless there is a huge political will to open up other spaces in education. The disaffiliation in the past of white music studies from the history and performance of black music has also created an enormous lacuna between the two. This has not necessarily been the case with other school and university subjects. As David Attwell notes, English literature students, for example, became aware as early as the 1970s of having to 'immerse [them]selves in the literature of our continent' and 'begin a journey into African literatures', which turned out to be 'as compelling now [2005] as it as when it began'.[4] The context in which David Attwell made this remark was that of 're-writing modernity'; and one can very easily superimpose onto this the idea of what rewriting modernity in South African black classical music might be. The effect such immersion had on Attwell and his peers during the 1970s was electrifying: 'disallowing everyone from remaining unchanged and therefore [keeping both Black and white] histories, traditions and identities radically in flux.'[5] This is precisely the effect that a missing history of Moerane still might have – even in retrospect and on however small a scale – on South African music education and music studies. For simply to contemplate what was missed and then do nothing about it 'places us at the edge of the abyss'.[6]

Finally, what needs to change in the way Moerane is perceived, studied and taught, if there were indeed curricula, facilities and teachers in state educational institutions? His blackness and his background in rural Africa counted against him profoundly throughout his career as a composer. It also counts against him now, as a subject of study in colleges and universities, most especially in the United States. I end, therefore, where the Preface to this book began, by referring to the subject areas mentioned there (musicology, ethnomusicology, popular music studies), and how little choral music and those composers who predominantly compose choral music feature in them. Moerane seems to belong neither to the realm of ethnomusicology, because he wrote Western-sounding notated music, nor to the realm of musicology, because almost all his music is for *a cappella* choir. As a black composer of classical music whose music to most scholars and other composers worldwide does not sound either like 'new' or 'African' music, he is unlikely to be valued in composition studies or music analysis. This, I suggest, reflects on the disciplines, which *can* change: not on Moerane and his musical life – which cannot.

This brings us to the second of the main points from the Preface: how much or how little material a biography can cope with. In some cases, such as the magisterial three-volume biography of Arnold van Wyk by Stephanus Muller,[7] there is almost too much, and the reason is not hard to find. Many composers are born into families where record-keeping, photographs, documents, writings and sketches for compositions, among many other things, are kept as precious documents that later find their way into libraries and archives. This puts a burden of another kind on the biographer. The burden of this book is that of gaps and fragments, which I have woven together as best I can with historical and musical detail and personal testimonies. This is why this work is called a 'musical life' rather than a 'biography'. There are many other composers whose lives would be similarly challenging to write about for lack of an archive, but I think Moerane's case is a remarkable one.

Born into a middle-class African homestead of great self-sufficiency, Moerane proved to be 'an excellent example of an African, who, in spite of almost insurmountable difficulties, succeeded in obtaining a basic education which not only led to him becoming a qualified schoolmaster [...] but also to his being the first [Basuto] to obtain a degree in music at a South African university.'[8] This accolade by Percival Kirby, who showed a keen appreciation of the difficulties Moerane faced, forms part of the original dictionary entry Kirby wrote for Malan's 1979 South African Music *Encylopedia*. Yet very little of the sympathy and interest Kirby expresses in his detailed four-page manuscript made it into the dictionary. Malan apparently reduced the piece to one paragraph, giving the bare essentials. The entry just before, by contrast, spends more than four pages on the 'distinguished music educationist' Franz Bernhard Migcod Moeller, who uplifted the white musical life of East London. This kind of intervention promoting a white nonentity and effacing a successful black composer, by the most influential musicologist of his time, shows how incalculable damage not only to Moerane, but to countless other black composers, was done. The influence of the past on the musical landscape of southern Africa has skewed both national and international views of it right up to the present day.

Coupled with this, the archive of black southern African musical scores remains pathetically small and often inaccessible in family homes, where manuscripts are sometimes lost or destroyed after a composer's death. Much of the legacy of Moerane has been preserved, thankfully; but this is not the case with many other African composers. Thousands of manuscripts remain in tonic solfa notation and in African languages, rendering them increasingly intangible as an African heritage. Many choirs still copy music illegally, and many performance venues are not licensed, or performance details are not submitted to agencies for the collection of royalties. Moerane and his family have lost out for decades, as have countless others, because of this.

Moerane is an individual musical figure of great importance in southern Africa's past; but his musical life also affords the opportunity to change our view of that past. Most of all, his life and music challenge the ways in which we teach, perform and curate music of this kind, this place and this time, in the present.

Appendix: Catalogue of Works by Michael Mosoeu Moerane

Title	English translation	ACE Cat. no.	MMM Cat. no.	Duration based on ACE Sibelius score incl. repeats	Key major unless otherwise stated	Scoring vocal scoring is always *a cappella*
Fatše La Heso	(My Country) Full score	450	001	10'–11'	C	Full orchestra
Fatše La Heso	(My Country) Set of 30 orchestral parts	451	002	10'–11'	C	Various
'Mankokotsane	The Rain Game	452	003	4'52"	E	SATB
'Mitsa-Mahosi	A Call To Kings	453	004	2'26"	F	SATB
Alina		454	005	2'15"	A♭	SATB
Barali Ba Jerusalema	Daughters of Jerusalem	455	006	1'43"	C	SATB
Della	Della	456	007	4'06"	F	SATB
Ea Hlolang	The Triumphant One	457	008	4'16"	D	SATB
Ha Ke Balahē	Who Says I'm Running Away?	458	009	1'53"	F	SATB
Hoja Ke Nonyana	If I Were a Bird	459	010	3'00"	F	SATB
Jehova Oa Busa	Jehova Reigns	460	011	1'52"	F	SATB
Khati	Skipping Game	461	012	2'04"	F	SATB

Title	English translation	ACE Cat. no.	MMM Cat. no.	Duration based on ACE Sibelius score incl. repeats	Key major unless otherwise stated	Scoring vocal scoring is always *a cappella*
Lebili	*Wheel*	462	013	2'01"	G	SATB
Leseli La Hao	*Your Light*	463	014	3'04"	F	SATB
Letsatsi	*The Sun*	464	015	1'43"	E	SATB
Likhohlo	*Gorges*	465	016	0'44"	G	SATB
Liphala	*Whistles*	466	017	2'08"	F	SATB
Mahakoe	*Jewels*	467	018	1'28"	F	SATB
Matlala	*Matlala*	468	019	5'30"	A	SATB
Monyaka Oa Pelo	*A Joyful Heart*	469	020	2'17"	G	SATB
Morena Tlake	*King Vulture*	470	021	2'15"	Dmin-Gmaj	SAATB
Naleli Ka 'Ngoe	*One Star at a Time*	471	022	2'44"	G♭	SATB
Ngokuba Sizalelwe Umtwana	*For Unto Us a Child is Born*	472	023	3'26"	F	SATB
Ntate Ea Mohau	*Lord of Mercy*	473	024	2'00"	F	SATB
Paki Ha Li Eo	*No Witnesses*	474	025	2'28"	F	SATB
Ruri!	*Truly!*	475	026	3'36"	G♭	SATB
Satane A Tšeha (Le Joe-leputsoa)	*The Devil Laughed (Johannesburg)*	476	027	2'20"	G	SATB
Seotsanyana	*Rock Kestrel*	477	028	2'32"	F	SATB
Sylvia		478	029	2'30"	G♭	SATB
Vumani KuYehova (Anthem)/ (Merabe, Rorisang)	*Sing To Jehovah (Anthem)*	479	030	1'35"	C	SATB
Liflaga	*Flags*	503	053	3'00"	D	SSAA
'Mankholikholi	*Yellow-billed Kite*	480	031	0'36"	D♭	SAA
Bonukunyana	*My Little Baby! [fragment]*	481	032	[fragment]	B♭	SAA

APPENDIX: CATALOGUE OF WORKS BY MICHAEL MOSOEU MOERANE

Title	English translation	ACE Cat. no.	MMM Cat. no.	Duration based on ACE Sibelius score incl. repeats	Key major unless otherwise stated	Scoring vocal scoring is always a cappella
Lia Qhomaqhoma	They Frolic	482	033	0'52"	D♭	SAA
Ma-Homemakers (Ingoma Ka Zenzele)	Homemakers	483	034	2'44"	D	SAA
Mohokare	The Caledon River	484	035	3'22"	F	SAA
Mosele	Mosele	485	036	2'08"	E	SAA
Ngeloi La Me	My Angel	486	037	3'02"	F	SAA
Ntsoaki	Ntsoaki	487	038	1'21"	E	SAA
Paka-Mahlomola	Creator of Sorrow	488	039	2'48"	E	SAA
Sa 'Mokotsane	Wailing	489	040	1'12"	B♭	SAA
Sekolo Se Koetsoe	School's Out	490	041	1'35"	F	SAA
Tsatsi La Pallo	Judgement Day	491	042	1'19"	D	SAA
Nonyana Tse Ntle	Beautiful Birds	492	043	0'49"	E♭	SA
Pelo Le Moea	Heart and Soul	493	044	1'16"	E♭	SA
By An' By (arr.)		494	045	1'33"	F	SATB
Go Tell It On The Mountains (Christmas) (arr.)		495	046	3'30"	G	SATB solo & choir
I Got A Home In-a Dat Rock (arr.)		496	047	1'18"	F	SATB
I Stood On De Ribber (arr.)		497	048	2'06"	F	Sop. solo & SATB choir
It's Me, O Lord (arr.)		498	049	2'00"	G	SATB
Nobody Knows The Trouble I've Seen (arr.)		499	050	1'10"	A	SAA

Title	English translation	ACE Cat. no.	MMM Cat. no.	Duration based on ACE Sibelius score incl. repeats	Key major unless otherwise stated	Scoring vocal scoring is always *a cappella*
Shenandoah (arr.)		500	051	1'00"	E	SSAT TBB
Witness (arr.)		501	052	2'35"	B♭	SATB

Glossary of Musical Terms

a cappella	without accompaniment
Adagio	tempo marking in music scores meaning very slow
Agitato	tempo marking in music scores meaning quickly, with excitement
Allegro	tempo marking in music scores meaning fast, moving along
Alto	low female voice (short for contralto)
Andante	tempo marking in music scores meaning fairly fast, ambling along
anthem	short choral work often sung by a church choir
antiphonal	two lines of music answering each other
arrangement	new version of a piece, for different voices and/or instruments
art music	classical music
articulation	general term for clarity and attention to detail in vocal presentation
augmented interval	distance between two notes enlarged by one semitone
aural	by ear
bar	very short measure of time in music and space in a music score
Baroque	a style in music history from early-seventeenth to mid-eighteenth century
Bass	low male voice
bass clef	sign in staff notation denoting lower notes

cadence	two or more chords that denote a point of rest or an ending
chamber music	music written for intimate spaces, for two to nine players
choral music	music for choir: in this book, unaccompanied choir
chord	vertical structure of notes played simultaneously
chromatic	using some of the 12 consecutive black and white keys on the piano melodically or harmonically
coda	the final section of a piece of music, sometimes just a few bars
contrapuntal	using counterpoint
counterpoint	musical lines combined to sound well against ('counter') each other
crescendo (or *cresc.*)	Italian word meaning 'growing'; in music it means 'get louder'
crotchet	note usually lasting a single beat
Da Capo	go back to the beginning and repeat a section
diatonic	using only the notes of a major scale (e.g. the white notes on the piano)
diminished interval	distance between two notes reduced by one semitone
dissonance	perceived clash of pitches, usually in a chord
divisi	voice or instrumental part divided into more than one note
dolce	sweetly or serenely
dominant	fifth note of the major or minor scale
dotted notes	a way of lengthening notes: dotted notes are usually followed by shortened notes in such a way that the two together constitute a complete note and this figuration of long-short notes is often used in sequence
dynamics	letters or words in a score that indicate required loudness or softness

GLOSSARY OF MUSICAL TERMS

eisteddfod	music competition with different sections and age groups
expression marks	words written in a score that indicate required changes of mood or speed
Expressionist	somewhat attenuated, dissonant style of composition associated with early twentieth-century composers such as Schoenberg
figured bass	lowest line of a composition written with figures attached to indicate what chords should be played above it
forte	Italian word meaning 'strong', used in music scores to indicate 'loud'
fortissimo	Italian word meaning 'very strong', used in music scores to indicate 'very loud'
functional harmony	arrangement of chords whereby each one has a function in the key
hairpin *crescendo*	indication in music scores to get louder, written as a long V on its side, open to the right
harmonisation	adding harmonies (chords) to a melody
harmony	vertical structure of chords one after the other
hemiola rhythm	a two-beat rhythm going against the metre of three beats in a bar
homogenous	in choral music, voices moving together on the same beats
hymn	short musical form sung by the congregation in religious services
interval	distance between notes, for example a second, fifth or octave
inversion	a chord such as C-E-G (d-m-s) sung E-G-C (m-s-d') or G-C-E (s-d'-m')
key	a note on a keyboard or the scale on which a piece is based
Lento	tempo marking in music scores meaning slow
LPs	long-playing records
lyrical	melodious, tuneful
lyrics	the words, in music that has sung text

major key	key based on the major scale e.g. d, r, m, f, s, l, t, d' forms a major scale
major scale	sequence of seven consecutive notes: on a keyboard, the white notes constitute a major scale – C major
manuscript	hand-written music score
melody	tune, sometimes quite long
mezzo	middle or medium, as in *mezzo forte* (fairly loud)
Mezzo-Soprano	middle-range female voice, lying between Soprano and Alto
minim	note usually lasting two beats
minor key	key based on the minor scale (l, t, d, r, m, f, se, d')
Modernism	style of music in the early twentieth century that used experimentation
modulation	change of key, for example from C major to F major
motet	more elaborate or longer form of anthem, usually polyphonic
non troppo	expression mark in music scores meaning 'not too much'
octave	distance of eight scale-notes above or below another note, e.g. d-d'
open score	music in which each vocal or instrumental part has its own stave
orchestra	group of Western instruments varying in size from 40 to 70 players
orchestration	allocation of musical lines to different instruments or families of instruments (strings, wind, brass, percussion) in an orchestra
ostinato	urgent repetition of a musical sequence
part-writing	music written for several voices simultaneously
passage	stretch of music lasting from a few to many bars
phrase	short group of notes or a few bars of music

GLOSSARY OF MUSICAL TERMS

piano	Italian word used in music scores to indicate 'soft'
pianissimo	Italian word used in music scores to indicate 'very soft'
piano score	music in which all parts are reduced to two staves for two hands to play
pitch	highness or lowness of a sound
polyphony	vocal music with several lines that move independently
Presto	tempo marking in music scores meaning 'very fast', pressing along
quadruple metre	four beats in a bar
quaver	note usually lasting half a beat
repertoire	collection or body of music by the same composer or known by a particular performer
rhythm	regular, repeated pattern of sounds
ritenuto	indication to slow down the tempo
Romanticism	style of nineteenth-century music emphasising passion and longing
root position	a chord such as C-E-G (d-m-s) given in an arrangement with C (the root) at the bottom
sacred song	work for voice(s) with a spiritual or ritual message
sarabande	dance in triple metre, like a slow waltz
score	written form of a piece of music
scoring	allocating music to particular voices or instruments
semiquaver	note usually lasting quarter of a beat
sequence	repetition of a phrase up or down in pitch, sometimes more than once
shanty	song traditionally sung by sailors at sea
sheet music	music written or published on loose or bound pages
solfa	tonic solfa notation
solfège	system of writing music using ut, re, mi, fa, sol, la, si, equivalent to doh, re, me, fah, soh, lah, te

solmization	system of singing music at first sight using ut, re, mi, fa, sol, la, si
sonata	classical instrumental work, often solo, often in three movements
sonata form	musical structure in three sections often called the exposition, development and recapitulation; sometimes has a concluding coda
song (in this book)	music for unaccompanied choir in three, four or five parts
song (generally)	music for solo voice, usually with accompaniment
songbook	book of solo songs, usually with accompaniment
Soprano	high female voice
sostenuto	indication to performers to sustain the notes or play them smoothly
sotto voce	with a hushed voice
spiritual	religious choral work based on a north American slave song
staccato (or *stacc.*)	indication to performers to separate notes by making them very short
staff notation	music written on a five-line stave or staff
string quartet	two violins, viola and cello or a work written for this combination
symphonic poem	short work for orchestra in one movement, sometimes descriptive
syncopation	rhythm in which notes other than the main beat are emphasised
syncretic	crossover; mixing two or more styles or cultures
tempo/tempi	speed/s
Tenor	high male voice
tenuto	indication to performers to cling to notes or lean into them
text (in this book)	lyrics of a song or poem
tonic	first note of the major or minor scale (doh)

tonic solfa	system of writing music using doh, re, me, fah, soh, lah, te, doh', normally reduced to the letters d, r, m, f, s, l, t, d'
transcribed	rewritten in a different notation, for example tonic solfa to staff
treble clef	sign in staff notation denoting higher notes
triple metre	three beats in a bar
triplet	three notes fitted into a beat normally divided into two
typescript	typed music score, which in Moerane's day would be typed on a manual typewriter
unison	everyone playing or singing the same notes
voice leading	one voice beginning and another or others following; often found in counterpoint and polyphony

Notes

Timeline of Political Events 1880–1991

1 First conference of African political organisations in the eastern Cape Colony, mainly to review the Voters Registration Act, by which 'some 20,000 voters, or 25 per cent of the electorate, were struck off the lists. Most of these were African and coloured people'; the conference was 'a landmark in African organisational politics' (André Odendaal, *The Founders: The Origins of the ANC and the Struggle for Democracy in South Africa* [Johannesburg: Jacana Media, 2012], 126; 128).

2 'Because of Basutoland's close proximity to the other colonies, news from these areas appeared regularly in the *Naledi* [which kept people] in touch with African opinion in the rest of South Africa' (Odendaal, *The Founders*, 281).

3 'The [revived] Progressive Association campaigned against the abuses of the chieftaincy and called for changes in the Basutoland National Council to make it representative of all classes of our people and not merely a council of chiefs and headmen' (Bernard Leeman, *Lesotho and the Struggle for Azania: The Origins and History of the African National Congress, Pan Africanist Congress, South African Communist Party and Basutoland Congress Party 1780–1994* [London: Bernard Leeman, 2015], 135).

4 Reduced African-owned land to twelve per cent of national total.

5 The Commoners League was a liberatory, nationalist (rather than a communist-inspired) movement, following the example of Marcus Garvey's Universal Negro Improvement Association (UNIA) in the United States, whose leader's ideas should be seen as part of the same pattern of thinking that emerged in the writings of Anton Lembede in the 1940s, Robert Sobukwe in the 1950s, Potlako Leballo in the 1960s, the Black Consciousness Movement in the 1970s and the Azanian People's Organisation (AZAPO) in the 1980s (Leeman, *Lesotho and the Struggle*, 161; 149). The Comintern was the small group that mobilised the Russian Revolution of 1917 under the leadership of Lenin and Trotsky.

6 It was also 'in close contact with the Garvey Movement, the Comintern, and the Pan African Movement' (Leeman, *Lesotho and the Struggle*, 138).

7 Colonial Africa was a recruiting ground for the spread of communism internationally (Leeman, *Lesotho and the Struggle*, 156–159).

8 'The racial policy of the Nazis resulted in the arrest and imprisonment of Padmore and the expulsion of all blacks from Germany. Comintern headquarters in Germany was raided and the German Communist Party's offices were sacked all over the country' (Leeman, *Lesotho and the Struggle*, 166).

9   'Umbrella African political movement established [to] try to halt the passage of legislation removing Cape African voters from the common voters' roll' (Christopher Saunders and Nicholas Southey, *A Dictionary of South African History* [Cape Town and Johannesburg: David Philip, 1998], 9), at which 'over three hundred Africans of differing political persuasions met together in a state of gloom' (Leeman, *Lesotho and the Struggle*, 168).

10 The Act 'scrapped the Common Cape [voters] Roll', 'froze the numbers of enfranchised Cape Africans, who totalled about 11,000' and 'strengthened the process of land segregation, apportion[ing] a mere 13.7% of South Africa for African ownership' (Leeman, *Lesotho and the Struggle*, 87).

11 Anti-imperialist, anti-colonialist Pan-African organisation started in New York by Paul Robeson and WEB Du Bois, accessed 6 August 2018, http://www.oxfordreference.com/view/10.1093/oi/authority.20110803095642748.

12 Under Xuma's leadership, an African Bill of Rights was drawn up in 1943. This demanded an equal part in governance through a universal franchise. '*African Claims*, the new constitution, and a call for the establishment of a Youth League, were presented to the ANC 1943 Conference at Kimberley' (Leeman, *Lesotho and the Struggle*, 172).

13 Formed by 'Coloured and African intellectuals in reaction to the nascent African exclusivism of the ANC Youth League. Whereas the Native Leaders sat on the Native Representative Council and Govan Mbeki served in the Transkei Bhunga, the NEUM called for the boycott of both, and it developed, throughout the 1940s and 1950s, a severe and uncompromising anti-collaborationist stance' (Mark Gevisser, *Thabo Mbeki: The Dream Deferred* [Johannesburg and Cape Town: Jonathan Ball, 2007], 80).

14 Lembede and Mda's work in the ANCYL 'marked the launching of the Africanist Movement, which eventually developed into the Pan Africanist Congress, the Black Consciousness Movement and the National Forum' (Leeman, *Lesotho and the Struggle*, 173).

15 Bernard Leeman, 'Mandela, Sobukwe and Leballo: The South African Communist Party and the Pan Africanist Congress' (2016), 2, accessed 31 May 2023, https://www.scribd.com/document/317895751/Mandela-Sobukwe-and-Leballo-5-July-2016. Mda was the writer Zakes Mda's father.

16 Africanist movement founded 'against ANC wishes' mainly in order to combat the South African government and British Basutoland Administration's joint intention to incorporate Basutoland into South Africa (Leeman, 'Mandela, Sobukwe and Leballo').

17 'The authors at the time did not acknowledge their work, but Ruth First, Lionel Bernstein, Mrs S. Muller, Mike Muller, Michael Harmel, Charles Baker, Fred Carneson and Joe Slovo were all suspected of having a hand in it [...] After the contents of the Charter had been fully examined and elucidated, many ANC members felt tricked. Eventually many refused to accept the consequences of its adoption and formed the PAC' (Leeman, *Lesotho and the Struggle*, 237). 'Africanists were against it because it was a means for minority ethnic groups, mostly elitist professionals, to take over the ANC' (Leeman, *Lesotho and the Struggle*, 238).

NOTES

18 156 people initially arrested, in the wake of the threat posed to the South African government by the Congress of the People in 1955, accessed 29 March 2023, https://www.sahistory.org.za/article/treason-trial-1956-1961.
19 Nkrumah 'did much to convince the Africanists that their ideology for liberation was correct. For his part, Mokhehle advised Sobukwe [to] form a new political party [...] In April 1959, the Africanists founded the Pan Africanist Congress (PAC) under Sobukwe and Leballo' (Leeman, *Lesotho and the Struggle*, 248).
20 'The AAPC had a larger vision than the eventual OAU and nothing has since served to replace it' (Leeman, *Lesotho and the Struggle*, 340).
21 The Robert Sobukwe Papers in the Historical Papers Research Archive, University of the Witwatersrand, record the history of his involvement, accessed 26 May 2023, http://researcharchives.wits.ac.za/papers-of-robert-sobukwe.
22 In March 1960, police killed 11 protesters in Pondoland. People retaliated by killing 20 collaborators. In November, a state of emergency was declared in Transkei and 'eventually, 4,769 peasants were detained (officially) of whom twenty were hanged' (Leeman, *Lesotho and the Struggle*, 323).
23 'A paramilitary, formed ostensibly for border security [but] in fact created to combat the activities of the BCP [and] commanded by British officers until 1974' (Leeman, *Lesotho and the Struggle*, 332).
24 'Leballo evades capture for six months. Sobukwe detained after completing his sentence and sent to Robben Island' (Leeman, 'Mandela, Sobukwe and Leballo', 3).
25 In October 1963, 'ten leading opponents of apartheid went on trial for their lives on charges of sabotage', including Nelson Mandela. The trial ended on 12 June 1964 'with the court sentencing eight people to life imprisonment' including Mandela, Walter Sisulu and Moerane's brother-in-law Govan Mbeki, accessed 6 June 2023, https://www.sahistory.org.za/article/rivonia-trial-1963-1964.
26 'Overconfidence, neglect of eastern mountains, and SACP funding costs BCP election win' (Leeman, 'Mandela, Sobukwe and Leballo', 3).
27 'Lesotho became independent under an inexperienced missionary-backed government, allied to South African interests. During its term as the legitimate government of Lesotho between 1966 and 1970, the BNP was aided by South African officials and industrialists to further the political and economic integration of the country into South Africa. There was also international sympathy for a small country totally surrounded by South Africa, irrespective of the political attitudes of its leadership' (Leeman, *Lesotho and the Struggle*, 383).
28 Jonathan's seizure of power was supported by a 'British mercenary led coup with links to rogue South Africa intelligence operatives' (Leeman, *Lesotho and the Struggle*, 4).
29 A Black Consciousness student organisation formed after the banning of the ANC and PAC, accessed 29 March 2023, https://www.sahistory.org.za/dated-event/black-people-convention-formed.
30 Accessed 30 July 2018, https://en.wikipedia.org/wiki/1973_in_South_Africa.
31 Zulu National Cultural Liberation Movement.
32 Biko was 'designated PAC deputy leader' at the time (Leeman, 'Mandela, Sobukwe and Leballo', 4).

33 American and Nigerian money supports David Sibeko's reform faction in the PAC but when Leballo is elected PAC chair 'Sibeko seizes power when Leballo leaves for England, although he is then assassinated (Leeman 'Mandela, Sobukwe and Leballo', 4).
34 Accessed 29 March 2023, https://www.sahistory.org.za/article/united-democratic-front-timeline-1983-1990.

Preface

1 Sigmund Freund quoted by Peter Gay, *Freud: A Life for Our Time* (New York and London: WW Norton & Company, (2006 [1988]), xv–xvi.
2 African Composers Edition, 'Michael Mosoeu Moerane', accessed 30 July 2024, https://african-composers-edition.co.za/composers/michael-moerane/.

Introduction: Moerane in Life and Literature

1 Thuso Moerane, 'Biography of Michael Mosoeu Moerane B.Mus. (21-09-1904)–(27-01-1980)', Tsepo Moerane private collection, Komani.
2 David Ambrose, 'Death of Epainette Mbeki, Mother of Former South African President, Thabo Mbeki', *Summary of Events in Lesotho* 21, no. 2 (2014): 25.
3 Mark Gevisser, *Thabo Mbeki: The Dream Deferred* (Johannesburg and Cape Town: Jonathan Ball, 2007), 28.
4 Thuso Moerane, 'Biography'. This would take Moerane to the equivalent of Grade 5 in present-day South Africa.
5 Thuso Moerane, 'Biography'. This is equivalent to today's Grade 7.
6 Thuso Moerane, 'Biography'.
7 Manasseh Tebatso Moerane, 'An Address by M.T. Moerane on the Occasion of the Unveiling of the Tombstone of his Elder Brother Michael, Mosoeu at Hlotse, Lesotho on December 17, 1988', Tsepo Moerane private collection, Komani, 1. The level is equivalent to Grade 10.
8 MT Moerane, 'Address'. This is the equivalent of Grades 11–12. The South African Native College was the only place in southern Africa at that time where Africans could complete the highest level of schooling.
9 Thuso Moerane, 'Biography'.
10 Thuso Moerane, 'Biography'.
11 Paul Maylam, *Rhodes University, 1904–2016: An Intellectual, Political and Cultural History* (Grahamstown: Institute of Social and Economic Research, Rhodes University, 2017), 32.
12 Gilbert Ramatlapeng, interview, Maseru, 4 April 2014.
13 Thuso Moerane, 'Biography'; Maylam, *Rhodes University*, 82.
14 Thuso Moerane, 'Biography'.
15 Thuso Moerane, 'Biography'.
16 Gevisser, *Thabo Mbeki*, 77–84; Ziphezinhle Msimango, 'Full Version of Sunday Times Interview with Former President Thabo Mbeki', Facebook, 2 April 2013, https://www.facebook.com/permalink.php/?story_fbid=10151430788504713&id=38131714712.
17 Thuso Moerane, 'Biography'.

NOTES

18 Bennett Makalo Khaketla, *Lesotho 1970: African Coup Under the Microscope* (Bloomsbury: C. Hurst and Co., 1971).
19 Mango Tshabangu, *Footprints in Stone: Women and the Zenzele Movement in South Africa* (Harare, Johannesburg, Cairo and London: Themba Books, 2015).
20 Gevisser, *Thabo Mbeki*, 25.
21 In April 1980. Thuso Moerane, interview, Komani, 12 May 2014.
22 *Rand Daily Mail*, 3 March 1966: 3.
23 Tsepo and Neo Moerane, interview, Komani, 20 September 2019.
24 Mofelehetsi Moerane, interview, Atteridgeville, 14 May 2014.
25 Eric Lekhanya, interview, Maseru, 2 March 2011.
26 Pretoria Bureau, 'Lesotho Burial for Composer', *Rand Daily Mail Extra*, 6 February 1980: 5.
27 It is the custom in African societies in southern Africa to erect the tombstone and gravestone some years after a person's burial. This then becomes the occasion of a family gathering and an honouring of the deceased.
28 MT Moerane, 'Address'.
29 How Moerane belonged to the family of Pelesana is discussed in Chapter 1.
30 When teaching tonic solfa and music theory to mission students, teachers did not teach 'composition' as such, which students had to pick up from other composers, either aurally at choir practices, or by swopping manuscript scores. Composers were probably not aware, therefore, of the custom in other countries of putting the date and place of composition at the end of a completed work.
31 *Leselinyana le Lesotho* [*The Little Light of Lesotho*], 'May Esther Bedford Prizes (South African Native College) Music', *Leselinyana le Lesotho* 70, no. 2 (13 January 1937): 3. The prize was £20, and it was the only composition prize Moerane ever received.
32 Michael Mosoeu Moerane, 'Barali ba Jerusalema: O Daughters of Jerusalem', in *South Africa Sings, Volume 1: African Choral Repertoire in Dual Notation*, ed. James Steven Mzilikazi Khumalo (Johannesburg: Southern African Music Rights Organisation, 1998), 14–21; 'Della', in *South Africa Sings, Volume 2: African Choral Repertoire in Dual Notation*, ed. James Steven Mzilikazi Khumalo (Johannesburg: Southern African Music Rights Organisation, 2008), 95–107.
33 See also https://african-composers-edition.co.za/m-m-moerane-catalogue-of-works/, accessed 9 July 2024. This book draws on many sources, in some of which spellings, diacritical marks or accents differ from those used by Moerane. This causes apparent typographical inconsistencies in the text. These are retained here rather than corrected, so as to stay as close as possible to the historical materials we had to work with.
34 Mavis Mpola, personal communication to author, 3 April 1999; the trophy is in Moerane's house in Tsifalimali.
35 Michael Blake, 'Parallel Streams: An Overview of South African Composition', *World New Music Magazine*, no. 10 (2000): 13–19.
36 Kenneth Grundy, 'Cultural Politics in South Africa: An Inconclusive Transformation', *African Studies Review* 39, no. 1 (1996): 1–24.
37 Louise Meintjes, *Sound of Africa! Making Music Zulu in a South African Studio* (Durham and London: Duke University Press, 2003).

38 Antonio Gramschi, *Selections from the Prison Notebooks of Antonio Gramschi*, edited and translated by Quentin Hoare and Geoffrey Nowell Smith (London: Lawrence and Wishart 1971), 556.
39 Accessed 28 July 2024, https://bach.wursten.be/portraits/1748%20Haussmann.htm.
40 Deirdre Hansen, *The Life and Work of Benjamin Tyamzashe: A Contemporary Xhosa Composer* (Grahamstown: Institute of Social and Economic Research, Rhodes University, 1968); Yvonne Huskisson, *Die Bantoe-Komponiste van Suider-Afrika/The Bantu Composers of Southern Africa* (Johannesburg: South African Broadcasting Corporation, 1969); Yvonne Huskisson and Sarita Hauptfleisch, eds., *Black Composers of Southern Africa: An Expanded Supplement to The Bantu Composers of Southern Africa* (Pretoria: Human Sciences Research Council, 1992).
41 Khabi Mngoma, 'The Correlation of Folk Music and Art Music Among African Composers', in *Papers Presented at the Second Symposium on Ethnomusicology*, ed. Andrew Tracey (Grahamstown: International Library of African Music, 1981), 61–69; Bongani Mthethwa, 'The Songs of Alfred A. Kumalo: A Study in Nguni and Western Musical Syncretism', in *Papers Presented at the Seventh Symposium on Ethnomusicology, 1987*, ed. Andrew Tracey (Grahamstown: International Library of African Music, 1988), 28–32.
42 Veit Erlmann, *African Stars: Studies in Black South African Performance* (Chicago: The University of Chicago Press, 1991).
43 PJ Nhlapo and Sibongile Khumalo, *The Voice of African Song* (Johannesburg: Skotaville Publishers, 1993).
44 Christopher Ballantine, 'Making Visible the Invisible: Creative Process and the Compositions of Joseph Shabalala', in *Papers Presented at the Symposium on Ethnomusicology Number 14, 1996*, ed. Andrew Tracey (Grahamstown: International Library of African Music, 1997), 56–59.
45 Markus Detterbeck, 'South African Choral Music (Amakwaya): Song, Contest and the Formation of Identity' (DPhil diss., University of Natal, 2002); Grant Olwage, 'Scriptions of the Choral: The Historiography of Black South African Choralism', *South African Journal of Musicology: SAMUS* 22 (2002): 29–45; 'Music and (Post)Colonialism: The Dialectics of Choral Culture on a South African Frontier' (PhD diss., Rhodes University, 2003); 'John Knox Bokwe, Colonial Composer: Tales About Race and Music', *Journal of the Royal Musical Association* 131 (2006): 1–37; 'Apartheid's Musical Signs: Reflections on Black Choralism, Modernity and Race-Ethnicity in the Segregation Era', in *Composing Apartheid: Music for and Against Apartheid*, ed. Grant Olwage (Johannesburg: Wits University Press, 2008), 35–53; 'John Knox Bokwe: Father of Black South African Choral Composition', *NewMusicSA Bulletin* 9/10 (2010/2011): 18–19.
46 Ndwamato George Mugovhani, 'The Manifestation of the "African Style" in the Works of Mzilikazi Khumalo' (MMus diss., University of the Witwatersrand, 1998); '*Muzika Wa Dzikhwairi*: An Essay On the History of Venda Choral Music', *Muziki: Journal of Music Research in Africa* 10, no. 2 (2013): 75–89; Ndwamato George Mugovhani and Ayodamope Oluranti, 'Symbiosis or Integration: A Study of the Tonal Elements in the Choral Works of Mzilikazi Khumalo and Phelelani Mnomiya', *Muziki: Journal of Music Research in Africa* 12, no. 2 (2015): 1–21;

NOTES

Christine Lucia, 'Back to the Future? Idioms of "Displaced Time" in South African Composition', in *Composing Apartheid: Music For and Against Apartheid*, ed. Grant Olwage (Johannesburg: Wits University Press, 2008), 11–34; 'Mohapeloa and the Heritage of African Song', *African Music: Journal of the International Library of African Music* 9, no. 1 (2011): 56–86; 'Composing Towards/Against Whiteness: The African Music of Mohapeloa', in *Unsettling Whiteness*, eds. Samantha Schulz and Lucy Michaels (Oxford: Inter-Disciplinary Press e-Book, 2014), 219–230; '"Yet None with Truer Fervour Sing": *Coronation March* and the (De)Colonisation of African Choral Music', *African Music: Journal of the International Library of African Music* 10, no. 3 (2017): 23–44; '"The Times Do Not Permit": Moerane, South Africa, Lesotho, and *Fatše La Heso*', *Muziki: Journal of Music Research in Africa* 16, no. 2 (2019): 87–112; 'Michael Mosoeu Moerane in the Museum', *Fontes Artis Musicae* 67, no. 3 (2020): 187–215.

47 Vivien Pieters, 'Music and Presbyterianism at the Lovedale Missionary Institute, 1841–1955' (PhD diss., University of South Africa, 2021), 246–258.

48 Christine Lucia, 'General Introduction', in *Michael Mosoeu Moerane Scholarly Edition*, general ed. Christine Lucia (Cape Town: African Composers Edition, 2020); African Composers Edition, accessed 9 July 2024, https://african-composers-edition.co.za/general-introduction; Lucia, Moerane Catalogue.

49 Gevisser, *Thabo Mbeki*, 18–30.

50 These are in the South African History Archives (SAHA) in Johannesburg.

51 Huskisson, *Bantu Composers*, 1969; Yvonne Huskisson, 'Moerane, Michael Mosoue' [sic], *New Dictionary of South African Biography*, ed. EJ Verwey and Nelly E Sonderling (Pretoria: Vista, 1980), 114–115; Huskisson and Hauptfleisch, *Black Composers*; Percival Robson Kirby, 'Moerane, Michael Mosoeu', in *South African Music Encyclopedia Volume III, J-O*, ed. Jacques P. Malan (Cape Town: Oxford University Press, 1984), 253–254; William McNaught, 'Broadcast Music', *The Listener*, 30 November 1944, 612–613; Deirdre Larkin, 'The Symphonic Poem and Tone Poem in South Africa', *Ars Nova* 26 (1994): 5–42; Elizabeth Kriek, 'Die Simfonie in Suid-Afrika: 1889–1989' (MMus diss., University of South Africa, 1991); Elizabeth Kriek, 'Die Simfonie in Suid-Afrika, 1970–1990: 'n Styl- en Struktuurstudie' (DMus diss., University of South Africa, 1995); Mavis Noluthando Mpola, 'An Analysis of Oral Literary Music Texts in IsiXhosa' (PhD diss., Rhodes University, 2007); Jeffrey Brukman, 'Tribute to Michael Moerane', *CueOnline*, accessed 22 October 2009, http://cue.ru.ac.za/music/2009/tribute-michaelmoerane.html and no longer available; Patricia Lawrence, *Viva Musica! A Bird's Eye View of Music at Unisa* (Pretoria: Unisa Press, 2011), 18; Denis-Constant Martin, *Sounding the Cape: Music, Identity and Politics in South Africa* (Cape Town: African Minds, 2013), 13; Carmel Rickard, 'Moerane and the Lost Chord Detectives', *Weekly Mail* Arts supplement, December 1988; Mokale Koapeng, 'Michael Mosoeu Moerane (1909–1981)', in *2009 African Prescribed Music* Old Mutual National Choir Festival Music Prescription Guidelines and Information Package (Old Mutual National Choir Festival, 2009), [0]–12; Zakes Mda, *Sometimes There is a Void: Memoirs of an Outsider* (New York: Macmillan, 2011), 99–108; 123–127.

52   Accessed 22 May 2023, https://africlassical.blogspot.com/2015/09/michael-mosoeu-moerane-born-20.html; accessed 22 May 2023, https://en.wikipedia.org/wiki/Michael_Mosoeu_Moerane.
53   Rickard, 'Lost Chord Detectives'.
54   Two interviewees independently told me that most of his belongings were destroyed.
55   Mofelehetsi Moerane, interview, Atteridgeville, 14 May 2014.
56   FZ van der Merwe and Jan de Graaf, *Suid-Afrikaanse Musiek-Bibliografie 1787–1952 deur F.Z. van der Merwe en 1953–1972 Bygewerk vir die Raad vir Geesteswetenskaplike Navorsing deur Jan van de Graaf* (Cape Town and Johannesburg: Tafelberg, 1974 [1958]), 275.
57   Huskisson, *Bantu Composers*, 157; Huskisson, 'Moerane', 214; Kirby, 'Moerane', 253. On Moerane's tombstone, engraved in 1988, the date is 21 September, however. It seems that Thabo Moerane, who was working in Geneva at the time, returned to Lesotho too late to change the 21 to 20 (Nthabiseng, interview, Bronkhorstspruit, 4 October 2017).
58   James Steven Mzilikazi Khumalo, 'Michael Mosoeu Moerane', in *South Africa Sings, Volume 1: African Choral Repertoire in Dual Notation*, ed. James Steven Mzilikazi Khumalo (Johannesburg: Southern African Music Rights Organisation, 1998), 14; SAMRO, *Catalogue: Works by Michael Mosoeu Moerane 1901–1981* (Johannesburg: SAMRO, 2003), [1]; James Steven Mzilikazi Khumalo, 'Michael Mosoeu Moerane', in *South Africa Sings, Volume 2: African Choral Repertoire in Dual Notation*, ed. James Steven Mzilikazi Khumalo (Johannesburg: Southern African Music Rights Organisation, 2008), 95 Mpola, 'Analysis', 49.
59   Koapeng, *2009 African Prescribed Music*, 2–12.
60   Pretoria Bureau, 'Lesotho Burial for Composer'.
61   Huskisson 'Moerane'; Kirby, 'Moerane'; Huskisson and Hauptfleisch, *Black Composers*, 25; Lawrence, *Unisa Musica*.
62   Pieters, 'Music and Presbyterianism', 246.
63   The entry has since been corrected to 'Michael Mosoeu Moerane (1904–1980), South African-Basotho Composer, Teacher, Pianist & Conductor', accessed 9 July 2024, https://chevalierdesaintgeorges.homestead.com/Moerane.html. The UP website http://sacomposers.up.ac.za, accessed 16 February 2017, is no longer available.
64   Pallo Jordan, 'MaMbeki's passing marks the end of an era', accessed 15 June 2014, http://www.bdlive.co.za/opinion/columnists/2014/06/12/mambekis-passing-marks-the-end-of-an-era and no longer available; Josias Makibinyane Mohapeloa, *From Mission to Church: Fifty Years of the Work of the Paris Evangelical Missionary Society and the Lesotho Evangelical Church 1933–83* (Morija: Morija Sesuto Book Depot, 1985).
65   Lebohang Mofelehetsi, personal communication to author, 21 May 2014. BNP = Basotoland National Party (now the Basotho National Party).
66   Bernard Leeman, *Lesotho and the Struggle for Azania: The Origins and History of the African National Congress, Pan Africanist Congress, South African Communist Party and Basutoland Congress Party 1780–1994* (London: Bernard Leeman, 2015), 113. The 2015 publication is 'a revised and slightly updated edition' of

Leeman's doctorate, originally published in 1985, whose title was *Africanist Political Movements in Lesotho and Azania (South Africa) 1780–1984: The Origins and History of the Basutoland Congress Party of Lesotho and the Pan Africanist Congress of Azania.*

67 Marumo Moerane, interview, Durban, 7 October 2017.
68 Khumalo, 'Moerane' *Volume 1*, 14.
69 Tasmina Viljoen, 'Choral Tribute to Michael Moerane', *Sowetan*, 3 September 2004: 5.
70 Huskisson, *Bantu Composers*, 157; Anton Hartman, internal memo to Yvonne Huskisson, 17 July 1973, SAMRO Archive, Yvonne Huskisson Collection, file 'Moerane, M', subfile 'Korrespondensie'; Mia Hartman, *Anton Hartman: Dis Sy Storie [This is His Story]* (Pretoria: Mia Hartman, 2003), 67.
71 This may have been at Moerane's insistence, but there is no documentation to support this view.
72 Hartman to Huskisson, 1973.
73 Marumo Moerane, interview 2017.
74 Van der Merwe and van de Graaf, *Musiek-Bibliografie*, 275.
75 Huskisson, *Bantu Composers*, 157–158.
76 Pretoria Bureau, 'Lesotho Burial for Composer'.
77 Ambrose, 'Epainette Mbeki', 24.
78 William Edward Burghardt Du Bois, *The Souls of Black Folk* (New York: Barnes & Noble Classics, 2003 [1903]), 45; 122.
79 Tessa Joughlin, ' The Gumtree Mill', accessed 25 February 2023, http://www.pbase.com/tessajoughin/the_gumtree_mill.
80 Mda, *Memoirs*, 99; 98; see also *Leselinyana le Lesotho [The Little Light of Lesotho]*, '1969 Cambridge Certificate Results', 20 January 1970, 4, David Ambrose Archive, Ladybrand.
81 South African History Online, accessed 30 July 2024, https://sahistory.org.za/dated-event/michael-mosoue-moerane-pianist-choirmaster-and-composer-born-gumtree-basutoland-now. The entry was only partially corrected when I pointed out some mistakes.
82 Kirby, 'Moerane', 254; De Jager telex to Yvonne Huskisson, 9 May 1969, SAMRO Huskisson Collection, File 'Moerane, M.M.', Subfile 'Korrespondensie'.
83 *Rand Daily Mail*, '36 Control Posts on Borders of S.A.', 30 April 1963: 2.
84 Tseliso Makhakhe, interview, Maseru, 20 May 2014.
85 Shadrack Mapetla, interview, Midrand, 15 May 2014.
86 *Rand Daily Mail*, 'PEKA High School (Basutoland) … Wanted: Deputy-Headmaster. Clerical or Lay. Graduate with Teaching Diploma. Willing to Share Administrative Duties. Physical Fitness More Important Than Age. January 1963', 30 June 1962, 8. This sounds cut out for Moerane, who did in fact become deputy-headmaster (Makhakhe, interview 2014).
87 *Rand Daily Mail*, 30 June 1962.
88 Moerane built a small cottage in Peka village and lived in a staff house in the grounds of Peka High School.
89 Letter from Mrs RW Levine to Percival Kirby, 29 June 1965, University of Cape Town Manuscripts and Archives, PR Kirby Collection BC 750.

90 Letter from Percival Kirby to Michael Moerane, 21 January 1966, University of Cape Town Manuscripts and Archives, PR Kirby Collection BC 750; Letter from Michael Moerane to Percival Kirby, 16 February 1966, University of Cape Town Manuscripts and Archives, PR Kirby Collection BC 750; author's emphasis.
91 Manasseh Tebatso Moerane, '"I Chose Freedom": The Autobiography of Mr. M.T. Moerane of South Africa', Johannesburg: South African History Archive, AL3284, Mark Gevisser's Research Papers for *Thabo Mbeki: The Dream Deferred*, Box 3.2.17 (n.d.), 16. The original has 'dear' but Gevisser has marked it 'tear'.

Chapter 1 The House of Moerane

1 'House' refers to far more than Moerane's immediate ancestors or the home he was born in, and is used in the same sense in which Jeff Peires uses the word in his landmark history, *The House of Phalo: A History of the Xhosa People in the Days of Their Independence* (Johannesburg: Ravan Press, 1981).
2 The historiographic sources include Paul Maylam, *A History of the African People of South Africa: From the Early Iron Age to the 1970s* (London: Croom Helm, 1986); Julian Cobbing, 'The Mfecane as Alibi: Thoughts on Dithakong and Mbolompo', *The Journal of African History* 29, no. 3 (1988): 487–519; Bernard Leeman, *Lesotho and the Struggle for Azania: The Origins and History of the African National Congress, Pan Africanist Congress, South African Communist Party and Basutoland Congress Party 1780–1994* (London: Bernard Leeman, 2015); Stephen Gill, *A Short History of Lesotho: From the Late Stone Age Until the 1993 Elections* (Morija: Morija Museum and Archives, 1993); Carolyn Hamilton, et al., eds., *The Cambridge History of South Africa: Volume 1, From Early Times to 1885* (Cambridge: Cambridge University Press, 2009); Robert Ross, et al., eds., *The Cambridge History of South Africa: Volume 2, 1885–1994* (Cambridge: Cambridge University Press, 2011); Scott Rosenberg and Richard F Weisfelder, *Historical Dictionary of Lesotho*, 2nd edition (Lanham, MD: Scarecrow Press, 2013); South African History Online, accessed 9 July 2024, https://www.sahistory.org.za/.
3 Martin Chatfield Legassick, *The Politics of a South African Frontier: The Griqua, the Sotho-Tswana, and the Missionaries, 1780–1840* (Basle: Basler Afrika Bibliographien, 2010).
4 Manasseh Tebatso Moerane, '"I Chose Freedom": The Autobiography of Mr. MT Moerane of South Africa.' Johannesburg: South African History Archive, AL3284, Mark Gevisser's Research Papers for *Thabo Mbeki: The Dream Deferred*, Box 3.2.17 (n.d.), 4.
5 MT Moerane, 'Autobiography', 5. Mark Gevisser corrected Moerane's '1890s' to '1880s' in the typescript.
6 Mark Gevisser, *Thabo Mbeki: The Dream Deferred* (Johannesburg and Cape Town: Jonathan Ball, 2007), 24.
7 MT Moerane, 'Autobiography', 5.
8 Leeman, *Lesotho and the Struggle*, 14.
9 Among the Gevisser papers in the South Africa History Archives in Johannesburg are two Moerane family trees, one typed and one handwritten by Gevisser while he was interviewing informants.
10 Susan Cook, 'Chiefs, Kings, Corporatization, and Democracy: A South African Case Study', *The Brown Journal of World Affairs* 12, no. 1 (Summer/Fall 2005): 125,

NOTES

accessed 9 July 2024, https://www.jstor.org/stable/24590671. The prefix 'Ba' in Sesotho and Setswana means 'the' (pl) and I therefore usually refer in this book to 'Bafokeng' (for example) rather than 'the Bafokeng'.

11 Isaac Schapera, 'Notes on the Early History of the Kwena (Bakwena-bagaSechele)', *Botswana Notes and Records* 12 (1980): 83. This is how social anthropologist Schapera put it in 1980, drawing on interviews that he conducted in 1938 with senior chiefs who were the acknowledged guardians of oral history at that time.
12 Leeman, *Lesotho and the Struggle*, 14.
13 Leeman, *Lesotho and the Struggle*, 1. The source Leeman gives for this is the 1973 *Oxford History of South Africa*; see also Maylam, *History*, 42.
14 Gill, *Short History*, 65–66.
15 Gill, *Short History*, 68.
16 Leeman, *Lesotho and the Struggle*, 3.
17 Leeman, *Lesotho and the Struggle*, 3.
18 Leeman, *Lesotho and the Struggle*, 5.
19 Leeman, *Lesotho and the Struggle*, 4.
20 Leeman, *Lesotho and the Struggle*, 7.
21 When Sir Philip Wodehouse, the British High Commissioner and Cape Governor, 'expressed reservations about the crowding of the Basotho behind the new border, President Brand (OFS) replied: "A plan is now being devised by which such Basutos as are unable to find a livelihood in Basutoland will be permitted to enter the Free State to seek service"' (Brand, quoted in Leeman, *Lesotho and the Struggle*, 13). This marked the beginning of an economic dependence on migrant labour that continues to this day: the land on the Free State side of the Caledon River is still contested by Lesotho. See the report by Al Jazeera in March 2023, 'Lesotho Lawmakers to Debate Reclaiming Parts of South Africa', accessed 16 May 2023, https://www.aljazeera.com/news/2023/3/29/lesotho-lawmakers-to-debate-reclaiming-parts-of-south-africa.
22 Gevisser, *Thabo Mbeki*, 21.
23 Gevisser, *Thabo Mbeki*, 22.
24 Gevisser, *Thabo Mbeki*, 22. 'Le Jakane' can mean Christian (Lebohang Mofelehetsi, personal communication to author, 21 May 2014) or 'foreigner' (Gevisser, *Thabo Mbeki*, 23–24). See also Adolphe Mabille and Hermann Dieterlin, reclassified, revised and enlarged by RA Paroz, *Southern Sotho–English Dictionary*, 7th edition (Morija: Morija Sesuto Book Depot, 1988 [1950]), 127, where the meaning of the root verb, 'jaka' is given as 'to go and live in a foreign country'.
25 MT Moerane, 'Autobiography', 1.
26 MT Moerane, 'Autobiography', 3.
27 Thuso Moerane, 'Biography of Michael Mosoeu Moerane B.Mus. (21-09-1904)–(27-01-1980)', Tsepo Moerane private collection, Komani.
28 Mabille and Dieterlin, *Dictionary*, 46.
29 Adolphe Mabille and Hermann Dieterlin, reclassified, revised and enlarged by RA Paroz, *Southern Sotho-English Dictionary: New Edition Using the 1959 Republic of South Africa Orthography*, 8th edition (Morija: Morija Sesuto Book Depot 1988 [1961]), 63.
30 Gevisser, *Thabo Mbeki*, 21.

31 Thabo Tseko Ei Pitso, interview, Maseru, 5 April 2014.
32 David Ambrose and Mamhlongo Maphisa, interview, Ladybrand, 22 May 2014.
33 It was not only the home but also the constituency of BCP candidate Mofelehetsi Moerane (Leeman, *Lesotho and the Struggle*, 659).
34 Tseliso Makhakhe, interview, Maseru, 20 May 2014.
35 Gevisser, *Thabo Mbeki*, 18. The image of Moerane as a child challenges his date of birth yet again. If the photo *is* from 1920 – and it must be, because it shows the two youngest girls – and if he was indeed born in 1904, he would have been 16, whereas in the photograph he only looks about 10 or 11, unless he was unusually short as a child. Moreover, he cannot be older than the first-born, Daniel.
36 Gevisser, *Thabo Mbeki*, 19.
37 The irony, as Bennett Khaketla points out in his 'Genealogy of the Royal House of Moshoeshoe', is that Moshoeshoe I's first wife Mamohato 'begat four sons: (a) Letsie I, (b) Molapo, (c) Masopha, and (d) Majara' (*Coup* 338); and that the line of succession from Letsie I led to Constance Bereng (1938–96) who became King Moshoeshoe II, while the line of succession from Molapo led to Chief Leabua Jonathan (1914–1987) who became first Prime Minister of Lesotho in 1966. Both men – who ended up on diametrically opposed sides of Lesotho's political spectrum – were great grandsons of Moshoeshoe I (Bennett Makalo Khaketla, *Lesotho 1970: African Coup Under the Microscope* [Bloomsbury: C. Hurst and Co., 1971]), 338–339.
38 Gevisser, *Thabo Mbeki*, 28.
39 Leeman, *Lesotho and the Struggle*. Other sources include Maylam, *History*; André Odendaal, *The Founders: The Origins of the ANC and the Struggle for Democracy in South Africa* (Johannesburg: Jacana Media, 2012); Gill, *Short History*; Ross et al., *Cambridge History Volume 2*; Christopher Saunders and Nicholas Southey, *A Dictionary of South African History* (Cape Town and Johannesburg: David Philip, 1998), 173.
40 Gevisser, *Thabo Mbeki*, 80. Gevisser describes the lines Moerane set from 'The Song of Songs' in *Barali Ba Jerusalema* as 'the Bible's proto-Black Consciousness lines' (80).
41 Saunders and Southey, *Dictionary*, 173.
42 Nelson Mandela, *Long Walk to Freedom: The Autobiography of Nelson Mandela* (London: Little, Brown and Company, 1994), 33.
43 William Beinart and Colin Bundy, *Hidden Struggles in Rural South Africa: Politics & Popular Movements in the Transkei & Eastern Cape 1890–1930* (Johannesburg: Ravan Press, 2017 [1987]), 199.
44 MT Moerane, 'Autobiography', 32–33; Gevisser, *Thabo Mbeki*, 19.
45 David Ambrose, 'Death of Epainette Mbeki, Mother of Former South African President, Thabo Mbeki', *Summary of Events in Lesotho* 21, no. 2 (2014), 25. She later became a staunch member of the ANC until her son, President Thabo Mbeki was 'deposed by Jacob Zuma, who had once been his Vice-President but had been relieved of his duties in 2005 because of his role in the Arms Deal corruption scandal' (26). Thabo Mbeki's 'downfall', says Ambrose, 'resulted in Epainette breaking with the ANC and joining the newly founded opposition party, COPE (Congress of the People with President Mosiuoa Lekota)' (26).
46 Thabo Mbeki, quoted in Gevisser, *Thabo Mbeki*, 783.
47 *Rand Daily Mail*, 'Benson Banned from Meetings', 5 March 1966: 3.

48 Tsepo and Neo Moerane, interview, Komani, 20 September 2019.
49 Thuso Moerane, interview, Komani, 12 May 2014.
50 Margaret Naidu, personal communication to author, 4 March 2017. Mrs Naidu told me that she used to go next door to have piano lessons with Todd. I was made aware, inside her house, of how spaciously Victorian these properties were.
51 Tsepo and Neo Moerane, interview.
52 'Marumo Moerane, interviewed by Danny Massey in 1999', Wits Historical Papers, William Cullen Library, University of the Witwatersrand, A3193f.
53 'Trials: State vs. Mofelehetsi Moerane & 31 others, 1975', Wits Historical Papers, William Cullen Library, University of the Witwatersrand, AK2290, 2.
54 State vs. Mofelehetsi Moerane, 21–22; 87; 90–91.
55 David Bellin Coplan, *In the Time of Cannibals: The Word Music of South Africa's Basotho Migrants* (Chicago: The University of Chicago Press, 1994), 172.
56 Makhakhe, interview 2014.
57 Leeman, *Lesotho and the Struggle*, 339; 471; 486; 517. Makhakhe's involvement came at a high cost: 14 years of exile in Botswana, during which time he heard that Peka students 'brutally assaulted' a teacher, and that the headmaster, Mr Mabote, was kidnapped by police and soldiers, who 'made him stand on the back of a van and shout all the way from there to Maseru that he was not a member of the opposition, the BCP […] That was the end of his life as a teacher' (Makhakhe, interview 2014).
58 Victor Lechesa, interview, Maseru, 27 February 2017.
59 Matsobane Putsoa, interview, Maseru, 27 February 2017.
60 Putsoa, interview 2017.
61 Zakes Mda, interview on Zoom, 17 May 2022.
62 Thuso Moerane, interview 2014.
63 Mofelehetsi Moerane, interview, Atteridgeville, 14 May 2014.
64 Sophia Metsekae [Moerane], quoted in Gevisser, *Thabo Mbeki*, 79.
65 Pitso, interview 2014. Among the main points of the 1959 orthography were the replacement of 'l' with 'd' before the letter 'i', 'oa' with 'wa' and 'ea' with 'ya'.
66 Mofelehetsti Moerane, interview 2014.
67 Thuso Moerane, interview 2014.
68 The language isiXhosa is classified by linguists as belonging in the Bantu language group, while Sesotho is in the Sotho-Tswana group.
69 Mandela, *Long Walk*, 44–45.
70 Epainette Mbeki, interview, East London, 27 May 2014.
71 Gilbert Ramatlapeng, interview, Maseru, 4 April 2014.
72 Mosa Ndlula, interview, Muizenberg, 22 October 2019.
73 Nthabiseng, interview, Bronkhorstspruit, 4 October 2017.

Chapter 2 Moerane the Student

1 Average ages of schoolchildren in rural southern Africa have always varied widely (and still do) because of their isolation and limited resources. Because of our patchy knowledge of Moerane's childhood, it is unclear what age he was when he left his father's school, but it is likely that despite the enormous advantages his upbringing gave him, he would have been a year or so older.

2   Manasseh Tebatso Moerane, '"I Chose Freedom": The Autobiography of Mr. MT Moerane of South Africa', Johannesburg: South African History Archive, AL3284, Mark Gevisser's Research Papers for *Thabo Mbeki: The Dream Deferred*, Box 3.2.17 (n.d.), 17.
3   Thuso Moerane, 'Biography of Michael Mosoeu Moerane B.Mus. (21-09-1904)–(27-01-1980)', Tsepo Moerane private collection, Komani.
4   MT Moerane, 'Autobiography', 20.
5   Epainette Mbeki, interview, East London, 27 May 2014.
6   Veit Erlmann, *Music, Modernity and the Global Imagination: South Africa and the West* (New York: Oxford University Press, 1999), 128.
7   Mark Gevisser, *Thabo Mbeki: The Dream Deferred* (Johannesburg and Cape Town: Jonathan Ball, 2007), 28. Gevisser refers to it as a hammond organ, which in such a sorry state could be confused with a harmonium, but a hammond organ is a later, larger keyboard instrument and requires electricity while a harmonium uses air pumped by the feet on two pedals.
8   Josias Makibinyane Mohapeloa and MK Phakisi, *Likheleke tsa Pina Sesothong* [*The Eloquence of Song in Sesotho*] (Maseru: Lekhotla la Sesotho [Sesotho Academy], 1987), 4. Translated for the author by Mantoa Motinyane.
9   Morija Sesuto Book Depot, *Lifela tsa Sione* (Morija: Morija Sesuto Book Depot, 24th edition, 53rd impression, 2015). For accounts of PEMS as a mission and (later) a church, see Josias Makibinyane Mohapeloa, *From Mission to Church: Fifty Years of the Work of the Paris Evangelical Missionary Society and the Lesotho Evangelical Church 1933–83* (Morija: Morija Sesuto Book Depot, 1985); Stephen Gill, *A Short History of Lesotho: From the Late Stone Age Until the 1993 Elections* (Morija: Morija Museum and Archives, 1993); and Martin Chatfield Legassick, *The Politics of a South African Frontier: The Griqua, the Sotho-Tswana, and the Missionaries, 1780–1840* (Basle: Basler Afrika Bibliographien, 2010).
10 Thabo Moerane quoted in Carmel Rickard, 'Moerane and the Lost Chord Detectives', *Weekly Mail* Arts supplement, December 1988.
11 Friedrich Hartmann to Percival Kirby, 11 March 1958, University of Cape Town Manuscripts and Archives, PR Kirby Collection BC 750.
12 Tsepo and Neo Moerane, interview, Komani (Queenstown), 30 September 2019.
13 Mohapeloa and Phakisi, *Likheleke*, 12.
14 Christine Lucia, 'General Introduction to the J.P. Mohapeloa Critical Edition', in *Joshua Pulumo Mohapeloa Critical Edition in Six Volumes* (Cape Town: African Composers Edition, 2016): xlii. Accessed 29 July 2024, https://african-composers-edition.co.za/general-introduction-to-the-mohapeloa-critical-edition/.
15 Mohapeloa and Phakisi, *Likheleke*, 13.
16 Mohapeloa and Phakisi, *Likheleke*, 13–14.
17 'St Johns College', accessed 11 April 2023, https://www.exool.co.za/st-johns-college.
18 Enrolment List 1841–1928 (Lovedale Missionary Institution), Cory Library for Historical Research, MS 16299: n.p.
19 *Lovedale Missionary Institution, South Africa: Annual Report for 1923* (Lovedale: The Mission Press, 1924), 2–3; *Lovedale Missionary Institution, South Africa: Annual Report for 1924* (Lovedale: The Mission Press, 1925), 16; 83; 94–95; 89; 86.

20 *Lovedale Report 1923*, 3; *Lovedale Report 1924*, 2.
21 Thuso Moerane, interview, Komani, 12 May 2014.
22 Manasseh Tebatso Moerane, 'An Address by M.T. Moerane on the Occasion of the Unveiling of the Tombstone of his Elder Brother Michael, Mosoeu at Hlotse, Lesotho on December 17, 1988', Tsepo Moerane private collection, Komani; *Lovedale Report 1923*, 79.
23 *Lovedale Missionary Institution, South Africa: Report for 1925* (Lovedale: The Mission Press, 1926), 45.
24 *Lovedale Report 1924*, 89.
25 Graham Alexander Duncan, 'Coercive Agency: Lovedale Missionary Institution Under Principals Arthur Wilkie and RHW Shepherd', *Missionalia: Southern African Journal of Mission Studies* 38, no. 3 (2010): 430.
26 Duncan, 'Coercive Agency', 430.
27 Timothy Raymond Howard White, 'Lovedale 1930–1955: The Study of a Missionary Institution in its Social, Educational and Political Context' (MA diss., Rhodes University, 1987), 20–21.
28 Cory Library for Historical Research, MS 16602.
29 *Lovedale Missionary Institution, South Africa: Report for 1931* (Lovedale: The Mission Press, 1932), 13; White, 'Lovedale', 33; 36; 39; 41; 42.
30 White, 'Lovedale', 49–73; 77.
31 White, 'Lovedale', 45; 46.
32 White, 'Lovedale', 106–107.
33 White, 'Lovedale', 114–115; Jabavu quoted in White, 'Lovedale', 134.
34 *Lovedale Report 1924*, 82.
35 Vivien Pieters, 'Music and Presbyterianism at the Lovedale Missionary Institute, 1841–1955' (PhD diss., University of South Africa, 2021), 258.
36 Kofi Agawu, 'Tonality as a Colonizing Force in Africa', in *Audible Empire: Music, Global Politics, Critique*, ed. Ronald Radano and Tejumola Olaniyan (Durham, NC: Duke University Press, 2016).
37 *Lovedale Missionary Institution, South Africa: Report for 1926* (Lovedale: The Mission Press, 1927), 70.
38 *Lovedale Report 1926*, 66–68.
39 *Lovedale Missionary Institution, South Africa: Report for 1930* (Lovedale: The Mission Press, 1931), 65.
40 *South African Native College Fort Hare, Alice, Cape Province, South Africa. Calendar 1930* (Lovedale: The Lovedale Press), 96; *South African Native College Fort Hare, Calendar 1928* (Lovedale: The Lovedale Press), 123; *South African Native College Fort Hare, Calendar 1934* (Lovedale: The Lovedale Press), 84.
41 Nelson Mandela, *Long Walk to Freedom: The Autobiography of Nelson Mandela* (London: Little, Brown and Company, 1994), 55; MT Moerane, 'Autobiography', 27.
42 MT Moerane, 'Autobiography', 31; 27.
43 Mandela, *Long Walk*, 56–57.
44 Epainette Mbeki, interview 2014.

45 Tseliso Makhakhe, interview, Maseru, 20 May 2014; Mosa Ndlula, interview, Muizenberg, 22 October 2019; Nthabiseng, interview, Bronkhorstspruit, 4 October 2017.
46 Mofelehetsi Moerane, interview, Atteridgeville, 14 May 2014.
47 Silesu's song *Love, Here is my Heart* is there, too, but it has the signature 'Sophia Moerane' at the top, and was bought at Music Mecca in Vermeulen Street. It must have been bought by Sophia and not her father, given that she studied in Pretoria.
48 Sheet Music Warehouse, 'From Manger to Cross – a Sacred Cantata - Vocal Score With Organ Accompaniment', accessed 6 May 2023, https://www.sheetmusicwarehouse.co.uk/vocal-scores/from-manger-to-cross-a-sacred-cantata-vocal-score-with-organ/.
49 *Leselinyana le Lesotho* [The Little Light of Lesotho], 'May Esther Bedford Prizes (South African Native College), Music', *Leselinyana le Lesotho* 70, no. 2 (1937): 3.
50 *South African Native College Fort Hare, Alice, Cape Province, South Africa. Calendar 1928* (Lovedale: The Lovedale Press), 123.
51 *Lovedale Annual Report 1925*, 44; 47.
52 *Lovedale Annual Reports 1926*, 22; *1929*, 39; *1931*, 13; *1932*, 35; *1933*, 55; *1934*, 50; *1935*, 59; *1936*, 56; *1937*, 57; *1938*, 15.
53 Thabo Mbeki quoted in Brown Bavusile Maaba, 'The History and Politics of Liberation Archives at Fort Hare' (PhD diss., University of Cape Town, 2013), 63; Maaba, 'Liberation Archives', 62; 75.
54 MT Moerane, 'Autobiography', 26; source's emphasis.
55 *The South African Native College Fort Hare, Alice, Cape Province, South Africa. Calendar 1926* (Lovedale: The Lovedale Press), 118–20 and *1927*, 138–40.
56 Marumo Moerane, Wits Historical Papers, File A3193f, 1999.
57 Mandela, *Long Walk*, 51.
58 Mandela, *Long Walk*, 52; 53.
59 Manasseh Moerane's home was recorded as 'Far View, Cape' (*The South African Native College* Fort Hare, Alice, Cape Province, South Africa. *Calendar 1934* [Lovedale: The Lovedale Press], 104), a mission station south of Mangoloaneng.
60 Mandela, *Long Walk*, 51–62. See also South African History Online, 'Alexander Kerr', accessed 30 July 2024, https://www.sahistory.org.za/people/kerr-alexander.
61 MT Moerane, 'Autobiography', 29.
62 Universiteit van Suid-Afrika/University of South Africa, 'This is to certify that Michael Mosoeu Moerane passed the following courses for the B.Mus. degree at this University' (Pretoria: University of South Africa, 1962), University of Cape Town Manuscripts and Archives, PR Kirby Collection BC 750, A: Correspondence.
63 1932, 88 – 'passed 1st year Mus. Bac. 1930'; 1935, 105 – 'passed 3rd year Mus. Bac. 1930'; 1944, 50 – 'B.Mus (S.A.) 1941'.
64 Hartmann to Kirby, 11 March 1958, UCT Kirby Collection.
65 Kirby, Percival Robert, 'Michael Mosoeu Moerane', Pretoria: National Archives of South Africa, HSRC Collection (Kirby Folder), n.d. I am indebted to Mieke

Struwig for knowledge of this unpublished four-page essay, which she located in the unsorted archive of material relating to Malan's *South African Music Encyclopedia* held in the National Archives, Pretoria. Although the essay is undated, its contents strongly indicate that it was intended as the entry on Moerane for the *Encyclopedia*. The final entry edited by Malan as published, however, is much shorter (one paragraph) and blunter, ignoring Kirby's sympathetic tone and most of his detail.

66 Thuso Moerane, 'Biography' and Thuso Moerane, interview 2014.
67 Mofelehetsi Moerane, interview 2014.
68 Hartmann to Kirby, 11 March 1958, UCT Kirby Collection.
69 Michael Moerane to Percival Kirby, 27 June 1968, UCT Kirby Collection.
70 *Rhodes University College Grahamstown: Calendar 1930* (Grahamstown: Grocott and Sherry), 48.
71 *Rhodes University Calendar 1930*, 143–44.
72 Universiteit van Suid-Afrika 1962.
73 *Rhodes University College Grahamstown: Calendar 1931* (Grahamstown: Grocott and Sherry), 148.
74 Universiteit van Suid-Afrika 1962.
75 *Rhodes University College Grahamstown: Calendar 1933* (Grahamstown: Grocott and Sherry), 93.
76 Universiteit van Suid-Afrika 1962.
77 Bernarr Rainbow with Gordon Cox, *Music in Educational Thought and Practice: A Survey from 800 BC* (Aberystwyth: Boethius Press 1989), 239; 241.
78 Paul Maylam, *Rhodes University, 1904–2016: An Intellectual, Political and Cultural History* (Grahamstown: Institute of Social and Economic Research, Rhodes University, 2017), 10.
79 Universiteit van Suid-Afrika 1962.
80 *The Zionist Reporter*, 14 August 1936, 35, accessed 9 July 2024, SUNdigital Collections, https://digital.lib.sun.ac.za, zr-1936-08-14-p35.pdf; Christine Lucia, 'Travesty or Prophecy? Views of South African Black Choral Composition', in *Music and Identity: Transformation and Negotiation*, ed. Eric Akrofi, Maria Smit and Stig-Magnus Thorsén (Stellenbosch: African Sun Media, 2007), 161–180, 163.
81 Hartmann to Kirby, 11 March 1958, UCT Kirby Collection.
82 Kirby, 'Moerane', National Archives. BMus degrees included Harmony, Counterpoint and Orchestration until the final year, a system based on the Oxbridge and London BMus degrees introduced in the later nineteenth century.
83 Maylam, *Rhodes University*, 52.
84 Ronald Currey, *Rhodes University 1904–1970: A Chronicle* (Grahamstown: Rhodes University, 1970), 77.
85 Currey, *Rhodes University*, 83; 73. In 1949, Rhodes was allowed to affiliate with Fort Hare and admit full-time non-European students who wanted to do courses not on offer at Fort Hare (Currey, 112). However, in 1959 under the 'Extension of University Education Act' the two universities were disaffiliated (139). This Act was almost as damaging to tertiary education as the Bantu Education Act was to school education.

86 Maylam, *Rhodes University*, 58; 81–100; 82.
87 Maylam, *Rhodes University*, 83; 99.
88 Maylam, *Rhodes University*, 84.
89 *Rhodes University College Grahamstown Calendar 1940* (Grahamstown: Grocott and Sherry), 17.
90 They are at the home of his grandson, Tsepo Moerane, in Komani. The gown is very short, giving an indication of Moerane's physical stature.
91 MT Moerane, 'Address'.
92 Maylam, *History*, 153–157. Bell's composition students included Hubert du Plessis, Stefans Grové and John Joubert.
93 Friedrich Hartmann to Percival Kirby, 11 March 1958.
94 *Lovedale Missionary Institution, South Africa: Annual Report 1937* (Lovedale: The Mission Press), 27–29.
95 Timothy Jackson quoted in Michael Haas, 'Friedrich Hartmann', Forbidden Music, 1 June 2013, https://forbiddenmusic.org/2013/06/01/friedrich-hartmann/. See also Michael Haas, *Forbidden Music: The Jewish Composers Banned by the Nazis* (New Haven, CT: Yale University Press, 2013) and Timothy Jackson, 'Friedrich Hartmann (1900–1973)', Johannesburg International Mozart Festival programme ([January] 2010): 18–22.
96 Maylam, *Rhodes University*, 82.
97 Ernest Frederick Dube, 'Yesterday's Nazi Sympathizers, Today's South African Leaders', Letter to the Editor, *The New York Times*, 5 August 1985, https://www.nytimes.com/1985/08/16/opinion/l-yesterday-s-nazi-sympathizers-today-s-south-african-leaders-195124.html.
98 Dube, 'Yesterday's Nazi Sympathizers'.
99 Annemie Stimie Behr, 'The Hans Kramer Collection at the National Library, Cape Town: An Archival Perspective on Jewish Patronage of Music in 20th-Century South Africa', *Journal of the Musical Arts in Africa* 12, no. 1–2 (2015): 1–22; Pamela Tansick, 'Tracing Joseph Trauneck: The Walking of a Persecuted Man', *Fontes Artis Musicae* 56, no. 2 (2009): 115–137.
100 Jeffrey Brukman, 'Tribute to Michael Moerane', *Cue Online* (n.d.), accessed 22 October 2009, http://cue.ru.ac.za/music/2009/tribute-michaelmoerane.html and no longer available.
101 Bernard S van der Linde, 'In Memoriam Friedrich Helmut Hartmann', *Ars Nova* 4 no. 1 (1972): 12–15.
102 White, 'Lovedale': 152; 155; 157; 158; 159.

Chapter 3 Moerane the Teacher and Composer

1 Manasseh Tebatso Moerane, '"I Chose Freedom": The Autobiography of Mr. M.T. Moerane of South Africa', Johannesburg: South African History Archive, AL3284, Mark Gevisser's Research Papers for *Thabo Mbeki: The Dream Deferred*, Box 3.2.17 (n.d.), 6.
2 Peter Kallaway, ed., *Apartheid and Education: The Education of Black South Africans* (Johannesburg: Ravan Press, 1984).

3 The Transvaal Education Department's *Report for School Year January–December 1903* quoted in Frank Molteno, 'The Historical Foundations of the Schooling of Black South Africans', in *Apartheid and Education: The Education of Black South Africans*, ed. Peter Kallaway (Johannesburg: Ravan Press, 1984), 67; The 1936 *Report of the Interdepartmental Committee on Native Affairs* 1935–36 quoted in Molteno, 'The Historical Foundations', 62; *Inkundla ya Bantu* XI (119) quoted in Molteno, 'The Historical Foundations', 63.
4 Hendrik Verwoerd, *Bantu Education Policy for the Immediate Future* (Pretoria 1954) quoted in Molteno, 'The Historical Foundations', 92–93.
5 Tom Lodge, 'The Parents' School Boycott: Eastern Cape and East Rand Townships, 1955', in Kallaway, *Apartheid and Education*, 265–295: 266; 268.
6 Grant Olwage, 'Music and (Post)Colonialism: The Dialectics of Choral Culture on a South African Frontier' (PhD diss., Rhodes University, 2003), 67. The situation in state schools is no better today.
7 Khabi Mngoma, 'Music in African Education', in *Music Education in Contemporary South Africa: Proceedings of the First National Music Educators' Conference*, ed. Christine Lucia (Pietermaritzburg: Natal University Press, 1986), 115–121: 115; 116.
8 *Lovedale Missionary Institution, South Africa: Report for 1938* (Lovedale: The Mission Press), 15.
9 De Jager telex to Yvonne Huskisson, 9 May 1969, SAMRO Huskisson Collection, File 'Moerane, M.M.', Subfile 'Korrespondensie'.
10 Olwage, 'Music and (Post)Colonialism', 129. Even closer to an 'oratorio' might have been Bokwe's 1905 'cantata' *Indoda Yamadoda/Man of Men* (Olwage, 'Music and (Post)Colonialism', 163).
11 *Lovedale Annual Report 1924*, 16.
12 *Lovedale Annual Report 1925*, 44; 47.
13 *Lovedale Annual Report 1925*, 44.
14 *Lovedale Annual Report 1926*, 22.
15 *Lovedale Annual Report 1926*, 47.
16 *Lovedale Annual Report 1929*, 39.
17 *Lovedale Annual Report 1938*, 15.
18 Vivien Pieters, 'Music and Presbyterianism at the Lovedale Missionary Institute, 1841–1955' (PhD diss., University of South Africa, 2021), 260.
19 Jonathan Hyslop, 'Food, Authority and Politics: Student Riots in South African Schools 1945–1976', paper presented at the African Studies Seminar, University of the Witwatersrand African Studies Institute, Johannesburg (29 September 1986), 6.
20 Gilbert Ramatlapeng, interview, Maseru, 4 April 2014.
21 Oswin Boys Bull, 'To the Teachers of Basutoland', *Basutoland Teachers' Magazine* 1 (November 1937), 3.
22 Ramatlapeng, interview 2014.
23 Ramatlapeng, interview 2014.
24 Veit Erlmann, *African Stars: Studies in Black South African Performance* (Chicago: The University of Chicago Press, 1991), 142–149.

25 Todd Matshikiza, quoted in Mark Gevisser, *Thabo Mbeki: The Dream Deferred* (Johannesburg and Cape Town: Jonathan Ball, 2007), 78.
26 Gevisser *Thabo Mbeki*, 79. Visiting the Lukhanji Museum in Komani on 23 February 2017, I was struck by the absence of Moerane: the curators had heard of him only vaguely, but had a large newspaper display in the foyer about the 'Great Little Jazz Town'.
27 Mofelehetsi Moerane, interview, Atteridgeville, 14 February 2017.
28 Thuso Moerane, interview, Komani, 12 May 2014.
29 Gevisser, *Thabo Mbeki*, 78.
30 Gevisser, *Thabo Mbeki*, 79.
31 Thuso Moerane, interview 2014.
32 Mofelehetsi Moerane, interview 2014.
33 Mofelehetsi Moerane, interview 2014.
34 Mosa Ndludla, interview, Muizenberg, 22 October 2019.
35 Marumo Moerane, interview, Durban, 7 October 2017.
36 Thuso Moerane, interview 2014.
37 Thuso Moerane, interview 2014.
38 Thuso Moerane, 'Biography of Michael Mosoeu Moerane B.Mus. (21-09-1904)–(27-01-1980)', Tsepo Moerane private collection, Komani..
39 Thuso Moerane, interview 2014.
40 Mofelehetsi Moerane, interview 2014.
41 Mofelehetsi Moerane, interview 2014.
42 Mofelehetsi Moerane, interview 2014.
43 Mofelehetsi Moerane, interview 2014.
44 Manasseh Tebatso Moerane, 'An Address by M.T. Moerane on the Occasion of the Unveiling of the Tombstone of his Elder Brother Michael, Mosoeu at Hlotse, Lesotho on December 17, 1988', Tsepo Moerane private collection, Komani.
45 Gevisser, *Thabo Mbeki*, 80.
46 Sophia Metsekae [Moerane] in Gevisser, *Thabo Mbeki*, 80.
47 'Memorandum Subsequent to the Interview of the 21 March 1955 with the Division of Bantu Education, Native Affairs Department, Pretoria', Wits Historical Papers, William Cullen Library, University of the Witwatersrand, AD1715.
48 Cape African Teachers Association Executive Committee, 'The Choice Before the Cape African Teachers', BC 925 (Box 5), Manuscripts and Archives Department, University of Cape Town Libraries.
49 CATA statement quoted in Phyllis Ntantala, *A Life's Mosaic: The Autobiography of Phyllis Ntantala* (Johannesburg: Jacana Media, 2009 [1992]), 147; 148.
50 '[A] form of communal education [wherein] Africans would only be educated to the level that they were capable of attaining [and remain unable] to reach the heights which were open to White South Africans' (Timothy Raymond Howard White, 'Lovedale 1930–1955: The Study of a Missionary Institution in its Social, Educational and Political Context' [MA diss., Rhodes University, 1987], 163).
51 White, 'Lovedale', 208; 210; 11.

NOTES

52 Thuso Moerane, interview 2014; Thuso Moerane, 'Biography'. Moerane must have been in Mpondoland by 1958 because one of the letters in Chapter 4 is addressed from there in April 1958.
53 MT Moerane, 'Address'.
54 Mofelehetsi Moerane, interview, Atteridgeville, 14 February 2017.
55 Tsepo and Neo Moerane, interview, Komani (Queenstown), 30 September 2019.
56 Hyslop, 'Food, Authority and Politics', 12.
57 1960 was the year in which the farmers in Pondoland began 'agitating' against local injustices. Their protests turned violent, leading to the deaths of 11 farmers and 20 collaborators. In response, the government declared a state of emergency and detained thousands of people, with 20 eventually being hanged. (Bernard Leeman, *Lesotho and the Struggle for Azania: The Origins and History of the African National Congress, Pan Africanist Congress, South African Communist Party and Basutoland Congress Party 1780–1994* [London: Bernard Leeman, 2015]), 323).
58 Nthabiseng, interview, Bronkhorstspruit, 4 October 2017.
59 Ndludla, interview 2019.
60 Accessed 30 July 2024, https://www.guidetomusicaltheatre.com/shows_p/princess_ju-ju.htm.
61 Thuso Moerane, 'Biography'.
62 Mary McVicker, *Women Opera Composers: Biographies from the 1500s to the 21st Century* (Jefferson, NC: McFarland & Company, 2016), 214.
63 Robin Malan, *Drama-Teach: Drama-in-Education and Theatre for Young People* (Cape Town: David Philip, 1973), 25.
64 Mofelehetsi Moerane, interview 2014.
65 Ndludla, interview 2019.
66 Tseliso Makhakhe, interview, Maseru, 20 May 2014.
67 Victor Lechesa, Maseru, interview, 26 February 2017.
68 Makhakhe, interview 2014.
69 Makhakhe, interview 2014. For identification of the students in the photograph, I am indebted to Mpho Ndebele and Zakes Mda.
70 Zakes Mda, interview on Zoom, 17 May 2022.
71 Matsobane Putsoa, interview, Maseru, 26 February 2017.
72 Bathsheba Everdene is the heroine of Hardy's novel.
73 Shortly before Sydney Carton is guillotined, Madame Lafarge says, 'It was nothing to her, that an innocent man was to die for the sins of his forefathers.'
74 Putsoa, interview 2017.
75 Tsepo and Neo Moerane, interview 2019.
76 Tsepo and Neo Moerane, interview 2019.
77 Ndludla, interview 2019.
78 Thabo Tseko Ei Pitso, interview, Maseru, 5 April 2014.
79 Makhakhe, interview 2014.
80 Lechesa, interview 2017.
81 Putsoa, interview 2017.
82 Shadrack Mapetla, interview, Midrand, 15 May 2014.
83 Mapetla, interview 2014.

84 Mda, interview 2022.
85 Mr Eric Lekhanya, interview, Maseru, 2 March 2011.
86 Josias Makibinyane Mohapeloa and MK Phakisi, *Likheleke tsa Pina Sesothong* [*The Eloquence of Song in Sesotho*]. Maseru: Lekhotla la Sesotho (Sesotho Academy) L/P 1139, 1987), 100. [Translated for the author by Mantoa Motinyane.]
87 Although the two men clearly knew each other and some of their respective work, Moerane may well have been intolerant of Mohapeloa's politics, which supported the BNP. Mohapeloa stood as the BNP candidate for Thabana Ntsonyana in 1960 (losing to the BCP) (Leeman, *Lesotho and the Struggle*, 679).
88 There was a hospital in Maseru, but the one in Bloemfontein then available to 'non-whites', Pelonomi, was far bigger.
89 I could not verify Moerane's death in Bloemfontein: my research took me to the Magistrate's Office Registry Room (401) in January 2018, where I was told that African people's death certificates were not issued in January 1980. They directed me to Pelonomi Hospital to see if there were records of the death there, but they had no records that went back that far.
90 Nthabiseng, interview 2017.

Chapter 4 Moerane in Correspondence

1 Letters 1–14 are reproduced by kind permission of the Curator, PR Kirby Collection, the South African College of Music, University of Cape Town. Letters 15–17 are reproduced by kind permission of SAMRO.
2 University of Cape Town Manuscripts and Archives, PR Kirby Collection BC 750, A: Correspondence. The signature was removed or covered but from the content, it was clearly written by Friedrich Hartmann, who seems to be replying to queries about both Moerane and (at the end) 'Mohapela'. The latter is Joshua Pulumo Mohapeloa, Moerane's major contemporary in the field of Sotho choral music, who studied part-time at Wits from 1939 to 1943, and who remembered Kirby with respect (Christine Lucia, 'Travesty or Prophecy? Views of South African Black Choral Composition', in *Music and Identity: Transformation and Negotiation*, ed. Eric Akrofi, Maria Smit and Stig-Magnus Thorsén [Stellenbosch: African Sun Media, 2007], 170). Hartmann could not have known Mohapeloa personally at Wits, however, since he was only appointed there in 1954 (Bernard van der Linde, 'In Memoriam Friedrich Helmut Hartmann', *Ars Nova* 4, no. 1 [1972], 12).
3 UCT Kirby Collection. The letter from Kirby that prompted Moerane's reply is not among the UCT Kirby Papers. Note how Moerane adds the š that is absent from most spellings, including his own later ones.
4 UCT Kirby Collection. The enclosure, which we would now call a 'student record' and which is frequently referred to in Chapter 2, was generated on the same date as the letter, 24 October 1962.
5 UCT Kirby Collection.
6 UCT Kirby Collection. The only evidence of a reply to this letter is a scrap of paper numbered '97' in the UCT Kirby Papers, at the top of which Kirby writes, 'With kindest regards, I remain Yours sincerely Percival R. Kirby', and at the

bottom of which, sideways, he writes, 'Percival R. Kirby 4 Constitution St West Hill Grahamstown S. Africa' followed by 'Dean Dixon Esq. Sinfonie Orchestra do. Chef Dirigigent Hessischer Rundfunk Frankfurt am Main (Postfach 3294) W. Germany'. The contents of the correspondence are missing.
7. UCT Kirby Collection.
8. UCT Kirby Collection. This was sent as an aerogramme letter to 'Recorded Programmes Librarian, 533 B.H., The British Broadcasting Corporation, Broadcasting House, London WI' and posted on 25 May 1964. Kirby copied its contents by hand.
9. UCT Kirby Collection.
10. UCT Kirby Collection.
11. UCT Kirby Collection.
12. UCT Kirby Collection.
13. UCT Kirby Collection.
14. UCT Kirby Collection.
15. UCT Kirby Collection.
16. SAMRO Archive, Johannesburg, Yvonne Huskisson Collection, File 'Moerane, M.M.', Subfile 'Korrespondensie'.
17. SAMRO Huskisson Collection.
18. SAMRO Huskisson Collection.

Chapter 5 The Symphonic Poem *Fatše La Heso* (*My Country*)

1. The translation of the title is Moerane's.
2. Scott David Farrah, 'Signifyin(g): A Semiotic Analysis of Symphonic Works by William Grant Still, William Levi Dawson, and Florence B. Price' (PhD diss., Florida State University, 2007), xii.
3. Grant Olwage, 'Apartheid's Musical Signs: Reflections on Black Choralism, Modernity and Race-Ethnicity in the Segregation Era', in *Composing Apartheid: Music for and Against Apartheid*, ed. Grant Olwage (Johannesburg: Wits University Press, 2008), 42–43.
4. Farrah 'Signifyin(g)', xii.
5. Walter Nhlapo, 'Music for Urban Natives', *The Star* (2 October 1947). University of Cape Town Manuscripts and Archives, PR Kirby Collection BC 750.
6. Chris Walton, 'Bond of Broeders: Anton Hartman and Music in an Apartheid State', *The Musical Times* 145 no. 1887 (2004): 70–71.
7. Christine Lucia, 'How Critical Is Music Theory?' *Critical Arts* 21 no. 1 (2006): 176–183.
8. Peter Klatzow, ed., *Composers in South African Today* (Oxford: Oxford University Press, 1987).
9. Deirdre Larkin, 'The Symphonic Poem and Tone Poem in South Africa', *Ars Nova* 26 (1994), 10; Jeffrey Brukman, 'Tribute to Michael Moerane', *CueOnline* (n.d.), accessed 22 October 2009, http://cue.ru.ac.za/music/2009/tribute-michaelmoerane.html and no longer available; Veronica Mary Franke, 'South African Orchestral Music: Five Exponents', *Acta Musicologica* 84 no. 1 (2012): 93.

10 Franke, 'Five Exponents', 93.
11 Some of the information in this chapter previously appeared in Christine Lucia, '"The Times Do Not Permit": Moerane, South Africa, Lesotho, and *Fatše La Heso*'. *Muziki: Journal of Music Research in Africa*, 16, no. 2 (2019): 87–112. https://doi.org/10.1080/18125980.2020.1787860.
12 *Rhodes University College Grahamstown: Calendar 1943* (Grahamstown: Grocott and Sherry), 264; *Rhodes University Calendar 1942*, 19.
13 Paul Maylam, *Rhodes University, 1904–2016: An Intellectual, Political and Cultural History* (Grahamstown: Institute of Social and Economic Research, Rhodes University, 2017), 32.
14 Franke, 'Five Exponents'.
15 James Steven Mzilikazi Khumalo, '"Serious" Music in an African Context, *NewMusic SA: Bulletin of the International Society for Contemporary Music – South African Section*, 3–4 (2004–2005): 14.
16 Marie Slocombe to Percival Kirby, 7 June 1964, University of Cape Town Manuscripts and Archives, PR Kirby Collection BC 750, A: Correspondence. The performance was in Bedford rather than central London because London was under bombardment at the time. Most of the BBC's work during World War II was carried on outside London.
17 Friedrich Hartmann to Percival Kirby, 11 March 1958, UCT Kirby Collection.
18 Slocombe to Kirby, 1964. These recordings were unfortunately destroyed, as we saw in Chapter 4.
19 Alastair Mitchell and Alan Poulton, eds., *A Chronicle of First Broadcast Performances of Musical Works in the United Kingdom, 1923–1996* (London and New York: Routledge, 2019), 90.
20 Mitchell and Poulton, *Chronicle*, 90. Spelling and other mistakes in this quotation are in the original.
21 Obviously, the genesis of the performance ('brought to the attention of Dr Hartman [...] in 1944') was misunderstood.
22 Accessed 30 July 2024, https://en.wikipedia.org/wiki/Fela_Sowande.
23 Accessed 30 July 2024, https://www.classicfm.com/discover-music/fela-sowande-nigerian-composer-music-life-career-african-suite/.
24 William McNaught, Broadcast Music', *The Listener* (30 November 1944), 612–613.
25 McNaught, 'Broadcast Music', 613.
26 'B.B.C. Broadcasts Work by Bantu Composer', *Rand Daily Mail*, Johannesburg, 18 November 1944, 3. The work was evidently broadcast again in 1946: 'Work of Bantu Composer to be Broadcast', *Rand Daily Mail*, Johannesburg, 20 July 1946, 8; 'BROADCASTING PROGRAMMES … Johannesburg To–morrow', *Rand Daily Mail*, Johannesburg, 20 July 1946, 6.
27 Izak Khomo, 'Nephew of Michael Mosoeu Moerane (1909–1981[sic]) Adds Details for Composer's Page at AfricClassical.com' (28 September 2011), 10 July 2024, https://africlassical.blogspot.com/2011/09/nephew-of-michael-mosoeu-moerane-1909.html.
28 Accessed 29 July 2024, https://www.wcml.org.uk/wcml/en/our-collections/international/pan-african-congress/.

NOTES

29 Hakim Adi, *Pan-Africanism: A History* (London: Bloomsbury Academic, 2018), 125.
30 Adi, *Pan-Africanism*, 125–126.
31 Extract from the second resolution quoted by Adi, *Pan-Africanism*, 126.
32 Bernard Leeman, *Lesotho and the Struggle for Azania: The Origins and History of the African National Congress, Pan Africanist Congress, South African Communist Party and Basutoland Congress Party 1780–1994* (London: Bernard Leeman, 2015), 248.
33 Hollis Ralph Lynch, *Black American Radicals and the Liberation of Africa: The Council on African Affairs, 1937–1955* (Ithaca: Cornell University Press, 1978).
34 Michael Moerane to Percival Kirby, 21 April 1958, UCT Kirby Collection.
35 *The Carolina Times*, 'Negro Composers' Works Featured in Symphonic Recital', *The Carolina Times*, 10 June 1950, 4, accessed 30 July 2024, https://newspapers.digitalnc.org/lccn/sn83045120/1950-06-10/ed-1/seq-4/#words=Composers+Featured+Negro+Recital+Symphonic+Works.
36 Sophia Metsekae Moerane, personal communication to the author, May 2014.
37 Memo from WA Hunton to WB Du Bois 2 June 1950, University of Massachusetts, Amherst, WEB Du Bois Papers, accessed 30 July 2024, https://credo.library.umass.edu/view/full/mums312-b128-i105.
38 Letter from WEB Du Bois to MM Moerane 30 November 1951, University of Massachusetts, Amherst, WEB Du Bois Papers, accessed 21 May 2023, https://credo.library.umass.edu/view/full/mums312-b133-i322.
39 Letter from Council on African Affairs to WEB Du Bois 30 January 1952, University of Massachusetts, Amherst, WEB Du Bois Papers, accessed 30 July 2024, https://credo.library.umass.edu/view/full/mums312-b136-i394.
40 Moerane to Kirby, 21 April 1958, UCT Kirby Collection.
41 Slocombe to Kirby, 1964, UCT Kirby Collection.
42 Kirby to Moerane, 21 January 1966, UCT Kirby Collection.
43 Moerane to Kirby, 9 March 1966, UCT Kirby Collection.
44 Moerane to Kirby, 27 June 1968, UCT Kirby Collection.
45 Michael Mosoeu Moerane, 'Fatše La Heso (My Country) Symphonic Poem'. Cory Library for Historical Research, Rhodes University, MS 14467 (1941), accessed 30 July 2024, https://african-composers-edition.co.za/product/fatse-la-heso-orchestral-score/; https://african-composers-edition.co.za/product/fatse-la-heso-set-of-orchestral-parts/.
46 Yvonne Huskisson quoted by Carmel Rickard, 'Moerane and the Lost Chord Detectives', *Weekly Mail* Arts supplement, December 1988.
47 Anton Hartman, internal memo to Yvonne Huskisson, 17 July 1973, SAMRO Archive, Yvonne Huskisson Collection, file 'Moerane, M', subfile 'Korrespondensie'.
48 Michael Moerane to Yvonne Huskisson, 20 May 1973. What Moerane seems to be implying here is that he has learnt that Yvonne Huskisson had ensured that the work was not only played on a 'Bantu' radio station, but also on the national 'white' English–medium station, 'Radio South Africa', which was a fairly unusual move in those days.
49 Rickard, 'Lost Chord Detectives'.

50 It can be heard on https://african-composers-edition.co.za/product/fatse-la-heso-orchestral-score/.
51 Dorothy C Shea, *The South African Truth Commission: The Politics of Reconciliation* (Washington, DC: United States Institute of Peace Press, 2000), 10.
52 Phil du Plessis, *Timbila: Orchestral Works Inspired by Elements in African Music*, Claremont Records, CD GSE 1513, 1991, liner notes (1991): 2.
53 Du Plessis, *Timbila* liner notes, 4; 6.
54 *South African Orchestral Works Vol I*, Marco Polo/Naxos DDD 8.223709 (1994) Track 6. This CD was followed in 1995 by *South African Orchestral Works Vol. 2* (Marco Polo/Naxos DDD 8.223833), which includes a symphony by William Bell, Moerane's external examiner in 1941.
55 Khomo, 'Nephew of Moerane'.
56 Abiola Irele, *The African Imagination: Literature in Africa and the Black Diaspora* (Oxford: Oxford University Press, 2001), 6.
57 Michael Mosoeu Moerane, 'Fatše La Heso'. Cory Library, 1. The Edgar Cree and Peter Marchbank recordings of the work can be heard on the ACE webpage. https://african-composers-edition.co.za/product/fatse-la-heso-orchestral-score/.
58 The audio examples are used by kind permission of Musa Nkuna, Director of the Internationales Chor- und Orchestermusikfestival in Kassel, Germany. They were recorded live at a performance of *Fatše La Heso* on 8 December 2023 by the Kyiv Symphony Orchestra conducted by Arjan Tien. If URL links from musical examples fail, contact info@african-composers-edition.co.za.
59 Hartmann to Kirby, 1958, UCT Kirby Collection.
60 Robin Wells, *An Introduction to the Music of the Basotho* (Morija: Morija Sesuto Book Depot, 1994). He and Moerane must have known each other.
61 Wells, *Introduction*, 60; 77; 112.
62 Wells, *Introduction*, 58; 60–62.
63 Wells, *Introduction*, 63.
64 Wells, *Introduction*, 77. The opening of the 'pina ea polo' that Wells transcribes (77–78) has more affinity with the second section of a choral work by Joshua Pulumo Mohapeloa, *U Ea Kae?*, a work that is also based on a Sotho threshing song than it appears to have with Example 5.2.
65 Wells, *Introduction*, 77; 79.
66 Wells, *Introduction*, 112–13. Khumalo ('Serious Music') calls the tune *Ho Koeetsa Ngoana*.
67 Wells, *Introduction*, 112–113.
68 MM Moerane, 'Fatše La Heso' Cory Library, 1.
69 MM Moerane, 'Fatše La Heso' Cory Library, 1.
70 Thabo Moerane quoted by Rickard, 'Lost Chord Detectives'.
71 Brukman, 'Tribute'.
72 Huskisson quoted by Rickard, 'Lost Chord Detectives'.
73 Bernarr Rainbow with Gordon Cox, *Music in Educational Thought and Practice: A Survey from 800 BC* (Aberystwyth: Boethius Press 1989), 239.
74 Larkin, 'Symphonic Poem', 7.

75 Thomas Pooley, 'Composition in Crisis: Case Studies in South African Art Music, 1980–2006' (MMus diss., University of the Witwatersrand, 2008), 28.
76 I am grateful to Matildie Wium for giving me access to a conference paper in which she analyses the work.

Chapter 6 Moerane and the Choral Movement in Southern Africa

1 Many of them were only published in 2020 on https://african-composers-edition.co.za/composers/michael-moerane/, accessed 8 May 2023.
2 Thembela Vokwana, 'Expressions in Black: A History of South African Black Choral Music: "Amakhwaya/Iikwayala"', unpublished paper delivered at the Department of Art, Visual Arts and Musicology, University of South Africa (2004).
3 Philip Timothy Burnett, 'Music and Mission: A Case Study of the Anglican-Xhosa Missions of the Eastern Cape, 1854–1880' (PhD diss., University of Bristol, 2020).
4 Kofi Agawu, 'Tonality as a Colonizing Force in Africa', in *Audible Empire: Music, Global Politics, Critique*, edited by Ronald Radano and Tejumola Olaniyan (Durham, NC: Duke University Press, 2016), 337.
5 Morija Sesuto Book Depot, *Lipina tsa Likolo tse Phahameng* (Morija: Morija Sesuto Book Depot, 6th impression, 1985 [1907]), 1.
6 Morija Sesuto Book Depot, *Lipina*.
7 James Steven Mzilikazi Khumalo, '"Serious" Music in an African Context, *NewMusic SA: Bulletin of the International Society for Contemporary Music – South African Section*, 3–4 (2004–2005), 15.
8 Khabi Mngoma, 'Music in African Education', in *Music Education in Contemporary South Africa: Proceedings of the First National Music Educators' Conference*, ed. Christine Lucia (Pietermaritzburg: Natal University Press, 1986), 116–117. Sadly, this is as true today for most state schools in South Africa as it was in 1986.
9 Markus Detterbeck 'South African Choral Music', 203, quoted in Mokale Koapeng, 'I Compose What I Like: Challenges Facing a Composer in the Black Choral Field in South Africa' (MMus Research Report, University of the Witwatersrand, 2014), 48.
10 Detterbeck, 'South African Choral Music', 203.
11 Koapeng, 'I Compose What I Like', 48.
12 Koapeng, 'I Compose What I Like', 48.
13 Koapeng, 'I Compose What I Like', 49, quoting Veit Erlmann, *Nightsong: Performance, Power and Practice in South Africa* (Chicago: The University of Chicago Press, 1996), 226.
14 Joshua Pulumo Mohapeloa, 'Khoro', in *Meloli le Lithallere tsa Afrika ka J.P. Mohapeloa*, 2nd edition (Morija, Lesotho: Morija Sesuto Book Depot, 1953), 3. See also https://african-composers-edition.co.za/general-introduction-to-the-mohapeloa-critical-edition/, accessed 29 July 2024.
15 Radebe quoted in Koapeng, 'I Compose What I Like', 50.
16 Christine Lucia, 'Back to the Future? Idioms of "Displaced Time" in South African Composition', in *Composing Apartheid: Music For and Against Apartheid*, ed. Grant Olwage (Johannesburg: Wits University Press, 2008), 27–30.

17 Vivien Pieters, 'Music and Presbyterianism at the Lovedale Missionary Institute, 1841–1955' (PhD diss., University of South Africa, 2021), 256.
18 Accessed 23 April 2023, https://african-composers-edition.co.za/general-introduction/.
19 Gideon Roos to MM Moerane, 29 June 1973, SAMRO Huskisson Collection, File 'Moerane, MM', Subfile 'Korrespondensie'. Before 1973, composers' royalties were handled by the South African Broadcasting Corporation (SABC). SAMRO is based in Braamfontein, Johannesburg and protects the intellectual copyright invested in the music of composers throughout the southern African region and on behalf of overseas collection agencies.
20 'Sunny South' is the title of a small collection of piano works.
21 SAMRO's website explains how to obtain a license, accessed 30 July 2024, https://www.samro.org.za/user.
22 Tsepo Moerane private collection, Komani.
23 Carmel Rickard, 'Moerane and the Lost Chord Detectives', *Weekly Mail* Arts supplement, December 1988.
24 Tsepo Moerane private collection.
25 Thuso Moerane, interview, Komani, 12 May 2014.
26 Thuso Moerane, interview, Komani, 23 February 2017.
27 Rickard, 'Lost Chord Detectives'.
28 Mofelehetsi Moerane, interview, Atteridgeville, 14 February 2014.
29 Victor Lechesa, interview, Maseru, 26 February 2017.
30 Tseliso Makhakhe, interview, Maseru, 20 May 2014.
31 Lechesa, interview 2017.
32 Manasseh Tebatso Moerane, 'An Address by M.T. Moerane on the Occasion of the Unveiling of the Tombstone of his Elder Brother Michael, Mosoeu at Hlotse, Lesotho on December 17, 1988'. Tsepo Moerane private collection.
33 Makhakhe, interview 2014.
34 Mpho Ndebele, 'On Translating Moerane's Song Texts', presentation given at the Andrew Mellon Moerane Critical Edition Research Workshop, Stellenbosch (30 September 2017). See also https://african-composers-edition.co.za/composers/joshua-mohapeloa/.
35 Makhakhe, interview, 2014.
36 Makhakhe, interview 2014.
37 Makhakhe, interview 2014.
38 Makhakhe, interview 2014.
39 Harold Steafel, 'Randfontein Is Choir Winner. Steafel: Ford Choirs National Competition '79', *Rand Daily Mail Extra*, Johannesburg, 13 December 1979: 11.
40 Basil (Doc) Bikitsha, 'Beaming Out a Spiritual Message', *Rand Daily Mail Extra*, 19 March 1980: 13.
41 Basil (Doc) Bikitsha, 'Jack Jones Takes over from Vereen at Sun City Feast', *Rand Daily Mail Extra*, 25 March 1981: 21.
42 Basil (Doc) Bikitsha, 'Its conductor Nehemiah Ramasiah is a sight on stage – a flurry of gestures and graceful swerves', in Bikitsha, 'Jack Jones Takes Over', 21.

43 Basil (Doc) Bikitsha, 'It's Doc Bikitsha's Finger on Your Pulse', *Rand Daily Mail Extra*, 7 June 1976: 13.
44 SAMRO, *Catalogue: Works by Michael Mosoeu Moerane 1901–1981* (Johannesburg: Southern African Music Rights Organisation, 2003), 7; 12.
45 Mofelehetsi Moerane, interview 2014; Makhakhe, interview 2014; Epainette Mbeki, interview, East London, 27 May 2014; Nthabiseng, interview, Bronkhorstspruit, 4 October 2017; Thuso Moerane, interview 2017; Marumo Moerane, interview, Durban, 7 October 2017.
46 Yvonne Huskisson, *Black Composers of Southern Africa: An Expanded Supplement to The Bantu Composers of Southern Africa*, ed. Sarita Hauptfleisch (Pretoria: Human Sciences Research Council, 1992).
47 *Rand Daily Mail*, 6 February 1980: 5.

Chapter 7 Moerane's Spiritual Songs

1 https://african-composers-edition.co.za/product/ea-hlolang/, https://african-composers-edition.co.za/product/jehova-oa-busa/, https://african-composers-edition.co.za/product/ntate-ea-mohau/. *Jehova Oa Busa* was reproduced by SAMRO, *Catalogue: Works by Michael Mosoeu Moerane 1901–1981* (Johannesburg: Southern African Music Rights Organisation, 2003), 7.
2 Tim Couzens, *Murder at Morija* (Johannesburg: Random House, 2003), 206.
3 Morija Sesuto Book Depot, *Lifela tsa Sione* (Morija: Morija Sesuto Book Depot, 53rd edition, 2015).
4 Morija Sesuto Book Depot, *Lifela tsa Sione*, 138; 176.
5 Patrick Harries, *Butterflies & Barbarians: Swiss Missionaries and Systems of Knowledge in South-East Africa* (Oxford: James Currey, 2007), 32; 18.
6 Audio and scores samples of all the music discussed in this book, and all musical extracts (unless otherwise stated) are published by African Composers Edition and are from Christine Lucia, general ed., *Andrew Mellon-Michael Mosoeu Moerane Critical Edition* (Stellenbosch: African Sun Media, 2020). Accessed 30 July 2024, https://african-composers-edition.co.za/composers/michael-moerane/.
7 Moerane groups and underlines the hummed notes in the manuscript, his syllable 'Hm' often occurring in the middle of a phrase, so that one imagines he wants the humming to continue without interruption.
8 Thuso Moerane, interview, Komani, 12 May 2014.
9 Thuso Moerane, interview 2014.
10 Accessed 30 July 2024, https://www.kingjamesbibleonline.org/Isaiah-Chapter-9/.
11 John Knox Bokwe, *Ntsikana, the Story of an African Hymn* (Alice: Lovedale Press, [n.d. c. 1904]).
12 Mofelehetsi Moerane, interview 2014. The ellipses are not words cut out of the interview but Mofelehetsi searching for words to express what he meant.
13 Harry Thacker Burleigh, ed., [Preface], in *Negro Spirituals: Arranged for Solo Voice*, (New York: Ricordi, 1917), [2], accessed 30 July 2024, https://digital.library.temple.edu/digital/collection/p15037coll1/id/5266.
14 Samuel A Floyd, 'The Invisibility and Fame of Harry T. Burleigh: Retrospect and Prospect', *Black Music Research Journal* 24 no. 2 (2004): 179. Burleigh studied at

the newly established National Conservatory of Music in New York just after Dvořák had been appointed its head in 1892. He became Dvořák's 'chief source of African-American music' for a compositional project that aimed 'to use the characteristics of this music to discover a national style of music in the United States' (Floyd, 'Invisibility', 182).
15 WEB Du Bois, *The Souls of Black Folk* (New York: Barnes & Noble Classics, 2003 [1903]); James C Scott, *Domination and the Arts of Resistance: Hidden Transcripts* (New Haven, CT: Yale University Press, 1990).
16 *The Musical Times*, 'The Fellowship Songbook' by Hugh Walford Davies' [Review] *The Musical Times* 57 no. 884 (1916): 456, accessed 30 July 2024, https://digital.library.temple.edu/digital/collection/p15037coll1/id/5266.
17 Veit Erlmann, *African Stars: Studies in Black South African Performance* (Chicago: The University of Chicago Press, 1991), 23.
18 Erlmann, *African Stars*, 152; 193; 152–53; Alexander Sandilands, *Negro Spirituals: 120 Songs, with Tonic Sol-fa Music* (Morija: Morija Sesuto Book Depot, 1981 [1951]).
19 Sandilands, *Negro Spirituals*, 61; 86.
20 The solo version sung by Paul Robeson (to slightly different words), can be heard on https://www.youtube.com/watch?v=pwYpqJVHHmo, accessed 30 May 2023.
21 Eugenio Clausetti to MM Moerane, 6 November 1937. An internal memo from the Manager of Lovedale Missionary Institution's Book & Stationery Department concerning *Nobody Knows* states that 'The Copyright of this piece is held by the Hampton Normal and Agricultural Institution' and asks, 'Would we not need to get their permission before printing Mr. Moerane's version?' (Cory Library, Lovedale Archive MS 16376). There is no reply in the Lovedale Archive.
22 Monroe Work, compiler, *A Bibliography of the Negro in Africa and America* (New York: The HW Wilson Company, 1928) (pages 420, 435 and 440 list seven books of spirituals and folksongs published by Ricordi between 1917 and 1921); Burleigh, *Negro Spirituals*.
23 The letters held in the Lovedale Missionary Institution, Lovedale Mission Press Archive MS 16376, and cited from are as follows: Morija Sesuto Book Depot to Moerane, 7 September 1937; RW Shepherd to Morija Sesuto Book Depot, 17 September 1937; Morija Sesuto Book Depot to the Director of Publications, 6 October 1937; Eugenio Clausetti to MM Moerane, 6 November 1937; RW Shepherd to Moerane, 3 May 1938.
24 Accessed 30 July 2024, https://www.youtube.com/watch?v=8W59quHJr_A.
25 Jean Snyder, '"A Great and Noble School of Music": Dvořák, Harry T. Burleigh, and the African American Spiritual', in *Dvořák in America, 1892–1895*, ed. John Tibbetts (Portland, OR: Amadeus Press, 1993), 123–148.
26 Accessed 30 July 2024, https://www.musicroom.com/product/musjc50572/r-r-terry-sailor-shanties-ttbb.aspx.

Chapter 8 Songs about Family, Community and Tradition
1 SAMRO, *Catalogue: Works by Michael Mosoeu Moerane 1901–1981* (Johannesburg: Southern African Music Rights Organisation, 2006), 6.

2 Bernice Mohapeloa, 'Basutoland Homemakers Association', *Basutoland Witness* 7, no. 1 (1953): 5–6. David Ambrose Archive, Ladybrand.
3 John Aerni-Flessner, 'Homemakers, Communists, and Refugees: Smuggling Anti-Apartheid Refugees in Rural Lesotho in the 1960s and 1970s', *Wagada: A Journal of Transformational Women's and Gender Studies* 13 (2015): 183–209.
4 Adolphe Mabille and Hermann Dieterlen, reclassified, revised and enlarged by RA Paroz, *Southern Sotho–English Dictionary*, 7th edition (Morija: Morija Sesuto Book Depot, 1988 [1950]), 225.
5 Adolphe Mabille and Hermann Dieterlen, *Southern Sotho-English Dictionary: New Edition Using the 1959 Republic of South Africa Orthography*, revised and enlarged 8th edition (Morija: Morija SesutoBook Depot, 1988 [1961]), 241.
6 Gordon Lindsay Maclean, *Roberts' Birds of Southern Africa* (Cape Town: John Voelcker Book Fund, 5th edition, 1985), 139–148; 162–163.
7 Maclean, *Roberts*, 162.
8 Maclean, *Roberts*, 112–113.
9 Mabille and Dieterlen, *Dictionary*, 240.
10 Kgaugelo Mpyane, personal communication to the author, 13 October 2018.
11 Zacharias Aunyane Matšela, *Dipapadi tsa Sesotho: Tholwana ya patlisiso dipapading tsa meetlo* (Mazenod, Lesotho: Mazenod Press, 1987), 50.
12 The Alto voice was usually called 'Contralto' in those days.
13 Maclean, *Roberts*, 655–656; 188.
14 Robin Wells, *An Introduction to the Music of the Basotho* (Morija: Morija Sesuto Book Depot, 1994), 9.
15 Cory Library for Historical Research, Rhodes University, Grahamstown, Lovedale Missionary Institution MS 16376.
16 Tseliso Makhakhe, interview, Maseru, 20 May 2014.
17 Victor Lechesa, interview, Maseru, 26 February 2017.
18 Lechesa, interview 2017.
19 Makhakhe, interview 2014.
20 Trod Ledwaba, 'Notes on Morena Tlake', in *Souvenir Programme 10th National Finals*, Ford–Old Mutual Choirs (1987): [8–9].

Chapter 9 Songs of Love and Loss

1 'Mabasiea Jeannette Mahalefele, *Lireneketso* (Morija: Morija Sesuto Book Depot, 1971).
2 https://african-composers-edition.co.za/product/della/.
3 Pretoria Bureau, 'Lesotho Burial for Composer', *Rand Daily Mail Extra*, 6 February 1980: 5. The three songs are the ones mentioned in this newspaper notice of Moerane's death.
4 Chris Dunton, 'The Works of Bennett Makhalo Khaketla', *The Post* [Lesotho] (24 February 2020), accessed 30 July 2024, https://menafn.com/1099758142/The-works-of-Bennett-Makalo-Khaketla is a reprint of this article.
5 Tseliso Makhakhe, interview, Maseru, 20 May 2014.
6 Bernard Leeman, *Lesotho and the Struggle for Azania: The Origins and History of the African National Congress, Pan Africanist Congress, South African Communist Party and Basutoland Congress Party 1780–1994* (London: Bernard Leeman, 2015), 214; 215.

7   Dunton, 'Works of Khaketla'.
8   Bennett M Khaketla, *Lesotho 1970: African Coup Under the Microscope* (Bloomsbury: C Hurst and Co., 1971), 213–214.
9   Africa Bureau, 'SA prohibits entry for Lesotho choir', *Rand Daily Mail*, 8 November 1974, 2.
10 Bennett Khaketla, *Lipshamathe* (Morija: Morija Sesuto Book Depot, 2nd edition, 1985).
11 Rodney Moffett, *Grasses of the Eastern Free State: Their Description and Uses* (Phuthaditjhaba: Uniqwa campus of the University of the North, 1997), 244.
12 Accessed 30 July 2024, https://www.britannica.com/place/Lesotho.
13 Khaketla, *Lipshamathe*, 85–86.
14 Ketlalemang Clement Maimane, 'Confluences of Lithoko, Religious and Traditional Beliefs and Western Poetry in Modern Sesotho Poetry: An Intertextual Perspective' (PhD diss., University of KwaZulu-Natal, 2016), 31.
15 For more on this and other books by Ntsane, see Johannes Malefetsane Lenake, *The Poetry of K.E. Ntsane* (Pretoria: J.L. Van Schaik, 1984). Accessed 30 July 2024, https://searchworks.stanford.edu/view/1568447.
16 Maimane, 'Confluences', 37.
17 Makhakhe, interview 2014.
18 Adolphe Mabille and Hermann Dieterlen, *Southern Sotho–English Dictionary: New Edition Using the 1959 Republic of South Africa Orthography*, revised anad enlarged 8th edition (Morija: Morija Sesuto Book Depot, 1988 [1961]), 298.
19 Accessed 30 July 2024, https://www.kingjamesbibleonline.org/Song-of-Solomon-Chapter-1/.
20 Mark Gevisser, *Thabo Mbeki: The Dream Deferred* (Johannesburg and Cape Town: Jonathan Ball, 2007), 80.
21 James Steven Mzilikazi Khumalo, 'Michael Mosoeu Moerane', in *South Africa Sings, Volume 1: African Choral Repertoire in Dual Notation* (Johannesburg: Southern African Music Rights Organisation, 1998). Khumalo later embellished the point slightly, saying that it was 'discovered by chance some years ago in an unpublished manuscript housed in the SAMRO Music Archive' (Khumalo, '"Serious" Music in an African Context', *NewMusic SA: Bulletin of the International Society for Contemporary Music – South African Section*, 3–4 [2004–2005], 15).
22 Khumalo, 'Serious Music', 15.
23 Christine Lucia, 'Back to the Future? Idioms of "Displaced Time" in South African Composition', in *Composing Apartheid: Music For and Against Apartheid*, ed. Grant Olwage (Johannesburg: Wits University Press, 2008), 22–27.
24 SAMRO, *Catalogue: Works by Michael Mosoeu Moerane 1901–1981* (Johannesburg: Southern African Music Rights Organisation, 2003), 2–3.
25 Mahalefele, *Lireneketso*. A second edition was published in 1982, accessed 30 July 2024, https://openlibrary.org/works/OL1786442W/Lireneketso?edition=key%3A/books/.
26 Accessed 30 July 2024, http://www.sesotho.web.za/publications.htm.
27 William Butler Yeats, *The Works of W.B. Yeats with an Introduction and Bibliography* (Ware, Hertfordshire: Wordsworth Editions Ltd., 1994 [1899]), 59.

28 The word 'gauda' (gold) is repeated quite often in the song, sometimes split into two syllables, 'gau-da', as in bar 2 Soprano/Alto, and sometimes three, 'ga-u-da', as in bar 2 Tenor/Bass. The vowel 'au' is a diphthong in Sesotho, pronounced 'ah–oo'.
29 Sibongile Khumalo, 'Dela', Heita! Records, South Africa, CD HEITA 009, Track 4 (2005), accessed 30 July 2024, https://www.youtube.com/watch?v=uIKVnPg4Jt4.
30 Sampson Synor Mputa, Letter to the Director, Lovedale Press, 30 September 1937. Cory Library for Historical Research, Rhodes University, Grahamstown, Lovedale Missionary Institution MS 16376.
31 Moerane to the Director, Lovedale Press, 4 February 1938. Cory Library for Historical Research, Rhodes University, Lovedale MS 16376.
32 MM Moerane (n.d.), 'Della' [Typescript] SAMRO A02913.
33 Yvonne Huskisson, *Die Bantoe-Komponiste van Suider-Afrika/The Bantu Composers of Southern Africa* (Johannesburg: South African Broadcasting Corporation, 1969), 158.
34 Some voice parts have *'ndithwele'* which means 'I bear', while *'ndilithele'* means 'I bear it'.
35 https://african-composers-edition.co.za/product/della/.
36 Huskisson, *Bantu Composers*, 158.
37 Nthabiseng, interview, Bronkhorstspruit, 4 October 2017.
38 Nthabiseng, interview 2017.
39 Mosa Ndludla, interview, Muizenberg, 22 October 2019.
40 Ndludla, interview 2019.
41 Nthabiseng, interview 2017.
42 Accessed 30 July 2024, https://www.youtube.com/watch?v=Wi7jXp59At8.
43 Thuso Moerane, interview, Komani, 12 May 2014.
44 Veit Erlmann, *African Stars: Studies in Black South African Performance* (Chicago: The University of Chicago Press, 1991), 123.
45 Ndludla, interview 2019.
46 I am indebted to Kgaugelo Mpyane for this information.
47 Nthabiseng, interview 2019.

Chapter 10 Conclusion

1 Percival Robert Kirby, 'Michael Mosoeu Moerane', Pretoria: National Archives of South Africa, HSRC Collection (Kirby Folder).
2 Carolyn Hamilton et al., *Refiguring the Archive*, 2nd edition (New York: Springer, 2002).
3 Kofi Agawu, 'Tonality as a Colonizing Force in Africa', in *Audible Empire: Music, Global Politics, Critique*, edited by Ronald Radano and Tejumola Olaniyan (Durham, NC: Duke University Press, 2016), 337.
4 David Attwell, *Rewriting Modernity: Studies in Black South African Literary History* (Pietermaritzburg: University of KwaZulu-Natal Press, 2005), 19.
5 Attwell, *Rewriting Modernity*, 17.
6 Christine Lucia, 'A Personal Reflection on the Moerane Project 2013–2020', *SAMUS: South African Music Studies* 41/42 (2022): 316–326.
7 Stephanus Muller, *Nagmusiek* (Johannesburg: Fourthwall Books, 2014).
8 Kirby, 'Michael Mosoeu Moerane', National Archives.

Bibliography

Secondary Sources

Adi, Hakim. *Pan-Africanism: A History*. London: Bloomsbury Academic, 2018.

Aerni–Flessner, John. 'Homemakers, Communists, and Refugees: Smuggling Anti-Apartheid Refugees in Rural Lesotho in the 1960s and 1970s'. *Wagada: A Journal of Transformational Women's and Gender Studies* 13 (2015): 183–209.

Agawu, Kofi. 'Tonality as a Colonizing Force in Africa'. In *Audible Empire: Music, Global Politics, Critique*, edited by Ronald Radano and Tejumola Olaniyan, 334–55. Durham, NC: Duke University Press, 2016.

Ambrose, David. 'Death of Epainette Mbeki, Mother of Former South African President, Thabo Mbeki'. *Summary of Events in Lesotho* 21, no. 2 (2014): 24–27.

Attwell, David. *Rewriting Modernity: Studies in Black South African Literary History*. Pietermaritzburg: University of KwaZulu-Natal Press, 2005.

Ballantine, Christopher. 'Making Visible the Invisible: Creative Process and the Compositions of Joseph Shabalala'. In *Papers Presented at the Symposium on Ethnomusicology Number 14, 1996*, edited by Andrew Tracey, 56–59. Grahamstown: International Library of African Music, 1997.

Beinart, William, and Colin Bundy. *Hidden Struggles in Rural South Africa: Politics & Popular Movements in the Transkei & Eastern Cape 1890–1930*. Johannesburg: Ravan Press, 2017 [1987].

Blake, Michael. 'Parallel Streams: An Overview of South African Composition'. *World New Music Magazine* 10 (2000): 13–19.

Bokwe, John Knox. *Ntsikana, the Story of an African Hymn*. Alice: Lovedale Press, [n.d. c.1904].

Brukman, Jeffrey. 'Tribute to Michael Moerane', *CueOnline*, accessed 22 October 2009, http://cue.ru.ac.za/music/2009/tribute-michaelmoerane.html

Bull, Oswin Boys. 'To the Teachers of Basutoland'. *Basutoland Teachers Magazine* 1 (November 1937), 3.

Burleigh, Henry Thacker. *Negro Spirituals: Arranged for Solo Voice*. New York: Ricordi, 1917.

Burnett, Philip Timothy. 'Music and Mission: A Case Study of the Anglican-Xhosa Missions of the Eastern Cape, 1854–1880'. PhD diss., University of Bristol, 2020.

The Carolina Times. 'Negro Composers' Works Featured in Symphonic Recital'. *The Carolina Times*, 10 June 1950. https://newspapers.digitalnc.org/lccn/sn83045120/1950-06-10/ed-1/seq-4/#words=Composers+Featured+Negro+Recital+Symphonic+Works

Cobbing, Julian. 'The Mfecane as Alibi: Thoughts on Dithakong and Mbolompo'. *The Journal of African History* 29, no. 3 (1988): 487–519.

Cook, Susan. 'Chiefs, Kings, Corporatization, and Democracy: A South African Case Study'. *The Brown Journal of World Affairs* 12 no. 1 (Summer/Fall 2005): 125–137.

Coplan, David Bellin. *In the Time of Cannibals: The Word Music of South Africa's Basotho Migrants*. Chicago: The University of Chicago Press, 1994.

Couzens, Tim. *Murder at Morija*. Johannesburg: Random House, 2003.

Currey, Ronald. *Rhodes University 1904–1970: A Chronicle*. Grahamstown: Rhodes University, 1970.

Detterbeck, Markus. 'South African Choral Music (Amakwaya): Song, Contest and the Formation of Identity'. PhD diss., University of KwaZulu-Natal, Durban, 2002.

Dube, Ernest Frederick. 'Yesterday's Nazi Sympathizers, Today's South African Leaders'. Letter to the Editor, *The New York Times*, 5 August 1985. https://www.nytimes.com/1985/08/16/opinion/l-yesterday-s-nazi-sympathizers-today-s-south-african-leaders-195124.html

Du Bois, William Edward Burghardt. *The Souls of Black Folk*. New York: Barnes & Noble Classics, 2003 [1903].

Duncan, Graham. 'Coercive Agency: Lovedale Missionary Institution under Principals Arthur Wilkie and RHW Shepherd'. *Missionalia: Southern African Journal of Mission Studies* 38 no. 3 (2010): 430–451.

Dunton, Chris. 'The Works of Bennett Makhalo Khaketla'. *The Post* [Lesotho], 24 February 2020. https://menafn.com/1099758142/The-works-of-Bennett-Makalo-Khaketla

Du Plessis, Phil. *Timbila: Orchestral Works Inspired by Elements in African Music*. Liner notes. CD GSE 1513, Claremont Records, 1991.

Erlmann, Veit. *African Stars: Studies in Black South African Performance*. Chicago: The University of Chicago Press, 1991.

——. *Music, Modernity and the Global Imagination: South Africa and the West*. New York: Oxford University Press, 1999.

——. *Nightsong: Performance, Power and Practice in South Africa*. Chicago: The University of Chicago Press, 1996.

Farrah, Scott David. 'Signifyin(g): A Semiotic Analysis of Symphonic Works by William Grant Still, William Levi Dawson, and Florence B. Price'. PhD diss., Florida State University, 2007.

Floyd, Samuel. 'The Invisibility and Fame of Harry T. Burleigh: Retrospect and Prospect'. *Black Music Research Journal* 24, no. 2 (2004): 179–194.

Franke, Veronica Mary. 'South African Orchestral Music: Five Exponents'. *Acta Musicologica* 84, no. 1 (2012): 87–125.

Gay, Peter. *Freud: A Life for Our Time*. New York and London: WW Norton & Company, 2006 [1988].

Gevisser, Mark. *Thabo Mbeki: The Dream Deferred*. Johannesburg and Cape Town: Jonathan Ball, 2007.

Gill, Stephen, with a foreword by LBBJ Machobane. *A Short History of Lesotho: From the Late Stone Age Until the 1993 Elections*. Morija: Morija Museum and Archives, 1997 [1993].

Gramschi, Antonio. *Selections from the Prison Notebooks of Antonio Gramschi*, edited and translated by Quentin Hoare and Geoffrey Nowell Smith. London: Lawrence and Wishart, 1971.

Grundy, Kenneth. 'Cultural Politics in South Africa: An Inconclusive Transformation'. *African Studies Review* 39, no. 1 (1996): 1–24.

Haas, Michael. *Forbidden Music: The Jewish Composers Banned by the Nazis*. New Haven, CT: Yale University Press, 2013.

Hamilton, Carolyn, Verne Harris, Michele Pickover, Graeme Reid, Razia Saleh, and Jane Taylor. *Refiguring the Archive*. 2nd edition. New York: Springer, 2002.

Hamilton, Carolyn, Bernard K Mbenga, and Robert Ross, eds. *The Cambridge History of South Africa: Volume 1, From Early Times to 1885*. Cambridge: Cambridge University Press, 2009.

Hansen, Deirdre. *The Life and Work of Benjamin Tyamzashe, A Contemporary Xhosa Composer*. Grahamstown: Institute of Social and Economic Research, Rhodes University, Occasional Papers Number Eleven, 1968.

Harries, Patrick. *Butterflies & Barbarians: Swiss Missionaries & Systems of Knowledge in South-East Africa*. Oxford: James Currey, 2007.

Hartman, Mia. *Anton Hartman: Dis Sy Storie*. Pretoria: Mia Hartman, 2003.

Huskisson, Yvonne. *Black Composers of Southern Africa: An Expanded Supplement to the Bantu Composers of Southern Africa*, edited by Sarita Hauptfleisch. Pretoria: Human Sciences Research Council, 1992.

———. *Die Bantoe-Komponiste van Suider-Afrika/The Bantu Composers of Southern Africa*. Johannesburg: South African Broadcasting Corporation, 1969.

———. 'Moerane, Michael Mosoue' [sic]. In *New Dictionary of South African Biography*, edited by EJ Verwey and Nelly E Sonderling, 114–115. Pretoria: Vista, 1980.

Hyslop, Jonathan. 'Food, Authority and Politics: Student Riots in South African Schools 1945–1976'. Paper presented at the African Studies Seminar, University of the Witwatersrand African Studies Institute, Johannesburg, 29 September 1986.

Irele, Abiola. *The African Imagination: Literature in Africa and the Black Diaspora*. Oxford: Oxford University Press, 2001.

Jackson, Timothy. 'Friedrich Hartmann (1900–1973)'. Johannesburg International Mozart Festival programme ([January] 2010), 18–22.

Kallaway, Peter, ed. *Apartheid and Education: The Education of Black South Africans*. Johannesburg: Ravan Press, 1984.

Khaketla, Bennett Makalo. *Lesotho 1970: African Coup under the Microscope*. Bloomsbury: C. Hurst and Co., 1971.

———. *Lipshamathe*. 2nd edition. Morija, Lesotho: Morija Sesuto Book Depot, 1985.

Khumalo, James Steven Mzilikazi. 'Michael Mosoeu Moerane'. In *South Africa Sings, Volume 1: African Choral Repertoire in Dual Notation*, edited by James Steven Mzilikazi Khumalo, 14. Johannesburg: Southern African Music Rights Organisation, 1998.

———. 'Michael Mosoeu Moerane'. In *South Africa Sings Volume 2: African Choral Repertoire in Dual Notation*, edited by James Steven Mzilikazi Khumalo, 95. Johannesburg: Southern African Music Rights Organisation, 2008.

———. '"Serious" Music in an African Context'. *NewMusicSA: Bulletin of the International Society for Contemporary Music – South African Section* 3/4 (2004/2005): 13–15.

———, general ed. *South Africa Sings, Volume 1: African Choral Repertoire in Dual Notation*. Johannesburg: Southern African Music Rights Organisation, 1998.

———, general ed. *South Africa Sings Volume 2: African Choral Repertoire in Dual Notation*. Johannesburg: Southern African Music Rights Organisation, 2008.

Khomo, Izak. 'Nephew of Michael Mosoeu Moerane (1909–1981[sic]) Adds Details for Composer's Page at AfricClassical.com' (28 September 2011). Accessed 10 July 2024, https://africlassical.blogspot.com/2011/09/nephew-of-michael-mosoeu-moerane-1909.html

Kirby, Percival Robson. 'Michael Mosoeu Moerane'. Pretoria: National Archives of South Africa, HSRC Collection (Kirby Folder), n.d.

———. 'Moerane, Michael Mosoeu'. In *South African Music Encyclopedia Volume III, J–O*, edited by Jacques Philip Malan, 253–254. Cape Town: Oxford University Press, 1984.

Klatzow, Peter, ed. *Composers in South African Today*. Oxford: Oxford University Press, 1987.

Koapeng, Mokale. 'I Compose What I Like: Challenges Facing a Composer in the Black Choral Field in South Africa'. MMus Research Report, University of the Witwatersrand, 2014.

———. Michael Mosoeu Moerane (1909–1981). In *2009 African Prescribed Music*, [0]–12. Old Mutual National Choir Festival Music Prescription Guidelines and Information Package, 2009.

Kriek, Elizabeth. 'Die Simfonie en Suid-Afrika: 1889–1989'. MMus diss., University of South Africa, 1991.

———. 'Die Simfonie en Suid-Afrika, 1970–1990: 'n Styl- en Struktuurstudie'. DMus diss., University of South Africa, 1995.

Larkin, Deirdre. 'The Symphonic Poem and Tone Poem in South Africa'. *Ars Nova* 26 (1994): 5–42.

Lawrence, Patricia. *Viva Musica! A Bird's Eye View of Music at Unisa*. Pretoria: Unisa Press, 2011.

Ledwaba, Trod. 'Notes on Morena Tlake'. In *Souvenir Programme 10th National Finals*, [8–9]. Ford–Old Mutual Choirs, 1987.

Leeman, Bernard. *Lesotho and the Struggle for Azania: The Origins and History of the African National Congress, Pan Africanist Congress, South African Communist Party and Basutoland Congress Party 1780–1994*. London: Bernard Leeman, 2015.

Legassick, Martin Chatfield. *The Politics of a South African Frontier: The Griqua, the Sotho-Tswana, and the Missionaries, 1780–1840*. Basle: Basler Afrika Bibliographien, 2010.

Lenake, Johannes Malefetsane. *The Poetry of K.E. Ntsane*. Pretoria: J.L. Van Schaik, 1984.

Lodge, Tom. 1984. 'The Parents' School Boycott: Eastern Cape and East Rand Townships, 1955.' In *Apartheid and Education: The Education of Black South Africans*, edited by Peter Kallaway, 265–295. Johannesburg: Ravan Press, 1984.

Lucia, Christine. 'Back to the Future? Idioms of "Displaced Time" in South African Composition'. In *Composing Apartheid: Music for and Against Apartheid*, edited by Grant Olwage, 11–34. Johannesburg: Wits University Press, 2008.

———. 'Composing Towards/Against Whiteness: The African Music of Mohapeloa' In *Unsettling Whiteness*, edited by Samantha Schulz and Lucy Michaels, 219–230. Oxford: Inter-Disciplinary Press e-Book, 2014.

———. 'General Introduction to the J.P. Mohapeloa Critical Edition'. In *Joshua Pulumo Mohapeloa Critical Edition in Six Volumes*, edited by Christine Lucia, xxiv–lix. Cape Town: African Composers Edition, 2016.

———. 'How Critical Is Music Theory?' *Critical Arts* 21, no. 1 (2006): 166–189.

———. 'Introduction'. In *Michael Mosoeu Moerane Scholarly Edition*, general ed. Christine Lucia. Cape Town: African Composers Edition, 2020. Accessed 9 July 2024, https://african-composers-edition.co.za/general-introduction

———, general ed. *Michael Mosoeu Moerane Critical Edition in Four Volumes*. Stellenbosch: African Sun Media, 2020.

———. 'Michael Mosoeu Moerane in the Museum'. *Fontes Artis Musicae* 67 no. 3 (2020): 187–215.

———. 'Mohapeloa and the Heritage of African Song'. *African Music: Journal of the International Library of African Music* 9, no. 1 (2011): 56–86.

———. 'A Personal Reflection on the Moerane Project 2013–2020'. *SAMUS: South African Music Studies* 41/42 (2022): 316–326.

———. '"The Times Do Not Permit": Moerane, South Africa, Lesotho, and *Fatše La Heso*'. *Muziki: Journal of Music Research in Africa* 16, no. 2 (2019): 87–112.

———. 'Travesty or Prophecy? Views of South African Black Choral Composition'. In *Music and Identity: Transformation & Negotiation*, edited by Eric Akrofi, Maria Smit, and Stig-Magnus Thorsen, 161–180. Stellenbosch: African Sun Media, 2007.

———. '"Yet None with Truer Fervour Sing": *Coronation March* and the (De)Colonisation of African Choral Music'. *African Music: Journal of the International Library of African Music* 10, no. 3 (2017): 23–44.

Lynch, Hollis Ralph. *Black American Radicals and the Liberation of Africa: The Council on African Affairs, 1937–1955*. Ithaca, NY: Cornell University Press, 1978.

Maaba, Brown Bavusile. 'The History and Politics of Liberation Archives at Fort Hare'. PhD diss., University of Cape Town, 2013.

Mabille, Adolphe, and Hermann Dieterlin, reclassified, revised and enlarged by RA Paroz. *Southern Sotho–English Dictionary*. 7th edition. Morija: Morija Sesuto Book Depot, 1988 [1950].

———, reclassified, revised and enlarged by RA Paroz. *Southern Sotho–English Dictionary: New Edition Using the 1959 Republic of South Africa Orthography*. 8th edition. Morija: Morija Sesuto Book Depot, 1988 [1961].

Maclean, Gordon Lindsay. *Roberts' Birds of Southern Africa*. 5th edition. Cape Town: John Voelcker Bird Book Fund, 1985.

Mahalefele, 'Mabasiea Jeannette. *Lireneketso*. Morija, Lesotho: Morija Sesuto Book Depot, 1971.

Maimane, Ketlalemang Clement. 'Confluences of Lithoko, Religious and Traditional Beliefs and Western Poetry in Modern Sesotho Poetry: An Intertextual Perspective'. PhD diss., University of Kwa-Zulu Natal, 2016.
Malan, Robin. *Drama–Teach: Drama-in-Education and Theatre for Young People*. Cape Town: David Philip, 1973.
Mandela, Nelson. *Long Walk to Freedom: The Autobiography of Nelson Mandela*. London: Little, Brown and Company, 1994.
Martin, Denis-Constant. *Sounding the Cape: Music, Identity and Politics in South Africa*. Cape Town: African Minds, 2013.
Matšela, Zacharias Aunyane. *Dipapadi tsa Sesotho: Tholwana ya patlisiso dipapading tsa meetlo*. Mazenod, Lesotho: Mazenod Press, 1987.
Maylam, Paul. *A History of the African People of South Africa: From the Early Iron Age to the 1970s*. London: Croom Helm, 1986.
——. *Rhodes University, 1904–2016: An Intellectual, Political and Cultural History*. Grahamstown: Institute of Social and Economic Research, Rhodes University, 2017.
McNaught, William. 'Broadcast Music'. *The Listener* (30 November 1944), 612–613.
McVicker, Mary. *Women Opera Composers: Biographies from the 1500s to the 21st Century*. Jefferson, NC: McFarland & Company, 2016.
Mda, Zakes. *Sometimes There is a Void: Memoirs of an Outsider*. New York: Macmillan, 2011.
Meintjes, Louise. *Sound of Africa! Making Music Zulu in a South African Studio*. Durham and London: Duke University Press, 2003.
Mitchell, Alastair, and Alan Poulton, eds. *A Chronicle of First Broadcast Performances of Musical Works in the United Kingdom, 1923–1996*. London and New York: Routledge, 2019 [2001].
Mngoma, Khabi. 'The Correlation of Folk Music and Art Music Among African Composers'. In *Papers Presented at the Second Symposium on Ethnomusicology*, edited by Andrew Tracey, 61–69. Grahamstown: International Library of African Music, 1981.
Moerane, Michael Mosoeu. 'Barali ba Jerusalema: O Daughters of Jerusalem'. In *South Africa Sings Vol. 1: African Choral Repertoire in Dual Notation*, edited by James Steven Mzilikazi Khumalo, 14–21. Johannesburg: Southern African Music Rights Organisation, 1998.
——. 'Della'. In *South Africa Sings Vol. 2: African Choral Repertoire in Dual Notation*, edited by James Steven Mzilikazi Khumalo, 95–107. Johannesburg: Southern African Music Rights Organisation, 2008.
Moffett, Rodney. *Grasses of the Eastern Free State: Their Description and Uses*. Phuthaditjhaba: Uniqwa campus of the University of the North, 1997.
Mohapeloa, Joshua Pulumo. 'Khoro'. In *Meloli le Lithallere tsa Afrika ka J.P. Mohapeloa*, 3–4. 2nd edition. Morija: Morija Sesuto Book Depot. 1953. [Translated into English for the author by Mantoa Motinyane.]
Mohapeloa, Josias Makibinyane. *From Mission to Church: Fifty Years of the Work of the Paris Evangelical Missionary Society and the Lesotho Evangelical Church 1933–83*. Morija: Morija Sesuto Book Depot, 1985.

—— and MK Phakisi. *Likheleke tsa Pina Sesothong* [*The Eloquence of Song in Sesotho*]. Maseru: Lekhotla la Sesotho [Sesotho Academy] L/P 1139, 1987. [Translated into English for the author by Mantoa Motinyane.]

Molteno, Frank. 'The Historical Foundations of the Schooling of Black South Africans'. In *Apartheid and Education: The Education of Black South Africans*, edited by Peter Kallaway, 45–107. Johannesburg: Ravan Press, 1984.

Morija Sesuto Book Depot. *Lifela tsa Sione*. Morija: Morija Sesuto Book Depot, 24th edition, 53rd impression, 2015.

——. *Lipina tsa Likolo tse Phahameng*. Morija: Morija Sesuto Book Depot, 6th impression, 1985 [1907].

Mpola, Mavis Noluthando. 'An Analysis of Oral Literary Music Texts in IsiXhosa'. PhD diss., Rhodes University, 2007.

Mthethwa, Bongani. 'The Songs of Alfred A. Kumalo: A Study in Nguni and Western Musical Syncretism'. In *Papers Presented at the Seventh Symposium on Ethnomusicology, 1987*, edited by Andrew Tracey, 28–32. Grahamstown: International Library of African Music, 1988.

Mugovhani, Ndwamato George. 'Music in African Education'. In *Proceedings of the First National Music Educators' Conference*, edited by Christine Lucia, 115–121. Pietermaritzburg: Natal University Press, 1986.

——. 'The Manifestation of the "African Style" in the Works of Mzilikazi Khumalo'. MMus diss., University of the Witwatersrand, 1998.

——. '*Muzika Wa Dzikhwairi*: An Essay On the History of Venda Choral Music', *Muziki: Journal of Music Research in Africa* 10, no. 2 (2013): 75–89.

——, and Ayodamope Oluranti. 'Symbiosis or Integration: A Study of the Tonal Elements in the Choral Works of Mzilikazi Khumalo and Phelelani Mnomiya', *Muziki: Journal of Music Research in Africa* 12, no. 2 (2015): 1–21.

Muller, Stephanus. *Nagmusiek*. Johannesburg: Fourthwall Books, 2014.

The Musical Times. '*The Fellowship Songbook* by Hugh Walford Davies' [Review]. *The Musical Times* 57, no. 884 (1916): 456.

Ndebele, Mpho. 'On Translating Moerane's Song Texts'. Presentation given at the Andrew Mellon Moerane Critical Edition Research Workshop, Stellenbosch, 30 September 2017.

Nhlapo, PJ, and Sibongile Khumalo. *The Voice of African Song*. Johannesburg: Skotaville Publishers, 1993.

Nhlapo, Walter. 'Music for Urban Natives'. *The Star* (2 October 1947). University of Cape Town Manuscripts and Archives, PR Kirby Collection BC 750.

Ntantala, Phyllis. *A Life's Mosaic: The Autobiography of Phyllis Ntantala*. Johannesburg: Jacana Media, 2009 [1992].

Odendaal, André. *The Founders: The Origins of the ANC and the Struggle for Democracy in South Africa*. Johannesburg: Jacana Media, 2012.

Olwage, Grant. 'Apartheid's Musical Signs: Reflections on Black Choralism, Modernity and Race-Ethnicity in the Segregation Era'. In *Composing Apartheid: Music for and Against Apartheid*, edited by Grant Olwage, 35–53. Johannesburg: Wits University Press, 2008.

——. 'John Knox Bokwe, Colonial Composer: Tales About Race and Music'. *Journal of the Royal Musical Association* 131 (2006): 1–37.
——. 'John Knox Bokwe: Father of Black South African Choral Composition'. *NewMusicSA Bulletin* no. 9/10 (2010/2011): 18–19.
——. 'Music and (Post)Colonialism: The Dialectics of Choral Culture on a South African Frontier'. PhD diss., Rhodes University, 2003.
——. 'Scriptions of the Choral: The Historiography of Black South African Choralism'. *South African Journal of Musicology: SAMUS* 22 (2002): 29–45.
Peires, Jeff. *The House of Phalo: A History of the Xhosa People in the Days of Their Independence*. Johannesburg: Ravan Press, 1981.
Pieters, Vivien. 'Music and Presbyterianism at the Lovedale Missionary Institute, 1841–1955'. PhD diss., University of South Africa, 2021.
Pooley, Thomas. 'Composition in Crisis: Case Studies in South African Art Music, 1980–2006'. MMus diss., University of the Witwatersrand, 2008.
Rainbow, Bernarr, with Gordon Cox. *Music in Educational Thought and Practice: A Survey from 800 BC*. Aberystwyth: Boethius Press, 1989.
Rickard, Carmel. 'Moerane and the Lost Chord Detectives'. *Weekly Mail* Arts supplement, December 1988.
Rosenberg, Scott, and Richard F Weisfelder. *Historical Dictionary of Lesotho*. 2nd edition. Lanham, MD: Scarecrow Press, 2013.
Ross, Robert, Anne Kelk Mager, and Bill Nasson, eds. *The Cambridge History of South Africa: Volume 2, 1885–1994*. Cambridge: Cambridge University Press, 2011.
SAMRO (Southern African Music Rights Organisation). *Catalogue: Works by Michael Mosoeu Moerane 1901–1981*. Johannesburg: Southern African Music Rights Organisation, 2003.
Sandilands, Alexander. *Negro Spirituals: 120 Songs, with Tonic Sol-fa Music*. Morija: Morija Sesuto Book Depot, 1981 [1951].
Saunders, Christopher, and Nicholas Southey. *A Dictionary of South African History*. Cape Town and Johannesburg: David Philip, 1998.
Schapera, Isaac. 'Notes on the Early History of the Kwena (Bakwena-bagaSechele)'. *Botswana Notes and Records* 12 (1980): 83–87.
Scott, James. *Domination and the Arts of Resistance: Hidden Transcripts*. New Haven, CT: Yale University Press, 1990.
Shea, Dorothy C. *The South African Truth Commission: The Politics of Reconciliation*. Washington, DC: United States Institute of Peace Press, 2000.
Snyder, Jean. '"A Great and Noble School of Music": Dvořák, Harry T. Burleigh, and the African American Spiritual'. In *Dvořák in America, 1892–1895*, edited by John Tibbetts, 123–148. Portland, OR: Amadeus Press, 1993.
Stimie Behr, Annemie. 'The Hans Kramer Collection at the National Library, Cape Town: An Archival Perspective on Jewish Patronage of Music in Twentieth-Century South Africa'. *Journal of the Musical Arts in Africa* 12, no. 1–2 (2015): 1–22.
Tansick, Pamela. 'Tracing Joseph Trauneck: The Walking of a Persecuted Man'. *Fontes Artis Musicae* 56, no. 2 (2009): 115–137.

Tshabangu, Mango. *Footprints in Stone: Women and the Zenzele Movement in South Africa*. Harare, Johannesburg, Cairo and London: Themba Books, 2015.
Van der Linde, Bernard. 'In Memoriam Friedrich Helmut Hartmann'. *Ars Nova* 4, no. 1 (1972): 12–15.
Van der Merwe, FZ, and Jan de Graaf. *Suid-Afrikaanse Musiek–Bibliografie 1787–1952 deur F.Z. van der Merwe en 1953–1972 Bygewerk vir die Raad vir Geesteswetenskaplike Navorsing deur Jan van de Graaf*. Cape Town & Johannesburg: Tafelberg, 1974 [1958].
Viljoen, Tasmina. 'Choral Tribute to Michael Moerane'. *Sowetan* (3 September 2004).
Vokwana, Thembela. 'Expressions in Black: A History of South African Black Choral Music: "Amakhwaya/Iikwayala"'. Unpublished paper delivered at the Department of Art, Visual Arts and Musicology, University of South Africa (2004).
Walton, Chris. 'Bond of Broeders: Anton Hartman and Music in an Apartheid State'. *The Musical Times* 145, no. 1887 (2004): 63–74.
Wells, Robin. *An Introduction to the Music of the Basotho*. Morija: Morija Sesuto Book Depot, 1994.
White, Timothy Raymond Howard. 'Lovedale 1930–1955: The Study of a Missionary Institution in its Social, Educational and Political Context'. MA diss., Rhodes University, 1987.
Work, Monroe, compiler. *A Bibliography of the Negro in Africa and America*. New York: The HW Wilson Company, 1928.
Yeats, William Butler. *The Works of W.B. Yeats with an Introduction and Bibliography*. Ware, Hertfordshire: Wordsworth Editions Ltd., 1994 [1899].

Archival Documents
University of Cape Town Manuscripts and Archives, PR Kirby Collection BC 750, A: Correspondence
Letter from Friedrich Hartmann to Percival Kirby, 11 March 1958.
Letter from Michael Moerane to Percival Kirby, 21 April 1958.
Letter from the Unisa Registrar to Percival Kirby, 24 October 1962.
Letter from Percival Kirby to Dean Dixon, 9 January 1964.
Letter from Dean Dixon to Percival Kirby, 25 March 1964.
Letter from Marie Slocombe to Percival Kirby, 22 May 1964.
Letter from Percival Kirby to Marie Slocombe, 7 June 1964.
Letter from Mrs RW Levine to Percival Kirby, 29 June 1965.
Letter from Percival Kirby to Michael Moerane, 21 January 1966.
Letter from Michael Moerane to Percival Kirby, 16 February 1966.
Letter from Percival Kirby to Michael Moerane, 22 February 1966.
Letter from Michael Moerane to Percival Kirby, 9 March 1966.
Letter from Michael Moerane to Percival Kirby, 27 June 1968.
Letter from Percival Kirby to Michael Moerane, 3 July 1968.
Universiteit van Suid-Africa/University of South Africa: 'This is to certify that Michael Mosoeu Moerane passed the following courses for the B.Mus. degree at this University'. Pretoria: University of South Africa (1962).

University of Cape Town Manuscripts and Archives, Cape African Teachers Association BC 925, Box 5

Cape African Teachers Association Executive Committee. 'The Choice Before the Cape African Teachers'.

SAMRO Music Archive, Johannesburg

Moerane, Michael Mosoeu. 'Alina'. Typescript, 3pp. File A02919.

——. 'Barali ba Jerusalema'. SABC CD29056A, Trk 2. Nation Building: Celebrating 10 Years in Music. Sowetan, Caltex, SABC 1 Massed Choir Festival. Bonisudmo Choristers, Soweto Songsters, National Symphony Orchestra, Jabulani Simelane, Joyce Mogolagae, Peter Mcebi, Sibongile Khumalo, cond. Mzilikazi Khumalo. Janus CD JANP33 (1998).

——. 'Barali ba Jerusalema'. Typescript. File A02038 (1996). (For the Sowetan–Caltex Massed Choir Festival.)

——. 'Della'. File A006993. (Arranged for Oboe and Piano.)

——. 'Della'. File A00769. (Arranged for Violin and Piano.)

——. 'Della'. File A00770. (Arranged for Violin, Horn, Bass Clarinet and Strings.)

——. 'Della'. Typescript, 2pp. File A02913.

——. 'Fatše La Heso–Symphonic Poem St: My Country'. Lead Sheet. File Q00144. (Copy of first few pages of ms. in Cory Library.)

——. 'I Got A Home In-A Dat Rock'. Typescript, 1p. File A02917.

——. 'I Stood On De Ribber'. Typescript, 1p. File A02918.

——. 'Jehova Oa Busa'. Typescript, 1p. File A02916.

——. 'Leseli La Hao'. Manuscript, 1p and typescript, 1p. File A07134.

——. 'Liflaga'. Manuscript, 2pp. File A06800.

——. 'Liphala'. Manuscript, 1p. File A02920.

——. 'Mahakoe'. Manuscript, 2pp. File A02921.

——. ''Mankokotsane'. Typescript, 3pp. File A02914.

——. ''Mitsa-Mahosi'. Typescript, 2pp. File A07140.

——. 'Mohokare'. Manuscript, 1p. File A02920.

——. 'Mohokare'. Manuscript, 2pp. File A07140.

——. 'Morena Tlake'. Typescript, 3pp. File A06462.

——. 'Mosele'. Typescript, 1p. File A02953.

——. 'Paka-Mahlomola'. Typescript, 2pp. File A02911.

——. 'Paki Ha Li Eo'. Typescript, 4pp. File A02910.

——. 'Ruri. 'Massed Choir Festival 10th Anniversary (1998)', 50–62. File A06048.

——. 'Vumani kuJehova'. Manuscript, 4pp. File A02915.

——, arr. Hans Roosenschoon. 'Barali ba Jerusalema: O Daughters of Jerusalem'. File A02425 (1997). (For Sop/pf or Ten/pf. Commission: SAMRO Endowment for the National Arts 1997 for Deon v d Walt Gala Benefit Concert.)

——, arr. Hans Roosenschoon. 'Barali ba Jerusalema: O Daughters of Jerusalem'. File A02436 (1997). (For Ten/orch. Commission: SAMRO Endowment for National Arts 1997 for Deon v d Walt Gala Benefit Concert.)

——, ed. and orchestrated by Walter Mony. 'Barali ba Jerusalema: O Daughters of Jerusalem' (1998). File Q00413. (For reduced orchestra. Commission: SAMRO Endowment for the National Arts 1998 for accompaniment of work in *South Africa Sings Vol. I.*)

——, ed. James Steven Mzilikazi Khumalo. 'Barali ba Jerusalema: O Daughters of Jerusalem' (1998). File A04323. (Instrumental parts for work in *South Africa Sings Vol. I.*)

SAMRO Archive, Johannesburg, Yvonne Huskisson Collection, File 'Moerane, M.M.', Subfile 'Korrespondensie'
Telex from De Jager to Yvonne Huskisson, 9 May 1969.
Letter from Michael Moerane to Yvonne Huskisson, 20 May 1973.
Letter from Gideon Roos to Michael Mosoeu Moerane, 29 June 1973.
Internal memo from Anton Hartman to Yvonne Huskisson, 17 July 1973.
Letter from Yvonne Huskisson to Michael Moerane, 19 July 1973.

Cory Library for Historical Research, Rhodes University, Grahamstown
Enrolment List 1841–1928 (Lovedale Missionary Institution). MS 16299.
Letter from Percival Kirby to Zachariah Keodirelang Matthews, 1959. MS 11071.
Lovedale Missionary Institution, South Africa: Annual Reports for 1922–1938. Lovedale: The Mission Press (1923–1939).
Lovedale Missionary Institution, Lovedale Mission Press Archive, Letters, MS 16376:
  Morija Sesuto Book Depot to Moerane, 7 September 1937.
  RW Shepherd to Morija Sesuto Book Depot, 17 September 1937.
  SS Mputa to the Director, Lovedale Press, 30 September 1937.
  Morija Sesuto Book Depot to the Director of Publications, 6 October 1937.
  Eugenio Clausetti to MM Moerane, 6 November 1937.
  Moerane to the Director, Lovedale Press, 4 February 1938.
  RW Shepherd to Moerane, 3 May 1938.
Lovedale Missionary Institution, Lovedale Mission Press Archive, Lovedale Press Publications, MS 16602.
Moerane, Michael Mosoeu. Fatše La Heso (My Country) Symphonic Poem. MS 14467 (1941).
Rhodes University College Grahamstown: Calendars 1930–1943. Grahamstown: Grocott and Sherry (1929–1943).
South African Native College Fort Hare, Alice, Cape Province, South Africa. Calendars 1925–1944. Lovedale: The Lovedale Press, 1925–1944.

South African History Archives, Johannesburg, Mark Gevisser's Research Papers for Thabo Mbeki: The Dream Deferred, AL3284
Moerane, Manasseh Tebatso. '"I Chose Freedom": The Autobiography of Mr. M.T. Moerane of South Africa'. Johannesburg: South African History Archive, AL3284, Mark Gevisser's Research Papers for *Thabo Mbeki: The Dream Deferred*, Box 3.2.17. (n.d.).

Tsepo Moerane private collection, Komani
Moerane, Manasseh Tebatso. 'An Address by M.T. Moerane on the Occasion of the Unveiling of the Tombstone of His Older Brother Michael Mosoeu at Hlotse, Lesotho on December 17, 1988'.
Moerane, Thuso. 'Biography of Michael Mosoeu Moerane B.Mus. (21-09-1904)–(27-01-1980)' [n.d.].

David Ambrose Archive, Ladybrand
Leselinyana le Lesotho [*The Little Light of Lesotho*]. '1969 Cambridge Certificate Results'. 20 January 1970: 4.
Mohapeloa, Bernice. 'Basutoland Homemakers Association'. *Basutoland Witness* 7, no. 1 (1953), 5–6.

Morija Museum and Archives, Morija, Lesotho
Leselinyana le Lesotho [The Little Light of Lesotho]. 'May Esther Bedford Prizes (South African Native College), Music.' *Leselinyana le Lesotho* 70(2), January 1937: 3.

University of Massachusetts, Amherst
Robert S Cox Special Collections & University Archives Research Center, WEB Du Bois Papers, 1803–1999 (bulk 1877–1963), MS 312.

Rand Daily Mail Archive, Johannesburg
'36 Control Posts on Borders of S.A.', *Rand Daily Mail*, Johannesburg, 30 April 1963, 2.
Africa Bureau. 'SA Prohibits Entry for Lesotho Choir', *Rand Daily Mail*, Johannesburg, 8 November 1974, 2.
'B.B.C. Broadcasts Work by Bantu Composer', *Rand Daily Mail*, Johannesburg, 18 November 1944, 3.
'Benson Banned from Meetings', *Rand Daily Mail*, Johannesburg, 5 March 1966, 3.
Bikitsha, Basil (Doc). 'Beaming Out a Spiritual Message'. *Rand Daily Mail Extra*, Johannesburg, 19 March 1980, 13.
Bikitsha, Basil (Doc). 'It's Doc Bikitsha's Finger on Your Pulse', *Rand Daily Mail Extra*, 7 June 1976: 13.
Bikitsha, Basil (Doc). 'Jack Jones Takes Over from Vereen at Sun City Feast'. *Rand Daily Mail Extra*, Johannesburg, 25 March 1981, 21.
'BROADCASTING PROGRAMMES … Johannesburg To-morrow', *Rand Daily Mail*, Johannesburg, 20 July 1946, 6.
'PEKA High School (Basutoland) … Wanted: Deputy–Headmaster', *Rand Daily Mail*, Johannesburg, 30 June 1962, 8.
Pretoria Bureau. 'Lesotho Burial for Composer', *Rand Daily Mail Extra*, Johannesburg, 6 February 1980, 5.
Steafel, Harold. 'Randfontein Is Choir Winner. Harold Steafel: Ford Choirs National Competition'79', *Rand Daily Mail Extra*, Johannesburg, 13 December 1979, 11.
'Work of Bantu Composer to be Broadcast', *Rand Daily Mail*, Johannesburg, 20 July 1946, 8.

Research Archive Historical Papers, William Cullen Library, University of the Witwatersrand

'Massey, Danny', 1999. File A3193f. (Interviews conducted by Massey with people who were at Fort Hare in the 1950s and early 60s: Marumo Moerane, Stanley Mabizela, Herby Govinden, Ambrose Mkiwane, and Ivy Matsepe-Casaburri.)

'Memorandum Subsequent to the Interview of the 21 March 1955 with the Division of Bantu Education, Native Affairs Department, Pretoria'. File AK1715.

'Robert Sobukwe papers', 1954-2013. File A2618.

'Trials: State vs. Mofelehetsi Moerane & 31 others, 1975'. File AK2290.

Author's Interviews

Dr David Ambrose and Mrs Mamhlongo Maphisa, Ladybrand, 22 May 2014.
Mr Victor Lechesa, Maseru, 26 February 2017.
Mr Eric Lekhanya, Maseru, 2 March 2011.
Mr Tseliso Makhakhe, Maseru, 20 May 2014.
Mr Shadrack Mapetla, Midrand, 15 May 2014.
Mrs Epainette Mamotseki Mbeki, East London, 27 May 2014.
Dr Zakes Mda, on Zoom, 17 May 2022.
Advocate Marumo Moerane, Durban, 7 October 2017.
Mr Mofelehetsi Moerane, Atteridgeville, 14 May 2014 and 14 February 2017.
Mr Thuso Majalla Moerane, Komani, 12 May 2014 and 23 February 2017.
Mr Tsepo and Ms Neo Moerane, Komani (Queenstown), 30 September 2019.
Mrs Mosa Ndludla, Muizenberg, 22 October 2019.
Mrs Nthabiseng [name redacted], Bronkhorstspruit, 4 October 2017.
Mr Gilbert P. Ramatlapeng, Maseru, 4 April 2014.
Mr Thabo Tseko Ei Pitso, Maseru, 5 April 2014.
Mr Matsobane Putsoa, Maseru, 26 February 2017.

Scores Published in Four Volumes by African Composers Edition

Lucia, Christine, general ed. *Andrew Mellon–Michael Mosoeu Moerane Critical Edition Volumes I–IV*. Stellenbosch: African Sun Media, 2020.

Index

Page numbers in *italics* indicate graphics and tables.

A

African choral *see also* choral
  competitions 8, 14, 61, 63, 113, 116–119, 128, 131–132, 164, 187, 190
  composition 57, 61, 62, 111, 115, 118–119, 199
  music 10, 114, 117, 132
African composers 9, 12, 61, 87, 94–95, 99, 116, 121, 129, 181, 189, 203, 206
African Composers Edition (ACE) xxvi, xxvii, 103, 113, 121, 129, 147, 174, 181, 189, 207–210
African intellectualism 32, 170
African National Congress (ANC) 27, 31, 49, 70–71, 104
African Secondary School (Queenstown) 4, 32, 66
African Springtime Orchestra 4, 11, 44, 68–69
African-American composers 12, 95–96, 141, 142, 203
African-American spirituals *see also* spirituals 141
Agawu, Kofi 115
Album for the Young (Moerane) 8, 46, 47, 53, 126, 144
Alice, Eastern Cape 2–4, 46
Alina 122, *124*, 125, 151, 154, *155*
Ambrose, David 23
American spirituals *see* spirituals
Amu, Ephraim 200, 203
ANC *see* African National Congress
anthems 135, 137, 140, 146, 166, 180

apartheid 1, 5, 12, 13, 24, 27, 33, 59, 71, 73, 105, 111, 132, 152, 179, 186, 199
Apartheid and Education: The Education of Black South Africans 60
Attwell, David 204

B

Bachelor of Music degree (BMus) 1, 3, 39, 50–52, 56–57, 60, 84, 97, 111
Bafokeng, royal house of 18, 125
Bakoena, royal house of 18
Bantu Education xxiv, 5, 57–58, 71–72
Bantu Education Act 42, 60
Barali Ba Jerusalema (Daughters of Jerusalem) 8, 10, 117, 122, *124*, 125–126, 130, 169, 180, *207*
Basotho 13, 17–20, 30, 85, 107, 156, 171
  chiefs 2, 19–21
  nation 17, 20, 171
  royal family 2
Basutoland *see also* Lesotho 2, 3, 5
Basutoland Congress Party (BCP) 5, 12, 13, 30, 31, 74, 79, 80, 170
Basutoland High School *see also* Lesotho High School 3, 4, 13, 34, 48, 64
Basutoland Homemakers Association 152
Basutoland National Party (BNP) 5, 80
BBC *see* British Broadcasting Corporation
BCP *see* Basutoland Congress Party
BCP Youth League 29
Bell, William Henry 55, 84, 102
Biko, Steve xxiv, 28

267

Black Consciousness Movement 49, 142
BMus *see* Bachelor of Music degree
BNP *see* Basutoland National Party
Bokwe, John Knox 42, 44, 61–62, 91, 139
Bonukunyana (My Little Baby!) 122, *124*, 125, 126, 151–152, *209*
Boputsoa 122, *124*, 125, 126
Botleng ba naha 124, 125
British Broadcasting Corporation (BBC) 68, 84–89, 98–99, 102–103
   African Service 87, 98–99
   Music Library 88
   Symphony Orchestra 68, 87, 98–99
British Cape Colony 2, 17–18, 39–41, 47, 49, 59, 65, 105, 161
British colonialism 19, 32, 170
British Protectorate of Basutoland 2, 105, 163
Bull, Oswin Boys 48, 65
Burleigh, Henry Thacker 96, 142–143, 146, 149
By An' By 135, 142, *145*, *209*

C
Caledon River *see also* Mohokare 128, 180
Caluza, Reuben 10, 42, 66, 143, 193
Cape African Teachers Association (CATA) 5, 31, 70, 71, 60
Catalogue of Works by Michael Mosoeu Moerane 8, 10, 113, 121, 122, 123, 125, 126, 131, 152
Catholic Church 12, 47, 63, 68, 80, 191
Catholic Mazenod Institute, Maseru 38
choral
   competitions 14, 61, 113, 117–119, 132, 166
   composers 9, 61, 116, 132–133, 193
   composition 57, 115, 118, 199
   music 9–10, 61, 80, 113–114, 116–117, 119, 121, 131–133, 152, 203, 205
   works 8, 105, 113, 116, 121, 127, 164, 186
Choral Movement in Southern Africa 113–118
choralism 30, 104, 118, 121
Chronicle of First Broadcast Performances of Musical Works in the United Kingdom, 1923–1996, A 98
Coleridge-Taylor, Samuel 101, 203
Commonwealth, British xxiii, 86
Communist Party of South Africa (CPSA) 27, 31

Coplan, David 30
Council on African Affairs xxii, 68, 100
Cree, Edgar 93–94, 103

D
Della 8–9, 56, 117, 122, *124*, 125, 130–132, 140, 169–170, 186–189, *190*, *207*
Department of Bantu Education and Development 71
Dixon, Dean 83, 85–87, 88, 89, 101, 102
Domination and the Arts of Resistance: Hidden Transcripts 142
DSRAC *see* Eastern Cape Department of Sport, Recreation, Arts and Culture
Du Bois, William Edward Burghardt 83, 100–102, 105, 142
Du Plessis, Phil 104–105, 111
Dvořák, Antonín Leopold 47, 79, 88, 95–96, 99, 109, 146

E
Ea Hlolang (The Triumphant One) 122, *124*, 135–137, *207*
East Griqualand *see also* Transkei 2, 23, 27
Eastern Cape 2, 9, 10, 12, 14, 18, 41, 68, 72, 97, 128, 132, 193, 200
Eastern Cape Department of Sport, Recreation, Arts and Culture (DSRAC) 9
Eiselen Commission on Native Education 57
Eiselen, Werner Willi Max 56
eisteddfodau 11, 116, 118
Erlmann, Veit 10, 143
European models for African music 114–116
Extract from Moerane's 'A General Note on Modern Music' *120*

F
Fatše La Heso (My Country) 8, 12–13, 53, 68, 91–94, 101–102, *110*, 111, 142, 151–152, 184, 202, *207*
   country of 104
   genesis of 97
   music of 97, 105
   orchestral work 4, 9, 59, 85, 95, 97, 100
   reception history of 98–99, 103
   symphonic poem 95
   themes 106, 107, *108–109*
Ficksburg 15, 72, 79, 191, 193
Field, Leslie 54–55

INDEX

Fisk Jubilee Singers 143
folksong 46, 105, 115, 147, 159
Fort Hare University 2, 3, 8, 42–45, 48–50, 53, 55, 62–63, 65–66, 84, 97, 107, 129
French–Swiss missionaries 38, 115, 136

G

Gevisser, Mark 5, 10, 18, 20, 21, 24–26, 32, 39, 67, 180
Go Tell It On The Mountains 124, 135, 142, *146, 209*
Grahamstown (Makhanda) 3, 15, 33, 50, 53, 56, 62, 66, 83, 84, 90, 99, 102
Grundy, Kenneth 9
Gumtree 13–16, 89

H

Ha Ke Balahē (Who Says I'm Running Away?) 124, 151–152, 156, *207*
Hallelujah Chorus 129, 164
Hampton Book of Spirituals 143
Harlem Renaissance 95
harmonium 37, 39
Hartman, Anton Carlisle 83, 94
Hartmann, Friedrich Helmut 4, 39, 50, 53–57, 83, 97–98, 102, 105, 107, 109, 111, 112, 184
Henderson, James 42
Hoja Ke Nonyana (If I Were a Bird) 123, *124,* 125, 169, 182, *207*
Hunton, Alpheus 101–102
Huskisson, Yvonne 10, 11–13, 15, 83, 93–94, 103, 111, 187, 200–202
hymns 39, 44, 78, 108, 114–115, 139, 160, 179–180, 203

I

I Got A Home In-a Dat Rock 136, 142, 147, *209*
International Missionary Conference 43
isiXhosa 9, 67, 105, 126, 138–139, 152, 186–187, 193, 200
I Stood On De Ribber 124, 126, 136, 142, 145, 147, *210*
It's Me, O Lord 136, 142–143, 147, *210*

J

Jabavu, Davidson Don Tengo 43, 49, 55

Jehova Oa Busa (Jehovah Reigns) 122, 123, *124,* 125, 135, *137, 208*
Jonathan, Joseph Leabua 5, 24, 30, 35, 170

K

Kajeno 124, 126
Kepe sa me 124, 125, 126
Ke rata Jehova 122, *124*
Kerr, Alexander 39, 50, 53, 66, 84, 97
Khaketla, Bennett Makalo 169–171, 183
music to poems by 171–176
Khaketla, 'Masechele Caroline Ntseliseng 183
Khati (Skipping Game) 78, 122, *124,* 125, 169, 171–172, *173, 208*
Khomo, Izak 100, 104, 111
Khumalo, Mzilikazi Steven 97, 116, 181
Kirby, Percival Robson 15–16, 50, 53, 83–92, 99, 102–103, 199–202, 206
Koapeng, Mokale 118, 121
Kroonstad 3, 21, 33, 50, 59, 66

L

Lebili (Wheel) 122, *124,* 125, 126, 169, *208*
Lechesa, Victor 31, 74, 78, 164
Leeman, Bernard 12, 18, 20, 26
Lekhanya, Eric 81
Leribe District, Lesotho 6, 15
Leseli La Hao (Your Light) 124, 135, 137, *208*
Lesotho 5, 12–15, 22–24, 26, 29–35, 68–69, 71, 163, 172, 176–179
politics of xxi–xxv, 80
rural 39, 108–109, 176, 200
Lesotho 1970: An African Coup Under the Microscope 170
Lesotho African National Teachers' Association 130
Lesotho and the Struggle for Azania 26
Lesotho Evangelical Church (LEC) 39, 76, 80, 136
Lesotho High School *see also* Basutoland High School 4, 13, 64
Lesotho Teachers Training College 6, 81
Letsatsi (The Sun) 122, *124,* 125–126, 151–152, 156, *208*
Lia Qhomaqhoma (They Frolic) 169, *124,* 125, 172, *209*
Life's Mosaic, A 71
Lifela tsa Sione (Songs of Zion) 39, 136

Liflaga (Flags) 122, 151, 163, *209*
Likhohlo (Gorges) 123, *124*, 125, 169, 172, 174, *208*
Liphala (Whistles) 7, 8, 56, 62, 73, *124*, 129, 131, 151, 160–161, *162*, 163, *208*
Lipina tsa Likolo tse Phahameng (Songs for High School) 115
Loram, Charles Templeman 58
Lovedale High School, Alice 2, 40, 41, 43, 48, 61, 62, 63
Lovedale Missionary Institution 40, 41
Lovedale
  brass band 44
  Drama Society 45
  Literary Society 44
  music at 44–47
  Musical and Dramatic Association 44–45
  principal of 15, 42
  riot 43
Lovedale Practising Schools 2, 48, 63
Lovedale students c. 1924 *41*
Lovedale Training School 2, 48, 62
Luvuyo Lerumo Senior Secondary School 66

M
M.M.M. Compositions and Harmonized Negro Spirituals (list) 123, *124*
Ma-Homemakers (Ingoma Ka Zenzele) (Homemakers) 5, *124*, 125, 151–152, *153*, *209*
Macpherson, Stewart 51, 52, 55
Mahakoe (Jewels) 122, *124*, 169, 183, *184*, *185*, *208*
Mahalefele, Mabasiea Jeannette 169, 181
Maholosiane 124
Maholotsane 124, 125, 126
Makhakhe, Tseliso 15, 23, 31, 73, 77, 80, 128–130, 161, 164–165, 170
Malan, Jacques Philip 206
Mandela, Nelson Rolihlahla 33, 45, 49, 104
Mangoloaneng 2, 16, 18, 23–24, *25*, 37, 39, 172
'Mankholikholi (Yellow-billed Kite) 122, *124*, 126, 151, 156, *158*, *159*, *209*
'Mankokotsane (The Rain Game) 122, *124*, 125, 151–152, 156, *207*
Mapetla, Chief Justice 30
Mapetla, Shadrack 79
Mariazell Roman Catholic Mission 2, 37–40

Maseru 50, 61, 65, 81
Mashologu, Bennie 44, 129
Masiza, Hamilton 118
Matlala 7, 117, 122, *124*, 125–126, 128–130, 151, 164–165, *208*
Matshikiza, Todd 6, 28, 61, 66–67
Matthews, Zachariah Keodirelang 42, 49
May Esther Bedford Prize for Musical Composition 8, 47, 65, 144
Mbeki, Epainette 'MaMotseki (née Moerane) (sister) 5, 12, 25, 27, 33, 37–39, 45
Mbeki, Govan Archibald Mvunyelwa 22, 27, 70
Mbeki, Thabo Mvuyelwa 5, 10, 22, 24, 27, 40
Mda, Zanemvula Kizito Gatyeni (Zakes) 14, 31, 47, 74, 79, 140
Meintjes, Louise 9
Mfundisweni Teacher Training Institute (College of Education) 5, 34, 63, 71, 72, 191
missing works by Moerane 126–127
mission schools 2, 37–38, 40, 42–43, 63, 67, 115, 191, 204
mission stations 21, 38, 114, 118
missionaries 20, 32, 40, 41, 43, 58, 114, 160
'Mitsa-Mahosi (A Call to Kings) 122, *124*, 125, 169, 171, *207*
Mngoma, Khabi 10, 61, 66, 117, 118
Moea oa ka 124, 126
Moerane, Beatrice Betty (née Msweli) (wife) 2, 5, 6, 13, 22, 33, 41–42, 65, 97, 152, 191, 197
Moerane, Daniel Mokhakala (brother) 22, 27, 70
Moerane, Eleazar Ramaphome Jakane (father) 2, 18, 21, 22, 24, 37, 38, 50, 105
Moerane family at Mangoloaneng c. 1920 *25*
Moerane, Fraser Masole (brother) 22, 49
Moerane, Halieo Lucinda (second-born daughter) 4, 22, 127
Moerane home at 10 Scanlen Street c. 1960 *28*
Moerane in correspondence 83–91
Moerane, Lenare (grandson) xxiv, 27, 28–29, 197
Moerane, Manasseh Tebatso (MT) (brother) 6, 8, 16, 18, 21–22, 27, 37, 45, 49, 89
Moerane, Marumo Tsatsi Khabele (nephew) 22, 29, 49

INDEX

Moerane, Mathabo Lineo (first-born daughter) 3, 22, 69–70, 127
Moerane, Michael Mosoeu 1, 6, 18, 21, 98, 131, 142, 147, 187, 198
  childhood and early life 2–4, 24–26
  death 5, 12–13, 35, 61, 81–82, 103, 125, 181
  family lineage 17–22, 26–27, 34
  later life 5–8, 14, 47
  in the literature 10–15
  marriage 3, 5, 33–34
  Moerane Scholarly Edition 10, 129
  musical education 4, 37–38, 40, 57, 61, 104, 116, 121, 132, 200, 204
  musical output 8–10, 199
  piano (instrument) 46
  score-reading 50, 52
  surname, meaning 22
  surname, origin 21
  politics 5, 6, 26–27, 29, 30–32, 49, 57, 66, 70, 112, 142, 200, 202, 203
  teacher and composer 59–70
  teaching his son Thabo the piano c. 1964 *7*
Moerane, Mofelehetsi Count (eldest son) 3, 11, 13, 46, 52, 63, 66–70, 127, 140
Moerane, Mofelehetsi (nephew) 29–30
Moerane, Neo (granddaughter) 71, 76
Moerane, Sofia (née Majara) (mother) 2, 5, 22, 24, 105
Moerane, Sophia Metsekae (Sophie) (last-born daughter) 4, 22, 32, 65, 71–72, 75, 127
Moerane, Thabo Kabeli (last-born son) 11, 22, 24, 29, 32, 34, 35, 55, 73–74, 82, 125, 167, 191, 197, *198*
  musician xxvi, 6, *7*, 11, 39, 67–69, 74, 109, 127
Moerane, Thuso Majalla (second-born son) 3, *4*, 6, 22, 33, 41, 50, 66, 68, 70–73, 76, 127, 138, 187, 191
  banning order xxiv, 6, 27–28, 102, 154
  curation of father's music xxvi, 11, 123–126
Moerane, Tsepo (grandson) 11, 49
Mofelehetsi, Lebohang (nephew) 21, 32
Mohapeloa, Joshua Pulumo 39–40, 81, 119, 129, 131, 160, 161
Mohapeloa, Josias Makabinyane 39
Mohokare (Caledon River) 15, 20, 176–177, 179

Mohokare (Caledon River) (composition) 122–125, 169, 177, 179, *209*
Mona, Lex 6, 28, 67
Monyaka Oa Pelo (A Joyful Heart) 31–54, 122, *124*, 125, 169, 174, *175*, *208*
Morena Tlake (King Vulture) 7, 117, 122, *124*, 125, 128, 132, 151, 164–166, *167*, *168*, 170, *208*
Morija 18, 24, 37–38, 40, 115, 136, 144
Morija Sesuto Book Depot 144
Morija Training Institution 2, 18, 22, 40
Mosele 122, *124*, 125, 151–152, *209*
Moshoeshoe I 17–20, 176
Mosotho 9, 156, 178, 200
Mossop, Douglas 53
'Mote 124, 126
Mount Fletcher district 2, 17, 18, 21
Mpola, Mavis Noluthando 9
Mpondoland 5, 33–34, 71–72
Mputa, Sampson Synor 169, 186–188
music degree *see* Bachelor of Music degree
Music of the Basotho 107

N

Naleli ea meso 122, *124*, 126
Naleli Ka 'Ngoe (One Star at a Time) 124, 169, 174, *208*
National Teachers Training College (NTTC) *see* Lesotho Teachers Training College
Nazism 56, 57
Ndebele, Mpho Kathleen 74, 129, 155, 164, 180, 183
Ndludla, Mosa (granddaughter) 34, 68, 73, 77, 191
Negro spirituals *see* spirituals
NEUM *see* Non-European Unity Movement
Ngakana-ntsonyana 124, 125
Ngeloi La Me (My Angel) 122, *124*, 125, 152, 155, 169, 176–178, *209*
Ngokuba Sizalelwe Umtwana (For Unto Us a Child is Born) 124, 135, 138, *139*, *208*
Nobody Knows The Trouble I've Seen 8, 56, 62, 125, 131, 136, 142–143, *144*, 145, *210*
Non-European Unity Movement (NEUM) 5, 31, 70
Nonyana Tse Ntle (Beautiful Birds) 122, *124*, 126, 151, 156, *159*, 160, *209*
Ntantala, Phyllis 71

Ntate Ea Mohau (Lord of Mercy) 208, *124*, 135–136, *208*
Ntsane, Kemuel Edward 169
  music to poems by 176–179
Ntsoaki 124, 125, 155, 169, 181, *182*, *209*
NTTC *see* Lesotho Teachers Training College

O

Old Mutual National Choir Festival 11, 116, 166
orthography 32–33

P

Paka-Mahlomola (Creator of Sorrow) 117, *124*, 169, 176–177, *178*, *209*
Paki Ha Li Eo (No Witnesses) 122, *124*, 125, 169, 179, *208*
Pan-Africanism 26, 29–31, 33, 35, 48, 100, 104, 112, 107, 200
Pan Africanist Congress of Azania (PAC) 100
Paris Evangelical Missionary Society (PEMS) 2, 39, 40, 136
Peka Bridge 15, 193
Peka district, Lesotho 30
Peka High School 6, 13–16, 34, 45, 72–73, 76–77, 128, 161, 166, 171, 177, 191
Peka High School Orchestra 5, 74, *75*, 137
Peka village 14, 15, *34*, 45, 76, 191, 197
Pelo Le Moea (Heart and Soul) 122, *124*, 125, 126, 151–152, *154*, *209*
Pelonomi Hospital, Bloemfontein 6, 81
Pester, Ernest Frank 40
Pieters, Vivien 10, 44, 121
Pitso, Thabo Tseko Ei 23–24, 77
Police Mobile Unit (Lesotho) xxiii, 30
political
  changes 35, 104, 186
  events xxi–xxiv, 26, 80, 100
  history xxvi, 1, 10, 15, 17, 24, 26, 54, 75, 95, 176
  leaders 26, 31, 40, 95, 203
politicians 31, 43, 74–75
politics 9, 26, 30–32, 44, 48, 57, 66, 70, 74, 80, 170, 203
  in Moerane's family 27–29
Presbyterian 12, 42, 44
Price, Florence 95, 203

Prince Ferdinand (operetta) 63, 114, 161
Putsoa, Matsobane 31, 74, 76, 78, 171–172

Q

Qhafutso 122, *124*, 127
Queen Elizabeth Hospital, Maseru 6
Queenstown (Komani) *see also* Scanlen Street 4–6, 12, 33–34, 70–73, 84–85, 101–102, 152, 191, 197
Queenstown Bantu Secondary School 66

R

Radebe, Mark 118–119
Raybould, Clarence 87, 98, 99
Rhodes University 11, 53–54
Rhodes University College 3, 50, 52, 55, 97, 99
Rhodes University Library 92, 93, 102
Rhodes University Main Building 1946 54
Rickard, Carmel 11, 103, 109, 127, 202
Ricordi (publisher) 143–145
Robeson, Paul 100, 142, 145
Roos, Gideon 122, 126
Ruri! (Truly!) 117, 128–131, 135, 140, *141*, 190, *208*

S

Sa 'Mokotsane (Wailing) 124, 125, 151, 153, 175, *209*
SABC *see* South African Broadcasting Corporation
SABC National Symphony Orchestra 7, 12, 94, 103–105
sacred songs *see* spiritual songs
Sailor Shanties 147
SAMRO *see* Southern African Music Rights Organisation
Sandilands, Alexander 143
Satane A Tšeha (Le Joeleputsoa) (The Devil Laughed (Johannesburg)) 124, 125, 169, 176, 179, 180, *208*
Scanlen Street, Queenstown 6, 27–28, *29*, 32, 67–68, 71, 140, 154
school songs 140, 160–163
Sekolo Se Koetsoe (School's Out) 124, 125, 140, 151, 160, 163, 175, *209*
Sentebale 124, 125, 127
Seotsanyana (Rock Kestrel) 124, 151, 156, *157*, *208*

INDEX

Sesotho 4, 19–20, 22–23, 65, 74, 123, 160, 169–170, 174, 180, 183
  home language 24, 31, 105, 152, 200
  lyrics 9, 32–33, 121, 126, 128–129, 138, 152, 158–159, 164, 166, 171, 176, 180, 183
Shenandoah 124, 126, 135, 142, 147, *148, 210*
Shepherd, Robert Henry Wishart 15, 42–43, 62, 144, 186–187
Slocombe, Marie 83, 87–88, 98–99
Sobukwe, Robert xxiii, 100
solfège 38, 115, 121, 215
songs about community 156–163
songs about family 151–155
songs about history and tradition 163–168
songs of love and loss 169
Sontonga, Enoch 42, 166
Sotho 12–13, 18, 32–34, 40, 181
Sotho folk themes 13, 106–109
Sotho music 105–107, 111, 131, 151–152, 156, 169, 199
Souls of Black Folk, The 142
South African Bantu Board of Music 118
South African Broadcasting Corporation (SABC) 12, 13, 15, 62, 94, 96, 117, 201–202
South African Institute of Race Relations 58, 143
South African Native College Calendars, The 50
South African Native College *see also* Fort Hare University 2, 48, 50
Southern African Music Rights Organisation (SAMRO) 8, 10–12, 122–123, 187, 189
  archive 122–123, 181, 187
  catalogue 122–123, 125–126, 131, 152
  membership 126
Sowande, Fela 87, 99, 200, 203
spiritual songs 135–149
spirituals 8, 95–96, 113, 123, *124*, 125, 135, 141–143, 146–147, 149
Still, William Grant 95, 101, 203
St John's College, Mthatha 2, 40
Students Christian Association 45
Sylvia 7, 9, 13, 117, 122, *124*, 125, 128, 130, 132, 140, 169–170, 186, 190–191, *192, 193–195, 196, 208*
symphonic poems 55, 61, 84, 92, 94–95, 99, 107–109, 111, 121, 151, 186, 200

T

Thabo Moerane, Sylvia Zongola and Michael Mosoeu Moerane 1968 *198*
Thaha e tala 124, 127
Thomas, John Smeath 54–55
tonality as a colonising force 115
Transkei 2, 15, 19, 26, 66
Transkei Bunga 22, 70
Transkeian Territories General Council 27
Tsatsi La Pallo (Judgement Day) 80, 123, *124*, 126, 135, 139–140, *209*
Tsifalimali, house in 2014 *35*
Tsifalimali, Lesotho 6, 9, 11, *35*, 76, 197
Tumeliso 124, 127
Tyamzashe, Benjamin 10, 42, 118

U

University of Cape Town (UCT) 11, 54
University of Lesotho 32, 197
University of Pretoria 12
University of South Africa (Unisa) 3, 11, 50, 51, 52, 53, 54, 55, 57, 83, 85
University of the Witwatersrand 83, 86
University of Zululand 66

V

Vokwana, Thembela 114, 116, 187
Vumani KuYehova (Merabe, Rorisang/Rorisang lebitso la Jehova) (Sing To Jehovah) 124, 125, 126, 135, *138, 208*

W

Ward, Clementine 72–73
Witness 124, 136, 142, 147, *210*
World War II xxii, 43, 50, 57

X

Xhosa *see* isiXhosa
Xhosa songs 138–139, 143, 187

Y

Yeats, William Butler 183–184
Yizani kum 124, 127

Z

Zedung, Mao 80
Zenzele movement 5, 152
Zongola, Sylvia Ntombentsha 34, 72, 191, 193, 197, *198*

www.ingramcontent.com/pod-product-compliance
Ingram Content Group UK Ltd.
Pitfield, Milton Keynes, MK11 3LW, UK
UKHW031306310125
4390UKWH00030B/533

9 781776 149193